Teunis Bergen

The Bergen family

The descendants of Hans Hansen Bergen, one of the early settlers of New York and

Brooklyn

Teunis Bergen

The Bergen family
The descendants of Hans Hansen Bergen, one of the early settlers of New York and Brooklyn

ISBN/EAN: 9783337197803

Printed in Europe, USA, Canada, Australia, Japan

Cover: Foto ©Raphael Reischuk / pixelio.de

More available books at **www.hansebooks.com**

THE
BERGEN FAMILY:

OR THE

DESCENDANTS

OF

HANS HANSEN BERGEN,

ONE OF THE

EARLY SETTLERS

OF

NEW YORK AND BROOKLYN, L. I.

WITH NOTES ON THE GENEALOGY OF SOME OF THE BRANCHES OF
THE COWENHOVEN, VOORHEES, ELDERT, STOOTHOOF CORTEL-
YOU, STRYKER, SUYDAM, LOTT, WYCKOFF, BARKELOO,
LEFFERTS, MARTENSE, HUBBARD, VAN BRUNT,
VANDERBILT, VANDERVEER, VAN NUYSE,
AND OTHER LONG ISLAND FAMILIES.

By TEUNIS G. BERGEN.

NEW YORK:
BERGEN & TRIPP, 114 NASSAU STREET.
M.DCCC.LXVI.

ABBREVIATIONS USED IN THIS WORK.

---

b.	for born.	N.	north.
d.	died.	N'ly.	northerly.
m.	married.	S.	south.
bap.	baptised.	S'ly.	southerly.
s.	son.	E.	east.
dau.	daughter.	E'ly.	easterly.
wid.	widow.	W.	west.
st.	street.	W'ly.	westerly.
ave.	avenue.	prob.	probably.
gl.	guilder.	sup.	suppose.
Do.	dominie.	O. S.	old style.

PREFACE.

THE compiler of this genealogy has devoted his leisure moments for some years past, in gathering materials and putting in its present shape, the work hereby presented. The labor has been much greater than he anticipated, and time and pecuniary means have been expended, without any expectation of a return, in the examination of public and private records, and traveling from place to place to obtain information. An examination of the work will show that it contains imperfections, that there are branches of the family which he has been unable to trace, names and dates which he has failed to obtain. In some cases the family records were lost, and in one the dates were refused, the female members of the family desiring secrecy as to their ages, intending to keep up the semblance of youth as long as possible.

The author has endeavored to make the work as perfect as possible, and has spared no pains or expense to effect this end, but perfection in a work of this kind can not be expected.

To the many members of the family, and others, who have cheerfully assisted him, he returns his sincere thanks. Especially are thanks due to the Rev. JOHN G. BERGEN, D. D., of Springfield, Illinois, from whom much valuable information has been obtained of the New Jersey branch of the family.

BAY RIDGE, NEW UTRECHT, Kings Co., N. Y., 1865.

particle of proof, as it is presumed some families among us, from similarity of names, have, with the aristocracy of the Fatherland. If any of the Bergens of this vicinity have fallen into this delusion, they may as well at once descend from the lofty eminence to which they have elevated themselves, and conclude that they are descended from the commonalty instead of the aristocracy.

They, however, are entitled to congratulate themselves, (if cause for congratulation it is,) that their paternal ancestor was a native of a country where the feudal system was never established: where, as in this country, the land was mainly held under no superior, not even the King: of the original seat of the Northmen, who, during the dark ages, made such frequent descents on the coasts of England and France; who were the ancestors of the Normans, a Scandinavian race, who conquered and carried their institutions to England and the fairer portions of Europe, who founded a kingdom in France and another in Southern Italy : and who discovered and visited the coasts of America centuries before the voyage of Columbus.

First Generation.

HANS HANSEN BERGEN, the common ancestor of the Bergen family of Long Island, New Jersey and their vicinity, was a native of Bergen in Norway, a ship-carpenter by trade, and removed from thence to Holland. From Holland he emigrated, in 1633, to New Amsterdam, now New York, probably arriving at Fort Amsterdam in April of that year with Wouter Van Twiller, the second Director General, in one of the vessels of the fleet, consisting of the West India Company's ships, the

Salt Mountain, (de zoutberg,) of 20 guns, commanded by Juriaen Blanck, the Carvel St. Martyn and the Hope, which vessels accompanied the Salt Mountain in her voyage from the Fatherland.

In the early colonial and other records, his name appears in various forms, his surname or patronymic, Bergen, derived from the place of his nativity, being generally omitted, as was the custom among the Hollanders and other Northern European nations in those days, and is the custom among some of them at the present time, and that of his father Hans, in the form of "Hansen," or "Hansz," representing the son of Hans, being generally added with other appendages referring to the land of his birth.*

Among these forms may be found that of "Hans Hansen Van Bergen in Noorwegan," "Hans Hansen Noorman," "Hans Noorman," "Hans Hansen de Noorman,"

---

* A man's name is the mark by which he is distinguished from other men. By our present almost universal practice it is composed of his Christian name and his surname. The one is given to him at his birth or baptism, the other, as at present practiced, derived from the common name of his parents. Anciently, among most European nations, there was but one name, surnames not commonly coming into use until the middle of the fourteenth century. The insufficiency of the Christian name to distinguish the particular individual where there were many bearing the same names, led necessarily to the giving of surnames. These in the great majority of cases were composed of the name of the place where the individual was born or dwelt, his occupation, some peculiarity in his appearance, character, history, qualities, or by adding to his Christian name that of his father, as Hans Hans, representing Hans, the son of Hanse. The latter was the common practice in this country among the descendants of the Netherlanders until about the beginning of the eighteenth century, when it gradually ceased, and true surnames from this have been since continued. Under it many families among us, although derived from a common ancestor, are now distinguished by different surnames, as for instance, the descendants of Adrueen Ryerse, of Flatbush, are now known by the surnames of Ryerse, Martense and Adriance. This change from generation to generation of surnames causes great difficulty in genealogical researches. The prefix of Van, meaning from, has also in many families been dropped. This is the case with the Couwenhovens, Ditmarses, and most of the Voorhees in our midst.

"Hans Hansz," "Hans Hausen,"* &c. The term "Noorman," meaning the Northman, evidently refers to Norway, and was applied to natives of that place, as for instance, Claes Carstensen, married at New Amsterdam in
1646, is said in the marriage entry to be from Norway,
and subsebuently he is called "the Noorman." Like
unto the great mass of the original emigrants to this
country, he probably belonged to an humble class in
society, and came hither to better his prospects and for-
tune. Of his European ancestry nothing is known,
which is the case with most of the early emigrants to
New Netherlands ; intercourse with their relatives in the
Fatherland having long ago ceased, and having, no
doubt, been obstructed in consequence of the piratical
conquest of the Colony by the English in 1664, during a
time of peace. Of the private letters which passed between the early settlers and their European relatives,
which might have thrown light upon their previous position, very few remain,† none having been found relating
to Hans Hansen. Many families can be traced by our
records with certainty to the first emigrant, but few beyond this without calling loudly upon the imagination
for assistance in the engrafting of them upon some European stock of a similar name.

In 1639, HANS HANSEN BERGEN married SARAH,
daughter of Joves, (George,) Jansen de Rapalie, (since
spelled Rapalje and Rapalye,) born according to the fam-

---

* On referring to the original records, which were generally signed by
the parties interested, we find the same mark affixed to these various
names by which Hans Hansen Bergen was known: thus clearly establishing that they were intended for the same person. It is common sense
and fact that a man's particular mark was intended for and is the evidence of his identity, as much as his full signature would be.

† The writer has in his possession several letters written by relatives
of the Voorhees family in the Fatherland, to their friends in this country,
and they are the only ones he has discovered in his examination of old
papers and documents among the descendants of the Netherlanders in
Kings County.

ily record on the 9th day of June, 1625, and who was the first white child of European parentage born in the Colony of New Netherlands, which then covered the present States of New York, New Jersey, and a portion of Connecticut. The early historians of this State and locality, led astray by a petition presented by her April 4th, 1656, (when she resided at the Waaleboght,) to the Governor and Council, for some meadows, in which she states that she is the first born Christian child in New Netherlands, assert that she was born at the Waaleboght. Judge Benson in his writings even ventures to describe the house where this took place. He says: "On the point of land formed by the cove in Brooklyn, known as the Waaleboght, lying on its westerly side, was built the first house, a one story log house, on Long Island, and inhabited by Joris Jansen de Rapalje, one of the first white settlers on the Island, and in which was born Sarah Rapalie, the first white child of European parentage born in the State." In this, if there is any truth in the depositions of Catalyn or Catalyntie Trico, (daughter of Jeronomis Trico of Paris,) Sarah's mother, (a copy of which may be seen on pages 49, 50, and 51 of Vol. 3 of New York Documentary History,) they are clearly mistaken. In her deposition taken on the 14th day of February, 1684-5, before Col. Thomas Dongan, Governor of the Province, she states that she came over in 1623 or 1624, to the best of her remembrance. In the other, taken "at her house on Long Island, in ye Wale Bought this 17th day of October, 1688" before William Morris, Justice of the Peace, she states, that she was aged about 83 years, and was born at Paris; that in 1623 she came to this country in the ship Unity, commanded by Arien Jorise, that as soon as they came to "Mannatans" now called N. York, they sent two families and six men to "harford River," two families and six men to Delaware River. 8 men they left at N. York to take possession, and the rest of the passengers went with the ship as far as Albany, then called "Fort Orangie." That deponent lived in Albany three years, that in 1626 she came from Albany and settled in New York, where she lived afterwards for many years, and then came to Long Island where she now lives."

Sarah therefore undoubtedly was born at Albany instead of the Waaleboght, and was probably married before she removed to Long Island, there being no reason to suppose that she resided there when a single woman, without her parents.

Joris, (George,) Janson de Rapalie, the father of Sarah, and the common ancestor of the Rapalie's of this country, is said by some writers to be a proscribed Huguenot, from Rochelle in France, an emigrant in 1623 in the ship Unity with Catalyn Trico, whom he probably married before the voyage (although the ceremony may have been performed after his arrival, having no date of the same,) appears to have resided for three years, until in 1626, in Albany, then removed to New Amsterdam, where he remained for more than 22 years, (occupying and owning a house and lot on the north side of the present Pearl Street, and butting against the south side of the Fort, for which he received a patent on the 18th of March, 1647,) and until after the birth of his youngest child in 1650.[*] During at least a portion of this time he kept a tavern or tap-house, as then styled, his name appearing as late as March 16, 1648, on the records in the book of the Burgomasters court[†] of said city, among the inn keepers and

---

[*] See Ricker's Newtown, p. 267. He sold his house and lot June 22d, 1654, to Hendrick Henderson, on which he probably removed to his farm, at the Wallabout.

[†] The records here referred to are proclamations, &c., issued prior to the establishment of the courts, and entered in the beginning of this book, containing said court records.

tapsters, inhabitants who promised to observe the procla mation of Gov. Stuyvesant of March 10, 1648, in relation to the regulation of such houses. Up to 1654 he figures frequently on the records of said court in numerous suits. His name however does not occur on a list of the tapsters of New Amsterdam of January 9, 1657, residing at this date on his farm at the Waalaboght, which he probably may have improved and partially cultivated while re siding in the city.

On the 16th of June, 1637, Rapalje obtained a patent and bought a tract of land of the Indians, Kakapeteyno, and Pewichaas, called " Rinnegackonck," situate on Long Island, south of the Island of Manhattans. On the 17th of June, 1643, his Indian purchase was patented to him by the Governor, and is described as "a piece of land called Rinnegaconck, formerly purchased by him of the Indians, as will appear by reference to the transport, lying on Long Island, in the bend of Mereckkawick,* (now Brooklyn.) East of the land of Jan Monfort, extending along the said land in a southerly direction, towards and into the woods 242 rods, by the kill and marsh easterly up 390 rods, at the sweet marsh 202 rods on a southerly di rection into the woods, and behind into the woods 384 rods in a westerly direction, and certain outpoints next to the marsh, amounting in all to the contents of 167 mor gens and 406 rods," (about 335 acres.)

On this land, which is situated in the City of Brooklyn, in the vicinity of the United States Hospital, and on the easterly side of the Waaleboght.+ Rapalie finally located,

---

*The bend of Mereckawick is tho same as the Waaleboght cove.

+Judge Benson in describing his imaginary house which he erects for Rapalie, places it on the westerly side.

and died soon after the close of the Dutch administration, having had eleven children.*

In August, 1641, Rapalie was one of the twelve men representing Manhattan, Breukelen and Pavonia, elected to suggest means to punish the Indians for a murder they had committed. In 1655, '56, '57 and 1660, he was one of the magistrates of Brooklyn.

March 1, 1660, Aert Anthonis, Meddagh, Tonis Gysbert Bogaert, Jorsey Rapalie, Jean LeCler, Jacob Kip and others, petitioned for permission to plant a village on the river opposite the Manhattans, in sight of Fort Amsterdam, between the lands of said Bogaert and Kip, but failed to obtain the same. Bogaert at this time possessed the lands patented to Hans Hansen Bergen, and the location of the proposed village was on the line between the towns of Brooklyn and Bushwick.

On the 26th of April, 1660, Rapalie petitioned to be allowed to leave his house standing on his farm for the present, which application appears to have been denied. At this period, in consequence of the Indian troubles, an order had been issued for those residing outside of the villages to abandon their dwellings, and remove to the villages, which were fortified, for safety.

Rapalie made the following mark for his signature to documents:

---

*His children as per an original family record preserved in the library of the New York Historical Society, were:—Sarah, b. June 9, 1625, m. successively to Hans Hansen Bergen and Teunis Gysbert Bogaert; Marritie, b. March 11th, 1627, m. Michael Vandervoort; Jannettie, b. August 18, 1629, m. Rem. Vanderbeeck; Judith, b. July 5th, 1635, m. Pieter Van Nest; Jan, b. Aug. 28th, 1637, m. Maria Fredericks, d. in 1662, without surviving issue; Jacob, b. May 28th, 1639, killed by the Indians; Catalyntie, b. March 28, 1641, m. Jeremias Westerhout; Jeronemus, b. June 27th, 1643, m. Anna Denyse; Annetie, b. Feb. 8, 1646, m. Marten Ryerse, and afterwards Joost Fransz; Elizabet, b. March 28th, 1648, m. Dirck Hooglandt; and Daniel, b. Dec. 29th, 1650, m. Sarah Klock.

His widow Catalyntie, died Sept. 11, 1689, aged 84, having been born in 1605, and must at least at the age of 20; and Sarah, her daughter, calculating from the birth of her oldest child, was married between that of 14 and 15. Cataly, the made her mark:

It has been asserted by our early writers that several families of Walloons, who emigrated with Reparie and his wife, in 1623, (who strictly speaking are the inhabetants of the frontier between Belgium and France,) settled as agriculturalists at the "Wahle-Bocht, or the Bay of the foreigners," since known as the Waaleboght in Brooklyn, as early as 1624 or 1625[*]. Of a settlement at so early a period at this location, there is believed to be no documentary proof, a rigid search failing to produce from our Colonial and early records evidence to sustain the assertion. The earliest recorded Indian grant to an individual for land in Kings County, is that to Jacob Van Corlear, on the 16th of June, 1636, for flats in Flatbush and Flatlands, and the earliest to the government or West India Company is dated the 1st of August, 1638, for land between Brooklyn and Mespath. There is also evidence showing that William Adriaanse, (Bennet,) and Jacques Bentyn, purchased in 1636, of the Indians, a large tract in Gowanus, and erected a dwelling house thereon, which was afterwards burned in the Indian wars. The earliest patents granted by the government (see book) for Brooklyn were to Thomas Bescher, on the 28th of November, 1639, of a plot of 300 paces in breadth, for a tobacco plantation, located probably at Gowanus[†]; and to Frederick Lubbertsen

---

[*] O'Callaghan's N. Netherlands, vol. I, p. 114

[†] April 5th, 1642, a patent was granted to Frederick Lubbertsen for a tract at "Gowanus," all being Walloon Association, District which land was formerly occupied by Jacob Van Remenis and Thomas Beets." A deed from Thomas Bescher ...

bertse, on the 27th of May, 1640, for a large tract opposite Governor's Island, neither being located at the Waaleboght. The first patents at the latter place, except that
of Rapalie, were those of Peter and Jan Monfoort of the
29th of May, 1641, of Lambert Huybertsen, (Mol,) of the
7th of September, 1641, of land formerly in the occupation of Cornelis Jacobsen Still : or Pieter Ceser Italien,
(the ancestor of the Alburtus family of Newtown,) for a
tobacco plantation, of the 17th of June, 1643 : of those
enlarging or more particularly describing the bounds of
the lands granted to the Monfoorts, of the 17th of August,
1643 : that of William Cornelissen, of the 19th of February, 1646, for premises formerly occupied by Michael
Picet : and that of Hans Hansen (Bergen,) of the 30th of
March, 1647. The Monfoorts and Huybertson may
have been Walloons : the name of Cornelissen indicates
that he was a Netherlander : Picet or Piquet was from
Rouen in France, which is located many miles from the
frontiers : he was banished in July, 1647, for slandering
and threatening ex-dire t or Kieft : pardoned by Stuyvesant, and in October of the same year, for threatening to
shoot the latter, sentenced to perpetual banishment and
eighteen years imprisonment in the work-house at Amsterdam. Pieter Ceser (Alburtus,) as his name indicates,
was an Italian : Hans Hansen Bergen was a Norwegian :
and Rapalie could not have been a Walloon by birth, if,

vidual known as Thomas Beets in the patent, to Cornelis Lambertsen,
(Cool,) of May 17th, 1639, (prior to the date of the first Brooklyn patent.)
recorded in the office of the Secretary of State at Albany, for the premises
covered in the patent, is the earliest conveyance from one settler to another which has been found for lands in Brooklyn. In this deed Bescher
conveys his right in "a plantation, before occupied by John Van Rotterdam,
and afterwards by him, Thomas Bescher, situate on Long Island, by Goawa-
nies, in the course towards the south by a certain creek or underwood, on
which borders the plantation of William Adriansen, (Bennet.) Cooper, and
to the north Claes Cornelise Smit's, reaching the woods in longitude ; for
all which Cornelis Lambertsen, (Cool,) shall pay to said Thomas Bescher
300 Carolus guilders, at 20 stuyvers the guilder." This is the earliest reference found in the records relating to a settlement in Brooklyn, and from
this deed it may be inferred that the first agricultural settlement in said
town was made on these lands, but however of this there is no certainty.

as asserted and claimed, he was a native of Rochelle, in France, a seaport on the Bay of Biscay, several hundred miles from the frontiers of Belgium. All Huguenots in those days may however have been known by the general title of Walloons, and the settlement of emigrants of this class at a later period in that vicinity, may account for the name, it being customary in Holland in those days to distinguish churches in their midst erected by French Huguenots, by the name of "Waale Kerken," or Walloon Churches, appears to favor this theory. The affidavits of Catelyn Trico, hereinbefore set forth, appear, however, to settle the point, that none of the families who came over with her located at the time of the emigration at the Waaleboght. It is not very reasonable to suppose that agricultural settlements existed in Brooklyn, and that improvements were made so many years prior to Indian purchases, or the granting of patents for the land. The most tempting locality on the west end of Long Island for settlers of the low and level lands of Holland or Belgium, who were experienced in the clearing of forests, were the flats in Flatlands and Flatbush, miniature prairies, void of trees, with a dark colored strong soil, similar to that of the prairies of the west, which had been subject to the arts and culture of the natives, and which were ready without much previous toil and labor for the plow. On these flats it is supposed, and almost certain, that the first agricultural settlements on Long Island were made, and their adaptation to cultivation accounts for their being first sought for and possessed.

Antony Jansen van Vaas, or Salee, generally written Antony Jansen van Salee, and designated in addition in portions of our early records with the appellation of "Turk," who on being banished from New Amsterdam in consequence of improper conduct on his part and that of his wife, Grietje Reiners, obtained in 1639 from Director

Kieft a grant of 100 morgens, (200 acres,) on the west end of Long Island, partly in the present towns of New Utrecht and Gravesend, on which he located and became the first settler in said towns, probably in consequence of the word Jansen, (meaning the son of Jan,) being common to both names. is fancied by some writers to have been a brother of Jores Jansen de Rapalie, but of this there is no proof. nor is this corroborated by our early records. they on the contrary going far to disprove it.

HANSE HANSEN BERGEN resided for some years in New Amsterdam. (now New York.) where he owned and probably occupied a lot on the present Pearl Street, butting against the fort, lying between the lots of Jan Snedeker, and that of Joris, (Jansen de) Rapalie, of one rod and two feet in breadth in front. one rod and nine feet in rear. with an average length of nine rods and five feet, Dutch measure. for which he received a patent. dated March 13th, 1647.[*] He also appears to have been interested in a plantation on Manhattan Island. as appears from a patent granted March 20th, 1642, to Thomas Hall,[+] in which the premises are described as "a piece of land lying on the Island of Manhatens. on the North River, formerly occupied by Edward Fiscock, Hans Hansen (Bergen, Maryn Adriansen, (having been owners.) bounded on the North by the plantation of the late Director Wouter Van Twiller and Laurens Dirckson. baker. and eastward by the swamp;" and as also appears by a note for 1000 carolus guilders. the purchase money of a plantation on the North River, on Manhatten Island, heretofore occupied by Hans Hansen, dated the 23d of January, 1643.[‡] It

---

[*] A Dutch rod is 12 feet and 3 inches, and a Dutch foot 11 three hundred and four one-thousandth inches English Measure.

[+] Vol. GG. p. 54. Dutch manuscripts, Secretary of State's office, Albany.

[‡] Vol. II. p. 43.

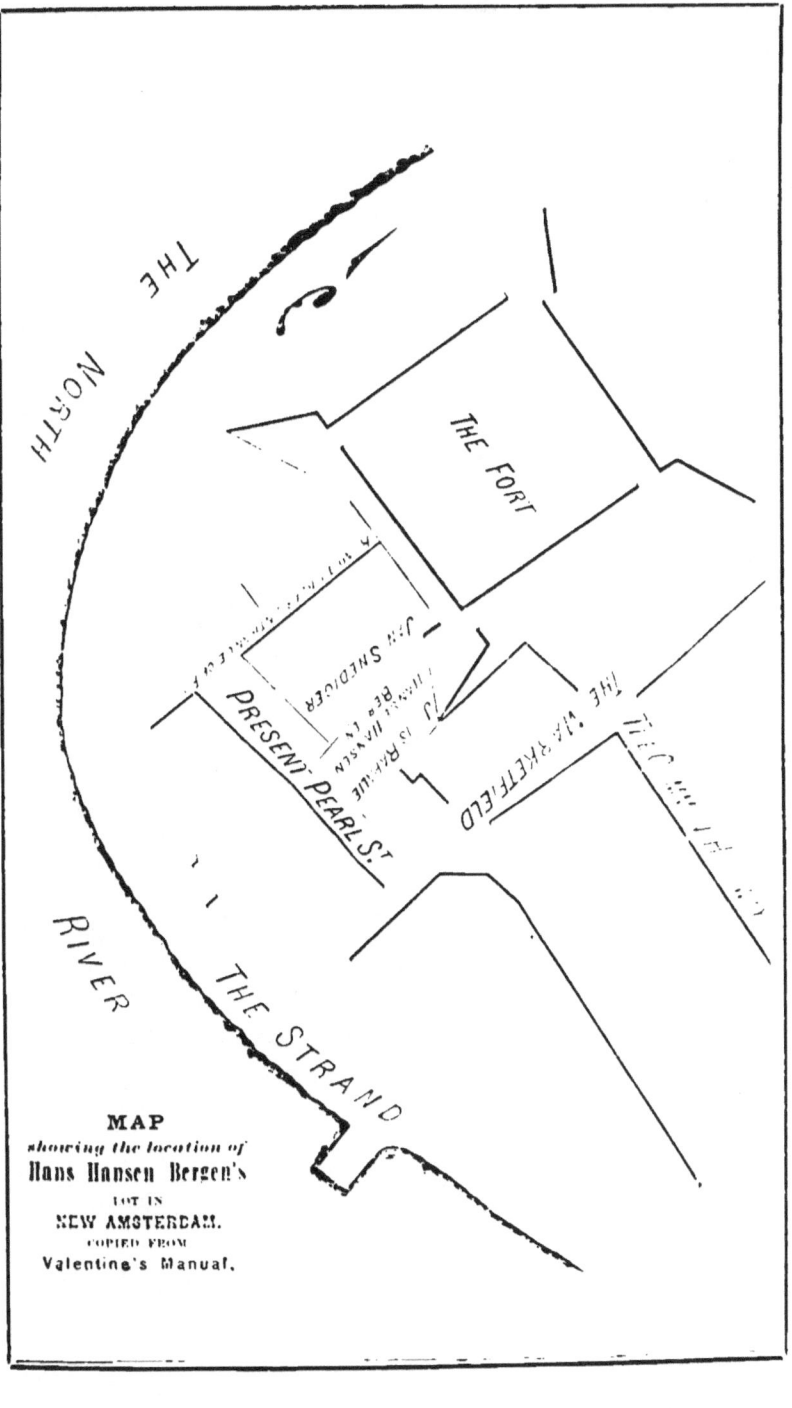

THE NORTH RIVER

THE

THE FORT

PRESENT PEARL ST.

JAN SNIDIGER

73 IS RAT-LINE
HANS HANSEN
BEG-LN

THE MARKETFIELD

THE STRAND

MAP
showing the location of
Hans Hansen Bergen's
LOT IN
NEW AMSTERDAM.
COPIED FROM
Valentine's Manual.

appears that Tunis Nyssen, (Denyse,) two of whose daughters married sons of Hans Hansen, also possessed a plantation in this vicinity. In 1638, Hans Hansen was engaged in the cultivation of a tobacco plantation or land of Andreas Holde, on Manhattan Island; and in 1643, from a law suit in relation to a shallop, (sloop,) it may be inferred he was engaged at his trade of shipwright, the agreement and minutes in relation to which are hereinafter given in full.

Hans Hansen's name with the mark "**H**" affixed, appears among those of the commonalty, who in 1643, at the request of Governor Kieft, met in the Fort to take into consideration the propositions which should be submitted to them for the general good. This was at a period when in consequence of Kieft's mismanagement they had aroused the hostility of the savages, with whom they were surrounded, and were in danger and trouble.*

By a receipt entered on the Register of the Provincial Secretary, it appears that on the 23d of April, 1644, Hans Hansen and George Rapalie, his father-in-law, hired cattle of William Smith of Stamford, and on the 29th of November of the same year he gave a note to Cornelis Maersen of Rensclaerswick for 250 guilders for wheat bought of him. George Rapalie also appears at the same time to have bought 215 guilders, worth of wheat from Maersen.†

On the 30th of March, 1647, he obtained from Governor Kieft a patent for "a piece of land situated on Long Island, in the kill of Jorse Rapalje, it extends from his house north by east till to Lambert Huybertse's (Mol) plantation, further on the kill of Jan the Swede, according to the old marks till to the land of Mesratches, to and along the Criplebush," &c. an patent to the premises

* See Vol. I. p. 191 of Colonial Documents.
† Vol. II. p. 136, Dutch Manuscripts, Secretary State

ion line of Derick Volkertsen's land, which he purchased
from Wilcock, and the division of Henry Satley, containing 200 morgen," (400 acres.)

This patent, as near as can be ascertained, covered at
least a portion if not the whole of the farms at the Waaleboght of the late General Jeremiah Johnson, and the adjoining one of the Remsens, and extended back to the old
Bushwick cross-roads, and to the meadows adjoining
Newtown; the land of Lambert Huybertsen Mol, on its
east side being the patent in the town of Bushwick which
adjoins the Brooklyn boundary. On this land he resided
as early as 1648, and may have resided at an earlier period, and there he continued to reside until his death, which
took place in the latter part of 1653, or the beginning of
1654.* He however must, either by extinguishing the
Indian title or otherwise, have been in possession of this
plantation prior to the date of his patent, for in the patent
of Abraham Rycken of August 8, 1640, his land is located on Long Island, opposite Rinnegakonck, bounded by
Gysbert Ryken, Hans Hansen, &c.; in a deed of the 29th
of July, 1641, of Cornelis Jacobson Selle to Lambert
Huybertsen Mol, he describes his plantation as next to
Hans Hansen, on Long Island,+ and in the patent to
Doughty and his associates of Mespat, on the 28th of
March, 1642, embracing nearly the whole town of Newtown, their lands are bounded by the meadows of Hans
Hansen.‡ Reference is also made to his lands in a survey
of the disputed bounds between Newtown and Bushwick,
made by Capt. James Hubbard of Gravesend, about 1669,
the draft of which is still preserved, and purports to be a

---

* He was probably living July 21, 1653, for on that date in a suit in the
Burgomaster's Court of New Amsterdam, of Jacob Vis against Hans Hansen, a default was entered against both parties, as was at the same term
of the court the case in a suit of the same plaintiff against Jores Rapalie,
the father-in-law of Hans.

† Vol. I. p. 251, Dutch Manuscripts, Sec'y. of State's Office, Albany.

‡ Riker's Newtown, p. 18 and 83.

"description of Mispath Kills see farre as to point out ye
situation of ye place, for some ffarther information of two
houses formerly inhabited, ye one by Hanse ye Boor,
(farmer,) which were Hance Hansonn, ye other called ye
Poles house." Riker, in his history of Newtown, states,
that from a careful survey of the patent, he arrives at the
conclusion, that Hanse's patent must have covered a part
and perhaps the whole of the present settlement at the
Bushwick cross roads.

His widow, Sarah, shortly after his death married Teu
nis Gysberts Bogaert, the ancestor of the Bogerts in this
vicinity, who emigrated from Holland in 1652, by whom
she had several children. Sarah early became a church
member in New York, and united with the Dutch Re
formed Church at Brooklyn, by certificate in 1664. She
died about 1685, aged about sixty, and the following is a
copy of her mark:

"S"

Her children by Bogaert, as near as has been ascer
tained were: Aertje, bap. Dec. 19, 1655, m. Oct. 14th,
1677, Theodorus Polhemius; Neeltje, bap. Feb. 22d, 1660,
d. young; Antje, bap. August 23d, 1665; Neesje, bap.
August 23d, 1665, m. August 22d, 1687, Cornelis Thni
son Denyse; Gysbert, m. April 16, 1689, Jannetje Sy
monse Van Aarsdalen; and Grietje, m. December 4th,
1687, Peter Jansen Haring of New York.

On the 4th of April, 1656,* "Sarah Jorese, (daughter of
Jores,) first born Christian child in New Netherlands and
widow of Hans Hansen," petitions the Governor and
Council for some meadows adjoining 200† morgen

* See Vol. VI. p. 53, of Dutch manuscripts in Secretary of State's
See, Albany.
† Two hundred morgen in the original Dutch records, erroneously trans
lated twenty by Vanderkemp.

granted her at the " Waalebocht:"[*] states that her neighbors mow the meadows in question and disturb her in the use of them, although they have meadows adjoining their own lands, and that she is burdened with 7 children; she also asks an exemption from taxes. The meadows were granted, but the exemption refused. Sarah, in stating in this memorial that she was a widow, neglected to state that she was again married and the wife of Bogaert, which latter must have been the case, judging from the New York baptismal record of their first-born child, Aartje, who is entered, as hereinbefore set forth, as baptised Dec. 19, 1655. No evidence has been found on the Colonial records showing that Sarah received a grant from the government or the Indians of 200 morgen, except her statement in the petition. She doubtless resided at this time on the farm patented to Hans Hansen Bergen, her late husband, and probably when referring to the land granted her, intended to be understood as referring to those lands. From this petition has probably arisen, with the aid of a little stretch of the imagination, the story of the Indians having presented her with a farm in consideration of her having been the first born white child in the colony.

The lot of Hans Hansen in New Amsterdam was sold by Sarah in 1654, shortly after his decease; the records at Albany showing "a patent granted upon a Transport made by Sarah Jooresay, the widow of Hans Hans, bearing date the 30th day of May, 1654, unto Caes Bording, for a certain lot of ground with the Housing thereupon within this city, lying on the south side of the Fort, between Jan Snediker's and Jores Rapalje's, containing in length on the east side 9 rod, 2 feet, and 2 inches, and on the west side 9 rod, 8 feet, and 3 inches; in breadth be-

---

* This is the earliest date that the word Waalebogt appears on the Colonial records, it being known previous to this as the bend of Merechkawick, the latter being the Indian name for Brooklyn.

hind on the west side 1 rod, 9 feet and 6 ... ...
south side 2 rod and 3 feet, by virtue of a ... ...
granted unto Hans Hansen aforesaid, ... 1 ... for a
confirmation," &c. This patent is dated June 1, 1667.

February 28th, 1656, a suit was brought in the Burgermaster's court in New Amsterdam, by Pieter Scher...
against Sarah Joris, (the widow of Hans Hansen) for the
payment of a note of 84 florits and 5 stuyvers,* signed
by her deceased husband in April, 1651. Defendant
stated "she knows nothing of the plaintiff, inasmuch as
the plaintiff hath not spoken to her for a long time, and
also it was not counted in the settlement of the deceased's estate." She requested a delay of payment until
next harvest, which was agreed to by the plaintiff.

On the conquest of the Colony of New Netherland by
the English in 1664, the Governor, as an acknowledg-
ment of their new masters, and perhaps to subserve for
the purpose of obtaining fees, required the inhabitants to
take out new patents. Bogaert, Sarah's second husband,
taking advantage of this, appears to have taken out the
new patent for Hans Hansen's 200 morgen in his own
name, instead of that of Hans's children, who were entitled to the same, and of whose possession of a portion
thereof no record has been found, nor any evidence showing that he made them any compensation for their patrimonial estate. It is possible, although not very probable,
that compensation was made, and that the written evidence has disappeared in the lapse of time. If Bogaert
defrauded the orphan children, it is probable he was not
the only guilty one, for the records show that in those
days there were others similarly situated, who took out
the new or confirmatory patents in their own names. To

* A florin or guilder is about 40 cents of our present ... ...
currency.

4

patent of Bogaert is as follows:—"Richard Nicolls, Esq. Whereas there was a patent or groundbrief heretofore granted by the Dutch Governor William Kieft unto Hans Hansen, bearing date the 30th day of March, 1647, for a certain parcel of land lying and being in the West Riding of Yorkshire upon Long Island, within the Kill then commonly called Jorse Rapalye's Kill, whose bounds did stretch along by the said Jorse Rapalye's House northeast and by east unto the Plantation then appertaining to Lambert Huberts, so on to John the Swede's Kill to the markt bounds, and then to the Kill belonging to Mespath by the swamp, from whence to run by the fence of Derick Volckersen's land which he bought of Willcocks, and so along by that belonging to the land of Henry Saetly, containing by estimation about 400 acres of ground, now the right and title to the said parcell of land being devolved upon Teunis Gisberts, who married the widow and Relict of Hanse Hansen aforesaid, for a confirmation unto the said Teunis Gisberts," &c.

Dated April 5, 1667.

In consequence of Hans Hansen Bergen and Jores Jansen de Rapalie both making their marks to documents,* it may perhaps fairly be inferred that they were illiterate men in an age when the natives of Holland were generally educated, and carried their schoolmasters as well as clergymen with them to their colonies; but this

---

* Other early emigrants also made their marks, among whom were Wolfert Garretse Van Couwenhoven, ancestor of the Cowenhoven or Conover family; Pieter Claesen, of the Wyckoff family; Albert Albertse, of the Terhune family; Jan Van Detmarsen, of the Ditmars family; Jan Van Kerke, of the Van Kerke family; Pieter Janse, of the Staats family; Jan Van Cleff, of the Van Cleef family; Pieter Cornelese, of the Luyster family; Ryck Hendrickse, of the Suydam family; Adriaen Andriesse, of the Onderdonk family; Derick Jansen, of the Hoagland family; Hendrick Willemse, of the Boerum family; Joost Durie, of the Duryea family; Nicholas Stillwell, of the Stillwell family; John Leeck, of the Lake family; Thomas Whitlock, of the Whitlock family, and nearly all the early residents of Gravesend, very few of the English settlers being able to write.

is not positive evidence, for it was customary in those days for persons who were able to write, in some instances to make a mark, the same as a seal is affixed to writings. The writer has, however, in no instance seen their signatures, and perhaps they were less educated than the Hollanders, being natives of other lands.

On the 12th of February, 1667, a patent was granted to Sarah, the widow of Hans Hans, upon a transcript bearing date the 10th day of March, 1663, made by Johannes Megapolensis, for a certain lot of ground in the City of New York, "lying and being on the south side of the Princes Graft, to the West of Michael Jans, and to the East of Susanna the Negrines, containing in breadth on the North and South sides one and fifty foot six inches, and on the West side nine feet."

On the 30 of July, 1671, a patent was granted to Cathaline, widow of Jores Rapalje, deceased, for a lot in New York.

The following are copies, or abridgements, of the entries on the early Colonial Records relating to *Hans Hansen Bergen*, and which have a bearing upon his biography :

"Conditions and stipulations agreed on between Andries Hudde and Hans Hansen Noorman on the 10th day of July, 1638.*

"1. Andries Hudde aforesaid shall, with the first opportunity of any vessel leaving a port of Holland, promise to Hans Hansen 6 or 8 persons, besides the tools required for the cultivation of Tobacco.

"2. Hans Hansen shall be holden to cultivate this plant on the plain situated on the Island Manhattan, behind Corlear's lot.

"3. Hudde shall be obliged to defray the expenses of transport, besides the sums paid in engaging them, and

* Vol. I. p. 19 of Dutch manuscripts in Secretary of State's office, Albany.

what might have been advanced before their arrival in port.

"4. Hans Hansen shall be obliged to provide the dwelling houses and stores for the tobacco as much as the time shall permit: he shall be further obliged to keep the persons emigrating from the Fatherland in constant employ to their mutual profit.

"5. Hans Hansen shall be invested with all power and authority over them in the absence of Hudde, without being subjected to any other control whatever. He, too, shall be obliged to pay half of all the expenses made by Hudde aforesaid. He shall further be holden to procure such a quantity of victuals as may be required for said number of persons, of which, however, Andries Hudde shall reimburse to him the half. Mr. Hudde shall be further obliged to pay Hans Hansen for his personal industry, in the manner as shall be agreed to by impartial men. Further shall Mr. Hudde not exact from Hans Hansen any payment for the land, but shall be obliged to assist him with such goods of his as may remain here, and all this till said Hudde shall have returned hither, when new measures may be adopted. While in regard to the above-mentioned stipulations, the parties submit their persons and goods to the judicature of the Supreme Court in Holland, or to any other lawful tribunal, all in good faith, without fraud or deceit. Signed as such. Done at Fort Amsterdam in New Netherlands, July 10, 1658.

A. HUDDE.

This is the ⊥ mark of
HANS HANSEN."

"This day appeared before me, Cornelis Van Tienhoven, Secretary of New Netherland, Hans Hansen van

Bergen in Noorwegan, and declared said Hans, that he had qualified as his attorney the Honorable, wise and prudent Wouter Van Twiller, who was before Director General of New Netherland, as he qualified him by this power of attorney, so that said Van Twiller may collect all money due him from Isbrant Adriaensen or his heirs, and that said Van Twiller shall make such an use of said money as Hanse shall direct him to do, which he Hans will consider any sum as paid to himself whenever the heirs shall have paid such money to said Director Van Twiller, and exonerate said heirs in such a case from all further demand.   Done in Fort Amsterdam in the Island of Manhattans this 18th of July, 1638."*

This is the mark of   I   HANS HANSEN VAN BERGEN.

+Augt. 30, 1640.
Jan Jacobsen from Vreeland,
vs.
David Davidsen and Hans
Noorman, defts.
In case of delivery of palisades.

After defendant had acknowledged to have purchased 800 palisades from the plaintiff, which they have not received, the plaintiff is bound to prove that he had said 800 palisades in the woods.

No further entry of the case, and probably settled.

‡ " Septr. 7, 1643.
Hans Hansen, plaintiff.
Lambert Clomp, defendant.

"On payment of 255 florens to deliver the half of a

* See Vol. I, p. 23 of Dutch manuscripts, Sec'y of State's office, Albany
† Vol. IV, p. 76, Dutch manuscripts, Secretary of State's office, Albany
‡ Vol IV, p. 246, Dutch manuscripts, Secretary of State's office, Albany

shallop (sloop). Defendant acknowledged he bought the shallop provided she was made tight and seaworthy. Decreed that if the seller can prove that the shallop was fitted to sail at the time when the bargain was struck or shortly after, &c., the defendant to pay as per contract." This matter of the shallop, (called Pernambuco,) was on the 8th of February, 1646, referred to arbitration.

\# "Appeared before me, Cornelis Van Tienhoven, Secretary in New Netherland, Hans Hansen, who in the presence of the witnesses acknowledged to owe Cornelis Maersen, residing in the colony of the Patroon Renselaer, the sum of 250 guilders, originating from the purchase of one hundred schepels wheat, which was delivered to him, Hans Hansen, by John Damon, which sum he Hans Hansen promises to pay on or before the first of April, 1645, next, and to a greater security so submits Hans Hansen, his person and property, real and personal, present and future, to the control of any court of justice. In truth whereof this was signed by him, and witnessed on the 9th of December, 1644. In Fort Amsterdam in New Netherland."

mark

+ This is the **H** of Hans Hansen,

made by himself.

‡ May 26th, 1648.
Hendrick Van Dyck,
      Attorney General,
        vs.
     Hans Hansen.

" On two metal chambers which the defendant assis-

---

* Vol. II. p. 136, Dutch manuscripts, Secretary of State's office, Albany.

† This mark, it will be perceived, differs from the preceding ones, and a question may be raised wherever it occurs whether the record does not refer to a different person, another Hans Hansen.

‡ See Vol. IV. p. 386, Dutch manuscripts, office Sec. of State.

|| A species of great guns or cannon.

ted one Bastiaensen in carrying. The Attorney General producing his written complaint, demanded execution. The defendant confessed that he assisted in carrying the chambers, but that he did not know from whence the sail maker Bastiaensen obtained them, and proved by witnesses that the sail maker offered them for sale long before.

The Director General and Council having seen the written conclusion of the Attorney General contra Hans Hansen, an inhabitant of this place, so is it, that the case being considered as pregnant with great consequences, but whereas Hans Hansen has borne a respectable character during his residence of 14 years in New Netherland, so are his faults with his opposition against the Director General for this time gratuitously remitted, although the aforesaid Hans Hansen must pray before the Council to God and justice for pardon, which has been performed by Hans Hansen, upon which the aforesaid faults have been pardoned, and the Attorney General non-suited with regard to the remainder of his conclusion."

*" Appeared before me in the absence of the Secretary, Jacob Hendrickse Kip, clerk of Cornelis Van Tienhoven, Secretary of New Netherlands, Mr. Harman Bastiaense, carpenter, residing at Fort Orange, who in the presence of the undersigned witnesses, appointed Isaac de Forest, an inhabitant of this place, to collect in his name from Hans Hansen, shipwright, now a resident of Long Island, the sum of 120 carolus guilders due to him, constituting, &c.

August 19th, 1649."

According to the entries on the record of the Protestant Reformed Dutch Church in the City of New York, the following are the children of HANS HANSEN BERGEN and *Sarah Rapalie:*—

† Vol. III. p. 59. Dutch manuscripts in Sec. of State's office, Albany.

Anneken, dau. of " Hans Noorman," bap. July 22d. 1640; sponsors, d' Heer Willem Kieft and Teuntje Jeurgien.

Breektje, dau. of " Hans Hanszen Noorman," bap. July 27th, 1642; sponsors, Jan Monfoort and Sarah Planck.

Jan, son of " Hans Hanszen de Noorman," bap. April 17th. 1643; sponsors, Jan Snyderkin and Annekin Bogardus.

Michiel, son of " Hans Hanzen Noorman." bap. Nov. 4th, 1645; sponsors, Michiel Pauluzen, Pieter Janszen. and Jannekin Rapalje.

Joris, son of " Hans Hanszen." bap. July 18. 1649; sponsors, Paulus Leendertszen and Marritie Lievens.

Marritje, dau. of " Hans Hanszen." bap. Oct. 8th. 1651; sponsors, Pieter Cornelszen. Judith Joris. and Annetie Laurens.

Jacob, son of " Hans Harszen." bap. Sept. 21, 1653 ; sponsors, Adriaen Blommart, Catalyn Joraszy. and Aert Willemszen and his wife.

Catalyn, dau. of " Hans Hanszen." (a twin with Jacob,) bap. Nov. 30th. 1653 ; sponsors, the same as at the bap. of Jacob.

Of these Catalyn probably died young, for Sarah their mother, as previously stated. in her petition of the 4th of April. 1656, sets forth that she is burdened with seven children, the old records showing no certain trace of Catalyn. with the exception of the entry of her baptism.

Second Generation.

Descendants of HANS HANSEN BERGEN and *Sarah Rapalie.*

ANNEKEN (or Annetje) HANSEN Bergen, bap. in New Amsterdam, July 20th, 1640; m. Jan. 17th, 1661, *Jan Clercq* of Brazil; witnesses, Teunis Gysbertse, step-father of the bride, and Jan Jorissen, (de Rapalie,) uncle of the bride. Jan Clercq d. Nov. 15th, 1661. She m. 2d Oct. 8th, 1662, *Derek Janse Hoogland*[*] of Maerseveen, in the Province of Utrecht. Sept. 27th, 1662, she became a communicant of the Reformed Dutch Church of Brooklyn; witness, Breckje Hanse (her sister.)

Supposed issue :—

Sarah, bap. Aug. 7th, 1681.
Lysbeth, bap. March 20th, 1684.
Neeltje, bap. June 11th, 1686.

The above are entered on the Flatbush Reformed Dutch Church records as children of Direk Janse Hoogland and Annetje Feddens, who may have been intended for Annetje Hansen, but of this there is no certainty and considerable doubt. If intended for her, it is singular that *Sarah*, her oldest child, should be born nineteen years after her marriage with Hoogland.

BRECKJE (or Rebecca) HANSEN Bergen, bap. in New Amsterdam, July 27th, 1642; m. *Aert Anthonise Middagh*,[†] the ancestor of the Middagh family of Brooklyn.

---

[*] Derek Janse Hoogland emigrated in 1657 and resided in Flat...

[†] Aert Anthonize (or Teunizen) Middagh emigrated from Holland in the ship Beaver in May, 1661. His descendants, who, in the first generation, generally added "Aertse" to their Christian name, owned large tracts of land in the City of Brooklyn in the vicinity of Henry and on the sides of Fulton street.

5

whose male descendants, although they have disappeared from among us, have left as a memorial Middagh street in said city. Sept. 27th, 1662, she became a communicant of the Dutch Church of Brooklyn. Issue :—

Jan, bap. Dec. 24th, 1662 ; sponsors, Jan Hansen (Bergen) and Catrina de Rappalie. On the baptismal record Middag is stated to be of the Wallabout. Jan signed his name Jan Aersen ; m. Adriaentje, dau. of Cornelis De Potter, owned some 200 acres of land on the East River, east of Fulton street, Brooklyn, afterward of Comfort and Joshua Sands, and had several children.

Garret, b. ———— ; m. Sept. 25th, 1691. Cornelia Janse Cowenhoven, and had children, Breekje, Jan, Dina, who m. George Rapalje, and Aert. His farm of 30 acres was located at Brooklyn ferry, on the west side of Fulton street.

Dirck, b. ———— ; m. Catalyntie ————, and had a s. Cornelius bap. June 13th, 1698.

JAN HANSEN Bergen, bap. in New Amsterdam, April 17th, 1644 ; living as late as 1715 ; m. *Jannetje Teunis*, dau. of Teunis Denyse, (sometimes written Nysen, Nyse, or Nyssen,) of Gowanus, who survived her husband and d. a short time previous to 1735. *Jannetje* was bap. Dec. 24th, 1641.

The first notice of Jan Hansen on our old records after his bap. is in the following :—March 18th, 1662, was made "a kind request to the Director General and Council of New Netherlands, if it will please them to present us the grant of a parcel of woodland situated between the

land of Joris Rapalje, next to the old path to the Bay.
Done at the Waelcboclit." Was signed

> JAN JORIS RAPALJE,
> TEUNIS GYSBERT BOGAERT,
> CORNELIS JACOBSEN,
> HENDRICK SWEERS,
> MICHEAL HANSEN (Bergen)*
> JAN HANSEN (Bergen).

"The request is granted to the supplicants, provided
that they shall place their dwellings within a concentration, which shall suit them best, but not to make a new
concentration."† *Jan Hansen* resided for some years at
Bedford, probably on land obtained through this application. His descendants have a tradition that he was the
owner of vessels engaged in voyages at sea, and that he
lost them in a great storm. From pages 452 and 456 of
Vol. 2 of Documents relating to the Colonial History of
New York it appears that a "Jan Bergen" was skipper
or captain of the ship St. Jan Baptist, Dec. 31st, 1661,
and that he was skipper of the ship "Bontekoe" or Spotted Cow, Dec. 31st, 1663. The Colonial records also
show that in May, 1661, he carried to New Amsterdam
in the St. Jan Baptist a cargo of emigrants; also in April,
1663, in the Bontekoe, and in April, 1664, in the ship
"d'eendracht," Concord, or Unity. From the books of
Warrants, Orders, &c., in the Secretary of State's office,
Albany, it appears that on the 5th of December, 1664,
Governor Nicolls, on petition, gave leave to "John Bergen," master of the ship Unity, to come to New York
with his ship and loading of Holland goods the next

---

* The part in parenthesis not in the original, which is the case in all
similar instances in this work where names in parentheses are added.
Under this application the petitioners obtained 20 morgen or 40 acres
apiece at Bedford.

† Vol. X. p. 88, Dutch manuscripts, office Secretary of State.

year; and on the 7th of the same month he gave him leave to transport to Holland in his ship a number of persons who were desirous of leaving the colony. Nov. 1st, 1664, a suit was pending in the Burgermaster's and Schepen's Court of New Amsterdam, between Skipper Jan Bergen, plaintiff, and Tamis Danidts, defendant, in which the plaintiff claimed 340 gl. 2 st. in beavers for freight, which, after several adjournments, he finally recovered. The Jan Bergen named in the above references may have been *Jan Hansen*, taking into consideration the fact of his father having been a ship carpenter and the family tradition of his having owned vessels, but if it was he had command of a vessel at the age of eighteen. The matter, however, cannot be determined with certainty at this late period.

March 14th, 1675–6, "*Jan Hansen*," of Bedford, on his own behalf, and by virtue of verbal authority of Jan Vennagar, conveyed to "Claes Pieterse," (Wyckoff,) about 12 morgens of land in Flatlands. On the same date he conveyed, on his own behalf, and by virtue of power from the aforesaid Jan Vennagar, to Dierek Jansen, about 16 morgens of land also located in Flatlands.*

In 1675 "*Jan Hansen*" was assessed in Brooklyn for 10 morgens, and in 1676 for 18 morgens of land.

In 1677 "John Hansz Bergen" and "Jannetje Teunis," his wife, of Bedford, were members of the Reformed Dutch Church of Brooklyn, and in the same year he is entered on the church records as removed to the town of Jamaica, where he continued to reside on a farm at Foster's River, with probably a mill attached, until his death.

March 13th, 1681, "Jan Hanse," Jerome Rapalje and John Tunison purchased land at Rockaway of the Indians.† March 2d, 1682, "Eenamant and Mongowack,"

---

* Flatland town records.

† Hempstead Records, Book C, p. 29.

Indians of "Recowack," petitioned the Governor and Council to confirm the sale and grant a patent to the purchasers for said lands. In this petition they set forth "that they, out of old acquaintance sake and Love, have freely Given and Granted, without any perswasion or seduction of any person or persons, unto Jan Hansen, Jerome De Rapale and Jan Theunissen a certain Neck of land being and Laying att Long Island, in the North West point of Recowack, Beginning from a certain Creeke called Cockwas, running from thence South by West to another Kill called Hapex, and farther to the other side of the River or Plaine."

March 13th, 1681, the commander-in-chief of the colony sent a letter to the constable and overseers of Hempstead, notifying them of the above application, and inquiring whether the premises had previously been purchased by the town, or were free and at the disposal of the Indians, and calling for a report.

March 20th, 1683-4, Hansen, Rapale and Theunissen again petitioned to have the above lands confirmed to them by a patent, in which the creek designated in the previous application as "Cockwas" is called "Coppwax."[*] On the remonstrance of Hempstead this Indian purchase was abandoned.

March 15th, 1684-5, "Jan Hansen" and Benjamin Coe had liberty from Jamaica to set up a corn and fulling mill on Foster's meadows in said town.[†] There was at this time a Dutch settlement at Foster's meadows.

March 6th, 1687-8, "John Hansen" exchanged six acres of land lying between Foster's River and Mill River.[‡] On a return of marriages, christenings and burials in the town of Jamaica for seven years preceding

* Vol. II. Land papers, in office of Sec. of State, Albany, p. 3 and 52
† Jamaica Records, Book 1, p. 190.
‡ Jamaica Records, Book 2, p. 142.

1688, "John Hansen" is entered as having had one burial.*

June 3d, 1692-3, Benjamin Coe conveyed to "John Hansen 60 acres of land in the bounds of Hempstead, near Foster's meadows.

In 1693-4 "John Hansen" subscribed toward the payment of the salary of the Presbyterian minister in Jamaica.

April 26th, 1697, he sold his lands, 40 acres, in Bedford, Brooklyn, to Lucas Coeverts.

May 12th, 1697, "John Hansen's" name appears on the town records of Jamaica, who, with others, his townsmen, received 20 acres of meadows at the farther East Neck.†

June 9th, 1706, Gersham Higgins conveyed to "Jan Hanse" two acres on the main street in the village of Jamaica.

July 13th, 1708, Jonathan Whitehead conveyed to "Johannes Berge" 11¾ acres at Jamaica in the hills; probably a wood lot.

February 19th, 1709, "John Hansen's" name appears on a petition as one of the elders of Dominie Freeman's congregation in Queens County, addressed to Governor Ingoldsby, complaining that Dominie Antonides intended to ordain an opposition consistory and preach illegally in their church, and praying for an order to restrain him. To this document are appended his initials "H. B."‡ This was at the period of the wranglings and disputes in the Reformed Dutch congregations in Kings and Queens counties between Dominie Freeman and Dominie Antonides, in relation to their respective claims to the Pastorship, in which partisan spirit arose to such a height as to

---

* Documentary History of New York, Vol III. p. 197.

† Jamaica Records, Book 2, p. 39.

‡ Documentary History of New York, Vol. III. p. 156.

cause, in at least one instance, the breaking down the church doors to obtain possession of the pulpit. The main foundation of this unhappy controversy appears to have been the question, whether the congregations had the right to call a minister without the intervention of the Governor. Freeman's friends favored the interposition of the Governor. This dispute was finally healed in 1714, a union took place, and both Pastors officiated alternately in all the Dutch churches.

April 29th, 1710, John Garretsen conveyed to "John Hansen" the one-half of a house and lot in the village of Jamaica, and in the same year he subscribed 12 shillings towards the salary of the Rev. Mr. Poyinslay, a Presbyterian clergyman.

April 29th, 1715, "Jan Hansen Bergen" subscribed £3 towards building a Dutch Reformed Church in Jamaica.

November 21st, 1735, the seat of "Jannetje Bergen," (widow of Jan,) in the Reformed Dutch Church in Jamaica was sold to Isaac Van Hoeck.

Jan Hansen Bergen in some instances made his mark thus, *H3* to documents; in others he signed his name, the following being a *fac simile* of his signature:

Issue:—

Hans, bap. Feb. 14th, 1677, in New York.

Teunis, bap. April 20th, 1679, in Brooklyn; sponsors, Lucas Teunis (Coevert) and Sarah Teunis.

Adriaantje, bap. Dec. 11th, 1681, in Brooklyn: sponsors, Hans Teunis (Denyse) and Antje Teunis (Denyse).

Marretje, bap. March 29th, 1685, in Flatbush, (by Flat

bush church records); sponsors, Jan Teunis (Denyse) and
Neeltje Teunis Boogaard.

Sarah.

MICHIEL OR MIGGUEL HANSEN Bergen, bap. Nov. 4th,
1645, in New Amsterdam · living as late as Jan. 22d,
1731, and d. about 1732 : m. *Femmetje Theunis*, dau. of
Theunis Denyse,* (sometimes written Nysen, Nysse or
Niessen.) of Gowanus, and sister of Denyse Teunis the ancestor of the Denyse family of Kings County and New
Jersey. Femmetje was bap. April 3d, 1650, in New Amsterdam.

March 10th, 1661, his name appears to the petition
herein before referred to in the account of Jan Hansen, to
the Governor and Council for more land. May 15th,
1664, he obtained from Gov. Stuyvesant a patent for 20
morgens at New Bedford in the Wallabout. After the re-
capture of the New Netherlands from the English by the

* *Tuenis Nyssen* emigrated from Binnck, or Bennekom, a village in the
province of Gilderland, in the Netherlands, as early as 1638, and d. prior
to August, 1663, having m. Femmetje Janse, wid. of Hendrick the
Boor or Farmer, and probably a dau. of Jan Evertse Bout. After
Nyssen's decease she m. August 24th, 1663, Jan Cornelisz Buys of
Brooklyn, and d. prior to 1667. Prior to 1639, Nyssen appears to have
possessed or occupied a plantation on Manhattan Island, and Dec. 1, 1646,
he bought of Leendert Arenden, a house and lot on the great highway,
opposite the company's garden, on said Island. March 28, 1647, he obtained a patent for a lot N. of the public wagon road, and E. of the company's land on Manhattan Island, which lot he sold on the 13th of May,
1649, to Govert Loockermans. April 3d, 1647, he obtained from Gov.
Kieft a patent for the plantation on the same Island, formerly occupied by
Jan Celes, adjoining the Rev. Everardus Bogardus's land, and the negroes
plantation, which he conveyed January 17th, 1651, to Augustyn Hermans.
He also obtained a patent for a plantation and meadows at Gowanus, in
the vicinity of 4th and 5th avenues and Carroll and President streets,
where he at one time resided. In 1656, he probably resided at Flatbush,
for on the 13th of Dec. 1656, "Teunis Nyson of Midwout," (as per Valentine's Manual of 1861, p. 591,) conveyed to Cousin Gerretsen a lot in New
Amsterdam. The plantation he owned in Flatbush, he bought in 1655, of
Evert Duycknigh, for 660 carolus guilders. He resided in Brooklyn in
1658 and 1661, and in said years was a magistrate in said town. His
children were Annetje, m. Hieronomus Rapalie ; Jannatie m. Jan Hansen
Bergen; Elsje, m. Gerrit Snediker; *Femmetje*, m. Michiel Hansen Bergen; Marretie, m. Dirck Janse Veerman, or the (ferryman;) Jan, m.
Catelina Teunis Bogaert; Dionys, m. first Elizabeth Pollemius, m. second, Helena, dau. of Jacques Cortelyou, whose descendants form the Denyse family of this vicinity.

Hollanders on the 25th of Oct. 1673, he was appointed a lieutenant of militia under the administration of Anthony Colve, the Netherland Governor. In 1676 and 1683, his name appears on the assessment rolls of Brooklyn, for 20 morgens, the amount of his patent, on which at the time he probably resided. Nov. 19th, 1679, the names of " Michiel Hansz Bergen and Femmetje Teunis, his wife," appear on the list of members of the Reformed Dutch Church of Brooklyn, and from 1680 to 1685, he appears to have held the office of deacon in said church.

March 2d, 1674, Michiel Hansen, of Bedford, agreed to purchase a plantation of Albert Cornelise Wantenaer, of Breukelen, for 8,500 guilders, 1,000 gl. down, one-fourth, (1,875 gl.) of the remainder to be paid at Christmas, 1675; one-fourth at Christmas, 1676; one-fourth at Christmas, 1677; and the balance at Christmas, 1678. The payments to be made one-third in wheat, one-third in peas, and one-third in all kinds of corn at the market value, and when all paid the deed to be delivered. In the agreement, Cornelise describes the premises as " his plantation situated here at Breukel, next to the land of Jan Evertse Bout, dec'd, but at present of Andriese Jurianse, southeast of the meadows; east 68 rods, southeast 30 rods, further the maize land* up to against the woods, northeast by north 60 rod, in the woods northeast by east 85 rod, in breadth in the woods to the land of said Andries Jurianse northwest 87 rods, again to the maize land next to the aforesaid Andries Juriansen, southwest and southwest by west 55 rods, the maize land through to the first descent southwest a little southerly 137 rods, containing 19 morgen and 105 rods; also yet another parcel of land joining

---

* By maize land is meant land used by the Indians in the cultivation of sea maize or Indian corn, which on account of being partly cleared was very desirable to early settlers.

the above mentioned land, thereafter to said Cornelisse allowed and on his patent noted, great about 9 or 10 morgen, so that the whole land contains about 29 morgens as it more particularly by the patent can be seen : with the above to be included the meadows by said plantation located, and by Albert Cornelisse previous to this bought of Theunis Niessen, dec'd which he promises to describe by the patent or deed from said Theunis Niessen." The boundary in the original patent of Gov. Kieft, of Feb. 22d, 1646, for this land to Huyck Aertsen van Rossum, accords mainly with the description in the above agreement, and is as follows : "a piece of land lying at Mareckka-wieck,* on the marsh of Gouwanos Kill, the maize land as well as woodland, lying on the southeast by the land of Jan Evertse along the marsh, east 68 rods, southeast 30 rods, further along the maize land till to the woods northeast by north 60 rods, in the woods northeast by east 85 rods, the breadth in the woods till to the land of said Jan Evertse, (Bout,) northwest 87 rods, again to the maize land next the land of the aforesaid Jan Evertse, southwest and southwesterly 55 rods, through the maize land to the first descent southwest a little southerly 137 rods, amounting in all to 19 morgen and 105 rods." Endorsed on the patent is also "yet another adjoining parcel granted so as his land to contain by the measurement of the surveyor 29 morgen." A confirmatory patent for these premises was granted, June 21, 1667, by Gov. Richard Nicolls to Albert Cornelissen, (Wantenaer,) who is stated therein to have married Trientye, the widow of the said van Rossum, in which the boundaries accord with the original patent, but the quantity is set forth to be in all 90 morgen or 180 acres.

March 7th, 1680-1, Cornelissen conveyed by endorse-

---

* The Indian name of Brooklyn.

ment on the back of both patents, to Micheal Hansen Bergen, all his rights in both patents ; also by a separate conveyance the adjoining meadows, which he had bought from Theunis Nissen, on the 16th of May, 1656, and which meadow was confirmed to Cornelissen by a patent from Gov. Nicolls, dated June 26, 1668.*

This is the farm, the main portion of which a few years ago was the property of the heirs of George Powers, deceased, distinguished as the Powers' farm on Butts' map of Brooklyn.

In consequence of Michiel Hansen holding and claiming 90 morgen, as per Gov. Nicoll's confirmatory patent, when the original one of Gov. Kieft covered but 29 morgen, the general boundaries in both being similar, the freeholders of Brooklyn, about 1722, commenced a suit in chancery against him to recover for their benefit the balance over the 29 morgen, but the dispute was finally settled after the title was vested in his son Hans, as will hereinafter appear.

In Dongan's patent of Brooklyn of May 13th, 1686, Michiel Hanse (Bergen) is named as one of the patentees. In 1681, 1682, 1686, 1688, and 1689, he held the office of one of the overseers or commissioners having in charge the town lands and to defend town rights, three citizens being customarily selected for this purpose.

In September, 1687, his name appears among those who took the oath of allegiance to the British government. Oct. 22d, 1688, he was commissioned as Captain of the Brooklyn company of militia, by Gov. Nicholson ; and Dec. 27th, 1689, he received a commission for the same office from the acting Governor, Jacob Leisler, whose side he seems to have espoused in the difficulties which at the time convulsed the colony, and which ended in the un-

* The first two patents and the conveyances are in the hands of the writer.

just condemnation and execution of Leisler, and his son-in-law, Milbourne.

November 21, 1692, Michiel Hansen (Bergen,) Aris Janse (Vanderbilt,) Johannes Nan Ekelen, Symon Hansen, and Daniel Remsen, were sent on behalf of a company, (mainly residents of Flatbush,) of which they were partners, to Pennsylvania to select a good tract of land for a settlement and residence, which when found to purchase for their joint use: the partners remaining at home, each to pay two pieces of eight towards the expenses of the journey. At this period and in the beginning of the next century, many families emigrated from the partially worn out lands of the west end of Long Island to the new and fertile lands of New Jersey and Pennsylvania, the cheapness of which afforded an opportunity to enlarge their borders and better their condition. This emigration at one period was so great that the Colonial Governors complained of it in their communications with the home government. Bergen's, Wyckoff's, Cowenhoven's or Conover's, Denyse's, Stoothoff's, Barkeloo's, Rapalye's, Cortelyou's and others, descendents of these emigrants are numerous in the above named States. Having found no result of this expedition, it may be presumed, from most of the parties remaining in the county, that no land was purchased.

Oct. 11th, 1698, Michiel Hansen was appointed a Justice of the Peace by the Governor, the Earl of Bellmont, and was one of the Justices of the Sessions, which office he held until 1703 ; in the same year his family is entered on the census of Brookland as consisting of "1 man, 1 woman, 3 children and 2 slaves." In 1701 he was fined eight shillings for not bringing his slaves and negro women before the court as bound to the sheriff. In 1702 he was assessed for one hundred acres of arible land.

In 1708, his name among others appears on an agreement to call a Minister from Holland, in the Reformed Dutch Church of Brooklyn.

April 20th, 1709, "Machielle Hansen" bought of Garret Middagh for £429, "a house, orchard and house lot at the ferry, Brooklyn, containing about 10 acres, bounded easterly in the front and to the street from a certain house now standing and formerly in possession of John Smith, deceased, and soe stretching from said house all along a certain fence and soe by the house abovesaid and barn thereto belonging, to the salt water river; northerly by said river called the East river from high water mark thereof, soe far along said river to the westward till it comes opposite the rear fence of said land that joynes upon the land of the heyres of Jores Remsen deceased; and southerly by the land and orchard formerly in the possession of said John Smith deceased, and the land of the said Garret Middagh, excepting always out of this deed and grant out of the bounds of the land abovesaid, the house and ground of John Evertse* to him sold formerly by John Gerretse Van Couwenhoven, as per deed thereof may appear, &c.; as alsoe all that ground on said river side to the westward of said John Evertse's house and ground soe far alongst said river till it comes opposite with the reare fence of said land that joynes upon the land of the heyres of Jores Remsen deceased, to begin from high water mark all alongst said river and within the limits aforesaid, and so to run 25 English floot up into the hill and noe more, as a reserve for the use and property of the grantor his heyres and assigns forever; And likewise the said Garret Middagh doth grant, &c., to the said Machielle, &c., all that spot of ground lying in the

---

* Probably John Everts's Boat. Thomas Everett a few years ago owned a plot in this vicinity, probably the plot above referred to, and said Thomas may be a descendant of said John Everts.

front and before said house, ground and bargained premises to the streetward, beginning from a certain house now standing and formerly in the possession of said John Smith deceased, all along said house and bargained premises to the salt water river, the length thereof and in breadth by the farthermost Pale that now stands in the sand, containing 66 English ffoot between said pale and the house, garden and barne of said bargained premises, together." &c. In this conveyance is the following singular provision :—" and if said Machielle or any of his heyres shall at any time hereafter see cause to sell and dispose of the abovesaid house, land and bargained premises, that the said Garrett Middagh or his heyres (if he or they see cause) shall have free privilege to purchase the same for the price of £429 current money of New York, and upon the payment of said sum a deed to be given for the same by the said Machielle or his heyres to the said Garrett Middagh or his heyres, and that the said Machielle or his heyres may not dispose of the said premises to any other person but to those of his or their offspring if the said Garrett or his heyres see cause to buy the same for the price aforesaid, he the said Garrett or his heyres paying over and above the price aforesaid for all new buildings that shall be at that time upon said land within fence, as any two indifferent men shall value it."* &c. June 4th, 1710, for £400, Michial Hansen, conveyed the above premises to his son Hans Bergen ; they were probably at some subsequent period conveyed back by Hans or his heirs to the Middagh's, the records showing nothing farther in relation to them, and they appear to have covered nearly all the land on Brooklyn heights from the vicinity of Clark street to about Doughty street, including a portion of the river front.

* See Lib. 3. p. 178 of con. K. C. Reg. Office.

In 1710 and 1711, Michiel Hansen's name again appears as a Justice of the Sessions; and Aug. 1st, 1711, as an elder of the church in "Brookland," with others on a petition to Gov. Hunter, for a charter for the church, which they failed to obtain. Oct. 9th, 1711, Cornelis Vander Hoove commenced a suit against him for £100.

August 21st, 1723, for £800, he conveys to his son Hans Bergen, of the ferry, his farm in "Brookland," (the land he bought of Albert Cornelisse Wantenaer,) "bounded S. E. by the fence of Martin Adriance; N. W. by Carel De Bevoise and the King's highway that goes to the ferry; and S. W. by the meadows; also, land at the east side of the Highway from Flatbush to Brookland, containing together with the land bounded as aforesaid and the woodland at the east side of the way aforesaid, 180 acres." Also, a lot of woodland in the second division of Brookland, and another lot in the same division both together containing 20 acres; also, the meadows in said town belonging to him.

August 21st, 1723, on the same date, an agreement was entered into between Hans Bergen, of the ferry, (son of Michiel,) of the one part, and Michiel Hansen Bergen, Femmetje Bergen, now the wife of John Vanderveer, Sarah Bergen, now the wife of John Strycker, and Mary Bergen, all daughters of said Michiel Hansen Bergen, of the other part, in which it is set forth that said Michiel Hansen Bergen, for the consideration of £800, has sold to his son Hans his lands, for which Hans is to defend without any liability or expense on the part of his father, a suit in Chancery, brought against said Michiel Hans by the inhabitants of Brookland for the recovery of part of his lands, the expense of said suit to be equal'y borne by himself and his three sisters, and to be deducted from the sums herein provided to be paid them by Hans; Hans to pay his sister Mary £200, Femmetje £200, and Sarah

£200, after the death of their father; Michiel Hans to hold possession and have the use of the premises during his life. The complaint in the above suit, was, that Michiel Hansen had taken up 120 acres of land more than what he was entitled to by Kieft's patent. Hans soon compromised the matter, and ended the suit, for it appears that January 7th, 1723-4, sixty-one of the freeholders of Brooklyn, (who were probably all, or nearly all who resided in the place,) for £40, released to Hans Bergen all their right in the 180 acres occupied by his father Michiel. Hans afterwards brought in a bill of £375, 7 sh. and 6 1-2d., up to January 19th, 1723, incurred for lawyer's fees, personal services, &c., (including the £40, paid the town,) in the defence of this suit, and a charge of interest from said date, to June 10th, 1732, of £252, and 10 sh. at 8 per cent. making a total of £693, 15 sh. 9 1-2d. which bill, if allowed, must have swallowed up the main portion of his sisters' patrimony.

January 22d, 1730-1, Michiel Hansen and Jeronimous Rapalje, two of the surviving patentees of " Brookland," convey to Cornelius Van Duyn, Carl de Bevois and Hans Michielse Bergen, for and in behalf of the freeholders of said town, their right in the common lands.* The object of this conveyance appears to be to confirm the several acts of the Trustees or Commissioners of said town in dividing their common lands: Michiel in some instances, if not in all, as a patentee having heretofore refused his assent to their divisions, perhaps on account of the dispute about his own lands herein before referred to.

The following is a fac simile of his signature :

*See Lib. 5, p. 96, of con. Kings Co., Reg. office.

Issue :

Sarah, bap. June 2d, 1678; sponsors, Theunis Gysbertse Boogaard and Sara Jorisen (Rapalie.)

Teunis, bap. May 16, 1680; sponsors, Teunis Guysbertsz Boogaard and Sarah Jores Rapalie.

Hans, bap. March 11, 1689.

Femmetje.

Mary.

JORES OR GEORGE HANSEN, bap. in New Amsterdam. July 18th, 1649. Living as late as 1723; m. August 11th, 1678, *Sara Stryeker*, dau. of Jan Stryeker* of Flatbush.

November, 1662, Jores Hansen's name appears among the catechumens, and in 1677 among the members of the Reformed Dutch Church of Brooklyn. November 19th, 1679, his wife's name also appears among the members of the same church.

In September, 1687, his name appears among those residing in Brooklyn, who took the oath of allegiance to the British government, in which year from a deed it appears he owned land in "Brookland," bounded on one side by land which Sophia Van Loedsteyn conveyed to Jurian Hendrickse Vander Breets. From 1690 to 1699 inclusive, he was one of the Commissioners or Trustees of the common lands of "Brookland." In December, 1695, George Hansen requested the court to be allowed to enclose his lands all together, between "Brookland" town and Flatbush, and for the making of a new highway within in his lands between said towns, &c.+

---

* *Jan Stryeker*, the common ancestor of the Stryker's of Kings County and vicinity, emigrated from the the province of Ruinen in the Netherlands in 1652, and married 1st Lambertje Seubering, the mother of Sara ; m. 2d, April 30, 1679, Swantje Jans, widow of Cornelis De Potter; and m. 3d, April 22d, 1687, Teuntje Teunis, widow of Jacob Hellakers.

+ See Kings County court records.

7

September 13th, 1698, Marretje Garitse, widow of
Nicholas Janse, baker, late of the City of New York,
dec'd, conveyed for £176 and 11s. to "George Hansen of
"Brookland," premises in Brooklyn containing 39 acres
and 40 rods, Dutch measure, as in fence and in possession
of said George, bounded southeast by land of Jurian
Andriese; northwest by land of Jacob Hansen (Bergen,)
and land of Derrick Woortman; southwest by Gowanos
Kill; and northeast by the Kings highway: formerly in
the possession of Gerret Wolpherste (Couwenhoven,) as
per patent to said Gerret of Gov. Wm. Kieft, of March
11th, 1647: also the just and equal part of all that Hook
or Neck of land in said township, containing 55 Dutch
rods broad, and 250 Dutch rods long, bounded south by
land of Jacob Brower; north by land of Machiel Hansen (Bergen;) west by Gowanos Kill or Mill Creek;
and east by the common woods; together with all the
meadows included in the bounds aforesaid: said Hook
or Neck of land being formerly in the possession of
Jan Evertse bout as per patent of Governor Nicolls, of
April 1, 1668, and now in possession of said George.*
The patent of March 11, 1647, to Gerret Wolpherste (Cowenhoven,) of the above first referred to plot, describes the
same as follows: "land lying at Recheweck.† both the
maize land and the woodland on the marsh of the Gowanos Kill, between the land of Jacob Stoffelson and Frederick Lubertsen, extending from the aforesaid marsh till
into the woods next the land of said Frederick till to the
land of Andries Hudden; northeast by north a little northerly 148 rods; behind through the woods till to the
land of the said aforesaid Jacob Stoffelsen, southeast by
east 80 rods: next the land of Jacob Stoffelsen aforesaid

* See Lib. 2, p. 181 of con. Kings County rec. off.
† The Indian name of Brooklyn.

till to the aforesaid marsh southwest a little westerly 165
rods; along the valley to the place of beginning 60 rods,
with a small projecting point, amounting in all to 19 morgen, 341 rods." This plot evidently fronted on the main
road leading from Flatbush and the village of Brooklyn*
to the ferry, extending back to the Gowanus Creek, and is
included in the plot designated as land of G. Martense on
Butts' map of Brooklyn.

In 1698, Joris Hansen Bergen's family, as per census of
"Brookland," consisted of "1 man, 1 woman and 11 children, and 2 slaves:" in the same year and in 1702, he was
an elder in the church in Brooklyn. In 1690, at a town
meeting he was elected one of the Trustees or Commissioners of common lands, which office he held until 1700.
In 1700, he was captain of the foot company of militia of
"Brookland." In 1701, "Jores Hansen," among others,
was fined 8 shillings for not bringing his slaves and negro
women before the court as bound to the sheriff. In 1703,
4 and 5, Capt. George Hansen (Bergen) was Supervisor of
Brooklyn. In 1706, he was assessed for 76 acres of arable land in Brooklyn; and January 3d of the same year,
he with others was styled "pretended deacons of Brookland," in a warrant issued by Gov. Cornbury, ordering
them to deliver the church property to Dominie Freeman.
This was during the unfortunate troubles in the Reformed Dutch Churches of Long Island, between Dominie
Freeman and Dominie Antonides, and their respective
followers, during which, the former, with his friends,
broke open the doors of the church in Brooklyn, to gain
possession thereof, and a duel came very near being
fought between Col. Beeckman and Col. Filkins, two of

---

* The village of Brooklyn was originally located on the present Fulton
avenue, in the vicinity of the junction of Smith and Hoyt streets with said
avenue, and southeast of the present City Hall; more than a mile from
the ferry.

the leading men of the colony. This dispute commenced in 1702, and was finally settled in 1714, by agreeing
to receive and support both ministers, who were to preach
alternately in all their churches. During these troubles,
for at least a portion of the time. George Hansen Bergen
was an Elder of the Church in Brooklyn, joining in the
call for a Minister from Holland, which brought over Antonides, with whom he sided.

His name also appears among the freeholders of Brooklyn in the deed of January 10th, 1723, to Hans Bergen,
herein before referred to.

The following is a fac simile of his signature :

Issue :

Lammetje, bap. Dec. 20th. 1679: sponsors, Jannetje
Joris Rapalie and Jan Strycker.

Sara, bap. March 13th. 1681: sponsors, Teunis Gis-
brechts Boogaard and Swaantje Strycker.

Aaltje, bap. Oct. 15th, 1682 : sponsors, Machiel Hansz
Bergen and Sara Strycker.

Hans, bap. August 31st, 1684: sponsors, Abraham
Jorisz (Brinckerhoff,) and Hendrick Strycker.

Jannetje, bap. May 27th. 1688 ; sponsors, Jakob Hansen (Bergen,) and Eytje Strycker.

Annetje, bap. March 9th. 1689-90.

Jan, bap. May 17th, 1694 : sponsors, Stoffel Probasco
and Femmetje Teunis (Denyse.)

Breehtje, bap. May 24th. 1696. New York records.

Joris.

MARRETJE HANSEN, bap. in New Amsterdam, Oct. 8th, 1651.

April 18th, 1680, Marretje Hansen Bergen and Jakob Rutgersz, were sponsors at bap. of Sara, dau. of Theodorus Polhemius, and Aurtje Tonis Bogaard. Nov. 17th, 1681, Marritje Hansen, of Esopus, Teunis Gysbertz, Aaltje Frederyks, and Cornelis Corzen were sponsors at bap. of Frederyk, s. of Jacob Hansz Bergen and Elsie Frederyk's.

The above are the only certain entries the compiler has seen of Marretje, and from them it may be inferred that she m. Jakob Rutgersz, and that they resided at Esopus.

JACOB HANSEN, bap. in New Amsterdam, Sept. 21st, 1653; living as late as 1738: m. July 8th, 1677, *Elsje Fredericks, of the Kreest*, dau. of Frederick Lubbertse and Tryntje Hendricks of Brookland.* At the time of his

---

* *Frederick Lubbertse*, emigrated at an early period to this country, was at one period a sailor, his name appearing as a boatswain among the officers in 1638, under Kieft's administration, and d. in 1680. He m. 1st Styntie Hendricks, and m. 2d, August 17th, 1657, Tryntie Hendricks, wid. of Cornelis Peterson (Vroom.) Tryntie had by her first husband at the time of her second marriage, children, Cornelis Corssen (Vroom,) aged 12; Peter, aged 6; and Hendrick, aged 3 years. Lubbertse had 3 dau., *Elsje*, who m. Jacob Hansen Bergen; Rebecca, who m. Oct. 19th, 1648, Jacob Leendertse van der Grift; and Aeltje, who m. Sept. 3d, 1682, Cornelis Seubering. Lubbertse resided at first in New Amsterdam, and in August, 1641, was one of the 12 men representing Manhatten, Breukelen and Pavonia, elected to suggest means to punish the Indians for a murder they had committed. April 14th, 1643, he bought of Laurens Cornelissen his house in the Smith's Valley, which on the 3d of June, 1653 he sold to Albert Cornelissen. Dec. 10, 1653, he was a representative from Brooklyn in the convention held at New Amsterdam to represent the state of the country to the authorities in Holland; and 1653, '54, '55, '64, and 1673, he was a magistrate of Brooklyn. April 17th, 1657, he was made a small Burgher of New Amsterdam. February 13th, 1660, he was assessed in said city for repairing the "Heere Graght," (canal,) owning a lot on the north side thereof; and Feb. 1st, 1662, he was a candidate for the office of Burgomaster in said city, but failed to secure an election. July 6th, 1663, he was a representative from Brooklyn in the convention called to engage the several Dutch towns to keep up an armed force for public protection. Of the children of Tryntie by her first husband, Cornelis Corssen or Corson (Vroom,) m. in 1680, Marretje Vander Grist of the village of Brookland; had sons, Jacob and Cornelius, and settled on Staten Island, where some of his descendants with the surname of Corson now reside. He d. in 1693. Peter Corssen (Vroom.) m. Catharine .... and resided in Brookland in 1689, in which year he conveyed to Dirck Janse

m. he resided at the Waaleboght. Frederick Lubbertse
in his will, dated Nov. 22, 1679, devised to his dau. Elsie,
wife of Jacob Hansen (Bergen,) "the farm whereupon
they live at present as it is at present in fence, as also the
back land by the mill until the fresh meadow, and by
their decease to their lawful offspring, paying unto Rebecca the aforesaid sum of 600 guilders wampum value;"
to their dau. "Aeltie the farm at the water side as it is at
present in fence;" "unto Peter and Hendrik Corson
(Vroom,) aforesaid, each the just moiety of the piece of
upland beginning from Job's land between the waggon
path and meadow and its length to the water place, with
this express condition that they jointly and every one
alike the value of the just third part of the aforesaid
land" pay to their brother Cornelius Corson, "who otherwise would have inherited therein" if he had not had
land of his own.*

The patent of Lubbertse by Gov. Kieft is dated May
27th, 1640, and is for land "on Long Island at Merckka-

Woortman, a small island and some meadows towards Red Hook, inside
of the Graver's Kill, since known as Remsen's Island; and he also mort-
gaged to Thomas Lambertse land and meadows at Frederick Lubbertse's
Hook in Brookland, and at the same time owned other land in the vicinity.
For particulars see Lib. 1, of Con. p. 157 and 180 in Kings Co. Reg. Office.
Aug. 19th, 1689 he entered into an agreement with John Marsh of East
Jersey for the erection of a water mill for grinding of corn, to be located
on the southeast side of the Graver's Kill, within the meadows of said
Corssen and those of Cornelis Subering, (see Lib. 1, p. 271 of Con. K. Co.
Reg. Office,) which was built, and in latter years known as Cornell's mill.
March 28th, 1698, Peter Corsen conveyed to Cornelis Seubering for £250,
his land on the Neck, called Frederick Lubbertse's Neck, bounded East by
land of Jacob Hansen (Bergen,) West by the Red Hook and Koolls Keys
Kill, so called, and North by the land of said Cornelis Subering, containing 100 acres, with all the meadows belonging to said land. See Lib. 2,
p. 162 of do. By a bond of March 26th, 1698, it appears that Cornelis
Subering bound himself to maintain Peter Corsen, and to furnish him with
reasonable board, clothing, &c, suitable for a person in his station in life,
or to pay the expenses of the same. (See Lib. 2, p. 164 of do.) From
this it may be inferred that Peter Corssen's wife at this time was dead,
and that he had no surviving children. Hendrick Corssen (Vroom,) in
1680, m. Josinie Pietersz Van Kesh of the village of Brooklyn, and settled
on the Raritans, where his descendants are numerous, among whom is
Gov. Vroom of New Jersey.

  * See Lib. 1 p. 130 Con. Kings Co. Reg. Office.

wickrigh, (Brooklyn,) near to Werpes, extending in breadth from the Kill and marsh coming from Gowanus northwest by north and from the beach on the East River with a course southeast by east 1700 paces of 3 feet to a pace, and in the length from the end of said Kill northeast by east and southwest by west to the Red Hook, with the express condition that whenever the Indians shall be willing to part with their maize land lying next to the aforesaid land there, Frederick Lubbertsen shall have the privilege of entering upon the same in the breadth of the aforesaid parcel of land, extending from that without his being hindered by any one."

A confirmatory patent was granted to Lubbertse by Gov. Nicolls on the 28th of March, 1667, with substantially the same boundaries, and covering the land in his possession and enjoyment. Lubbertse's patent appears to have covered a large tract of upland in that portion of Brooklyn adjoining the salt meadows and marsh which formerly separated Red Hook from the main land, extending from the East River opposite Governors Island to Gowanus Cove and the Mill Creek, including a portion of the surrounding salt meadows, and covered the plots laid down on Butts' map of Luqueer (formerly Sebring,) Jacob Bergen, Coles, Conover, Hoyt, Cornell, Kelsey and Blake, Johnson, Heeney and other parcels in that vicinity.

On the 7th of April, 1726, Aaltie Seabringh, (now a widow,) and Jacob Hansen (Bergen,) and Elsie, his wife, agreeable to an award made by Johannes Jansen, Jacobus Rip, Esq., Col. Joost Van Brunt, Abraham Lot, and Christopher Codwise, commissioners appointed for the purpose of dividing a portion of their father's estate, quitclaimed or released to each other certain premises. The part released by Elsie and her husband to Altie, contain-

ed 235 acres of upland and meadow, exclusive of said
Aaltie's old farm not covered by the release. Aaltie
Seberingh quit-claimed and released to Jacob Hansen
(Bergen) and Elsie his wife "all that certain tract of land
and meadows heretofore belonging to Frederick Lubbertsen, deceased, situate, lying and being in the town of
Brookland, near unto and adjoining the old farm of the
said Jacob Hansen (Bergen,) and Elsie his wife, beginning at a Saxafax tree with several young branches and
bushes of Saxafax about the same, and standing near
unto the range of the fence that divides the old farm of
the said Jacob Hansen (Bergen,) and Elsie his wife, and
of the said Aaltie Sebringh, running from the westward
most end of the said Jacob Hansen's (Bergen) orchard,
and runs from said Saxafax tree South 19 deg. 30 min.
east 8 ch. 70 links to a stake, thence South 40 deg. West
35 ch. 50 links, thence South forty-six degrees and
a half West 12 ch. 30 links to a stake standing at the
edge of the meadow, thence South 46 deg. then . . . . .
thence South 60 deg. West to an inlet of water, and
thence along the said inlet to Gowanus Bay, thence along
said Bay to Adam Brower's Creek so called, (since known
as the Mill Creek,) and so up the said Creek until it
meets the meadow formerly belonging to Rut Van Brunt
deceased, and thence from said Creek and along the said
meadow to the upland there, thence along the upland and
edge of the meadow to a certain old stump at the head of
a reed meadow, thence North 60 deg. West 14 ch. to a
stake to the Southward of Jacob Hansen's (Bergen) house
at the Southermost side of the said Jacob Hansen (Bergen's) orchard, thence North 34 deg. West along said
orchard 11 ch. to the division fence of the said Jacob
Hansen (Bergen,) and Aaltje Sebringh's old farms, thence
on a straight line to the first station (no part of the said

Jacob Hansen's old farm being included,) containing in all 140 acres of land and meadows." And also a small parcel of meadow lying to the Eastward of Thys Van Dyk's dwelling house adjoining to Graver's Creek or Kill, and runs along a small Creek at the North side of the meadow belonging to the heirs of George Remsen, and so along said Creek to a stake standing at the Northeast side of a branch or creek that runs out of said small creek Westwardly towards the East River, thence from said stake Northwest into the East River to a stake, and so along said River to Graver's Kill to where it began, containing ten acres more or less.

Nov. 19, 1679, Jacob Hansen Bergen and Elsie his wife, of the village of Brookland, were members of the Reformed Dutch Church, and in 1682 he was a deacon in said church. In 1687 he is on the list of those who took the oath of allegiance to the British government, and in 1698 he is styled on the old Kings County court records, "a newly chosen constable of Brookland," and complained of for non-appearance at court in pursuance of notice. In the same year his family is entered on the census as consisting of "1 man, 1 woman, 6 children and 2 slaves." From 1700 to 1708 inclusive, he was elected or appointed one of the Trustees of the Common lands and to defend town rights, of Brooklyn. In 1706 he was assessed for 150 acres of arable land. April 23d, 1708, his name, among others appears on an agreement to call a Minister in the Brooklyn Dutch Church. He appears to have had difficulties with his neighbor Cornelis Sebering, who owned a part of the Lubbertse patent. Sebering commencing a suit against him Nov. 12th, 1714, also Nov. 11th, 1715, one for £19, 19s. and 8d.; and another in Oct, 1718. In Oct. 1722, he sued Sebering for £19, and again in 1723.

In 1715, as per minutes of the Board of Supervisors,

8

Jacob Hansen (Bergen) held the office of Supervisor of Brooklyn.

April 13th, 1732, Jacob Hansen Bergen, and Elsje his wife, conveyed to Hans Bergen their son, "200 A. in Brookland, bounded easterly by land of Jores Bergen and Mill Creek to the River; southwesterly by said River; northwesterly by land and meadow of Aeltje Sebering; northeasterly by land of Rem. Remsen and Jores Bergen, excepting a certain piece of meadows formerly sold to Michiel Hanalle; and further a certain piece of meadow of ten acres joining northeasterly upon the meadow of Aeltje Sebering aforesaid, south by a certain creek, southerly by the Graver's Kill so called, and northwesterly by the river. Also two lots of woodland in the second division of Brookland woodlands, containing 10 A. each, (Nos. 60 and 61.)" The conveyance sets forth, that he and his wife "by and with consent of all their children, by name, Frederick Bergen, Jacob Bergen Junr., Johannes Slecht, and Catrina, his wife, Gisbert Bogaert Junr., and Marretje, his wife, Jan Croesen, and Breekje, his wife, Derick Croesen, and Cornelia, his wife, testified by their being parties to the ensealing and delivery hereof, &c.," which children joined in the conveyance.* In 1738, Jacob Hansen Bergen's name appears on the census of Brooklyn, his family consisting of one white male above ten years, one white female above ten, one black male under ten, and this is the last record of his being alive.

The following is a fac simile of his signature

Issue :—

Hans, bap. May 12th, 1678; sponsors, Theunis Gysbertsz (Boogaert,) and Sara Rapalie.

* See Lib. 5, p. 160 of K. Co. Con.

Frederick, bap. Nov. 27th, 1681; sponsors, Teunis Gys-
brechtsz. (Boogaert,) and Aaltje Fredericks (Lubbertse.)

Jacob, bap. Jan. 20, 1683-4.

Sara, bap. Aug. 5th, 1688; sponsors, Cornelis Se-
brinekse, and Femmetie Theunissen.

Catryna.

Marretje.

Breekje.

Elsje.

Cornelia.

CATALYN or CATHARINE HANSEN, (a twin with Jacob,)
bap. Nov. 30, 1653. No account of Catalyn beyond that
of her birth, she probably dying in childhood, for Sara
her mother, in her petition of April 4th, 1656, as herein
set forth, to the Governor and Council, states that she is
a widow burdened with seven children, which would have
been incorrect, having had eight by her first husband,
Hans Hansen, unless one had previously died.

For the purpose of simplifying the matter and avoid-
ing confusion, the descendants or issue, of the several
sons of *Hans Hansen Bergen*, are hereinafter taken up and
carried out separately.

JAN HANSEN BERGEN.

Descendants in the line of JAN HANSEN BERGEN,
(and *Jannetje Theunis Denyse*,) of Jamaica, Queens
County, N. Y., the eldest son of Hans Hansen Bergen,
the first settler :—

Third Generation.

TUNIS BERGEN, bap. April 20, 1679 ; d. in 1755 ; m.
Mary or Marritje. His will is recorded in Lib. 19, page
400, of the Surrogate's Office in the City of New York,
dated Oct. 8th, 1755, and proved February 24th, 1756.
Resided on and owned a farm near the village of Jamaica, and in 1715 he subscribed £2 towards building a Reformed Dutch Church in said village.

Issue :—
Maria, bap. March 21, 1710.
Jannetje, bap. July 10, 1715.
Derick, b. Dec. 10, 1717.
Sarah, bap. Sept. 10th, 1720.
Catlyn, bap. July 25th, 1726.

ADRIAANTJE BERGEN, bap. Dec. 11th, 1681 ; m. *Jan
or Johannes Garretse.*

Issue :—
Maria Garretse, bap. April 14th, 1707.
Johannes Garretse, bap. Aug. 16th, 1709.
Adriana Garretse, bap. Aug. 16th, 1709, a twin with Johannes.
Jennetje Garretse, bap. March 8th, 1711.

MARRETJE BERGEN, bap. Feb. 1st, 1684 ; m. (sup.)
Johannes Eldertse, the 3d son of Eldert Lucasse Voorhees
of Jamaica.

Issue : —

Crecia Elderts, bap. April 14th, 1707

Johannes Eldertse.

Grace Eldertse.

HANS OR JOHANNES BERGEN ; living in Nov. 1734 ; m. *Antie or Annetje Lucassen,* dau. of Eldert Lucassen

* Antie Lucassen is a descendant of Steven Coerte, or Steven Koers, as written by himself, from Voorhees or from before Hees, a small neighborhood of nine houses and fifty inhabitants, near Ruinen in the Province of Drenthe, in the Netherlands. The family subscribed themselves "Van Voorhies" and "Van Voorhyes." Steven is the common ancester of the Voorhees family of Long Island, N. J., &c., and he with all his family except his dau. Merghein, emigrated in 1660, in the ship Bontekoe, (Spotted Cow,) Capt. Pieter Lucassen. This family, like most of our early settlers, had no proper surname, adopting as such the name of the village from whence they emigrated. By means of letters yet in existence they are traced back one generation in the fatherland, the only instance of the kind known to the writer.

The father of *Steven* was Coert Alberts, a resident of Voorhees, who had brothers, Steven Alberts, of Voorhees ; Hendrik Alberts, of Twyel, who had five children living in 1684 ; Luytgen Alberts, of Haekes Welt, who had one child living in 1684 ; Jan Alberts, of Heffelying, who d. prior to 1684, leaving one dau. ; Hilbert Alberts, who d. prior to 1684, leaving two sons and one dau. ; and Wesvel Alberts, of Amsterdam, who also d. prior to 1684, leaving one dau. ; Coert also had sisters Gertien Alberts, of Oshaer by Veghten, who was m. and had children ; and Mergin Alberts who m. Jan Mewus, of the Hights, who d. prior to 1684, leaving children.

Steven Coerte had brothers who remained in Holland, Hilbert Coerte, of Voorhies b. in 1634 ; Jan Coerte, of Voorhies who occupied the homestead of his father ; Albert Coerte, of Bethuyn, a carpenter, who m. Aeltyn ; and Wesvel Coerte, of Veeninge ; also two sisters.

Steven Coerte, m. Willempie Roeleffse, purchased land and settled in Flatlands shortly after his arrival in this country, and d. about Feb. —, 1684, his will being dated Augt. 25, 1667. His children were Mergin, Merghein or Merchyn Stevense, who remained in the fatherland, d. Oct. 2d, 1702, N. S., m. 1st, Roelofs, m. 2d, Remmelt Willems, by whom a s. Willem Remmelts, schoolmaster of Saxum in Gronengen ; Hendrickyn Stevense who also remained in the fatherland and was alive in 1699 ; Cbert Stevense, of Flatlands, whose will is dated Aug. 26, 1677, who m. 1st . . . . m. 2d Marretje Gerretsz Van Couwenhoven, *Lucas Stevense*, of Flatlands, living in 1719, m. 1st Catharine Hanssen, m. 2d. Jan'y 26, 1689, Jannetje Monnes ; Jan Stevense of Flatlands, living in 1719, m. Mar. 17, 1678, Cornelia Reyniers Wizzel-penning, who d. Jan'y 7, 1680, m. 2d, Oct. 6th, 1680 Femmetje Aukes, da. of Auke Janse Van Nuyse ; Albert Stevense, m. Ap'l 24, 1681, Jielletje Reiniers Wizzel-penning, all of the above children except Mergin and Hendrickyn having emigrated with their father. . Abraham Stevense m. Altie Stryker ; Aaltje Stevense m. Barent Jurianusz ; Jannetje Stevensz. m. 1st Jan Martense Schenck, m. 2d Feb 29th, 1690, Alexander Symson ; and Hendrikje Stevense, who suppose m. 1st John Kiersted, and m. 2d Albert Albertsz Terhunen.

Lucas Stevense, s. of Steven Coerte and Willempe of Hackingsack in 1685, and of Flatlands in 1687, had issue by his 1st wife *Eldert Lucasz.*

Voorhees: bap. Feb. 24th, 1684, and living in 1735. Resided on and owned a farm near the village of Jamaica; in 1715, subscribed £2, 10s. towards building a Reformed Dutch Church in said village, and in 1731 subscribed £25 towards building a Reformed Dutch Church in Success.

Issue :—

Jannetje, bap. March 30, 1702.

Eldert, bap. July 3d, 1705.

Jan, bap. March 21, 1710.

Styntje, bap. March 25th, 1712.

Lucas, bap. July 10th, 1715.

Jacobus, bap. April 12th, 1719.

Tunis, bap. April 16th, 1721.

Antie, bap. May 26th, 1723 ; d. May, 1803, single.

---

whose will is dated in 1714 and proved in 1722. m. Styntje Hendricks and settled in Jamaica : Jan Lucas of Flatlands, bap. Feb. 19, 1675, living in 1737, m. Oct. 10, 1699, Anna Van Duyckhuysen who d. Jan. 5, 1702, m. 2d May 5, 1704, Mayke Schenck who d. Nov. 25, 1736, m 3d Jan. 25, 1737, Jaunetje Remsen who. d. Aug. 25, 1747 : Stephen Lucasz, bap. Sep. 16, 1677; Hans Lucasz, bap. Sep. 7, 1679, m. May 17, 1715, Neeltje Nevius ; Jannetje Lucasz, bap. Dec. 25, 1681, m. May 25, 1704, Martin Schenck ; Willemetje Lucasz bap. Nov. 9, 1683, d. young ; Anna Lucasz, bap. Ap'l 25, 1686, d. Sep. 30, 1774. m. June 5, 1709 William Couwenhoven of Flatlands ; Catryntje Lucasz, m. May 3d, 1712 Roelof Nevius ; Elsje Lucasz ; (sup.) by 2d wife Reinsche Lucasz, m. May 22d, 1712, Johannes Noostrant ; Willmetje Lucasz, bap. Nov. 15, 1694, m. Aug. 23d, 1715, Martin Nevius ; Albert Lucasz, b. May 10th, 1698, d. Oct. 28th, 1734, m. 1st May 10, 1720 Arrejeantje Ditmarse who d. April 14, 1721, m. 2d 1722 Catryntje Cornell ; Roelof Lucasz, m. Ap'l 26, 1715, Helena Stoothoff ; and Minna Lucasz of Flatlands, m. Ap'l 25, 1717, Antje Wyckoff.

Eldert Lucasz, s. of Lucas Stevense settled in the town of Jamaica, and had children, Lucas Eldertse of Jamaica, bap. Dec. 5, 1677 ; Rachel Eldertse, m. Adam Smith ; Hendrickje Eldertse, bap. Ap'l 4th, 1680, d. young ; Johannes Eldertse of Foster's Meadow, bap. Dec. 26th, 1681, m. (sup.) Marretje Bergen, d. prior to 1714 ; *Annetje Eldertse* bap. Feb. 17th, 1684, m. Hans Bergen of Jamaica : Egbertje Eldertse, m. Abraham Coevert ; and Hendrick Eldertse of Jamaica, bap. Mar. 4, 1691, m. 1st Greetje, m. 2d Tryntje.

The patronymic of Eldert (instead of Voorhees,) derived from Eldert Lucase, has been continued by the descendants of said Lucas to this day.

Fourth Generation.

Descendants of TUNIS BERGEN and *Mary or Marritje,*
of Queens County, N. Y.:

MARIA OR MARY BERGEN, bap. March 21, 1710; d.
prior to Oct. 8th, 1755; m. *Johannes Hardenbrook* of Jamaica.

Issue:

Tunis Hardenbrook, bap. Feb. 19th, 1740.
Maria Hardenbrook, bap. Oct. 18th, 1747.

JANNETJE BERGEN, bap. July 10th, 1715; d. prior to
the death of her father; m. *John Hegeman* of Dutchess
County.

Issue: –

Sarah Hegeman; m. John Fox of Dutchess County, N. Y.
Phebe Hegeman; m. Peter Van Kemp of Dutchess County.
Catharine Hegeman; m. John Lambertse of Jamaica.

DERICK BERGEN, b. Dec. 10th, 1717; d. June 12th,
1799; m. *Femmetje or Phebe,* who d. June 2d, 1779; resided on and owned a farm near Jamaica, and March 7th,
1792, sold about 70 acres of the easterly side of his farm
for £950 to Peter Stoothoff.

Issue:—

Mareya or Maria, bap. June 9th, 1751.
Yan or Jan, b. Sept. 9th, 1754.

SARAH BERGEN, bap. Sept. 10th, 1720; no farther
trace, and probably d. young, not being mentioned in her
father's will.

CATLYN BERGEN, bap. July 25th, 1726; no farther
trace, and probably d. young, not being mentioned in her
father's will.

Descendants of HANS or JOHANNES BERGEN and *Antie Lucassen* of Queens County, N. Y. :—

JANNETJE BERGEN, bap. March 30, 1702 ; m. (prob.) *Thomas Stringham.*

Issue :—
Jannetje Stringham, bap. Feb. 1st, 1727.
Samuel Stringham.
Johannes Stringham, bap. Jan. 14th, 1732.

ELDERT BERGEN, bap. July 3d, 1705 ; no farther trace, and probably d. young.

JAN BERGEN, bap. March 21, 1710 ; d. May, 1780 ; resided with his brother Jacobus, on a farm at Jamaica South ; no account of his marriage or issue.

STYNTJE BERGEN, bap. March 25th, 1712 ; m. (prob.) *Polhemus.*

Issue :—
Eldert Polhemus, bap. March 21, 1740
Mary Polhemus.

LUCAS BERGEN, bap. July 10th, 1715 ; d. March, 1803 ; m. *Susanna Schenck,* who d. Oct. 1810 ; will dated Nov. 18th, 1802, proved May 3d, 1803, and recorded in the office of the Surrogate of the County of Queens ; owned and resided on a farm in the hollow near Brushville. Signed his name "Lucas Barager."

Issue :—
Sara, bap. Aug. 27th, 1749 ; d. young.
Johannes, bap. Nov. 3d, 1751.
Sara, bap. April 2d, 1754.
Abraham, b. May 22d, 1757.
Ann, b. about 1760.

JACOBUS OR JACOB BERGEN, bap. April 12th, 1719 ; d. about 1790 ; m. *Mary or Marrytje Carpenter ;* will dated

April 2d, 1789; proved Sept. 7th, 1790, and recorded in the office of the Surrogate of the County of Queens. Resided on a farm of about 150 acres at Jamaica South, purchased by himself and his brothers Tunis, Luke and John, about 1770.

Issue:—

Antie, bap. Dec. 19th, 1740.
John.
Jacob, bap. July 25th, 1746.
Elizabeth.
Mary.

TUNIS BERGEN, bap. April 16th, 1721; m. Mattye; will dated March 20th, 1795, and proved July 15th, 1802. Left no surviving issue; resided on a farm at Jamaica South.

ANTIE BERGEN, bap. May 26th, 1723; d. May, 1803; single. Will dated May 21st, 1803, and proved May 25th, 1803. Resided at the time of her death with John Everett, who m. Antie, dau. of her brother Jacobus.

Fifth Generation.

Descendants of DERICK BERGEN and *Femmetje*, of Queens County, N. Y.:—

MAREYA OR MARIA BERGEN, bap. June 9th, 1751; d. Sept. 1st, 1828; married June 10th, 1798, *John Bergen*, s. of Jacobus and Marrytie. No issue.

YAN OR JAN BERGEN, b. Sept. 9th, 1754; d. Sept. 9th, 1828; m. Nov. 12th, 1780, *Miriam Oldfield*, b. Feb. 18th, 1763, d. June 9th, 1851; will dated October 27th, 1828, and that of his wife, August 17th, 1849. Owned

9

and resided on a farm within the boundaries of the town of Hempstead.

Issue:—

Phebe, b. Nov. 15th, 1781.
Miriam, b. Oct. 11th, 1783.
Oldfield, b. Jan. 27th, 1786.
Aletta, b. April 25th, 1788.
June, b. Jan. 4th, 1791, d. young.
John, b. Oct. 8th, 1793.
James, b. May 28th, 1796.
Jane, b. Sept. 18th, 1798.
Nicholas, b. April 10th, 1801.

Descendants of LUCAS BERGEN and *Susanna Schenck*, of Queens County, N. Y.:—

JOHANNES BERGEN, bap. Nov. 3d, 1751: d. Oct. 11th, 1776: m. July 12th, 1774. *Magdalena Boerum*. Resided on and owned a farm north of the village of Jamaica. June 14th, 1754, letters of administration were granted to Magdalena his wife, on his estate, as per records in the Surrogate's office in the city of New York.

Issue:—

Johannes, b. April 6th, 1775.
Mariel or Maria, b. Jan. 9th, 1777.

SARA BERGEN, bap. April 2d, 1754: m. about Dec. 1776. *Hendrick Emans*, Junr.

Issue:—

Lucas Emans, bap. Jan. 26th, 1783.
Sarah Emans, bap. March 26th, 1786.

ABRAHAM BERGEN, b. May 22d, 1757: d. Oct. 31st, 1802: m. about March, 1782. *Antie Springsteen*, who d. June 28th, 1846. Owned and occupied a farm at Brushville.

Issue :

Susan or Susanna, b. March 16th, 1783.

Caspart or Caspar, b. July 4th, 1784.

Johannes or John, b. Jan. 15th, 1786.

Phebe.

Gilbert or Gysbert Schenck, bap. June 6th, 1790.

Luke, bap. May 6th, 1792.

Roeleph Schenck, bap. April 6th, 1794 ; d. Oct. 21st, 1795.

Antye, bap. May 22d, 1796.

Abraham, bap. May 20th, 1798.

Roelof Schenck, bap. June 2d, 1802.

ANN BERGEN, b. about 1760 ; m. about June 1781, *Aury Ramson.*

Issue :

Jannetje Ramson, bap. Oct. 15th, 1786.

Allie Ramson, bap. Oct. 15th, 1786, a twin with Jannetie.

Rem Ramsen, bap. Nov. 2d, 1793.

John Ramsen, bap. Nov. 9th, 1798.

Descendants of JACOBUS or JACOB BERGEN and *Marrytie Carpenter*, of Queens County, N. Y. :—

ANTIE, bap. Dec. 19th, 1740 ; m. *John Everett.*

Issue :—

John Everett.

Benjamin Everett.

Sarah Everett, m. John Latham.

JOHN BERGEN, m. first *Mary Mills* ; m. second, Jan. 10th, 1798, *Mary or Polly*, dau. of Derick and Femmetje Bergen, by whom no children. Will dated March 14th, 1815, proved January 12th, 1826, recorded in office of Surrogate of Queens County. Resided on and owned a farm at Rushville. Name written "John Barrager."

Issue :—

Jacob, b. July 20th or (23d.) 1770.

Isaac, b. Oct. 1st, 1772 ; d. young.

Mary or Polly, b. Aug. 11th, 1774.

Jane, b. July 20, 1777.

John, b. May 4th, 1779.
Catharine. b. Nov. 18th, 1782.
Abigail, b. Jan. 8th, 1788.
Isaac, b. April 10th, 1790.

ELIZABETH BERGEN, m. *Ludlam Smith.*

Issue :—
William Smith.
Patience Smith.
Nathaniel Smith.

MARY BERGEN, m. *Isaac Baylis.*
Issue :—
Tabitha Baylis.
Ann Baylis.
Mary Baylis.
Daniel Baylis.
Jacob Baylis.
Isaac Baylis.

JACOB BERGEN, b. July 25th, 1746: d. Feb. 24th, 1816: m. *Mary Marsten*, b. June 25th, 1748: d. Sept. 7th, 1828: resided on and owned a farm at Jamaica, South, fronting the bay. A Jacob Bergen was a private in Van Akins' company and Pawling's regiment in the revolutionary war, who may have been this Jacob.

Issue :—
Tunis, b. June 1st, 1772.
Thomas, b. Oct. 11th, 1773.
Ann, b. March 15th, 1776 ; d. July 3d, 1795, single.
Jacob, b. Feb. 2d, 1782.
David, b. Nov. 6th, 1784.

Sixth Generation.

Descendants of YAN or JAN BERGEN and *Mariam
Oldfield* of Hempstead, Queens County. N. Y. :—

PHEBE BERGEN, b. Nov. 15th, 1781 ; m. Jan. 29th,
1823, *John Johnson*, a brewer, of Brooklyn. No issue.

OLDFIELD BERGEN, b. Jan. 27, 1786; d. Nov. 22d, 1835; m. Oct. 15th, 1808, *Elsy Demott*; m. 2d, July 2d, 1831, *Abigail Cornell*, of South Hempstead. Owned and cultivated a farm and followed the occupation of a butcher in Hemstead.

Issue:--

John Demott, b. July 30th, 1809; m. June 11th, 1834, Hannah Simonson; resides in the village of Jamaica. No issue.

Lefferts, b. Jan. 3d, 1813; m. Jan. 4th, 1832, Mary Ann Wiggins. Cultivates a farm near Hempstead Plains.

Issue:--Amelia Ann, b. Dec. 31st, 1835; d. Oct. 9th, 1836.

Aletta Ann, b. July 25th, 1815; d. Oct. 9th, 1836; m. Jan 5th (or 10th,) 1834, Benjamin Wiggins.

Issue.--Benjamin Wiggins, and Philip Wiggins.

Joseph Oldfield, b. March 20th, 1824; m. Nov. 5th, 1845, Sarah R. Rhodes of Flushing; is a farmer near Brushville.

Issue:--Joseph Lefferts, b. March 30th, 1847; Cornelius R., b. Nov. 5th, 1849; and Benjamin R., b. Feb. 11th, 1852.

Elsy, m. Nov. 1845, Daniel R. Burtis.

Catharine, m. Benjamin Allen.

ALETTA BERGEN, b. April 25th, 1788; d. about 1847; m. Christopher Loweree.

JANE BERGEN, b. Jan. 4th, 1791; d. Jan. 4th, 1795.

JOHN BERGEN, b. Oct. 8, 1793; d. May 19th, 1848; single.

JAMES BERGEN, b. May 28th, 1796; d. Feb. 9, 1861; m. 1st 1823, Naomi Deniee, b. 1804, and d. June, 1828; m. 2d, February 9th, 1852, Catharine wid. of Joseph Fish, by whom no children. Was a farmer near Brushville.

Issue by 1st wife :

Tunis Evereitt, b. Sept. 12th, 1804; m. Dec. 17th, 1851, Phebe Jane Shaw, b. Aug. 31st, 1833. Owns and cultivates a farm at Christian Hook, south of Hempstead, and has children. Naoma Emma, b. Oct. 27th, 1853; d. April 19th, 1858; George Everett, b. Oct. 21st, 1855; Mary Alma, b. April 5th, 1858; Naoma Ann, b. Feb. 4th, 1859; and Ida Emma, b. June 11th, 1863.

George Johnson, b. Oct. 21st. 1825; single; resides in Brooklyn, and engaged with his uncle, John Johnson, in his brewery.

JANE BERGEN, b. Sept. 18th, 1798 : m. May 16th, 1820, Tunis Everett, by whom children, Jane Maria, who m. Culver Wynants of California : and Phebe Ann, who m. Samuel Aymar of Jamaica ; m. 2d, Amos J. Saxton, by whom James, who m. a Miss Kennedy.

NICHOLAS BERGEN, b. April 10th, 1801 : d. July 17th, 1846 : m. Dec. 22d, 1824, Eliza Fowler : living in 1863. Was a farmer and resided about three miles east of Brushville.

Issue :—

Phebe Jane.
David A., resides on Hempstead Plains.
Margaret Ann.
Nicholas F.
Oliver M.

Descendants of JOHANNES BERGEN, and *Magdalena Berrum* of Jamaica, Queens County, N. Y. :—

JOHANNES OR JOHN BERGEN, b. April 6th, 1775; d. Sept. 16th, 1858; m. Sept. 2d, 1798, *Johanna*, dau. of Peter Wyckoff of Gowanus : b. Sept. 2d, 1778 : d. Sept. 20th, 1829. A farmer in Illinois, to which State he emigrated, his wife remaining on Long Island, where she died.

Issue :—

Lemma, b. June 10th, 1800; m. 1st, Dec. 22d, 1818, John Williamson, s. of William of Flatbush; m. 2d, Dec. 23d, 1841, Simon Rapalye of New Lots, by whom no children.

Issue :—William J. Williamson, b. Dec. 18th, 1819 ; Johanna Williamson, b. May 29th, 1822, d. Nov. 6th, 1831 ; and Peter Wyckoff Williamson, b. August 23d, 1825.

John, b. Dec. 28th, 1801 ; m. March 16th, 1822, Matilda C. Burkbee of Brooklyn, who d. Nov. 26th, 1826 ; m. 2d, July 15th, 1829, Phebe Wood, who d. April 29th, 1858. In his earlier days kept a shoe store in the city of Brooklyn, afterwards kept a public house in the village of Flatlands, and now, 1865, a farmer at Hempstead.

Issue by first wife :—John W., b. May 18th, 1823 ; d. June 21, 1861. m. Sept. 17th, 1844, Deborah W. Wood, b. Sept. 15th, 1829 ; Henry, b. March 15th, 1826, d. or last heard of in 1850.

Issue by 2d wife :—Mary Jane, b. Jan. 8th, 1831, m. Feb. 5th, 1851, Willington Simonson ; Leonard M., b. Dec. 30th, 1832, m. April 24th, 1861, Hannah Willet.

Peter J., b. Dec. 28th, 1803 ; m. in Ohio, Nov. 25th, 1827, Solace Pickering, who d. May 11th, 1833. A shoe maker by trade, and emigrated to Cincinnati, Ohio. After the death of his wife, removed to Vicksburgh, on the Mississippi River, and engaged in mercantile business. From Vicksburgh returned to Brooklyn, and for several years was in the employ of the Atlantic Bank, from which he has retired, and now, 1865, resides in East New York.

Issue :—Emma, b. Sept. 27th, 1828, d. Feb. 25th, 1829 ; Leonteum, b. Dec. 20th, 1830, d. Dec. 10th, 1831 ; Roland and Philander, twins, b. Feb. 14th, 1833 ; Philander d. March 16th, and Roland d. June 11th, 1833.

Charles, b. Jan. 21st, 1806 ; m. Helen Maples. Removed with his father to Illinois, where he owns and cultivates a farm.

Issue :—Solace P., b. Aug 18th, 1835, d. Oct. 8, 1835 ; Mary Elizabeth, b. Aug. 24th, 1836, d. Aug. 30th, 1836 ; Lodusky Ann, b. Nov. 19th, 1837 ; Angeline, b. April 28th, 1840, d. Nov. 29th, 1849 ; George Henry, b. Feb. 27th, 1843, d. Dec. 6th, 1849 ; Cornelia b. Feb. 14th, 1846 ; Lavina, b. Nov. 1st, 1848 ; and Peter J., b. April 5th, 1852, d. Oct. 20th, 1861.

Henry, b. July 10th, 1808 ; m. May 24th, 1827, Cornelia Beerum, b. April 9th, 1801. At first owned and occupied a farm at New Bushwick, Kings County, at present a farmer in Orange County, N. Y.

Issue :—Elizabeth Helen, b. March 12th, 1829, d. Nov. 17th, 1831 ; Lemma Ann, b. May 14th, 1832, m. May 12th, 1852, Henry Suydam of Kings County ; George B., b. April 27th, 1836.

Magdalen, b. Jan. 20th, 1811 ; m. Daniel Lawrence in Illinois ; removed with her father to Illinois, where she resides.

Issue:—Lemma Lawrence, b. Nov. 16th, 1830, d. April 30th, 1846; Johanna Bergen Lawrence, b. June 30th, 1832, d. June 28th, 1844; George W. Lawrence, b. April 7th, 1834; Peter J. Lawrence, b. Sept. 19th, 1836; Susanna Lawrence, b. Feb. 21th, 1839; Sarah Ann Lawrence, b. January 12th, 1841; William Lawrence, b. Feb. 20th, 1843; Charles Lawrence, b. Nov. 7th, 1345; Louisa Lawrence, b. March 15th, 1849; James Henry Lawrence, b. April 24th, 1853, and Magdalen Solas Lawrence, b. March 9th, 1856, d. Aug. 11th, 1856.

Elizabeth, b. March 20th, 1813 ; d. young.

George W., b. July 20th, 1814; m. July 19th, 1838, Susan, dau. of Thomas Carman of Hempstead, b. June 29th, 1818. In early life for a short period engaged in mercantile business in Vicksburgh, on the Mississippi River; for many years past a member of the firm of Valentine & Bergen, engaged in the wholesale grocery business in Brooklyn.

Issue:—Elizabeth C., b. Nov. 23d, 1839, m. Nov. 3d, 1857, Horace D. Badger; Charles M., b. Dec. 9th, 1842; George P., b. Sept. 18th, 1849; Annie Valentine, b. August 9th, 1856.

MARIAL or MARIA BERGEN, b. January 9th, 1777; m. *Reuben Decker* of New Lots.

Issue :—

Magdalena Decker, bap. July 26th, 1795.
John Decker.
Reuben Decker.
Stephen Lott Decker, b. Sept. 27th, 1801.
Richard Decker, b. Aug. 24th, 1805.
Williamson Decker.
Jacob Decker.

Descendants of ABRAHAM BERGEN and *Antie Springsteen* of Jamaica, Queens Co., N. Y. :—

SUSAN or SUSANNA, b. March 16, 1783; living 1863; m. *Nathaniel Mills*.

Issue :—

Nathaniel Mills, b. June 4th, 1802; d. 1862; m. Aletta Hendrickson. Kept a leather store in Brooklyn, and left several children.

Abraham Mills, b. March 16th, 1804; d. May 20th, 1847; m. 1st Maria Rape'ye; m. 2d, Ellen Lott.

Jacob Mills, b. April 6th, 1806; d. April 1st, 1838, single.

Isaac Mills, b. June 25th, 1808; d. May 15th, 1811; m. 1st, Frances Rudgerd; m. 2d, Mary Rudgerd, sister of Frances.

John Higby Mills, b. May 15th, 1811; m Susan Pepper

Casper Schenck Mills, b. Nov. 2d, 1813; d. Feb. 14th, 1832, single.

Phebe Ann Mills, b. June 7th, 1817; d. July 12th, 1837; m. Nathaniel Blydenburgh.

Sarah Maria Mills, b. Aug. 15th, 1822; m. Jacob Duryea.

CASPER OR CASPART BERGEN, b. July 4th, 1784; d. April 16th, 1828, single.

JOHANNES OR JOHN BERGEN, b. Jan. 15th, 1786; d. August 13th, 1828; m. July 30th, 1806, *Matie or Mary Hendrickson*, b. Oct. 11th, 1787, d. Dec. 14th, 1850. Owned and occupied a farm of about 160 acres on the Black Stump Road, in the town of Flushing.

Issue : –

Abraham, b. May 17th, 1807; d. April 13th, 1842; m. March 14th, 1832, Sally Bowne. Cultivated a farm in the town of Flushing, and had children, William, m. May 17th, 1854, Maria Louisa, dau. of Frederick and Maria Crommelin, whose children are Sarah Maria, b. Dec. 22d, 1855; John William, b. Oct. 1st, 1858; and Hannah B., b. March 28th, 1862; and John.

Sarah, b. Feb. 9th, 1809; d. Jan. 3d, 1851, single.

Ida Ann Winfred, b. July 23d, 1811; m. Dec. 12th, 1839, William R. Siney, s. of Robert, of Flushing, now of the city of New York, and the proprietor of a line of stages.

Issue :—Mary Elizabeth Siney, and Jerusha Ann Siney, living, and Robert Siney, Pierre William Siney, and Augusta C. P. Siney deceased.

Phebe Maria, b. May 20th, 1814; d. Jan. 6th, 1836, single.

Isaac Hendrickson, b. July 11th, 1816; d. Feb. 10th, 1851; m. Maria Mills. Was engaged in the feed business in the city of New York. No issue.

Gilbert Schenck, bap. Aug. 10th, 1818; d. July 9th, 1860; m. Oct. 5th, 1843, Mary J. Bowne, who d. Nov. 2d, 1854. Was engaged in the flour and feed business at East New York.

Issue :—John W., b. about 1849, d. Aug. 16th, 1854; and Anna Maria

10

Cornelius Monfort, b. Dec. 6th, 1820; m. May 12th, 1852, Sarah A Wright. b. Aug. 9th, 1830. Owns and cultivates a farm of eighty acres, (the one half of the homestead of his father,) on the Black Stump Road, in the town of Flushing.

Issue:—Mary Elizabeth, b. Feb. 23d, 1853.
Phebe Maria, b. Feb. 6th, 1824. single.

PHEBE BERGEN, d. some years ago; m. *Abraham Hendrickson*.

Issue :—

Isaac Hendrickson, bap. Feb. 15th, 1808.
Emily Ann Hendrickson, bap. Oct. 14th, 1810.
Abraham Cornelius Hendrickson, bap. June 6th, 1813.

GILBERT OR GYSBERT SCHENCK BERGEN, bap. June 6th, 1790; single. He and his brother Luke own and cultivate a farm consisting of a portion of the original tract owned and occupied by their ancestors, located in the hollow at Brushville, in the town of Jamaica.

LUKE BERGEN, bap. May 6th, 1792; single. Resides with his brother, Gilbert Schenck, together occupying a farm at Brushville.

ROELOF SCHENCK BERGEN, bap. April 6th, 1794; d. Oct. 21st, 1795.

ANTYE BERGEN, bap. May 22d, 1796; single. Resides with her brothers Gilbert Schenck and Luke, at Brushville.

ABRAHAM BERGEN, bap. May 20th, 1798; d. Dec. 5th, 1858; m. May 10th, 1820, Winfred Hendrickson, who d. Dec. 19th, 1846, aged 53. Owned and occupied a farm near the Beaver Pond, Jamaica.

Issue :—

Abraham Schenck Bergen, b. Oct. 31st, 1822; m. Sept. 25th, 1845, Maria Suydam. Owns and cultivates a farm at Fresh Ponds, near Mount Olivet in the town of Newtown.

Issue:—Catherine Winifred, b. May 7th, 1847; Sarah Maria, b. June 6th, 1849; Ida Ann, born Sept. 29th, 1851; Magdalin, b. Sept. 9th,

1853 ; Rufus Schenck, b. Oct. 1, 1855, d. Jan. 22d, 1856 ; Rufus Schenck, b. Nov. 16th, 1856, d. Jan. 31st, 1858 ; Gilbert Schenck, b. April 20, 1860, and Ann, b. June 15th, 1862.

Isaac C., b. May 2d, 1824 ; died March 4th, 1838.

John Luke, b. Nov. 1st, 1827 ; d. Nov. 1st, 1828.

John Luke, b. Nov. 1st, 1828 ; d. young.

Rufus Schenck, b. Sept. 13th, 13th, 1829 ; m. Oct. 9th, 1861, Angelike Raymond. Employed as a clerk in the City of New York, and has issue—Rufus Cameron, b. August 29th, 1862.

Sarah Ann Maria, b. March 11th, 1831 ; m. Henry Benjamin of the City of New York.

William Kissam, b. April 10th, 1835 ; m. Sarah Triquet.

ROELEF SCHENCK BERGEN, bap. Jan. 2d, 1802 ; d. at Zakatecas, in South America, without issue.

Descendants of JOHN BERGEN and *Mary Mills*, of Jamaica, Queens County, N. Y. :

JACOB BERGEN, b. July 20 (or 23,) 1770 ; d. Nov. 13th, 1842 ; m. Dec. 23d, 1790, *Mary Wiggins*, who d. March 23d, 1834, aged 69. Owned and cultivated a farm at Brushville. Will dated May 4th, 1838.

Issue :—

John Bergen, b. Nov. 11th, 1791 ; d. young.

Benjamin Bergen, b. May 18th, 1794 ; m. May 6, 1824, Phebe Skidmore, who died January 11th, 1834, aged 33 ; m. 2d, Dec. 13th, 1836, Elizabeth Jones. Formerly a farmer, at present residing in the village of Jamaica.

Issue :—Mary Ann, b. Dec. 5th, 1825 ; m. Dec. 15th, 1846, Benjamin T. Bergen, s. of Jacob, of Jamaica South ; Jacob b. April 2d, 1828 ; m. Oct. 11th, 1854, Aletta Maria Hendrickson ; Benjamin Alexander b. April 22d, 1838 ; d. Dec. 8, 1849 ; Charles Henry, b. Oct. 16th, 1839, m. Feb. 5th, 1862, Kate A. Way. Engaged in teaching school in Jamaica.

Jacob Bergen, bap. Sept. 2d, 1798 ; d. young.

Jacob Bergen, bap. March 10, 1799 ; m. April 5th, 1817, Nancy Seaman. Cultivates a farm at Brushville.

Issue :—Mary Elizabeth, b. Nov. 5th, 1821 ; m. Nov. 16th, 1847, John Lott Bergen, s. of Tunis and Ann of Brushville.

Aury Bergen, b. Aug. 3d, 1800 ; d. Sept. 29th, 1806.

Mary Bergen, b. July 30th, 1806.

MARY OR POLLY BERGEN, b. Aug. 11th, 1774; m. Aury Snediker. Living 1863, and no issue.

JANE BERGEN, b. July 20th, 1777; d. a young woman and single.

JOHN BERGEN, b. May 4th, 1779; single and living 1863, near the village of Jamaica. Owned and formerly cultivated one half of his father's farm at Brushville, which he sold in 1853, his brother Jacob owning the other remaining half.

CATHARINE BERGEN, b. Nov. 18th, 1782; m. Jan. 5th, 1808, Thomas Smith, of Jamaica.

Issue :

Nicholas Smith, b. May 27th, 1809; m. Mary dau. of Israel Smith.
Mary Smith, b. Jan. 19th, 1811; d. young.
Judith Smith, b. Nov. 8th, 1812; m. Daniel Ludlam.
John Bergen Smith, b. Oct. 15th, 1814.
Thomas Smith.
Rachel Smith, m. John J. Ryder.
Abigail Jane Smith, b. Aug. 23d, 1824.
Catharine Smith, m. Thomas Ryder.

ABAGAIL BERGEN, b. Jan. 8, 1788; d. about 1851; m. Aug. 31st, 1808, *Johannes Lott, Junr.*

Mary Lott, b. March 1st, 1810; m. Isaac Simonson.
Margaret Lott, b. March 9th, 1812; d. about 1854; m. Peter Nostrand.
John Bergen Lott, b. Dec. 16th, 1813.
James Lott, b. Sept. 17th, 1815.
Abagail Jane Lott, b. April 21st, 1818; m. Joseph Powell.
Hendrick Lott, b. April 6th, 1822.

ISAAC BERGEN, b. April 10th, 1790; d. Feb. 16th, 1829; m. Sept. 18th, 1815, Sarah Lambertson.

Issue :—

John S., m. 1st (sup.) Aug. 1834, Phebe R. Snediker; m. 2d, ——— Emigrated west.
David; living in 1863, single and insane.
Margaret Ann; m. July 9th, 1845, Jeremiah Cheshire.
Sarah Elizabeth; m. Feb. 30th, 1839, Jose de Monte, a Spaniard. Living 1863, in the village of Jamaica.

Descendants of JACOB BERGEN, and *Mary Marston*, of Jamaica South, Queens Co., N. Y. :—

TUNIS BERGEN, b. June 1, 1772; d. July 4th, (or 6th,) 1817; m. *Ann Lott*, b. April 1, 1782; d. March 28th, 1844. Cultivated a farm at Jamaica South, and also at Brushville. Will dated May 28th, 1844.

Issue : —

Mary or Maria, b. March 3d, 1800; m. 1834, Stimerson Powell, and have children; Stephen B., Phebe Ann, and Jacob.

Ann, b. Oct. 6th, 1802; m. Dec. 28th, 1824. John Gracie, and have children:—John, Daniel, and Tunis Bergen, who d. May, 1837.

John, b. Jan. 31st, 1806; d. April 3d, 1807.

Tunis, Junr., b. Dec. 7th, 1808; living 1863, and insane.

Jacob L., b. Nov. 9th, 1811; d. Jan. 3d, 1849, single.

John Lott, b. May 23d, 1813; d. Sept. 3d, 1854; m. Nov. 16th, 1841, Mary Elizabeth, dau. of Jacob Bergen and Nancy Smith. At first a merchant in the village of Jamaica, and afterwards purchased his father's farm at Brushville, to which he removed and where he d.

Issue:—John Wessel, b. Oct. 27th, 1843; Jacob Clark, b. June 4th, 1845; Catharine Ann, b. Oct. 8th, 1847; George Lott, b. Jan. 11th, 1850; Mary Lethelia, b. Jan. 19th, 1852; and Sarah Adelia, b. Oct. 18th, 1854.

David, b. Sept. 26th, 1815; d. 1863; m. March 4th, 1840, Mary Elizabeth Valentine. Formerly a merchant, and in 1862, a Justice of the Peace in the village of Jamaica.

Issue:—James V., b. Dec. 4th, 1842.

THOMAS BERGEN, b. Oct. 11th, 1773; d. March 30th, 1842; m. Feb. 15th, 1797, *Margaret Couvert*, who d. Jan. 1848, aged 70. Owned and cultivated a farm at Jamaica South.

Issue :—

Jacob T., b. Dec. 6th, 1798; m. Dec. 16th, 1826. Alice Ann Peck, b. Aug. 5th, 1805. Is a Teacher and Professor in the City of New York, and has children:—Mary, b. Dec. 16th, 1827, d. Jan. 16th, 1832; Thomas, b. April 29th, 1830, d. Dec. 25th, 1831; Margarite C., b. Nov. 1st, 1836, m. May 5th, 1860. Robert H. Kelly; David William, b. Sept. 24th, 1839, d. Oct. 23d, 1843; Phebe Catherine, b. March 13th, 1842; Thomas, b. Oct. 28th, 1844; and David William, b. Sept. 6th, 1847; d. May 18th, 1853.

Catharine, bap. May 9th, 1802; m. May, 1849, Isaac Hendrickson

ANN BERGEN, b. March 15th, 1776 ; d. July 3d, 1795, single.

JACOB BERGEN, b. Feb. 2d. 1782 ; m. April 9th, 1817, *Ann* (or *Nancy*) *Smith*, who d. Aug. 8th, 1857.   Resides on and owns a farm of about 150 acres on the bay at Jamaica South, which he and his brother purchased about 1820.

Issue :—

Phebe Ann. b. Jan. 22d, 1818, single.

Benjamin Thurston. b. Dec. 17th, 1819 ; m. Dec. 15th, 1846, Mary Ann, dau. of Benjamin Bergen of the village of Jamaica, and has children :— Anna, b. Oct. 11th, 1854 ; and Cornelius James, b. Nov. 21st, 1860.

Cornelius, b. Feb. 25th, 1823 ; d. Jan. 31st, 1854, by accidentally falling from a load of hay ; single.

David, b. March 27th, 1825 ; d. April 7th, 1826.

Mary Elizabeth, b. May 28th, 1827 ; m. Nov. 16th, 1841, John Lott, s. of Tunis and Ann Bergen.

Jacob James, b. March 13th, 1832 ; single.

DAVID BERGEN, b. Nov. 6th, 1784 ; d. April 23d, 1828 ; m. March 3d, 1830. Ann Marston, b. Sept. 2d, 1795, d. Dec. 23d, 1842.   No issue.   Cultivated a farm at Jamaica South.

MICHAEL HANSEN BERGEN.

Descendants in the line of MICHAEL HANSEN BER-
GEN, (and *Femmetje Theunis Denyse*,) of Brooklyn, the
second son of *Hans Hansen Bergen*, the first settler. :—

Third Generation.

Sarah Bergen, bap. June 2d, 1678; d. July 15th,
1760; m. Feb. 17th, 1722, *Jan Strycker*,* of Flatbush.

Jan Strycker, the ancestor of Jan who m. Sarah, emigrated to this
country from Ruinen, a village in the province of Drenthe, in the Netherlands, in 1652, and was among the first settlers in Flatbush, of which town
he was a magistrate most of the time from 1654 to 1673. He m. 1st Lambertje Seubering in the fatherland, where probably all of his children were
born; m. 2d April 30th, 1679, Swantje Jans, wid. of Cornelis De Potter, of
Brooklyn; m. 3d April 22d, 1687, Teuntje Tunis, wid. of Jacob Hellakers.
No children by his last two wives. Issue by Lambertje:—Altie, who m.
May 20th, 1660, Abram Jorisz Brinckerhoff; Jannetje, m. Cornelis Janse
Berrian; Garret Janse, of Gravesend, d. 1695, m. Dec. 25th, 1683,
Wyntie or Styntie Cornelis Boomgaert, by other accounts, Styntje Gerrits
Dorlant; Angenietje, m. Jan Cornelise Boomgaert; Hendrick d. 1689, m.
Feb. 11th, 1687, Catharine Hys, left no issue; Eytie, m. Stoffel Probasco;
Peter, of Flatbush; and Sarah, who m. Sept. 1st, 1678, Joris Hansz Ber-
gen.
Peter, s. of Jan, and Lambertje, b. Nov. 1st, 1653, d. June 11th, 1741, m.
May 30th, 1681, Annetje Barends or Joosten, who d. June 17th, 1717. He
resided in Flatbush, and was one of the patentees of the town named on
Dongan's patent. His children were: Lammetje, b. March 20th, 1682, d.
April 9th, 1682; Lammetje, b. Feb. 16th, 1683, d. July 26th, 1690, of
small pox; *Jan*, of Flatbush; Barent, b. Sept. 3d, 1686, d. July 9d, 1690,
of small pox; Jacob, b. Aug. 24th, 1688, m. (sup.) Dec. 17th, 1710 Annetie
Vander Beek; Barent, b. Sept. 14th, 1690, d. Oct. 27th, 1746, m. Feb. 16th,
1717, Libertje Hegeman, who d. June, 1758; Hendrick b. Dec. 3d, 1692,
d. May 17th, 1694; Sytje, b. Dec. 17th, 1694, m. (sup.) March 14th, 1717,
Aert Vanderbilt; Pieter, of Flatbush, b. Feb. 12th, 1697, d. Dec. 24th,
1776, m. May 18th, 1720, Jannetie Martens, dau. of Martin Adrian; Hendrick, a baker in Brooklyn, b. Feb. 18th, 1699, d. Aug. 19th, 1739, m.
(sup.) Marretje or Mary ———; and Lammetje, b. Dec. 21, 1700, d. Sept.
14th, 1763, m. 1st Nov. 4th, 1721, Johannes Lott, who d. in 1752, m. 2d
Christanus Lupardus, s. of Do. Lupardus.
Jan, s. of Peter and Annetje, of Flatbush, b. Aug. 6th, 1684, d. Aug.
18th, 1770, m. 1st Margerita Schenck, who d. Aug. 1721, m. 2d Feb. 17th,
1722, Sarah dau. of Michiel Hansen Bergen; children by Margereta: Pie-

Her descendants have in their possession a large folio family Bible, (Dutch.) presented to her by her father, and deemed of sufficient importance to be referred to in some of their wills.

Issue :—

Mighiel Strycker, b. March 4th, 1723: m. May 31. 1751, Hanna Strycker; d. Sept. 26th, 1807.

Femmetje Strycker, b. June 19th, 1725: m. May 25th, 1745, Jacobus Vanderveer.

Barent Strycker. b. Nov. 13th, 1728; d. young.

Sara Strycker, b. June 15th, 1731 : d. young.

TEUNIS BERGEN. bap. May 16th, 1680. He probably d. young. no record having been found in which he is named. excepting that of his birth.

HANS MACHIELSE OR HANSE BERGEN, bap. March 11th. 1689; d. in 1731 : m. *Rachel* dau. of Derick Bensing or Benson.[*] Rachel was b. April 13th, 1659, and d.

ter. b. Sept. 14th. 1705: Johannes. b. Feb. 12th, 1707: Annetje, b. Dec. 20th, 1708, m. Roelof Cowenhoven: Magdalena. b. Dec. 19th, 1710, m. Aert Middagh: Maragrita, b. March 24th, 1713, d. young: Abraham, b. Aug. 4th, 1715: Lammetje, Feb. 11th, 1716, m. Jan Ammerman; Jacobus b. Sept. 29th, 1718. m. (sup.) Geertje Duryea, settled in Somerset Co, N. J.: and Maragrita, b. Dec. 17th, 1719, m. Jacobus Cornell: children by 2d wife: *Mighiel*, Femmetje, Barent, and Sara.

Mighiel, s. of Jan and Sara, of Flatbush, b. March 4th, 1723, d. Sept. 26th, 1807, m. May 31, 1751, Hannah dau. of Cornelis Stryker. b. Feb. 13th, 1733, and d. Oct. 1st, 1807. Had children Jan of Flatbush, b. March 1st, 1752. d. Sept. 26th, 1817, m. July 12th, 1777, Jannetie Lott. and left no issue: Lezebet, b. Sept. 21st, 1753, d. March 27th, 1787, m. Dec. 1771, Roelof Lott: Sara, b. July 11th, 1756. d. May 23d, 1825, m. May, 1778, Peter Nevius or Nefus, of Flatbush; Rebecca, b. Nov. 6th, 1758, m. John Coevert, of Newtown: *Cornelius*. of Flatbush: Johannes, b. May 1st, 1763: Femmetje, b. Feb. 14th, 1765, m. David Springsteen, of Newtown: and Michiel, b. Nov. 15th, 1771, d. Oct. 13th, 1777.

Cornelius, s. of Mighiel and Hanna, b. April 26th, 1760, d. March 12th, 1841, m. Jan. 16th, 1789, Adrianna Schenck, b. Aug. 22, 1768, d. Sept. 1st, 1830. Had children: Wilhelmina, b. Jan. 31st, 1791, d. Feb. 16th, 1847, single: Hannah, b. Nov. 13th, 1793, d. July 26th, 1794; Hannah, b. May 10th, 1795, d. Aug. 12th, 1803: Ann, b. Aug. 23d, 1798, d. Aug. 5th, 1834, m. John Schenck: *Michael*, of Flatbush, b. Feb. 8th, 1803, d. Oct. 23d, 1817, m. Dec. 27th, 1827, Gitty Jane. dau. of Garret Kouwenhoven and Maria Bergen, of Flatlands, said Maria being a dau. of Cornelius Bergen, of Flatbush; and Nicholas, b. June 20th, 1805, d. Aug. 28th, 1809.

[*] *Derick Benson or Bensing*, was a s. of "Sampson Bensing." (who may have been a descendant of a Derick Bensick, who was in the colony as early as 1649.) of the city of N. Y., whose will is dated July 20th, 1726, and proved Feb. 23d, 1731. Sampson had children: *Derick* dec'd at the

in 1752. In 1707-8, the names of "Johannes Burger," appears on a petition of Cornelis Sebering, for a ferry from his lands in Brookland to New York. May 12th, 1708, it appears from the old Kings County court records that "Hans Machielse Bergen," was concerned in a riot at the house of Sarah Knight, a tavern keeper, in the village of Brookland. June 4th, 1710, "Hans Bergen" bought of his father for £400, the 10 acres at Brookland ferry, which he had purchased April 27th, 1709, of Garret Middah.*

By a deed of March 23d, 1715-16, Hans Bergen appears to have bought, and by a deed dated March 26th, 1715-16, Hans Bergen and Johannes Sebering bought of the freeholders and inhabitants of Brookland for £150, 10s., a plot or spot at the ferry, "bounded N. E. by the highway leading from Brookland to the river or ferry; S. E. by the highway lying between the house and ground of Master Parmeter and said spott of ground; S. W. by the highway lying between the ground of Hans Bergen

date of his will; Teunis, also, dec'd at the date of his will; Herman; Sampson; Robert, also, dec'd at the date of said will; Henricus; dau. Palo, also, dec'd; Elizabeth, w. of Egbert Van Burson; and Catena. "Dirck Benson," petitioned Nov. 7th, 1689, the Gov. and Council for a patent for a tract of 188 acres of land on Staten Island with some meadows, lying between Long Neck and Daniel's Neck. "Derick Bensing" in 1701, leased the ferry from New York to Brooklyn, for seven years at £130 per annum, on which lease it was said he lost money. Mar'ch 23d, 1707, "Derick Benson," of Brookland, gentleman, loaned on mort. to Cornelis Vanderhove, of Bedford, £121; Nov. 10, 1707, "Derick Benson m. Jannetie Vanderwater, a second wife. In 1710, on an assignment of a mort. he is styled a merchant of the city of New York. March 24th, 1710, "Derick Benson" petitioned the Gov. and Council for a grant of 1000 acres out of the land formerly granted to Capt. John Evans, in Ulster Co. Aug. 26th, 1711, "Derick Bensing" petitioned the Gov. and Council for a grant of 2000 acres of land lying between the south limits of the land granted to Dr. Samuel Staats and the south side of the Dunder Berg, on which a warrant for the survey of the same was granted.

Derick Benson d. prior to 1721, and from the will, etc, is stated to appears to have left children, among whom were *Racon*, &c, *bort 11th*, 1685, m. Hans Machielse Bergen; Eva, bap. March 19th, 1695, and Derick, bap. July 5th, 1696. His wife d. about 1732.

In Montgomery's charter of the city of N. Y., a "Derick Bensing" was appointed collector of the outward of the city. This Derick who d. in 1750, may have been the Derick b. in 1696, and brother of Rachel.

* See Lib. 5, p. 10 of conveyances, K. C. Reg. Off.

11

and said spott of ground ; and N. W. by the river."* On
the same date Sebering executed a mortgage to Hans for
£75 on the above premises. In 1715, " Hans Bergen's"
name appears on the militia list of the town as a private
in Capt. Remsen's company. April 16, 1717, " Hans
Bergen," baker. bought of Johannes Sebering, baker, for
£99, his interest or the one undivided half of the plot
they purchased of the freeholders and inhabitants of
Brookland, described as " lying to ye S. W. of ye ferry
house. Butted and Bounded W'ly by ye highway, S'ly
by ye highway, E'ly by ye highway, and N'ly by ye
river."† April 17, 1717, Hans Bergen and Rachael his wife,
for £10, conveyed to Johannes Sebering. a portion of the
plot " bounded E'ly by ye highway, N'ly by ye river,
W'ly by the grounds of said Hans Bergen. and S'ly also
to said Hans Bergen, being in breadth on both ends 7 ft.,
to be measured from ye northermost fence and soe upwards along ye highway and from said fence to ye river,
on both ends, and in length on both sides 20ft. all English measure.‡ This plot was evidently at the corner of
the present Fulton street and the then shores of the East
River.

May, 2d, 1717, "Hans Bergen of the ferry, baker,"
bought of Thomas Palmeter for £455, "all those several
dwelling houses, tenements and all that piece or parcel
of land, &c., lately belonging to John and Sarah Coa, as
ye same now lyes in fence : Bounded E'ly, W'ly and
N'ly to ye roads or highways, and S'ly to ye land in possession of ye wid. Middagh, containing within said fence
about two acres." This plot appears to have included

---

* This plot appears to have covered the whole westerly front of Fulton
st. from the alley known as Elizabeth st., adjoining Jones' tavern and liv-
ery stable located S. E. of the corner of Columbia and Fulton streets, to
the East river. See Lib. 4, p. 303 and 119 of con. in K. C. Reg. Off.

† See Lib. 4, p. 153 and con. in K. C. Reg. Off.

‡ See Lib. 4, p. 151 of con. in K. C. Reg. Off.

the lands fronting on Fulton street, from Elizabeth street to the Middagh lands, S. E. of Hicks street.*

Oct. 7th, 1720, Hans Bergen, baker, and Rachel his wife conveyed to William Baker of the city of New York for £110, a portion of the land bought of Palmeter, "as in fence, containing in breadth 72 feet, 4 in. fronting the road, and the same in the rear, and in the length from front to rear, 152 feet, all English measure, bounded S. E. by the land of the wid. Middagh, and N. W. by the land of the said Hans Bergen."†

April 7th, 1720, he sued Jacob Vandewater for a silver tankard.‡ March 7th, 1721, " Johannes Bergen " and Rachel his wife, heirs and executors of the estate of Derick Bensing, released a mortgage to Cornelis Vander Hoven. April 17th, 1721, Hans Bergen of the ferry, and Jan Rapalje, complained to the grand jury of the general sessions of the peace of encroachments on the public highway, on which indictments were found.§ Aug. 21st, 1723, Hans Bergen bought of his father his farm of one hundred and eighty acres, late of Albert Cornelissen, here-

* See Lib. 4. p. 154 of con. K. Co. Reg. office.

† See Lib. 4. p. 319 and 321 of con. K. C. Reg. office.

‡ Garret G. Bergen of Gowanus, one of the descendants of Hans Bergen, has in his possession an old family silver tankard marked H. R. B., the initials of Hans and Rachel Bergen, probably the one here referred to.

§ The following is a copy of the entry on the court records:—" Flatbush, April 19th, 1721. John Rapalje and Hans Bergen of the ferry, des'r s of ye grand jury that ye Commissioners now being should be presented for not doing their duty in laying out ye Kings Highway according to ye law, being ye Kings highway is too narrow from ye ferry to one Nicalis Cowenhoven, living at Brookland, and if all our neighbors will make ye road according to law, then ye said John Rapalje and Hans Bergen is willing to do ye same as aforesaid, being they are not willing to suffer more than their neighbors."

On this complaint the grand jury at the then April term of the General Sessions for the County, found indictments for encroachments on the " common highway of the King leading from the ferry to the church at Brookland," against John Rapalje, Hans Bergen, James Harding, and others, by which indictments it appears the road should have been four rods wide. These indictments do not appear to have been tried, the Colon'n Legislature in 1721 having passed a law regulating the road and establishing its width as it then was.

inbefore referred to. In 1724. "Hans Bergen" was Supervisor of Brookland.

January 11th, 1728. "Hans Bergen" and Rachel his wife, for £250 conveyed to Israel Horsfield a house and land at the ferry, "bounded S. W. on the land now in the possession of the said Hans Bergen, to the E. S. E. on the land now in the possession of Gabriel Cox, to the N. E. on a street or highway, and to the N. W. partly on a street or highway, and partly on the land of said Israel Horsfield and Cornelia Middagh; beginning at a street or highway at the E. corner, now in the possession of Gabriel Cox. and from thence running by the said street or highway towards the East River, N. 60 deg. W. 226 feet to another street or highway leading to the East River side, thence running by the said street, which leads to the said river; S. 60 deg. W. 120 feet to the lot of said Israel Horsefield. thence running by his lot S. 30 deg. E. as the said lot runs 40 feet to the rear thereof; thence running by the said Horsefield's lot S. 60 deg. W. as it runs 200 feet; thence S. 30 deg. W. by the said lot 15 feet to the rear of the lot of Cornelia Middagh; thence S. W. as the rear of that lot runs 25 feet to the S. W. bounds thereof; thence by the said Hans Bergen's land S. 54 deg. E. 429 feet to the land now in possession of Gabriel Cox, at the N. W. corner thereof; thence running by the said Cox's land to the N. N. E. as the said land runs 397 feet to the place of beginning.

May 2d, 1730. "Hans Machielse Bergen" and others, freeholders of Brookland, conveyed to Jan Bennet of Gowanus about three acres of woodland in the rear of Bennet's farm.

On the census of Brooklyn of 1738.* " Hans Bergen's family is entered as consisting of four white males above

* See Vol. IV. p. 197. Doc. His. of N. Y.

ten years, one white male under ten, six white females above ten, one black male under ten, and one black male above ten. This entry is supposed to be intended for the family of Hans Machielse Bergen, although he was dead at the time, the number and sex of the members of the family agreeing more nearly with his, than that of any other Hans Bergen.

Hans Bergen carried on the bakery business in Brooklyn from 1717 to about 1730, in conjunction with a store and stabling for the horses of the residents of the Island, when crossing to New York, in a stone building located as near as can be ascertained, on the westerly corner of Fulton and Elizabeth streets, a portion of the walls of which are supposed to form the easterly end of the building at present located there. His will is dated Jan. 18th, 1731, and proved Jan. 13, 1732. He devises to Michiel his oldest son the farm (of 180 acres, since Powers's,) on which he then resided, valued at £600, subject to the payment of a legacy of £200 to his dau. Femmetje, and also of £200 to be paid to his son Tennis, when 21 years of age; to his son Derick, the dwelling house at the ferry, wherein John Rjm now lives, with the bolting house and the ground whereon Thomas Browne now lives, all valned at £250, subject to a legacy of £50, to be paid to his son Hans when 21; and to his son Hans in addition, a lot at the ferry valued at £150.

The following is a fac simile of Hans Bergen's signature:—

$$\mathcal{Hans\ Bergen}$$

Issue: -

Annetje, bap. March 12th, 1710, in New York. No farther trace and probably d. young.

Tiesje, b. June 9th, 1711, and bap. in Brooklyn. No farther trace, and probably d. young.

Michiel, b. Dec. 22d, 1712, and bap. in New York.

Femmetje, b. July 29th, 1715.

Derick, b. Feb. 28th, 1716, and bap. in New York.

Hans, b. July 12th, 1721.

Teunis, b. Oct. 15th, 1730.

FEMMETJE BERGEN, m. Jan. 1695, *John Cornelissen Vanderveer,* who was b. in Flatlands.

Issue :—

Katryna Vanderveer, bap. March 29th, 1696.

Femmetje Vanderveer, m. Jacob Sebering.

Jan Vanderveer, m. Antje . . . .

MARY BERGEN, was unmarried Aug. 25th, 1723. No farther trace.

———

Fourth Generation.

Children of HANS MACHIELSE BERGEN and *Rachel Bensing* of Brooklyn, N. Y. :—

MICHAEL BERGEN, b. Dec. 20th, 1712, and bap. in N. Y.: d. prior to 1788, during the war of the Revolution ; m. *Catalyn,* dau. of Hanse Jacobse Bergen.

Oct. 7th, 1733, Rachel Bergen, widow of Hans Bergen, and Michael Bergen his son, for £180, 12s. convey to Israel Horsefield land at the ferry, " bounded N. E. by the highway leading from Brookland to the River : S. E. by the highway lying between the house and grounds of Master Parmerter, (now or late in the possession of the executors of the said Hans Bergen,) and said spot of ground: S. W. by the highway lying between the ground of the aforesaid Hans Bergen, deceased, (now in the possession and occupancy of Timothy Horsefield,) and said spot of ground: N. W. by the River. (except and always reserving out of this present bargain and sale, 7 feet in length of the River leading from Brookland, and 25 feet in breadth heretofore sold by Hans Bergen, deceased, to Johannes Sebering;" said land being the plot conveyed to Hans Bergen and Johannes Sebering by the Trustees of Brookland, and by said Sebering to said Bergen.*

April 12th, 1748, Rachel, widow of Hans Bergen, released to her son Michael Bergen, her right of dower in the farm (formerly of Albert Cornelissen,) in Brookland, which was devised to him by his father, said farm being bounded in the release, S'ly by land of Jacobus Debevoise; N'ly by land of Carl Debevoise and Israel Horsefield; E'ly by the Kings highway leading from Flatbush to New York ferry; and W'ly by the meadows, containing 120 acres :† also her right of dower in the meadows and woodland.

April 30th, 1750 Michael Bergen bought a negro man of the estate of his father-in-law, Hanse Jacobse Bergen. In 1751-2-3, he was a member of the consistory of the Reformed Dutch Church of Brooklyn. March 25th, 1754, Sylvester Marius Groen and Femmetje, his wife, (dau. of Hans Bergen,) executed a release to Michael Bergen for the legacy of £200, devised to Femmetje by the will of her father. In 1755, he is entered on the list of slaves in Brookland, as having one negro man named Tight, and one negro woman named Dine.

April 3d, 1767, the executors of Thomas Cornell of Queens County, sold to Michael Bergen for £1600, a house, grist mill and farm on the south side of the town of Jamaica, in Queens County, near the salt meadows, containing 220 acres, including uplands and bog mead-

---

* See Lib. 5, p. 155 of con. K. C. Reg. office.

† This farm originally contained 180 acres, if the contents here given are correct. 60 acres must have been sold off prior to this period, of which sale no deed has been seen.

ows, and also a plot of salt meadows.   In Nov., 1776, his name appears among those who took British protection.

April 15th, 1783, on Sunday night, Capt. Hyler of New Brunswick went over to Long Island, (Michiel Bergen's, Gowanus,) and brought off a Hessian Major, Ensign, &c.   During the war of the Revolution his house was robbed, and in a printed placard a reward was offered for the detection of the robbers.   During those perilous times robberies were frequent.

While on his death bed, Michael Bergen, by will, devised his real estate to his grandson, Michael Bergen Grant, son of his dau. Sarah.   The descendants of his dau. Tishe say that young Grant took advantage of his grandfather's infirmities, and unfairly induced him to devise his property in this manner, thus cutting them off from the inheritance.   This accusation may or may not be well founded.   In his life time he had given his dau. Tishe a deed for about forty acres of his farm, which deed during the troublesome times of the Revolution, she placed in the hands of her father for safe keeping.   On his death, this deed with his other papers fell in the hands of Grant, who in consequence of Tishe and her descendants having no papers in their possession to the contrary, took and held possession of all the land, the forty acres included.   Grant finally sold all the real estate to George Powers, and emigrated to Nova Scotia, leaving his papers with Garret Bergen of Gowanus, the deed for the forty acres included.   In 1836, the heirs of Tishe obtained this deed from T. G. Bergen, in whose hands the papers had fallen, and commenced proceedings to recover the land, employing Gerard of New York as their Attorney, but it appeared they were too late to succeed.

Issue :—

Sarah, b. Dec. 18th, 1743.
Tishe.

The following is a fac simile of Michael Bergen's signature :—

meighiel Bergen

FEMMETJIE BERGEN, b. July 29th 1715; d. Oct. 31st, 1793, ag. 79 years and 3 mo.; m. April 18th, 1745, *Sylvester Marius Groen*, a widower, whose descendants now write their sirnames "Morris," instead of Marius, having altogether dropped the Groen, one of whom, Jacob Morris, m. Leah, dau. of Simon Bergen, dec'd. Sylvester Marius Groen was a grocer, residing in the city of New York, and a descendant of Pieter Jacobs Marius Groen, who emigrated from Hoogwout, in the province of North Holland, and who m. Nov. 13th, 1655, Marritje Pieters, of Amsterdam. Pieter Jacobs Marius Groen, was a merchant and an alderman of New York, from 1677 to 1682. One of his ancestors while in command of one of the fleets of Holland, captured three Turkish vessels, for which he was authorized to add three crescents to his coat of arms.

Issue :—

Polly Marius. d. single, aged 86.

Letitia Marius, b. about 1749 ; d. single Sept. 19th, 1835.

Rachel Marius, d. aged 80 and single.

Jacob Marius, b. May 10th, 1755, m. Mary Van Riper. Left issue, Sylvester ; John ; Jacob, b. Sept. 6th 1792, m. Leah dau. of Simon Bergen ; Peter ; Maria ; and Phebe.

Sylvester Marius, m. Hannah Bear, and had children, Catharine, David, Effee, Sylvester, Henry, and Jacob, who all d. without issue.

Elizabeth Marius, m. Daniel Kemper, an officer of rank in the war of the revolution, on the termination of which he resided in the city of N.Y. where he held municipal positions, and afterwards removed to New Brunswick, where he died. Their children were Daniel, who was an officer in Miranda's unfortunate expedition to South America, in which he was taken prisoner and forfeited his life; Sylvester Marius; Jackson, who is Bishop of the Episcopal church, of the diocese of Wisconsin; Jane; and Eliza, who since the death of their father have resided with the Bishop.

DERICK BERGEN, b. Feb. 28, 1716, and bap. in New York; d. Nov. 19th, 1759; m. 1749, *Deborah*, dau. of Jacques Cortelyou, b. Nov. 29th, 1720, and d. Jan. 15th, 1808.*

Derick resided with his brother Hans in the old stone house standing near the bay or river in the vicinity of 55th street, Brooklyn, and late the property of the heirs of Theodorus Bergen, dec'd, in which house he died, his family after his decease removing to the farm he bought, July 21st, 1756, of his brother Hans in the vicinity of 15th street, in said city.

April 22d, 1740, Rachel Bergen, wid. of Hans Bergen, and Derick Bergen her son, conveyed for £340, to Samuel Hopson, a plot in Brookland, " Bounded partly E'ly upon the high road or street leading to the ferry; partly N'ly

---

* *Jaques Corteljou*, the surveyor, a Huegonot, private tutor of the children and agent of Mr. Cornelis Van Werckhoven, (said Cornelis was a member of the Privileged West India Company, one of the patrons of New Netherland, and the original patentee of the Nyack tract in New Utrecht, which tract fell in the hands of said Jaques,) emigrated to this country in 1652, was among the first settlers of New Utrecht in 1657, and the common ancestor of the Cortelyou family in this country. He d. about 1693; his wife Neeltje Van Duyn, a sister of Garret Cornelisse Van Duyn, dying prior to Dec., 1695. His children were Jaques, b. about 1662, d. about 1732, m. Marretie Hendricks Smock; *Peter* b. about 1664, d. April 10th, 1757, m. Deborah or Diewertje De Witt about 1694; Cornelis d. about 1690, ır. Neeltje Volckers; Helena d. about 1720, m. 1st Nicholas Rutgersz Van Brunt, Aug. 19th, 1683, m. 2d March 29th, 1685, Deonys Theunis, and m. 3d Hendrick Hendrickson; Maria m. William Barkeloo; and William, who probably died before his father, unmarried.

Peter the s. of Jaques had children, Neeltje, bap. Nov. 15, 1694; *Jaques* b. about 1698, d. Oct. 10, 1757, m. April 25th, 1718, Jacomintie Van Pelt, who d. Sept. 28th, 1769, aged 72; Peter b. Sept. 25th, 1699, d. 1764, m. Feb. 24th, 1720, Neeltje Van Pelt; Cornelis b. Aug. 17th, 1701, emigrated to Staten Island, and is the ancestor of the Cortelyou family in Richmond county; Helena, b. Sept. 21st, 1703; William b. Sept. 27th, 1705; Maria b. Aug. 10th, 1707; Dorothea or Deborah, b. Nov. 20th, 1709; and Neeltje, b. March 20th, 1712.

Jaques the son of Peter and Deborah had children: *Deborah* b. Nov. 29th 1720, d. Jan 15th, 1808, m. 1749, Derrick Bergen, of Gowanus; Peter b. Oct. 3d, 1722, d. March 21, 1777, m. Jan. 8th 1743, Agnes or Angenietie De Hart; and Nelthe, b. March 6th, 1726.

on the high road or street leading to Israel Horsefields;
partly W'ly by a back highway leading towards John
Middagh's; and partly S'ly upon land now in possession
of William Phillips, containing about one acre."*

In 1755, "Derick Bergen" is entered on the lists of
slaves in Brookland, as possessing two negro men named
Will and Cæser.

His will is dated Oct. 7th, 1759, proved May 17th,
1769, and recorded in the office of the Secretary of State
in Albany.

Issue:—

Rachel, b. 1753.
Jeromus? b. May 4th, 1755.
Tise?, b. Jan. 19th, 1756.
Nelly b. March 25th, 1758, d. Oct. 18th, 1761.

HANS (JOHN OR JOHANNES,) BERGEN, b. July 12th,
1721, and bap. in Brooklyn, d. April 28th, 1786, m.
Gertrude or *Trintje*. ——— b. July 25th, 1726, and d.
Oct. 6th, 1795.

Aug. 20th, 1744, Theodorus A. Van Wyck, of the city
of New York and Helen his wife, sole dau. and heiress
of Cornelius Sanford, late of Brooklyn, conveyed to
"John Bergen" for £610, the house and land at Yellow
Hook, Brooklyn, containing 200 acres as in fence, and in
the occupancy of Jacob Bloom and Gertrude Sanford wid.
of said Cornelius; bounded S. W. by land of Hendrick
Van Dyck; N. E. by land of Wouter Van Pelt; N. W.
by the river; and S. E. by land of said Van Dyck; also,
all their right in the undivided woodlands of Brooklyn.
Sandford's wid., Gertrude, was a dau. of Simon de Hart,
of Gowanus, having m. for a second husband Jores Remsen; John Bergen in addition to the £610, paid £100 for

* This may be a part of the part. Derick's Estate, Hans, purchased
of the freeholders, &c., of Brooklyn, on which a schoolery was situated. See
Lib. 5, p. 129 of con. in K. C. Reg. off.

Gertrude's dower right.* On this farm, Hans Bergen, after its purchase, resided the remainder of his life, occupying the old mansion, partly of stone, located near 55th
street, between First avenue and the bay, which his
grandson Theodorus Bergen lately occupied, and in which
he died. The above premises were conveyed, April 6th,
1724, for £824, by Claes Van Dyck to Joseph Hegeman;
and May 10th, 1734, for £500, by said Hegeman to said
Cornelius Sanford. This farm, located in the vicinity of
52d and 56th streets, is the first purchase made by the
Bergen family of the numerous farms they subsequently
owned on the bay at Gowanus, Yellow Hook and Bay
Ridge.

As early as in 1749, "Hans Bergen" was a member of
the consistory of the Reformed Dutch Church of Brooklyn.

March 7th, 1751, Christopher Scharse and Peter Van
Pelt, conveyed to "Johannes Bergen," for £225, a farm
at Gowanus, Brooklyn, bounded S. W'ly and N. E'ly by
land of Cornelius Van Duyne; N. W'ly as the river
runs; and S. E'ly by land of Garret Cowenhoven, containing 35 acres.† July 21st, 1776, "Hans Bergen" conveyed the above farm for £227, to his brother Derick Bergen. These premises are in the vicinity of 15th and 16th
streets, and designated on Butts' map as land of John
Dimon and heirs of Rachel Berry.

On the 24th of Aug., 1751, in consideration of £117,
Isaac Sebring of "Brookland," and Catharine his wife,
conveyed to Nicholas Vechte, Jurry Brouwer, Abraham
Brouwer, Peter Staets, Cornelius Van Duyn, Jun., Wynant
Bennet, Jacob Bennet, Wilhelmus Bennet, and Hans Bergen, the fee of "all that certain strip or piece of meadows
and marshes, situate, lying and being in the township of

---

* See Lib. 5, p. 170 and 175 of con. in K. C. Reg. off.

† See Lib. 6, p. 4 of con. in K. C. Reg. off.

Brookland aforesaid in the county aforesaid, butted and bounded as followeth, viz: beginning at the east side of a little island where John Van Dyck's long milldam is bounded upon, running from thence northerly into the river all over or through the meadows of said Isaac Sebring, being in breadth twelve feet and a half."* As a part of the consideration Sebring was to make a ditch over the whole of this strip at least six feet deep, for the use of the grantees, and to allow them the use of a "foot-path two foot and a half wide to dragg or hall up their canoes or boats," reserving to himself among other things, the privilege of navigating the ditch.

March 16th, 1744, the Colonial Assembly of the State passed an act which was approved of by Gov. Tryon, on the 19th, entitled "An Act to empower certain persons therein named to complete a ditch that is partly dug from Gowanus bay to the East river in Kings county, under certain restrictions."† The preamble to this act sets forth that the same is enacted in consequence of the difficult and dangerous navigation around Red Hook, and refers to the deed of 1751. The parties named in the act are, "Nicklaas Veghte, Peter Staets, Deborah Bergen, (wid. of Derick,) Anthony Holst, John Rapalje, Winaent Bennet, Jacob Bennet, Tennis Bergen, Tuenes Tiebout and Simon Bergen." Some of these parties were among the original purchasers of the strip of meadows, and some of the others at this period owned the farms held by the original purchasers in 1751. They were required to keep the bridge over the ditch or canal on the road leading to Van Dyck's mill in order, to keep up the dams along so much of the neighboring mill ponds as adjoined upon the canal, and were

*This deed is not recorded, but the original with other papers, of the heirs of Nicholas Vechte, was in the hands of Judge J. A. Lott, in 1862.

†This act is entered in full on the engrossed copy of the colonial laws on file in the office of the Secretary of State, Albany.

authorized to close the same when they thought proper, without detriment to their fee. A provision was also inserted making such inhabitants of Gowanus as might use the ditch, liable to contribute towards keeping the same in repair. This canal or ditch is delineated on Ratzer's map of Brooklyn and New York, and was partially closed some 25 years ago, by the improvements at the Atlantic Dock, persons being yet living, among whom is the writer, who frequently passed through it with their boats, in going or returning from New York.

The avoidance of the difficult and dangerous navigation around Red Hook by row boats engaged the attention of the neighboring residents at a much earlier period, for we find that on the 29th day of May, 1664, the inhabitants of Gouwanus petitioned the Director General and Council of New Netherlands for permission to clean out the kill at the end of Frederick Lubbertsen's land, and near Red Hook, so as to render it navigable to Gouwanus and the mill, and relieve them of the necessity of going around the Red Hook, which petition was granted.[*]

In 1755, "John Bargay," is entered on the list of slaves in Brookland, as possessing five negro men named Roger, Harry, Peter, Josey and Esquire, and two negro women named Mary and Pegg. This Mary, known as Mary Peterson, resided many years with his descendants and d. Nov. 1824, ag. 103 years.

June 9th, 1760, "Johannes Bergen" bought of Hendrick Van Dyck, for £950, a tract at Yellow Hook, Brooklyn, containing ninety and a half acres, adjoining and on the S. W'ly side of the lands he purchased of the heirs of Cornelius Sandford, and also a tract of woodland in the rear of the same, partly in Brooklyn and New Utrecht,

*Vol. X. p. 225, Dutch manuscripts, Sec'y of State's off.

containing twelve acres and four perches. These parcels are located in the vicinity of 56th and 59th streets.*

From 1762 to 1777, "Johannes Bergen" held the office of Justice of the Sessions and Common Pleas of the county of Kings. April 21st, 1762, "Johannes Bergen," Wynant Bennet and Peter Cortelyou, were presented by the grand jury for "that their nets or seines were used on Sunday, the 20th of April inst., and they are fined by this court each six shillings," which fines appear to have been paid in court.

From 1764 to 1775, inclusive, and in 1777 and 1782, "Johannes Bergen" held the office of Supervisor of Brooklyn. There are no minutes of the year 1776, and of some of the years prior to 1782, and the probability is that if any one acted during this period he was the person, and that he held the office during the war of the Revolution and until 1783. In March and April 1776, his name appears among the committeemen chosen by the towns of the county, to protect them from British aggression, but in November of the same year, after the conquest of the Island, it appears among those who took British protection and the oath of allegiance; the county and town Committees dissolved themselves in Dec. 1776. In those days of trial, our forefathers who had rebelled against the tyranny of England, residing in the portion of the country conquered and held by the British army, were compelled either to take the oath of allegiance and make their submission, or else abandon their homes and property, and remove beyond the British lines, with a small prospect of being able to maintain their families. The sacrifice was too great for the mass of the whigs and patriots of Long Island. They concluded to smother their detestation of English rule until a more fitting season, prefer-

* See Lib. 6, p. 4 of con. in K. C. Reg. off.

ing their old homes to banishment. During the great
Southern rebellion of our day no doubt thousands similarly situated have acted in the same manner.

July 17th, 1780, Hans Bergen's name appears among
the signers of an address to the British Gov. Robertson, the
successor of Gov. Tryon, on his accession to office. On the
establishment of peace his name appears among the signers of a congratulatory address to Gen. Washington. He
claimed after the revolution £216, 2s. of the government
for the loss of 25 cattle, 2 horses, 104 bu. wheat and 136
bu. rye, caused by the American army.

From the following entries in the records of the commissioners of the Land Office at Albany it appears he was
concerned in the purchase from the Indians of large
tracts of land in the northern part of this state. "Thomas Palmer, Derick Lefferts, John Lake, one of the heirs of
Robert Leake, dec'd, Simon Remsen, Abraham Brinckerhoff, Rem P. Remsen, dec'd, and 'Johannes Berger,' having exhibited their claim by virtue of an Indian purchase
prior to the 14th of Oct., 1775, for a tract of land lying
and being on the W. side of the W. branch of Hudson's
river, beginning at a certain marked tree about half a mile
above the big island, and runs from thence W. 46 chains
to the N. W. corner of the patent granted to Cornelius
Schuyler in 1742; thence N. 30 deg. W. 1040 ch.; thence
N. 60 deg. E. 1400 ch.; thence S. 30 deg. E. 1400 ch.; to
the said branch of Hudson's river; thence up along the
same as it runs to a tract of 9000 acres conveyed to John
Glen and others; thence along the E'ly, N'ly and W'ly
bounds thereof to the river again; thence up along the
same as it runs until it meets a tract granted to Philip
Livingston; thence along the W'ly and N'ly bounds
thereof until it meets a tract known by the name of Northampton; thence along the W'ly and N'ly bounds thereof

to beginning, computed to contain 157,000 acres, excepting out of the bounds and limits aforesaid 24,000 acres granted to John Berger; also for another certain tract of land lying and being on Sacondaga or the W. branch of Hudson's river, beginning at a certain marked tree on the W. side of the W. branch of Hudson's river about half a mile above the big island, and running thence W. 46 ch. to the N. W. corner of the patent granted to Cornelius Schuyler, in 1742 ; thence N. 30 deg. W. 1040 chains ; thence N. 60 deg. E. 205 ch. ; thence S. 30 deg. E. to Northampton patent ; thence along the different courses of said patent to the beginning, containing by estimation 24,000 acres."

The petition for the last mentioned tract of about 24,000 acres was presented as early as the 23d day of December, 1769, in which it was set forth that the "petitioners had lately discovered a certain tract of land in the county of Albany, as yet unpurchased of the native Indian proprietors thereof."[*] On the 31st day of July, 1772,[†] Hendrick, alias Tayahansara, Lourance alias Aggneragies, Hans alias Canelagaure, Hans Krine alias Anagoadhoje, native Indians, with the consent of the Gov. John, Earl of Dunmore, for £100, conveyed said tract of 24,000 acres to John Bergen and his associates, who it appears were:

" NICHOLAS C. LOWE.   JOHN BERGEN.
PHILIP LIVINGSTON.   SIMON REMSEN.
HUGH GAINE.   REM P. REMSEN.
TIMOTHY WOOD.   HENRY REMSEN.
EDWARD SMITH.   SIMEON BERGEN.
CHARLES MORSE.   PETER VAN SCHAACK.
SAMUEL BOWYER.   GERARD BANCHER.
JOHN GRUMLY.   DIRCK LEFFERTS.
JOHN BOWLES.   GERARD G. BEEKMAN.

* Vol. XXVI, p. 62, land papers, Sec. of State's off., Albany.

† Vol. XXXII, p. 42, land papers, Sec'y of State's off., Albany.

13

BENJ. J. JOHNSON.   WILLIAM BUTLER.
MALCOM W. ISAACS.   ROBERT HARDING.
EDMUND FANNING.   ISAAC LOW."*

Caveats were filed, claims and counter claims presented in relation to these lands, the principal portion of which appears to have been awarded to the heirs of Philip Livingston, dec'd and others, leaving for John Bergen and his associates the tract of 24,000 acres. On the final survey by S. DeWitt, the surveyor general, and division of this tract, there is nothing on the records shewing that any portion thereof was allotted to either John or Simon Bergen, they probably with many of their associates having sold out their interests, but of this no evidence has been seen. These lands continue to be known and described as the "Bergen purchase," on the tax lists of the counties in which they are located.

Sept. 23d, 1785, "Johannes Bergen" purchased of John Van Pelt and Jane his wife, for £600, the S'ly one half of the farm late of Tunis Van Pelt, dec'd, located in Brooklyn, and bounded N. W'ly by the river; N. E'ly by land of Wynant Van Pelt; S. E'ly by the Wedge lot; and S. W'ly by land of said Johannes Bergen, containing fifty acres; also one acre of salt meadow located near said farm, 2 1-2 acres woodland in Brooklyn on the rear of said farm, 5 acres of woodland in one plot in New Utrecht, and 11 acres in another plot.

Johannes Bergen and his brothers and their descendants, used for a burial plot, (until the establishment of Greenwood Cemetery, to which most of the remains have been removed,) a plot on the farm, late of Simon Bergen, between 3d and 4th avenues, and between 39th and 40th streets, Brooklyn, which plot was probably used for the same purpose by the DeHart family, the owners of the farm previous to Simon Bergen.

* Vol XXXII. p. 130, land papers. Sec'y of State's off, Albany.

Hans Bergen's will is dated Jan. 12th, 1786, and proved April 21, 1789. He devises one half the farm, he then occupied adjoining the part devised to his son Derick, to his son Michael; the N. E'ly one half part of said farm to his son Derick; to his son Tunis 100 acres of his farm adjoining land of James Bennet; to his son Peter the farm he lately bought of John Van Pelt, containing 69 acres and lying adjoining the N. E'ly portion of his farm devised to Derick, and S. W'ly of the lands of Wynant Van Pelt; all subject to legacies payable to his other children.

Issue: —

Rachel, d. young.
Simon, b. Oct. 13th, 1746.
Michael, b. Jan. 11th, 1751.
Hans, d. young.
Derick.
Tunis, b. Sept. 1759.
Cornelius, b. Dec. 10th, 1761.
Agnes.
Peter, b. Feb. 25th, 1765.
Jacob, b. April 16th, 1767.
Rachel, d. when 12 years old.

The following is a facsimile of the signature of Hans Bergen:

Johannes Bergen

TEUNIS BERGEN, b. Oct. 15th, 1730, at 1 o'clock. A. M., new style, and bap. on the 28th, at Brooklyn; d. May 21, 1807; m. April, 1760, ... or Johanna.*

*Capt. Elbert Elbertse Stoothoff, a Van .... ancestor of the Stoothoff family in this country, ... from New Netherland to the province of North Brabant in the Netherlands in 1637, and finally settled in New Amersfoort, now Flatlands, in the fall of 1656 or 7. He was one of the nine men appointed by the council of the com-

dau. of Garret Stoothoff, of Flatlands, b. Feb. 21st, 1743, old style, and d. July 23d, 1819.

Feb. 19th, 1763, he bought of Wilhelmus Bennet, for £1,025, a farm of 70 acres at Gowanus, located in 32d and 33d streets in the 8th Ward of Brooklyn, on which

munity in 1649 and 1650, who represented Manhattens, Breuckelen, Amersfoort and Pavonia whose duties were to promote the honor of God, the welfare of the country, the preservation of the reformed religion, and to give their opinion on matters submitted to them by the Director and Council. In 1648, they remonstrated to the States General of the Netherlands against the acts of the Director Generals and the West India Company. Van Tienhoven in his reply, on behalf of the Company, to the remonstrance, in describing the nine men, (to whom he did not intend to be very complimentary,) says: "that Elbert Elbertse went to the country as a farmer's boy, at about ten or eleven years of age, in the service of Wouter Van Twiller." In 1653, he represented Amersfoort in the convention held at New Amsterdam to represent the state of the country to the authorities in Holland. In 1654, '56, '57, '60, '61, '62, '63, '64 and 1673, he was one of the magistrates of Amersfoort. Feb. 27th, 1664, he was one of the representatives from Amersfoort in the convention held at Midwout, for the purpose of sending delegates to Holland to lay before the States General and West India Company, the distressed state of the country; and April 10th, 1664, he was one of the delegates from the same town to the General Assembly, held at the City Hall in New Amsterdam. On the 16th of June, 1661, he obtained a patent for 18 morgens in Flatlands. After this he purchased of Garret Wolpherson Van Couwenhoven a tract of 123 morgen on the S'ly end of the Westermost of the three flats, known by the Indian name of "Kaskutew." On the 25th day of November, 1665, he purchased of Thomas Spicer "Meutelaer," (as per patent.) Island, now known as Bergen Island, in Flatlands. This island was patented, May 14th, 1646, by Geo. Kieft to Capt. John Underhill, a mercenary soldier from New England, employ'd by Kieft to fight the Indians. Underhill sold his patent to Spicer, who, July 20th, 1652, extinguished the Indian title, the deed of which sets for h that the Island is called by the Dutch "Metlers" Island, and by the Indians "Wimbaccoe," and is signed by Specke Jon alias Aremaeus, Oranke, Qahsse, and Ohachama, in the presence of Ambrose Londdon, interpreter, and John Lake, (both of Gravesend,) as witnesses. He also purchased, April 27th, 1662, of the executors of Wolfert Gerretsen van Couwenhoven and his heirs, for 5,000 guilders in good strong "wompom," payable in four years, one fourth each year, the lands and farms with the improvements and cattle thereon, "known by the name of Achtervalt," which the said Wolfert possessed; said lands being the premises which Andries Hudden and said Wolfert purchased of the Indians, and which are described as the "westermost of the three flats named Kaskutenw, lying on the Island named by the Indians Suanhacky, between the bay of the North river and the East river, in breadth from a certain meadow or valey and strecling a' out westerly to and into the woods;' which lands were patented to them by Gov. Wouter van Twiller on the 16th day of June, 1636, and by a confirmatory patent of the 24th of August, 1658, granted by Gov. Stuyvesant to said Wolfert. Elbert Elbertsen received Nov. 1st, 1667, from Gov. Nicolls, a confirmatory patent for the above premises, and as per recorded deeds was in possession at the time of his death of at least 600 acres of uplands in Flatlands. There is no patent of an earlier date for land on Long Island than that to Hudden

he resided and died. April 13th, 1781, he bought of John Vanderbilt, for upwards of $600, a mortgage on the adjoining premises of Willielmus Bennet, containing 71 acres and 16 perches. Under a foreclosure of this mortgage, Sept. 14th, 1784, he purchased the premises through Michael Bergen, his nephew, and held the same during the remainder of his life. Bennet after the Revolutionary war, contested the legality of the foreclosure, on the ground of irregularity, &c., and obtained a verdict in his favor, declaring the sale invalid, but on an appeal to the court of final resort, the same was reversed, and the purchase and proceedings under the foreclosure were sustained; on which, under the then existing laws, Bennet the plain-

and van Couwenhoven, and from papers in the possession of the descendants of Elbert, it is evident that farm buildings were erected on this patent prior to 1639. He m. Aug. 27th, 1615, Aaltie Cornel's, wid. of Gerret Wolfertse van Couwenhoven, and m. 2d Aug. 8th, 1683, Sara Roeloffse, wid. of Cornelis van Boss in, of New York. Children by first wife: *Garret*; Helen or Heiltie, who m. Thomas Willet, Sen., of Flushing; and Aechye or Aegje, who m. John Teunisse Vandyckhuys; no children by his 2d wife.

Garret Elbertse, s. of Elbert Elbertsen and Aaltie, m. Aug. 10th, 1684, Johanna Nevius, of Brooklyn ferry, who d. about 1734. He resided in Flatlands and d. March 30, 1730. Issue: *Elbert*; Johanna who d. about 1735; Altie; Johannis, m. March 28th, 1711, Neeltje Schenck, and d. without issue, prior to his father; Sara, m. Lawrence Williamson; Petrus; Arinthe or Adriana, b. Aug. 6th, 1686; Helena, m. April 26th, 1714, Rulof Lucasse Voorhees; Cornelius, bap. 1698, d. March, 1781, having emigrated to N. J.; Garret, m. Catharine; and Wilhelmus, b. May 30th, 1705, d. Feb. 14th, 1783, m. Sara.

Elbert, s. of Garret Elbertse and Johanna, m. March 28th, 1714, Johanna Lupardius, b. in Dortrecht, Holland, (sister of the Rev. Wilhelmus Lupardius,) resided in 1726, in Somerset Co., N. J., and also in Flatlands, d. Sep. 19th, 1756. Issue: *Garret*; and Wilhelmus who d. about 1782, and m. Nov. 9th, 1728, Altje Coerten Voorhees.

Garret, s. of Elbert and Johanna, b. Aug. 13th, 1715, O. S., m. 1739, Lammetie Stryker, resided in Flatlands and Aug. 1st, 1746, O. S., was accidentally drowned in Flatlands bay in the presence of Michael Stryker, his brother-in-law. His widow afterwards m. John Ammerman, of Flatlands, who removed to Staten Island and owned and occupied a farm on the Kills west of New Brighton. Garret had issue: Eitie or Margrietie, b. Jan. 28th, 1740, m. Nov. 24, 1765, William Nabason or Nelson, d. without issue, prior to 1789; Aeootie or Johanna, b. Feb. 21, 1743, m. April, 1760, Teunis Bergen, of Gowanus, d. July 23d, 1819; and Saartie or Sarah, b. Sept. 6th, 1745, O. S., m. John Stephens of Byberry, in the county of Philadelphia, Pennsylvania. After the death of her husband she resided in Bucks county in the same state, where she d. and left numerous descendants.

tiff, in consequence of failing to pay the costs, was for a time imprisoned, but finally out of compassion, was released by Bergen, the defendant.

In 1834, the descendants of Wilhelmus Bennet, who were generally ignorant and uneducated, having the possession of the old title deeds and a tradition that they had a good claim upon the property and that their ancestors had been defrauded out of the same, under the advice of a hungry lawyer named Thompson, took forcible possession of a portion of the premises, erecting at night a shanty thereon, from which however they were soon ejected under an action for forcible entry and detainer, and mulched for costs and damages, which one of them, luckily, happened to be in possession of sufficient property to pay.

About 1764, a suit was commenced by Teunis Bergen and Anatie his wife, John Stevens and Saartie his wife, and William Nallison and Eitie his wife, against John Stiles, (a fictitious name,) and Wilhelmus Stoothoff for the recovery of the Island located in the meadows and on the shores of the bay in Flatlands, patented by Gov. Kieft to Capt. John Underhill, known as "Wynpaggne," Mentelaers, or Omety's Island,* (now Bergen's Island,) containing about 90 acres of upland, on the ground that their wives, the daughters and heirs of Garret Stoothoff, were entitled to the same by the will of Elbert' Elbertse Stoothoff, their ancestor, dated Dec. 18th, 1686, in which he bequeathed said Island to his eldest son Garret,' and after his death to his child or children in succession and on failure of

---

* The spelling of the Indian name varies on different documents; on some it is "Wynpaggne," on others "Wimbacoe," "Meutelaer, or Metlers." Meutelaer or Metler may be the name of an individual. There was a Philip, a Hendrick and an Abraham Metselaer, residing in New Netherlands in the latter part of the 17th century, from whom this name may have been derived, although no evidence has been found of any of them having resided or exercised ownership on it. Metselaer means mason or bricklayer, which occupation one of the Stoothoff's may have followed, and of which Metler may be a corruption, and hence the name, "Omety's" Island means Uncle's Island.

...the session to Garret's' two sisters, Heyltie and Aegje, and in case of their death upon their child or children, and in case of failure of them, then upon his nearest relations in blood, stating that it was his express will and desire, that the same should not go out of his family or generation, but should remain forever hereditary therein. After the decease of Elbert[1] Elbertse, Garret[1] went into possession, and by his (Garret's) will devised the Island, (supposing he had a legal right,) to Wilhelmus[1] one of his younger sons. However Elbert,[2] Garret's[1] eldest son entered on the Island on his father's death, and put his eldest son Garret[2] in possession, who died, (being accidentally drowned in the bay,) during his father's lifetime, leaving issue three dau., viz: Eitie or Margrietie, Anatie, and Saartie, plaintiff's together with their husbands in this suit. After the death of Garret,[2] Elbert[2] his father put his second son Wilhelmus[2] in possession, and on Elbert's[2] death, Wilhelmus[2] the second son delivered up possession to his uncle Wilhelmus,[1] a defendant in this suit who died in 1783, during its progress. On the death of the uncle, Wilhelmus,[1] his son Peter went into possession.

This suit was finally decided on the 3d of Sept, 1791, (about twenty-seven years after its commencement,) in favor of the plaintiffs, thus declaring the entailment by Elbert Elbertse to be lawful, but before its termination, Eitie or Margretie, died without issue, leaving her two sisters her heirs at law. After the termination of the suit, on the 10th of May, 1792, Teunis Bergen for £800, bought of John Stevens and Saartie his wife, their undivided half of the Island, placing his son John in possession.

June 2d, 1772, "Tunis Bergen" was commissioned a second Lieut. of Capt. John Carpenter's company of foot in the regiment of militia of Kings county, by Gov. Wm. Tryon. Nov. 1776, his name appears among those who took British protection and the oath of allegiance. After the revolution he claimed £78, for the loss of eight cattle, one horse, forty bush. wheat and forty bush. rye, destroyed by the American army, prior to the battle of Long Island. These claims were founded on an order issued, it is said by Gen. Washington to the farmers on the west end of the Island on the arrival of the British fleet and army in the lower bay, to stack their grain outside their barns, so that in case of necessity it might be burnt without endangering the buildings, (which burning took place); and their cattle to effect the same object were driven to the eastern part of the Island, and never recovered.

In 1784, he was supervisor of Brooklyn. His will is dated Sept. 23d, 1806, proved Oct. 28th, 1807, in which he devised his Brooklyn lands, (except some woodland to his son Tunis,) to his son Garret, and the Island in Flatlands to his son John, all subject to the use of his widow during life, and subject to legacies to his other children.

Issue :—

Rachel, b. Aug. 15th, 1761.

Lammetje, b. Oct. 13th, 1762.

Johannes or *Hans*, b. Sept. 23d, 1764.

Johanna or *Antje*, b. Oct., 1766, d. March 4th, 1771.

Femmetje, b. Aug. 4th, 1769.

Gerrit, b. Jan. 11th, 1772.

Tunis T., b. May 16th, 1774.

Johanna or *Annatie*, b. Oct. 2d, 1776.

Sarah, b. March 10th, 1782.

The following is a fac simile of the signature of Tunis Bergen:

Tunis Bergen

Fifth Generation.

Children of MICHAEL BERGEN, and *Catalyntie Bergen*, of Brooklyn, N. Y. :

SARAH BERGEN, b. Dec. 18th, 1743, d. ——, m. Aug. 30th, 1759, Capt. *John Grant*, of his Majesty's 42d Highland Reg., who was b. in 1729. According to tradition she was celebrated for her beauty which captivated the Captain. After their marriage they resided on the farm with the grist mill attached, which her father purchased of the executors of Cornell, on the south side of the village of Jamaica, in Queens Co. Being a loyalist, immediately after the revolution, Capt. Grant with his family, (excepting Micheal Bergen Grant, his eldest son,) emigrated to Kempt, about nine miles below Windsor, on the Avon river, near the bay of Fundy, in Nova Scotia, where for his services or losses in the war, he had a grant from the British government for 3,000 acres of good land in the wilderness. In Nova Scotia, on the western shores of the Bay of Fundy, reside the descendants of Long Island and New Jersey families, whose ancestors were tories in the revolution, and fled when this country achieved her independence. Those to whom the British government assigned lands in this locality were fortunate, the soil being generally good and productive. Others had lands assigned them on the Atlantic coast, some in the neighborhood of Sherbourne, an iron bound shore, on which the lands are rocky and sterile, where after the means they brought with them were exhausted, starvation stared them in the face, from which many of them fled, and some returned in poverty seeking the protection of the government they had opposed.

Micheal Bergen Grant, the oldest son, who inherited from

14

his grandfather the Brooklyn homestead farm, after a few years sold the same to George Powers, and then also emigrated to Kempt. Most of the descendants of Capt. John Grant continue to reside in Nova Scotia and occupy a respectable position in society.

Issue:—

*Michael Bergen Grant,** b. 1760; d. Nov., 1807; m. Sophia Nutting, of the state of Maine, who was alive in 1857.

John Grant, b. Dec. 21st, 1762 ; probably d. young.

Rachel Grant, b. 1766: lived to an old age, d. single.

Catharine Grant, bap. Dec. 4th, 1767 ; d. young in Nova Scotia.

Letitia Grant, b. 1771; m. William Parker and left issue.

Sarah Grant, b. April 28th, 1774: d. young in Nova Scotia.

Stephen Grant, b. Jan. 21st. 1776: d. young in Nova Scotia.

Nancy Grant, bap. Aug. 4th, 1777; d. young on Long Island.

Ann Grant, b. Aug. 20th, 1778; m. John Smith.†

Sarah Terhune Grant, b. Jan. 15th, 1787: m. John Parker, and left issue.

Stephen Grant, b. Feb. 24th, 1789, d. poor in the city of N. Y., m. and left issue.

Catharine Grant, b. Nov. 12th, 1791; m. her cousin, Albert Terhune, s. of Stephen.

TESCHE or LETITIA BERGEN, b. ———, d. ———; m. July 7th, 1759, *Stephen Terhune* of Hackingsack, N. J., a s. of Albert Albertse Terhune and Hendrickje Stephense Van Voorhees, at first of Flatlands, and afterwards of Hackingsack, and a grandson of Albert Albertse Terhune, ribbon weaver, the first emigrant of the name, who resided on the Nyack tract in New Utrecht in 1657 at

* Issue of *Michael Bergen Grant* and Sophia Nutting: *John Nutting* who had children by his first wife. Sophia Elizabeth m. Monson H. Goudge, Mary Matilda m. John Bennet, Micheal Bergen, Sarah Caroline and John Nutting; by his second wife, Henry Hugh, Mary Ann, Frederick Malcom, Peter McCullum and Susan: *Caroline Bergen,* who m. John Burgess: *Mary Ann* who m. George Allison a farmer: *Sophia Mary,* who m. Joseph Allison, sheriff in 1857, of the county: *Letitia Lefferts,* single: *Jannette McNeal,* who m. William Allison, a farmer, and *Susan Nutting,* who m. Theodore S. Harding a merchant.

† Issue of John Smith and Ann Grant: John; William; Bennet; and Sophia. Bennet Smith resided in 1857, at Windsor, Nova Scotia, was a ship builder and a large ship owner.

the time of the settlement of said town, and in 1666 and 1667, purchased land of the Van Couwenhovens and Stoothoff's and removed to Flatlands.

Issue:—

*Michiel B. T———, b. Feb. 20, 1769; d. Dec. 1st, 1849; m. Maria or Mary Terhune, a wid. Resided on and owned for many years a farm and grist mill, which he purchased at Bergen, formerly Constable Point, at the mouth of the kills between Staten Island and N. J., on the bay of N. Y., which farm he finally sold, and removed to the city of New York, where he d. His children were Stephen, b. March 21st, 1793, now (1863) of Greenville, near Jersey City, who m. 1st Eliza Vreeland, and m. 2d Mary Van Horn; Ursula, b. June 1st, 1791, m. Barent Van Horn; Margaret, b. June 17th, 1795, m. Andrew Brombush; and Ralph, b. May 19th, 1799, of Hackingsack, who m. Ann Brinckerhoff.

Catharine Terhune, m. John N. Romaine, of the city of N. Y., and had children, Cornelius, Elizabeth, who m. Walter Leggett, and Michiel, who d. single.

Elizabeth Terhune, m. John Berry, of N. J., and had children, William, Stephen, John, and several daughters.

John Terhune, of Saddle river, Bergen Co., N. J.; m. Elizabeth ———, and had several children among whom were Stephen and Henry.

Stephen Terhune, of Hackingsack, N. J.; m. and had children, Guilliame and others.

Jacob Terhune, of Polifly, N. J.; m. ——— Chappel, and had children, Stephen and John.

Albert Terhune, m. his cousin Catharine, dau. of Michiel Bergen Grant. Removed with his father-in-law to near Windsor, on the Avon river, Nova Scotia, where he has left surviving a number of children, one of whom in 1857 was Judge of the County.

Sarah Terhune, m. Peter Terhune of Polifly, N. J., and had a s. Stephen.

Letitia Terhune, m. James Houseman of Polifly, N. J., and had children, Letitia, Catharine, Elizabeth, Maria, James, Stephen and Abraham.

Children of HANS, JOHANNES or JOHN BERGEN and *Catryntie:*

SIMON BERGEN, b. Oct. 13th, 1746; d. Feb. 22d, 1777;

m. *Geshe*. dau. of Simon De Hart,[*] of Gowanus, b. Feb.
4th, 1744, and d. March 18th. 1781.

Resided on the farm containing 300 acres. at Gowanus,
in the vicinity of 37th and 42d streets, Brooklyn, which
his wife inherited from her brother Simon de Hart.   By a
conveyance from Simon and Gashe to his uncle Tunis
Bergen, and a conveyance of Tunis to Simon, the title of
this farm was vested in Simon.   In March, 1776, he held
the office of 1st Lieut. in the militia company of Brooklyn.
Gaine's Register of March 3d. 1777, says: "a few days
ago Simon Bergen was accidentally shot in the leg by a
musket he was buying of a sailor, and died from loss of
blood." The accident is said to have happened close to
and in front of the old stone house near 38th street and
the bay, in which he resided.   This house is among, if
not one of the oldest, in the city of Brooklyn, it being
laid down on a map of 930 acres purchased by William
Arianse Bennet and Jacques Bentin, Englishmen, of the
Indians in 1636, made Jan. 9th, 1695-6, by Augustus
Graham, surveyor general.   This purchase covered nearly
all the land S. of 27th street in the city of Brooklyn, and

---

[*]*Simon Aertsen Ter Haert* or *De Hart*, emigrated to this country in 1664,
and owned and occupied prior to 1679. the farm at Gowanus, since of Si-
mon and John S. Bergen, his descendants. He m. 1st Geertie Cornelissen,
and 2d. June 19th, 1691, Annetie Andrieas Willjard, wid. of William
Huycken, tailor of Gowanus. Had children by 1st wife. *Simon*; Elyas,
bap. March 21st. 1677; and Annetie, bap. July 6th, 1687.
  His son *Simon* inherited his plantation and m. Angenietje, dau. of Jan
Jansz Van Dyck, and had children. Simon; Augenietje or Annanetie, b.
Jan. 4th, 1722, m. Jan. 8th, 1743, Peter Cortelyou, of New Utrecht;
Tryntje, bap. Aug. 14th. 1726, m. Peter Conover, of Middletown, N. J.,
the father of Jacob Conover, who m. Rachel, dau. of Tunis Bergen, of Gowanus; Mayke, bap. May 18th, 1729, d. young; Teuntje, m. Jacobus
Lott, the ancestor of Charles Lott, of New Utrecht; Geertie, m. 1st Corne-
lius Santford, and m. 2d Jores Remsen; Jannetie; and *Geshe*, b. Feb. 4th,
1744, m Simon Bergen. Simon, s. of Simon and Gertie, d. in 1743, and by
his will dated July 13th, 1744, devised his plantation to his son Simon.
Simon, s. of Simon and Angenietje, m. Mary ——, and d. in 1769, without issue, devising by his will dated Sept. 26th, 1769, his plantation at
Gowanus to his sister *Gashe*, the wife of Simon Bergen.
  Elias De Hart, s. of Simon Aertsen, resided in Gowanus, in the begin-
ing of the 18th century, his wife was named Katie, and he had a son Elyas
bap. Sept. 18th, 1709.

the house being erected prior to 1696, is older than the
Cortelyou, formerly Vechte mansion, near 4th street and
5th avenue, the latter having been built in 1699.

Issue:

S____, b. April 15th, 1768.
John S., b. May 1st, 1777.

MICHAEL BERGEN, b. Jan. 11th, 1751; d. March 3d,
1825, m. 1st, *Antie Van Wyck*, dau. of Theodorus Van
Wyck and Sarah Martense, b. July 6th, 1752, d. Nov.
24th, 1784; m. 2d, 1784, *Rebecca* dau. of Leffert Lefferts,*
of Flatbush, b. June 17th, 1754, d. Oct 20th, 1828.

He inherited and resided on the S'ly one half of the
farm at Gowanus, which his father bought of Van Wyck,
to which he added by purchase the adjoining one half
(less 6 acres,) of his brother Derick's portion.

Issue by first marriage:

Johannes, b. June 10th, 1776, d. July 4th, 1783.
Theodorus, b. March 17th, 1775.
Sarah, b. Sept. 13th, 1781, d. Dec. 30th, 1829, single.

* *Leffert Lefferts*, was a descendant of Leffert Pieterse van Hoogewort,
(or from Hauwert, a village in the province of North Holland,) the common ancestor of the Lefferts family of Kings county, who emigrated in
1650, settled in Flatbush, and m. Abigail dau. of Auke Jouse Van Nuyse,
bap. Dec. 8th, 1704, and his wife d. July 1901, 1748, at a very old age.
His children were: Aucke, b. June 2d, 1676, d. July 15th, 1735; Auke,
b. April 4th, 1678, m. 1st, May 29th, 1703, Marytie ten Eyck, m. 2d, July
30th, 1735, Catharine Vonk; Peter, b. May 1st, 1680, d. Mar. 13th,
1774, m. Eytie Suydam; Rachel, b. Jan. 17th, 1682; Jan, b. Jan. 1416,
1684, m. Margrit' ——; Jacob, of Bedford, June 9th, 1686, d. 1768,
m. Oct. 7th, 1716, Jannetie Blom; Isaac, b. May 15th, 1688, d. Oct. 1st,
1746, m. Harmpie ——; Abraham, b. Sept. 1, 1692 m. Sarah ——;
Madalina, b. Aug 20th, 1694, m. Garret Martense, of Flatbush; Annor
Antien, b. March 1st, 1696; Abigail, b. Aug. 24th, 1698, d. Nov. 17th,
1704; Leffert, b. May 22d, 1701, d. Sept. 27th, 1754, m. Nov. 15th, 1724,
Catryntje Dorlant; and Benjamin, b. May 24, 1704, d. Nov. 17th, 1707.
    Isaac, s. of Leffert Pieterse and Abiza, resided in Flatbush, and had
children: Leffert, b. Feb. 20th, 1723, d. Sept 21st, 1800, m. ——, April
18th, 1747, Eltie or Elsie Lourum; Hendrick, b. July 3rd, 1725, d. Aug 26th,
1812; Isaac, bap. Aug. 16th, 1730, m. Sept April 19th, 1754, Agnetie
Lott; and Harmje, who m. Oct. 1766, Hendrik Suydam.
    Leffert, s. of Isaac and Harmpie, resided in Flatbush, and had children:
Rebecca, b. June 17th, 1754, d. Oct. 20th, 1828, m. 1784 Michael Bergen
and Elsie, b. March 11th, 1761, d. July 23d, 1841, m. Samuel Gerritsen.

Issue by second marriage :

Johannes, bap. Jan. 18th, 1~84, d. May 31st, 1784.

Leffert, b. July 10th, 1789.

Catharine, b. Oct. 29th, 1791.

DERICK BERGEN, b. ——: d. about 1791 ; m. 1st, May, 1778, *Maria*, dau. of Garret Boerum ; m. 2d —— *Kingsland.*

Inherited from his father the N'ly side of his farm at Gowanus, where he resided for some years, and then sold to his brothers Michael and Peter, and removed to Newark, N. J., where he died.

Issue :—

Catharine.

Maria.

Rebecca.

John.

Michael.

Garret.

TUNIS J. BERGEN, b. Sept., 1759: d. Nov. 26th, 1826 ; m. *Annie* dau. of Cornelius Vanderveer,* of Flatbush, b. in 1768, and d. July 16th, 1846.

He inherited and resided on the land in Gowanus, near

---

* *Cornelius Vanderveer*, was a descendant of Cornelis Janse Vander Veer, or from the ferry, farmer, the common ancestor of the Vanderveer's in this vicinity, who emigrated to this country from Alekmaer or Alekmaar, a province in North Holland, in the Netherlands, in the ship Otter, in Feb., 1659, and settled in Flatbush, where, on the 24th of Feb., 1677-8, he purchased of Jan Jansz, a farm. He m. Tryntje Gillis, and had children: *Cornelis* who m. Jannetje ——: Neeltje Cornelissen, m. Aug. 13th, 1685, Daniel Pollemius ; Maria Cornelissen, bap. July 30th, 1682; Hendrikje Cornelissen, bap. Aug. 17th, 1684 (sup.) m. Johannes Wyck; Jan Cornelissen, m. Jan. 6th, 1695, Femmetje, dau. of Micheal Hansen Bergen ; Dominicius, bap. Nov. 16th, 1679, m. Jannetje, and also (sup.) m. Feb. 7th, 1702-3, Maria Margreta Noortlyck or Van Orteck ; and Michiel who m. Beletje.

Cornelis, s. of Cornelis Jans~ and Tryntje, m. Jannetje, and had children: *Cornelius*, Jun., b. Dec. 5th, 1731, d. Feb. 13th, 1804, m. Nov. 1761, Leah, dau. of John Ver Kerk, b. Jan. 27th, 1741, d. May 23d, 1813 ; and Petrus, bap. Jan. 5th, 1735.

Cornelius, Jun, s. of Cornelis and Jannetje resided in Flatbush, and had children: John C., b. 1762, d. April 7th, 1845, m. Elizabeth, dau. of Adrian Van Brunt ; Garret, b. Aug. 12th, 1765, d. Dec. 12th, 1847, m. Catharine Lott ; *Annie* b. 1768, d. June 16th, 1846, m. Tunis J. Bergen ; and Jane, b. Nov. 15th, 1775, d. Sept. 26th, 1831, m. Simon Bergen.

the New Utrecht boundary, which his father bought of Van Dyck, and was commonly known as Major Bergen. He bought May 1st, 1807, for $5,050, of the heirs of Casper Cropsey, the common ancestor of the Cropsey's of Kings county, a farm of 109 acres on the bay at Yellow Hook, now Bay Ridge, New Utrecht, of which he conveyed to Jacobus Cropsey, one of the heirs, one half, which half is now owned by William C. Langley.

Issue : —

John T., b. 1786.

Cornelius, b. Feb. 22d, 1790.

CORNELIUS BERGEN, b. Dec. 10th, 1761; d. Oct. 9th, 1824; m. *Gertrude*, daughter of Hendrick Suydam,* of Flatbush, b. Jan. 28th, 1761, and d. Nov. 22d, 1840.

He resided on a farm in the village of Flatbush, which his wife inherited from her father, and was elected one of the Presidential Electors in 1804, and appointed Sheriff of the county from 1793 to 1798, and from 1800 to 1805.

Issue :—

John C., b. March 7th, 1786.

Maria, b. Dec. 29th, 1787.

*Hendrick Suydam, was a descendant of Heyndrycke Rycke, the common ancestor of the Suydam family of this vicinity, who emigrated in 1663, from "Suyt-dam" or "Zuyt-dam," (as appears in an indenture of Jonathan Mills as an apprentice to learn the blacksmith trade with Jacob a son of said Hendrick,) in Holland, meaning south of the dam, from which the family derive the name of Suydam, having dropped the sirname of Rycken. He m. Ida Jacobs, and finally settled in Flatbush, dying in 1701. His children were: *Jacob* ; Hendrick ; Ryck ; Ida ; Gertrude ; and Jane.

Jacob, s. of Hendrick Rycken and Ida, b. 1666, d. 1738, m. Seytie Jacobs, resided in Flatbush, and had children : Jacob ; *Hendrick* of Flatbush ; Johannes of Flushing ; Jan ; Ryck, of N. J. ; Cornelius, of Oysterbay ; Dow of Newtown ; Ida ; Adriana ; Gertrud ; Isabella ; Jannetje ; and Seytie.

Hendrick, s. of Jacob and Seytie, bap. March 29th, 1696, d. 1744, m. 1719, Geertie dau. of Evert Van Wickelen, of New Lots, had children : Evert, of New Utrecht ; Jacob of Flatlands ; *Hendrick*, of Flatbush ; John ; Seytie ; Metje ; Pieternella ; and Geertje.

Hendrick, s. of Hendrick and Geertie, bap. Feb. 13th, 1732, d. May 16th, 1791, a farmer in Flatbush, m. Maria Ammerman and had children : Jane, who m. Abraham Ditmars ; and *Geertie* who m. Cornelius Bergen.

AGNES BERGEN, b. ——, d. Feb. 10th, 1803; m. April 1770, *Daniel Rapalje*, farmer, of New Lots, who was b. in 1748, and d. Oct. 19th, 1795.

Issue :—

John Rapalje, b. Dec. 24th, 1770 ; m. Aug. 21st, 1804, Charity, dau. of Abraham Van Sicklen, of New Lots ; d. April 19th, 1810, and had children : Cornelia and Daniel.

Daniel D. Rapalje, b. Aug. 26th, 1772 ; m. Feb. 7th, 1799, Rensie, dau. of Joost Wyckoff ; d. Dec. 25, 1852, and had children : Agnes, Daniel Luyster, Sarah, Agnes, Johanna, Catharine, John and George Wyckoff. Resided at Newtown, where he owned a farm and grist mill.

Simon Rapalje b. Jan. 29th, 1775 ; m. 1st, Jan. 10th, 1802, Hieltie, dau. of Nicholas Williamson, by whom children : Williamson, Daniel and a dau.; m. 2d Lemma Bergen, dau. of John, and wid. of John Williamson, by whom no issue. Owned and occupied a farm at New Lots, and d. Jan. 10th, 1849.

PETER BERGEN, b. Feb. 25, 1765 ; d. Feb. 29th, 1844, m. March 3d, 1796, *Mary* or *Polly*, dau. of the Rev. Martinus Schoonmaker,* of Flatbush, and Pastor of the Reformed Dutch Churches in Kings county ; she was b. July 7th, 1777, and d. Jan. 29th, 1854.

Owned, resided on and cultivated the land in Gowanus,

---

* *Martinus Schoonmaker*, was a descendant of Joachim Schoonmaker and Lydia, who resided in the town of Rochester, in Ulster county, N. Y. Joachim and Lydia had children : Daniel, John, Jacobus, *Martinus*, and Helena.

Martinus, b. March 1, 1737, m. Jan. 27th, 1761, Mary Fassett, and d. May 20th, 1824, in Flatbush : Mary was b. Feb. 23d, 1739, and d. April 27th, 1819. He studied Theology, was licensed to preach, settled first over the churches of Haerlem and Gravesend, and afterwards over the Collegiate Reformed Dutch Churches of Kings county, and was the last of the pastors of said churches who habitually preached in the language of Holland, the father land. Martinus and Mary had children : Sarah, b. April 18th, 1762, m. John Emmaus, of Gravesend : Stephen, b. Jan. 25th, 1765, d. March 28th, 1842, m. Charity Vanderveer : Martinus, b. Aug. 3d, 1767; m. Catharine Bennam : John, b. Feb. 2d, 1770, m. Catharine Van Beuren, d. Feb. 27, 1824 : Michael, b. June 21st, 1772, d. Nov. 14th, 1845 ; m. 1st, Susan Ludlam, and m. 2d, ———— : Jacobus, b. Sep. 3d, 1774, m. Gitty Vandervoort : *Mary* or *Polly*, b. July 7th, 1777, m. Peter Bergen : Anne, b. Sep. 11th, 1779, d. May 28th, 1780 : Nicholas, b. April 9th, 1781, d. Aug. 31st 1817, m. Margaret Masterton, was a physician: Anna, b. Feb. 27th, 1784, d. Sept. 28th, 1785 ; and Ellenor, b. March 11th, 1787, d. Feb. 12th, 1849, m. Stephen Freeland, of N. J.

his father bought of John Van Pelt, and also the northerly
one half, (six acres in addition,) of the land devised by his
father Johannes, to his brother Derick, Derick having disposed of his lands to his brothers Michael and Peter. His
farm lay about between 49th and 52d streets, extending
from the bay to near the Patent line adjoining New
Utrecht.

Issue :

Catharine, b. June 3d, 1797; d. Aug. 12th, 1808.

Peter, b. July 25th, 1801.

Martinus, b. Feb. 21st, 1811.

JACOB BERGEN, b. April 16th, 1767; d. July 5th,
1845; m. *Catharine*, dau. of Isaac Eldert and Maria
Wyckoff, of New Lots, b. Feb. 22d, 1781, and d. Jan.
21st, 1836.*

Resided on and owned a farm of about 131 acres of up-
land and salt meadows on Court, Hoyt, Smith, Carrol,
President, Union and other streets in the city of Brooklyn.
The main portion (110 acres,) of this farm he purchased
Dec. 21st, 1799, of Robert Stoddard,† for $8,750, and the

* *Catharine Eldert*, is a descendant of Hendrick Eldertse, of Jamaica, a
s. of Eldert Lucase, grandson of Lucas Stevense and great grandson of
Steven Coerte, referred to in the foot note under Hans or Johannes Bergen
and Antie Lucassen, of Jamaica.

Hendrick Eldertse, bap. Mch. 4th, 1691, m. 1st, Grietje, m. 2d Tryntje, will
dated Feb. 6th, 1759, proved Dec. 12th, 1768, resided in Jamaica, and had
children; Grietje, bap. May 11th, 1722, m. John Stephens; *Johannes*, of
New Lots, m. Femmetje, will proved June 8th, 1781; Eldert, d. single;
Styntje, m. John Monny; Margaret, m. Godfrey Heyn; Ann, m. Hendrick
Emans; and Mary, m. Rem. Van Cleef.

Johannes Eldert, s. of Hendrick Eldertse, had children; Hendrick, b.
July, 16th, 1749, d. Sept. 27th, 1793, m. Cornelia, resided in Flatbush;
Isaac, b. March 31st, 1752, d. Oct. 31st, 1795, m. April 29th, 1775, Maria
Wyckoff, b. April 4th, 1758, d. July 31st, 1836 in her 94th year; and Mar-
garet m. John Vanderveer, Jun.

Isaac Eldert, of New Lots, s. of Johannes, had children; Johanes, b.
Sept. 4th, 1778, d. Dec. 8th, 1857, m. May 11th, 1805, Sarah Vanderveer,
no issue; Phebe, b. Sept. 30th, 1776, d. Sep. 30th, 1811, m. Dec. 2d, 1795,
Stephen Lott; *Catharine*, b. Feb. 22d, 1781, d. Jan. 21st, 1836, m. Jacob
Bergen; and Cornelius, b. Aug. 30th, 1783, m. 1st, Margaret, dau. of
Daniel Ryder, m. 2d, Jane Wiggins.

† The land purchased of Stoddard was a portion of the premises patented by Gov. Kieft to Frederick Lubbertse, May 22d, 1641. Lubbertse by
his will dated Nov. 22d, 1679, bequeathed to his dau. Else, wife of Jacob

15

balance from Mr. Reed. He held the office of associate Judge of the county courts in 1811.

Issue:—

Maria. b. May 23d, 1801.

Catharine. b. Feb. 16th, 1803.

Phebe. b. Feb. 20th, 1805.

Agnes. b. Oct. 25th, 1806.

Michael, b. July 28th, 1809.

Isaac E., b. July 7th, 1811.

Sarah E., b. April 3d, 1813, d. May 4th, 1813.

John Tunis, b. April 16th, 1815.

Eldert, b. May 27th, 1818.

Sarah. b. Aug. 22d, 1820.

Margaret. b. Aug. 25th, 1822.

Children of DERICK BERGEN and *Deborah Cortelyou,* of Brooklyn. N. Y. :—

RACHEL BERGEN. b. about 1753 : d. March 10th, 1824; m. Dec. 29th, 1771. *Walter Berry,* who owned and occupied a farm in Gowanus, in the vicinity of 12th and 14th streets, which he purchased of the heirs of Cornelius Van Duyne, and who was gored to death by a bull, Sept. 21st, 1813, aged 63. After the death of her husband she resided on her share of her father's farm.

Issue :—

Samuel Berry, b. Nov. 5th, 1772; d. May 31st, 1774.

Jemima Berry, b. Aug. 27th, 1774; d. March 9th, 1809; m. about 1793, William Barre, of New Utrecht, and had children : Catharine, Samuel, William W. and Walter.

Richard Berry, b. Feb. 7th, 1777; d. June 27th, 1848; m. Jane Voor-

Hansen (Bergen,) a part of his patent. Jacob Hansen Bergen and Elsje his wife, April 13 1, 1732, (see Lib. 5, p. 160, Kings Co. Reg. off.) convey to their son, Hans Bergen, 200 acres of the above premises. Hans Bergen by his will dated Sept. 11th, 1743, bequeathed one-fifth of his estate to each of his children. Jacob Bergen, his only son, who probably had purchased the interest of his sisters in the farm, and Antie his wife, April 18th, 1750, (see Lib. 5, p. 164, K. C. Reg. off.) for £700, convey to John Rapalje 139 acres of the above named premises. John Rapalje in 1794, by a deed not recorded, conveys the main body of the above premises to Robert Stoddard, having previously conveyed a portion thereof to the father of Jorden Coles

hees, b. June 25th, 1783, d. Feb. 16th, 1846, and had children, Rachel John and Cornelia. Owned and occupied his father's farm at Gowanus.

Deborah Berry, b. Sept. 25th, 1780; living in 1865; m. Adrian Martense, of Flatbush, and has children, Maria, Rachel and Elizabeth.

Mary or Polly Berry, b. April 3d, 1784; d. about 1853; m. James Powers, resided at Waterford, N. Y., and had issue, Jesse, Ann, George and Walter.

Rachel Berry, b. May 27th, 1786, living in 1865, and single.

Elizabeth or Betsey Berry, b. Dec. 21st, 1792; d. Nov. 21st, 1854; m. Oct. 1816, John Rutledge, a lawyer of New York; no issue.

JACAMYNTE or JEMIMA BERGEN, b. May 4th, 1755; d. Sept. 1824; m. Sept. 1769, *Joseph Smith,* who was b. Oct. 17th, 1739, and d. March, 1829. Owned and occupied a part of the farm on 15th street, Gowanus, which her father bought of his brother Hans Bergen.

Issue :—

Derick Bergen Smith, b. Dec. 11th, 1770; d. Sept. 8th, 1777.

Samuel Smith, b. July 13th, 1772; d. an old man and single.

Elizabeth Smith, b. Aug. 11th, 1774; d. about 1854 or 5; m. James Seaman and had children: Maria, Jemima, Eliza, Thomas, and Sarah.

Derick Bergen Smith, b. Aug. 20th, 1778; d. Sep. 10th, 1779.

Johannes or John Smith, b. Sept. 11th, 1780; m. (sec.) Maria, dau. of John Devauene ; living in 1865, and has issue.

Derick Smith, b. Jan. 16th, 1783 ; was mate of a vessel and perished at sea.

James Smith, b. March 17th, 1785; d. an old man in Queens Co.; m. ———, and had a son Joseph, who d. April 1828, at sea, ag. 19.

James Smith, b. March 12th, 1787; probably d. young.

Rachel Smith, b. Dec. 19th, 1789; living in 1865; m. 1st, Capt. Nicholls 2d, ——— Ford, and 3d, Calvin Camfield, of N. J., by whom issue.

Deborah Smith, b. March 26th, 1792; d. May 6th, 1836; m. Nov. 11th, 1813, Thomas Adams, by whom children: Thomas, William, Adaline and Elizabeth; m. 2d, John Wyckoff, of Gowanus, by whom a son, John, who m. Catharine Maria, dau. of Lefferts Bergen, of Gowanus, and d. 1865.

Joseph Smith, b. April 17th, 1795; d. Nov. 24th, 1854; res. near dau. of John Bennet of Yellow Hook, New Utrecht, and wid. of John States; had children: Anna Maria, Elizabeth, Mary Ann and Ella.

TIESIE BERGEN, b. Jan. 19th, 1758; d. April 19th,

1826: m. May 1780, *Ebenezer Carson*, an officer in the war of the Revolution Owned and resided on a part of her father's farm, in Gowanus.

Issue :—

Deborah Carson, b. March 4th, 1780: d. Feb. 7th, 1863; single, and resided solitary and alone after the death of her mother, in a house on part of her grandfather's farm, on 16th street and the old Gowanus road

John Carson, d. about 1829, in Trinidad, in the West Indies; m. Elizabeth Easterly, and was a cooper by trade. Had children: John, Richard and Edward.

Richard Carson, was a Captain in the merchant service, and d. single prior to 1826, in the East Indies.

Benjamin Carson, resided with an uncle in Philadelphia, and accidentally drowned June 6th, 1803, when a school boy, while bathing in the Schuylkill.

Children of TUNIS BERGEN and *Johanna Stoothoff*, of Brooklyn, N. Y.:—

RACHEL BERGEN, b. Aug. 15th, 1761: d. June 16th, 1817; m. May 10th, 1780, *Jacob Conover*, of Middletown, N. J., (a captain of infantry in the Revolutionary war,) while a prisoner on parole on Long Island. Prior to the occupation of New York by the British army, Capt. Conover was sent to Sandy Hook and smashed the lamps of the lighthouse, to prevent the expected British fleet from having the benefit of the same: was afterwards taken prisoner near Middletown Point, brought on board one of the enemies vessels and threatened to be hung on the yard arm as a rebel, the noose even being prepared for his neck, and subsequently confined among the prisoners in the Sugar House in New York. After the war he resided until after 1796, on his farm in N. J., and then on a small farm of some 16 acres which he purchased, in the vicinity of Hamilton avenue and Court street, Brooklyn.

Issue :—

Sarah Conover, b. Oct. 30th, 1780, on Long Island; living in 1865: m. Dec. 5th, 1806, Pearson Dey, of N. J., b. March 8th, 1780: they removed to Seneca Co., N. Y., and have issue: Jacob C., Anthony P., Richard, deceased; Peter P., Elizabeth, William, Catharine, dec'd, and Henry.

Peter Conover, b. April 16th, 1783, in Middletown, N. J.; d. Jan. 4th, 1842; m. Feb. 14th, 1819, Catharine, dau. of Joost and Ann Stillwell, of Gravesend, and wid. of Nicholas Van Dyck, of Red Hook, b. Jan. 9th, 1789, d. Sept. 16th, 1816. Resided at one time with his cousin Garret Bergen, of Gowanus, was an Adjutant in the war of 1812, and afterwards engaged in mercantile business in Brooklyn, and a Supervisor of said city. Had issue: George S., b. May 7th, 1824; Jacob, b. May 15th, 1827, and d. May 8th, 1847; and Ann, b. Nov. 13th, 1829

Johanna Conover, b. June 2d, 1785, in N. J., living in 1863, with Garret G. Bergen, of Gowanus, and single; d. Sept. 28th, 1864.

Catharine Conover, b. April 14th, 1787, in N. J.; d. Sept. 13th, 1833; m. William Jackson of Orange Co. N. Y., and left issue, a s. Richard.

Phebe Conover, b. March 7th, 1789, in N. J.; d. March 7th, 1853; m. Francis Dey, of Seneca Co., N. Y., and had issue: Philip, b. Sept. 16th, 1816; Jacob, d. when about two years old; and Frances Johanna, who m. Charles B. Platt, and d. March 5th, 1853.

Francis Conover, b. Oct. 25th, 1796, and d. when about three months old.

LAMMETIE BERGEN, b. Oct. 13th, 1762; d. Oct. 17th, 1830; m. June 20th, 1782, *Rutgert Van Brunt,** of New

* *Rutger Joost a Van Brunt,* or from Brunt, the common ancestor of the Van Brunt family of this vicinity, emigrated from Holland, in 1653, (probably from a villa known by the name of Brunt,) and in 1657, was among the first settlers in New Utrecht, where he held large tracts of land, and of which town he was one of the representatives in July 1663, in the convention held at New Amsterdam to engage the several Dutch towns to keep up an armed force for public protection. He was also, both under the Dutch and English governments, for several years a Magistrate and Justice of the Peace of the town. He m. 1st, Tryntie Claes, b. about 1618, m. 2d, Gretian, and he d. about 1718. His children were, Nicholas Rutgersz, who m. Helena, dau. of Jacques Cortelyou, the surveyor, Aug. 19th, 1683, and who d. in 1684; *Cornelis Rutgersz,* m. April 16th, 1687, Tryntje Arysen Bennet, d. about 1748; and Joost Rutgersz, m. Aeltie Coerten Van Voorhees, April 16th, 1687, d. about 1746.

Cornelis Rutgersz, had issue, *Rutgert,* m. Elizabeth Van Voorhees, d. April 7th, 1760; Nicholas m. Geesje, and emigrated to N. J., where he has numerous descendants; Willem; Adryan who had a dau. Jannetie; Anggenition, bap. June 30th, 1689; Maria or Marrytie, bap. Dec. 10th, 1694; Tryntien; Gretien or Marragreet; and Neeltie.

Rutgert, s. of Cornelis Rutgersz, had issue Cornelis C., b. March 6th, 1716, m. Hellitje; Sartie, b. May 4th, 1718, m. Aris Vanderbilt; *Albert,* b. Nov. 14th, 1720, d. Oct. 16th, 1784, m. his cousin Jannetie, dau. of Adryan Van Brunt; Wilhelmus, b. July 26th, 1725, d. Jan. 25th, 1790, m. Jannetie Van Voorhees; Catryntie, b. Feb. 14th, 1726, d. young; Rutgert, b. Sept. 13th, 1728, d. young; Joost, b. March 4th, 1731, d. Feb. 8th, 1814, m. 1st, Elizabeth Duryea, m. 2d, Lydia Griggs

Utrecht, who owned and resided on a farm of 70 acres, (now of Isaac F. Berger,) at Yellow Hook, now Bay Ridge.

Issue :—

Jane Van Brunt, b. July 2d, 1783; d. July 13th 1814, single.

Johanna Van Brunt, b. Jan. 14th, 1785; m. Morris Patterson, of N. Y., amd d. some years ago.

Albert Van Brunt, b. March 3d, 1787; d. April 28th, 1817, single.

Tunis Van Brunt, b, July 29th, 1780; emigrated west and d. in Michigan; m. Mary Matthews,

Elizabeth Van Brunt, b. Oct. 1st, 1793; d. Aug. 13th, 1794.

Phebe Van Brunt, b. Aug. 18th, 1795; m. John P. Dey, of Seneca Co., N. Y., living in 1865.

Nicholas Van Brunt, b. Aug. 25th, 1797; m. Dec. 7th, 1820, Ellen, dau. of Elias Hubbard, of Flatlands: residing in Brooklyn in 1865.

John Van Brunt, b. Feb. 17th, 1800; d. Sept. 18th, 1819, single.

Elizabeth Van Brunt, b. July 10th, 1802; d. Oct. 1802.

Garret Van Brunt, a twin with Elizabeth, b. July 10th, 1802; d. Oct. 1802.

JOHANNES or JOHN BERGEN, b. Sept. 23d, 1764; d. Aug. 12th, 1824; m. April 23d, 1793, *Rebecca,* dau. of Samuel Stryker,* of Gravesend, b. Jan. 8th, 1774, d. Jan. 28th, 1854.

of Gravesend, removed to Jamaica, Queens Co.: Rutgert, b. Jan. 16th, 1733, d May 18th, 1812, m. Altie Cortelyou, and resided in Gravesend; Adrian, b. Nov. 17th, 1734, d. Sept. 18th, 1785, m. Engletie Rapalje; Catryntie, m. Daniel Hendrickson: and Elizabeth, m. Hendrick Johnson.

Albert s. of Rutgert and Elizabeth, had issue: Elizabeth, bap. Sept. 9th, 1747, m. Nicholas Van Dyck, of Red Hook; Nicholas b. Aug. 27th, 1749, d. Sept. 5th, 1802, m. Mary Wyckoff; *Rutgert,* b. Nov. 18th, 1757, d. Sept. 5th, 1830, m. Lammetie dau. of Tunis Bergen; Cornelius, b. Aug. 21st, 1760, d. Sept. 26th, 1827, m. Jannetie, dau. of Rem Adriance: and Albert, b. July 28th, 1765, d. Aug. 14th, 1776.

* *Samuel Stryker,* was a descendant of *Garret Janse,* son of Jan Stryker, referred to in the foot note under Sarah Bergen, dau. of Michiel Hansen Bergen and Jan Stryker. Garret Stryker emigrated from Ruinen, in the Netherlands, in 1652 with his father, settled in Flatbush, afterwards in Flatlands, and in 1691, probably removed to Gravesend, where in said year, he purchased a farm of William Goulder.

Garret Janse, a s. of Jan and Lambertje, d. in 1695, m. Dec. 25th, 1683, Wyntie or Styntie Cornelis Boomgaert, or Styntie Garret Dorland, who d. in Gravesend, in 1700. Had children: Gezina, bap. Dec. 9th, 1677; Jannetje, bap. Dec. 26th, 1679, (sup.) m. Thomas Leake; Jacobus, of Gravesend, bap. Aug. 27th, 1682, m. Martha ——; Garret, of Stryker's bay on Manhatten Island, bap. Nov. 23d, 1684; Geesje, bap. Jan. 11th, 1685; *Cornelis,* of Gravesend, b. 1691, d. Oct. 23d, 1769, m. Rebecca Hubbard, b.

Resided on the farm which he inherited from his father on what was formerly known as Mentelaers Island, called by the Indians Wynpaggue, containing about 90 acres of upland, located in the salt marsh on the easterly side of the town of Flatlands, and at present known as Bergen's Island.

Issue :

Tunis, b Feb. 19th, 1794.

Maria, b. Jan. 3d, 1796, d. Sep. 14th, 1797.

Cornelius, b. Feb. 26th, 1798.

Maria, b. Dec. 30th, 1799.

John, b. Dec. 19th, 1802.

Johanna, b. Oct. 14th, 1805.

Ann, b. Nov. 17th, 1810.

Garret, b. Feb. 22d, 1813.

FEMMETJE or PHEBE BERGEN, b. Aug. 4th, 1769 ; d. Oct. 17th, 1831 ; m. May 23d, 1790, *Andrew Emmans*, of New Utrecht, where he resided and owned a farm of about 100 acres. Andrew was b. Jan. 21st, 1771, and d. Dec. 1, 1840.

Issue : —

Mary or *Maria Emmans*, b. May 21st, 1799 ; m. Jaques W. Cropsey, a farmer, of New Utrecht, and has children : William J. and Andrew J.

Johanna Emmans, b. Aug. 28th, 1801, and d. young.

1700, d. Sept. 8th, 1787 ; and Garretje, bap Nov. 14th, 1694, who (prob.) m. Oct. 11th, 1709, Jan Wyckoff.

Cornelis, s. of Garret and Wyntie, had children : Garret, b. March 2d, 1729, d. Sept. 27th, 1779, m. June 26th, 1756, Ida Van Deventer, who d. Feb. 7th, 1810, and (sup.) resided in Gravesend and Flatlands ; Hanna, b. Feb. 13th, 1733, d. Oct. 1st, 1807, m. May 31st, 1751, Mighiel Stryker, of Flatbush ; *Samuel*, of Gravesend, b. Oct. 20th, 1737, d. Feb. 7th, 1828, m. Nov. 17th, 1768, Maritje Schenck, b. May 29th, 1739, d. May 13th, 1813 ; Cornelius, of Gravesend, b. May 2d, 1739, d. Feb. 6th, 1829, m. Maria Lake, b. July 2d, 1748, d. July 3d, 1837 ; and Elizebeth, b. Sept. 28th, 1741.

Samuel, of Gravesend, s. of Cornelis and Rebecca, had children : Cornelius, b. Aug. 21st, 1769 ; Anny, b. Sept. 24th, 1771 ; Altie, bap. Oct. 11th, 1771 ; *Rebecca*, b. Jan. 8th, 1774, m. John Bergen, of Flatlands ; Stephen, b. Dec. 9th, 1776, d. June 1st, 1851, m. Merca Loth, 1798, Annatie or Johanna, dau. of Tunis Bergen, of Gowanus ; and Garret, b. Aug. 15th, 1781, d. Feb. 6th, 1861, m. Cornelia Ryder, b. April 1st, 1783, d. July 4th, 1850.

Johanna Emmans, b. Sept. 12th, 1804; m. Michael Hegeman, of New Utrecht, and has children: Phebe, b. Oct. 4th, 1823. d. Feb 4th, 1824; Belinda, b. Jan. 14th, 1825, Andrew, b. Aug. 31st, 1827; Thomas, b. Aug. 12th, 1830: Phebe M., b. Dec. 7th, 1833, d. March 5th. 1856; Peter A., b. Jan. 22d, 1837; and John C., b. Nov. 14th, 1842, d. Aug. 4th, 1843. Michael Hegeman, d. Oct. 20th, 1863.

John A. Emmans, b. Sept. 12th, 1804; m. Aug. 18th, 1830, Betsey Williams, and has issue, Phebe. b. Aug. 20th, 1831. m. 1st, Andy Van Blarcum, and 2d, Dr. Frederick De Mond. John A. owns and resides on the homestead of his father, purchased of Samuel Groenendyck by Andries Emans, great grandfather of John A., Jan. 25th, 1742–3.

GARRET BERGEN, b. Jan. 11th, 1772: d. Feb. 26th, 1845; m. Jan. 6th, 1806, *Jane,* dau. of Peter Wyckoff.*

---

* *Peter Claessen Wyckoff,* the common ancestor of the Wyckoff family in this country, emigrated from the Netherlands in 1636, settled in Flatlands, where he purchased land, and where in 1655, he superintended the bouwery and cattle of Director Stuyvesant. Of this town he was a magistrate in 1655, 1658, 1662 and 1663, and in Feb. 1664, one of the representatives at the convention held at Midwout, for the purpose of sending a delegation to Holland, to lay before the States General and West India Company the distressed state of the country, and also one of the patentees in the town charters of 1667 and 1686. He m. Gretie, dau. of Hendrick Van Ness, d. after 1695, and had issue: Annetje Pieterse, bap. (sup.) Nov. 27th, 1650; *Mayken* or *Maria Pieterse,* bap. (sup) Oct. 19th, 1653, m. Willem Willemse, of Gravesend, who emigrated to this country in 1657; Geertie Pieterse, alive in 1711, m. March 3d, 1678, Christoffel Janse Romeyn, of Flatlands; Claes Pieterse, of Flatlands, m. Sarah, dau. of Pieter Monfoort, who (prob.) d. in 1704; Cornelis Pieterse, of New Lots, in Flatbush, d. in 1746, m. Oct. 13th, 1678, Gertrude Simons, dau. of Simon Van Aersdalen, bought two tracts of land of 600 acres in N. J., one at Middlebush, and the other at six mile run; Hendrick Pieterse, of Flatlands, m. Helena ———. d. Dec. 6th, 1744. without issue, leaving by his will dated July 25th, 1741, his farm in Flatlands to Johannes Willemse, a grandson by his sister Mayken or Maria, on condition he assumed the surname of Wyckoff; Garret Pieterse, of Flatlands, m. Katharine ———. will da. Oct. 9th, 1704. pro. Jan. 12th, 1707; Martin Pieterse, of Gravesend, m. May 17th or 27th, 1683, Hannah Willemse, of Flatlands. m. 2d, (sup.) Moyeah ———, who after his death m. Thomas Van Dyke; he left female but no male issue; Pieter Pieterse, m. Willemtie ———: and Jan Pieterse, of Flatlands, b. Feb. 16th, 1665. m. Neltie, dau. of Willem Kouwenhoven, b. Feb. 3d, 1669. and sold his farm in Flatlands. May 14th, 1702, to Cornelis Coerte Van Voorhees.

Willem Willemse, of Gravesend and *Mayken* or *Maria* had issue: *Peter Willemse,* of Gravesend, bap. April 16th, 1682; Marretje Willemse, bap. April 12th, 1685; and Annetje Willemse, bap. May 29th, 1695.

Peter Willemse, of Gravesend, s. of Willem and Mayken or Maria, had issue: *Johannes Willemse,* (who assumed the surname of Wyckoff, in pursuance of his great uncle Hendrick Pieterse Wyckoff's will,) b. Jan. 1st, 1721, d. Jan. 12th, 1761. m. in 1742, Johanna or Annetie, dau. of Joost Debevoise, b. Oct. 20th, 1720, d. Aug. 30th, 1778.

Johannes Willemse Wyckoff, of Flatlands, s. of Peter Willemse, had

of Gowanus, b. April 3d, 1787, and living in 1865. He
inherited, owned and resided on the farm of 111 acres
his father bought of the Bennets, of Gowanus; held

issue: Henry or Hendrick, of Gravesend, b. Jan. 22d, 1712–3, d. (sup.)
Sept. 2d, 1819, m. Oct. 27th, 1761, Sarah Emmans, b. 1752, d. July 22d,
1780; Jacst or George, of Flatlands, b. Nov. 26th, 1715, d. Jan. 21st, 1787,
m. Dec. 15th, 1768, Sarah, dau. of Daniel Luyster, of Newtown, b. Oct.
30th, 1748; Feb , of Gowanus, b. May 19th, 1718, d. Sept. 1st, 1825, m.
Oct. 19th, 1771, Lammetie, dau. of Peter Lott, (a) of Flatbush, b. April 1st,
1750, d. Oct. 16th, 1821; Maria or Mary, b. April 2d, 1752, d. Sept. 13th,
1802, m. 1st, May 22d, 1768 John Emmans, of N. U., m. 2d, March 8th,
1783, Nicholas Van Brunt, of N. U.; John or Johannes of Jamaica, b.
March 6th, 1760, d. Oct. 22d, 1831, m. Feb. 9th, 1781, Etie or Margaret,
dau. of Albert Terhune, of Gravesend, b. May 2d, 1764, d. April 16th,
1840; and Johanna or Annatie, b. July 7th, 1761, d. June 10th, 1834, m.
1778, William Kouwenhoven, of Flatlands.

Peter Wyckoff, and Lammetie Lott, of Gowanus, had issue: Nelly, b.
Dec. 3d, 1772, d. May 2d, 1817, m. David Kelsey, of Suffolk Co., and left
no issue; Annatie b. April 3d, 1775, d. Sept. 16th, 1776; Joanna, b. Sept.
2d, 1778, d. Sept. 20th, 1829, m. Sept. 2d, 1798, John Bergen, of Queens
Co.; Peter, of Gowanus, b. Oct. 24th, 1781, d. Oct., 1815, m. Mayke, dau.
of Jaques Van Brunt, of N. U.; John, of Gowanus, b. Dec. 8th, 1784, d.
of cholera in 1855, m. 1st, Elizabeth, dau. of Stephen Hendrickson, m. 2d
Deborah Smith, wid. of Thomas Adams; *Jenn*, b. April 3d, 1787, m. Jan.
6th, 1806, Garet Bergen, of Gowanus; and Maria, b. Dec. 4th, 1789, d.
Feb. 11th, 1830, m. Dec. 28th, 1808, Peter Durvea, of N. U.

(a) *Peter Lott,* written "Lot" by himself, "Lodt " by his son Peter, and
sometimes "Loth" and "Loot," (most probably an abbreviation of Lodivicus, and meaning Peter, s. of Lodivicus,) the common ancestor of
the Lott family of Long Island, erroneously supposed by some to have
been an Englishman by birth, emigrated from Reynerwout or Ruiner-
wold, a village in the province of Drenthe, in the Netherlands, in
1652, and settled in Flatbush, where July 28th, 1653, "Bartel Lett,"
and "Pieter Loot," purchased of Edward Griffin 25 morgen of land on
the west side of the road, next to the minister's land No. 9, as conveyed to said Griffin by Garret Stryker. This Bartel is entered on the
N. Y. marriage records as "Bartel Englebertsen Lott," of Reynerwout,
m. Dec. 16th, 1662. Hermantje Barents, of the same place, and he was
probably either a brother or near relative of Peter, who less perpetuated
his name in his family. Peter Lot was a magistrate of Flatbush in 1656
and 1673, and one of the patentees on Long's patent of 1685. He m.
Gertrude ——, who d. in 1704, and had children; *F.....l....t,* of Flatbush,
b. Dec. 1654, d. April 30th, 1730, m. Oct. 20th, 1678, Cornelia, dau. of
Abraham De La Noy, of the city of N. Y., removed to and resided for a
time at New Castle, on the Delaware river, up in 1682, removed back to
Flatbush, and was high Sheriff of the county in 1698, Catrina m. Sept.
22d, 1687, Douwe Janse Van Ditmarsen, of Flatbush ; Peter, m. Sarah ——,
Abraham, m. Gertrye ———; and Hendrick, m. Cury..

Englebert, s. of Peter and Gertrude, had issue: Abraham, b. Sept. 7th,
1684, d. July 29th, 1754, m. Nov. 15th, 1709, Catherine, dau. of Elbert
Hegeman, b. Nov. 11th, 1691, d. Nov. 19th, 1741; Johannes, d. Jan. 29th,
1701, young; Gertruy, bap. Feb. 5th, 1696, d. Sept. 2d, 1701; Cornelia,
bap. July 31st, 1698, d. Sept. 11th, 1699; John..s, b. July 22d, 1701, d.

16

the office of Justice and associate Judge of the County Courts from 1802 to 1815, inclusive, and also, from 1819 to 1822; was a member of, and at times an Elder and Deacon of the Protestant Reformed Dutch Church, of Brooklyn, and of the South Church, Gowanus, of the same denomination.

Issue :—

Tennis G., b. Oct. 6th, 1806.

Peter G. b. March 31st, 1808.

Johannah. b. July 9th, 1810; d. Sept. 25th, 1813.

Lammetic, b. Oct. 6th, 1812.

John G., b. Dec. 4th, 1814.

Garret G., b. April 6th, 1817.

Johannah. b. Aug. 30th, 1819; d. Feb. 3d, 1827.

Jane Stryker, b. Nov. 4th, 1821; d. June 6th, 1823.

Jacob Conover, b. Jan. 22d, 1826; d. Feb. 3d, 1827,

Francis Henry. (a twin,) b. March 3d, 1828; d. Feb. 24th, 1844.

Michael Stryker. (a twin,) b. March 3d, 1828; d. Aug. 2d, 1828.

TUNIS T. BERGEN. b. May 16th, 1774; d. Oct. 3d, 1841; m. 1st. Dec. 12th, 1802, *Nelly*, dau. of Adrian Mar-

1732, m. Nov. 4th, 1721, Lammetie, dau. of Peter Stryker, who after the death of Johannes, m. Christianus Lupardius; Gertruy, b. Dec. 4th, 1703; and Elizabeth, bap. March 12th, 1715, on Staten Island.

John m. s. of Englebert and Cornelia, of Flatbush, had issue: Englebert, b. Sept. 23d, 1722; Annetie, b. Sep. 9th, 1724, m. Cornelis Van Duyne, of Newtown; *Peter*, of Flatbush, b. Aug. 14th, 1726, d. Aug. 12th, 1775, m. 1st. July 9th, 1749, Neeltie, dau. of Dominicus Vanderveer, who d. Aug. 28th, 1767, m. 2d. April 9th, 1769, Jane Eldert, a widow, by whom no issue, and who d. April 19th, 1801; Cornelia, b. Sept. 29th, 1728; and Johannes, of Flatland Neck, b. Sept. 2d, 1730, d. Nov. 23d, 1776, m. Sept. 22d, 1753, Hendrikje, dau. of Isaac Remsen, who is said to have weighed 300 pounds.

Peter, s. of Johannes and Lammetie, had issue: *Lammetje*, b. April 1st, 1750, d. Oct. 19th, 1824, m. Oct. 19th, 1771, Peter Wyckoff, of Gowanus; John, b. Feb. 28th, 1752, d. Oct. 7th, 1776, single; Jane, b. Nov. 11th, 1754, d. Sept. 6th, 1828, m. July 12th, 1777, John Stryker, of Flatbush, no issue; Johannes, b. July 9th, 1757, d. Oct. 3d, 1776, single; Catelyne, b. May 29th, 1760, d. Aug. 29th, 1767; Antie, b. June 27th, 1763, d. Jan. 19th, 1850, m. May 2d, 1781, William Williamson, of Flatbush, b. Nov. 11th, 1755, d. Aug. 26th, 1830; and Dominicus, b. Feb. 22d, 1766, d. Aug. 20th, 1767.

The Abraham Lott, b. Sept. 7th, 1684, is the great grandfather of the late Englebert Lott, of N. U., Jeremiah Lott, John Lott, and Abraham Lott, of Flatbush, all brothers, their father Johannes E. Lott, being a s. of Englebert, which Englebert was a s. of said Abraham.

tense,* of Flatbush, b. May 23d, 1785; d. Oct. 7th, 1811; m. 2d, *Jane Boice Stillwell*, b. March 7th, 1798, and living in 1865.

Resided first on a farm in New Utrecht, belonging to Adrian Martense, his father-in-law, now 1865, owned and occupied by his sons Adrian and Tunis, and 2d on a farm which he owned in the village of Flatbush, lying adjoin-

* *Adrian Martense*, is a descendant of Adrian Reyersz, the common ancestor of the Reyerse, the Adriance, and the Martense family in this country. Adrian Reyersz, emigrated to this country from Amsterdam, in 1646, settled in Flatbush, m. July 29th, 1659, Annetje Martens, dau. of Martin Roelofse Schenck, of Flatlands, and d. Nov. 24th, 1710. His children were Jannetje Adriance, b. July 25th, 1660; Elbert Adriance, b. Aug. 14th, 1663, m. April 18th, 1689, Catalyntie, dau. of Rem Janse Vanderbeeck, settled in Flushing, his descendants adopting the patronymic of Adriance and constituting the Adriance family; Maratie Adriance, b. Dec. 2d, 1665, O. S.; *Martin Adrian*, b. March 9th, 1668, d. Oct. 30th, 1754, m. Sarah (sup.) Hegeman, who d. April 30th, 1723, his descendants adopting the patronymic of Martense, and constituting the Martense family; Margaret or Grietje Adriance, b. March 28th, 1670; Sarah Adriance, b. June 9th, 1672, d. young; Reyer Adriance, b. May 28th, 1673, d. young; Neeltje Adriance, b. Dec. 7th, 1675; Reyer Adriance, bap. March 31st, 1678, d. young; Abraham Adriance, bap. Nov. 21st, 1680, probably settled at FishkIll; Sara Adriance, bap. Nov. 21st, 1680, and a twin with Abraham; Reyer Adriance, bap. May 6th, 1683; and Cosna Adriance, bap. April 29th, 1686, m. Femmetje Vanderb'lt.

Martin Adrian, had issue, Rem Martense, of Flatbush, b. Dec. 12th, 1695, d. June 14th, 1760, m. Susanna, b. March 4th, 1698, d. March 5, 1775; Garret Martense, of Flatbush, b. Oct. 24th, 1698, d. 1732, m. Magdalena, dau. of Leffert Pieterse, b. Aug. 20th, 1694; Jannetje Martense, b. July 31st, 1702, d. Jan. 1, 1794, m. May 18th, 1720, Peter Stryker, of Flatbush; Antje Martense, b. Nov. 5th, 1705; *Adrian Martense*, b. Oct. 24th, 1707, d. Sept. 17th, 1780, m. Neeltje, of Flatbush.

Adrian Martense, of Flatbush, s. of Martin Adriance, had issue; Sara Martense, b. March 17th, 1729, m. April 17th, 1747, Theodorus Van Wyck; Antje Martense, d. June 4th, 1732; Susanna Martense, b. Oct. 22d, 1734, single; Joris Martense, b. March 8th, 1737, d. Nov. 9th, 1801, single; Gerrit Martense, b. Sept. 19th, 1740, d. Nov. 9th, 1826, single; *Adrian Martense*, b. Dec. 9th, 1742, d. March 13th, 1817, m. 1st Nov. 3d, 1765, Adriaentje Ryder, b. Feb. 2d, 1711, d. May 27th, 1776, m. 2d, Femmetje Monfoor, b. Dec. 27th, 1750, d. Oct. 2d, 1801; Neeltje Martense, b. May 19th, 1745, d. Oct. 3d, 1799, m. John Van Duyne; Isaac Martense, b. d. m. 9th, 1748, d. Nov. 12th, 1778, m. Nov. 5th, 1775, Maria Martense, b. Oct. 22d, 1758, d. June 18th, 1816; and Jannetje Martense, b. Jan. 6th, 1754, d. Oct. 30th, 1828, m. Brinckerhoff.

Adrian Martense, of Flatbush, s. of Adrian and Neeltje .... by his first wife; Adrian, b. Aug. 17th, 1768, d. Dec. 12th, 1840, m. Gertrude, dau. of Jacob Suydam, b. Jan. 25th, 1770; .... 2d wife, M. rio, b. March 10th, 1781, d. Jan. 1st, 1784; and N...., b. May 23d, 1785; d. Oct. 7th, 1814, m. Dec. 12th, 1802, Tunis T. Bergen.

George Martense, the only s. of Adrian and Gertrude, m. Jan. 13th, 1818, Helen, one of the dau. of Jacob Van Brunt, of Brooklyn, a descendant of Jacob Hansen Bergen.

ing to and on the westerly side of the road known as the little lane. His mind was disordered about the time of the death of his first wife, but he finally recovered.

Issue by 1st wife :—

Johanna, b. June 15th, 1804.
Adrian, b. Nov. 24th, 1806.
Jane, b. Sept. 15th, 1808.
Tunis, b. Dec. 25th, 1810.
Maria, b. 1813.

By 2d wife :—

Daniel, b. March 5th, 1817.
John T., b. Oct. 4th, 1819.
Catharine J., b. July 31st, 1827.
Lemma Ann, b. July 9th, 1831.
Sarah Matilda, b. July 7th, 1836.
Elmira Rosetta, b. May 17th, 1839.

ANATIE or JOHANNA BERGEN, b. Oct. 2d, 1776; d. Aug. 22d, 1833: m. March 15th, 1798, *Stephen Stryker*, of Gravesend, b. Dec. 2d, 1777, d. June 1st, 1851.

She resided in Gravesend with her husband on his farm, now, 1865, of their son Samuel S. Stryker, located on the main road between the village of New Utrecht and Gravesend.

Issue :

Maria Stryker, b. Sept. 15th, 1798; living in 1865, and single.

Tunis Stryker, b. Dec. 7th, 1800; d. May 14th, 1852, m. March 31st, 1819, Ann Hubbard and had 8 children.

Samuel S. Stryker, b. Sept. 29th, 1803; m. June 25th, 1825, Ellen, dau. of Jaques Stillwell, of Gravesend: living in 1865, on the homestead of his father and has four children.

Johanna Stryker, b. July 4th, 1807; d. Oct. 15th, 1837; m. June 18th, 1825, Henry I. Wyckoff, of Gravesend: left issue, 4 children.

Ann Stryker, b. July 15th, 1809; m. March 1st, 1832, James A. Williamson, of Gravesend, and has two children.

Sarah Stryker, b. Jan. 30th, 1811: m. April 26th, 1831, John F. Voorath, a German, and resides in the city of N. Y.; has issue, two children.

SARAH BERGEN, b. March 10th, 1782; d. Jan. 22d, 1827; m. Aug. 12th, 1805, Dr. *Francis Henry Dubois*, b. May 21st, 1783, d. Dec. 27th, 1834. Dr. Dubois, a native of New Jersey, resided in the village of New Utrecht, was a skillful physician, and had an extensive practice in the towns of New Utrecht, Gravesend, Flatlands and Flatbush, and in Gowanus, to which his s. Dr. James E. Dubois, succeeded.

Issue:

Tunis Bergen Dubois, b. May 28th, 1806; m. April 15th, 1830, Eliza Williams; a carpenter by trade and has children: Francis Henry, b. March 9th, 1832; Sarah Elizabeth, b. May 31st, 1836; James, b. Aug. 19th, 1838; Simon Williams, b. Aug. 24th, 1840; John, b. Oct. 6th, 1842; Annie Louisa, b. Feb. 20th, 1845; Phebe Emmans, b. Nov. 19th, 1848; and Edwin, b. Oct 12th, 1851.

Margaret Dubois, b. Nov. 29th, 1807; d. Nov. 27th, 1808.

James Dubois, b. Fe. 4th, 1809; d. Sept. 6th, 1809.

James Engush Dubois, b. Feb. 24th, 1811; m. June 3d, 1852, Eliza Ellen, dau. of Adrian Bergen; d. Sept. 13th, 1856, of yellow fever, contracted in the faithful discharge of the duties of his profession, during the fatal ravages of this fever along the water front from Bath, in New Utrecht, to Gowanus cove in Brooklyn. Dr. James E. Dubois, was like his father, a skillful physician of extensive practice, popular in his profession, and his loss was deeply lamented, so much so, that to his memory and that of Dr. John L. Crane, his faithful associate, who d. about the same time and of the same disease, his friends erected in the burial ground in New Utrecht an imposing and expensive granite monument. He left children: Francis Adrian, b. Sept. 22d, 1854; and Sarah Louisa, b. Feb. 24th, 1857.

John Dubois, b. Dec. 27th, 1812; m. April 25th, 1841, Mary Riley, resides in Brooklyn, and has children: Henry, b. March 13th, 1842; Tunis, b. March 28th, 1843; Charles, b. Jan. 31st, 1845; Mary Ann, b. Sept. 16th, 1846; John, b. March 24th, 1848; Mary Jane, b. Aug. 23d, 1850; Sarah, b. Jan. 28th, 1852; Francis Chester, b. Jan. 2d, 1855; and James, b. Aug. 21st, 1857.

Sixth Generation.

Children of SIMON BERGEN and *Gashe De Hart*, of Brooklyn, N. Y. :—

SIMON BERGEN, b. April 15th, 1768; d. May 23d, 1830; m. Dec. 10th, 1795, *Jane* dau. of Cornelius Van-derveer,[*] of Flatbush, b. Nov. 9th, 1775; d. Sept. 26th, 1831.

Occupied and owned (150 acres,) the N. E'ly one-half of the De Hart farm in Gowanus, which his father occupied in his lifetime. His father having died intestate, under the British laws of primogeniture, he being the eldest son, was entitled to the whole of the real estate, one-half of which, he however, at the solicitation it is said of his grand-father, Johannes Bergen, and to secure an interest in his estate, and also to carry out an intention signified by his father before his death, he conveyed to his brother, John S. Bergen, by two deeds, the one dated June 22d, 1789, and the other April 4th, 1800. He also owned a farm of about 70 acres on the bay at Bay Ridge, New Utrecht, which he purchased of the Barkuloos and Cropseys. In his youth he accidentally lost the use of one of his eyes.

Issue :—

Gashe, b. July 24th, 1797; m. Dec. 29th, 1817, Johannes H. Lott, of Flatlands, and has issue, Jane Bergen, b. Aug. 6th, 1819, m. May 20th, 1847, Charles Burr Ditmas; Henry Dewitt, b. June 21st, 1821, m. Oct. 28th, 1863, Ann Bennet; Mary, b. Dec. 26th, 1823, single; Catharine Ann, b. Dec. 2d, 1825, m. 1st, May 23d, 1849, Chauncey Drummond, m. 2d, Oct. 14th, 1854, Samuel L. Clapp; Eliza, b. July 17th, 1828, m. Jan. 12th, 1858, Byron Whitcomb; Simon Bergen, b. Oct. 23d, 1830, m. March 28th, 1861, Martha J. Van Cleef; and Jurien, b. March 10th, 1835.

[*] For the ancestors of Cornelius Vanderveer, see foot note on Ann Vanderveer, wife of Tunis J. Bergen.

Leah, b. Sept. 25th, 1800; m. Dec. 22d, 1825, Jacob Morris, of the city of N. Y., a sailing master in the U. S. Navy, afterwards a farmer in Gowanus and in Orange Co., N. Y. Has issue: Simon B., b. July 6th, 1827, m. Dec. 23d, 1856, Ann Gridley; Mary Jane, b. Sept. 30th, 1821, m. —— Gridley; Silvester Jacob, b. Oct. 27th, 1832; John P., b. Jan. 9th, 1835; Catharine Letitia, b. June 23d, 1841, m. Dr. Matthew McCollum; and Emma Henrietta, b. Jan. 26th, 1844.

Ann, b. Sept. 28th, 1801; m. June 19th, 1819, Peter Bergen, Jun. Resided on a farm in Gowanus, and lately in the city of N. Y. Has issue:

Simon.

Peter.

Mary Catharine.

Jane Ann.

Virginia.

For births, &c., of the above see children of Peter Bergen.

Catharine, b. Feb. 16th, 1807; m. May 10th, 1832; d. Sept. 14th, 1835, Tennis S. Barkeloo, of Brooklyn, and left no issue.

Jane, b. Aug. 24th, 1811, m. 1st, Sept. 14th, 1835, Calvin F. Spear, a merchant in the city of N. Y., who resided after his marriage in Gowanus and d. Sept. 25th, 1854; issue: Elizabeth Flint, b. Aug. 16th, 1836, d. Jan. 24th, 1842; Jane Bergen, b. Dec. 3d, 1837, d. Feb. 9th, 1838; Austin Flint, b. Jan. 23d, 1839, d. Feb. 9th, 1839; Austin Flint, b. Feb. 13th, 1840, d. March 23d, 1840; Calvin Flint, b. June 2d, 1841, d. Sept. 27th, 1844; Edward Flint, b. Aug. 17th, 1843, d. Aug. 27th, 1843; Elizabeth Flint, b. July 22d, 1844, d. Nov. 11th, 1844; Josephine, b. Nov. 30th, 1846, d. Sept. 21st, 1849; Calvin Flint, b. Feb. 9th, 1849; and Lenister, b. Aug. 10th, 1852, d. Dec. 28th, 1852. She m. 2d, in 1858, James Millwood, an Englishman by birth.

JOHN S. BERGEN, b. May 1st, 1777, (bap. in New Utrecht, May 11th, 1777); d. Dec. 22d, 1854; m. Dec. 11th, 1799, *Mary* or *Polly*, dau. of Elias Hubbard,* of Flatlands, b. Nov. 28th, 1778, and living in 1865.

* *Elias Hubbard*, is a descendant of Henry Hubbard and Margaret, his wife, who resided in the town of Langham, in the county of Rutland, England, and had 11 sons and daus., among whom were, William, John, Henry, Margaret and *James* who was the youngest.

James, s. of Henry and Margaret, emigrated to New England, and in 1643, with Lady Deborah Moody and others, on account of their peculiar religious views and pretensions, left the latter place and settled in Gravesend, L. I., where he was known as Serjeant Hubbard. Of this town he was a magistrate in 1650, '51, '53, and 1663; he also represented the town in the convention held at New Amsterdam, Nov. 26th, 1653, to devise and recommend measures for the public security, and to put a stop to

Resided on and owned the S. W'ly one-half (150 acres.) of the De Hart farm, in Gowanus. Was a Lieut. of a uniform Company, in the war of 1812, one of the assistant Judges of the county Court, from 1834 to 1841, and an Alderman of the 8th Ward of Brooklyn, in 1835–6 and 7.

Issue :—

Gashe, b. Aug. 14th, 1800; d. Dec. 24th, 1801.

Simon J., b. Dec. 24th, 1802 ; d. Feb. 27th, 1841 ; m. Nov. 1834, Johanna, dau. of Timothy T. Cortelyou,* of New Utrecht, b. Nov. 8th, 1804.

the piracies and robberies of one Thomas Baxter, and in the convention of the 10th of Dec. 1653, held at the same place. to represent the state of the country to the authorities in Holland. In 1655, he had a wife named Martha. He m. Dec. 31st, 1664, Elizabeth Balies or Baylis, and d. prior to 1693, having issue : *James*, b. Dec. 10th, 1665, m. Rachel, and living as late as 1695 ; Rebecca, b. April 28th, 1667 ; Elizabeth, b. June 3d, 1669 ; John, b March 20th, 1670 ; Elias, b. April 11th, 1673 ; m. Dec. 15th, 1699, Jannetje, wid. of Jan Barentse Van Driest ; and Samuel, b. May 2d, 1676.

James, s. of James and Elizabeth, had issue : *James*, b. June 18th, 1706, m. Sept. 1729, Altye Ryder, b. March 8th 1712 ; and Elias, b. Dec. 1731, m. Sept. 29th, 1723, Femmetje, dau. of Lawrence Ditmars, b. May 23d, 1707.

James, s. of James and Rachel, had issue : Johanna, b. Aug. 30th, 1730, d. Nov. 24th, 1740 ; Bernardus, b. Feb. 1, 1732, m. Nov. 18th, 1756, Neeltie Lake ; Elizabeth, b. 1733, d. March 21st, 1740 ; Ariaentje, b. 1735, d. Oct. 5th, 1735 ; Ariaentie, b. Dec. 7th, 1736, m. (sup.) Nov. 1765, Jacobus Lake ; Phebe, b. Aug. 1st, 1739, d. Nov. 29th, 1740 ; Samuel, b. April 28th, 1742, d. Feb. 30th, 1835, m. Ann ——, who d. Dec., 1834 ; Jacobus, b. May 23d, 1744 ; *Elias*, of Flatlands, b. Feb. 13th, 1746, d. Dec. 13th, 1832, m. Margaret Lake, wid. of Cornelius Blanc, b. Feb. 28th, 1739, d. Oct. 15th, 1825 ; Johanna b. July 23d, 1748 ; Stephen, b. May 23d, 1752, d. March 22d, 1819, m. Maria Ryder ; and James, bap. March 25th, 1764, d. 1799.

Elias, s. of James and Altje, had issue : Catharine, b. Dec. 4th, 1774, m. Michael Sice ; Elias, of Flatlands, b. Dec. 1st, 1776, living in 1863, m. Jan. 14th, 1801, Huldah Holmes, of N. J., b. Oct. 27th, 1779, and d. April 4th, 1851 ; and *Mary or Polly*, b. Nov. 28th, 1778, m. John S. Bergen.

* *Johanna Cortelyou*, is a descendant of *Peter*, s. of Jaques and Jacamintie Cortelyou, referred to in the foot note under the head of Deborah, dau. of said Jaques and Jacamintie.

Peter, m. Agnes or Angenietje De Hart, and had issue : *Jaques*, b. Oct. 16th, 1743, d. Sept. 14th, 1815, m. 1st. Nov. 1st, 1767, Mary Hewlet, m. 2d, July 28th, 1773, Sarah Townsend, of Queens Co. ; Simon, b. March 11th, 1746, d. Aug. 15th, 1828, m. 1st, May 20th 1763, Sarah Van Wyck, m. 2d, Maria Bogert, wid. of Jaques Barkelow.

Jaques, s. of Peter and Agnes, had isssue by Mary his 1st wife : Peter, b. Nov. 28th, 1768, d. Sept. 12th, 1804, m. 1st, July 7th, 1789, Femmetje, dau, of Adrian Voorhees, m. 2d, May 1803, Mary Alstine ; by Sarah Townsend, his 2d wife, *Timothy Townsend*, b. Nov. 19th, 1774, d. May 1st,

Resided on and cultivated a portion of his father's farm at Gowanus.
Left issue: Anna Cortelyou, b. Feb. 25th, 1836; Mary Margaret, b. Sept.
19th, 1837; and John Simon, b. Feb. 21st, 1839, d. July 9th, 1862.

Margaret, b. Jan. 5th, 1803; m. Dec. 15th, 1824, John A. Bergen, of
Gowanus, who d. July 30th, 1856, of yellow fever and had issue: Mary
Gashe, Sarah Vanderbilt, (dec'd,) Margaret Maria, (dec'd,) Theodore,
(dec'd,) John DeHart, (dec'd,) Caroline H., (dec'd,) Miles H. Simon De
Hart, (dec'd,) and Ida.

Enos Hibbard, b. Dec. 6th, 1806, m. Jan. 14th, 1852, Johanna, dau. of
Henry Snydam, of Flatbush, who d. Jan. 17th, 1857, without surviving
issue. Was engaged as a clerk in mercantile business in the city of N. Y.
and resided in Brooklyn, and is now deceased.

John, b. May 6th, 1809; d. Sept. 6th, 1856, of yellow fever; m. Jan. 7th,
1834, Agnes, dau. of Jacob Bergen, of Brooklyn, she dying of the same
disease. Resided on and cultivated a portion of his father's farm at Gowanus. Held the office of Lieut. in the militia. Had issue: Catharine, b.
Feb. 22d, 1835; John S., b. Nov. 1st, 1837, is a Captain in the U. S. army,
engaged in suppressing the rebellion, (N. Y. S. V.); Jacob J., b. May 13th,
1839, d. Sept. 17th, 1856, of yellow fever; Maria, b. Jan. 6th, 1841, Phœ-
be Ann, b. Dec. 26th, 1842; Margaret, b. May 9th, 1844; Josiah S., b.
Nov. 5th, 1845; Simon, b. July 25th, 1847, an idiot; Tunis Henry, b.
April 26th, 1850; d. Sept 11th, 1852; and Tunis Henry, b. Nov. 5th,
1852.

Cornelius B., b. July 30th, 1811; d. Oct. 24, 1852, m. Dec. 20th, 1836,
Catharine, dau. of Parmenus Johnson of Brooklyn. Resided in the city
of Brooklyn, and engaged in the grocery business. In 1844, was one of
the Supervisors of the first seven wards of the city. Had issue: Edward
b. Feb. 11th, 1838; Cornelius De Hart, b. June 22d, 1844, and Parmenus
J., b. April 22d, 1845.

Michael, b. Sept. 16th, 1813; d. Feb. 9th, 1816.

1829, m. July 23d, 1801, Anna, dau. of Willard Kouwenhoven, of Flat-
lands, b. Nov. 5th, 1785, d. Feb. 28th, 1843.
Timothy Townsend, s. of Jaques and Sarah, had issue: Sarah, b. Oct.
Oct. 7th, 1802, m. Nov. 2d, 1819, Isaac, s. of Jacob or Jacques Cortelyou;
Johannes, b. Nov. 8th, 1804, m. Simon J. Bergen, Ratto, s. May 31, 1807,
d. Jan. 28th, 1812, single; Peter, b. June 25th, 1809, d. Oct. 11, 1809;
Anna Maria, b. Sept. 8th, 1810, d. Sept. 20th, 1841; Anna Maria, b. Sept.
27th, 1812, m. Dec. 17th, 1834, John L. Van Pelt, of New York;
Timothy T., b. July 22d, 1815, m. Ann, dau. of Robert L. Sowens of
Gravesend; Freelove Jane, b. April 28th, 1818, d. Aug. 9th, 1819;
Freelove Jane, b. Aug. 14th, 1820, insane; Ida, b. Feb. 25th, 1823, a ny-
phomaniac; William K., b. June 7th, 1825; and Mary F. b. Mar. 24,
1828.

17

De Hart, b. Aug. 1st, 1816; m. Oct. 25th, 1843, Margaret, dau. of Jacob Bergen, of Brooklyn. Resided (1863.) on and cultivated a portion of his father's farm in Gowanus. Has issue: Jacob De Hart, b. May 22d, 1845; Marietta, b. July 25th, 1848; Emma, b. April 12th, 1851.

Mary Gashe, b. Dec. 9th, 1818; d. March 28th, 1831.

Michael J., b. May 17th, 1823; m. Feb. 12th, 1854, Mary, dau. of Robert C. Bell, of Brooklyn, b. Dec. 19th, 1834. Occupies and cultivates (1865.) the farm of Thomas Hunt, at Gowanus. Has issue: Robert C. B., b. Feb. 12th, 1854; Frank S., b. July 14th, 1857; Mary Louise, b. Sept. 11th, 1859, and Ella Florence, b. Aug. 27th, 1861.

Children of MICHAEL BERGEN, and *Anthe Van Wyck*, his first, and of *Rebecca Lefferts*, his second wife, of Brooklyn, N. Y. :—

THEODORUS BERGEN, (by 1st wife,) b. March 17th, 1775; d. Jan. 21st, 1859; m. *Sarah Vanderbilt*,* of Flat-

---

* *Sarah Vanderbilt*, is a descendant of *Jan Aertsen Vanderbilt*, or Jan Aertsen, from the Bild or Bilt, a manor in the province of Friesland in the Netherlands, who emigrated at an early period, settled in Flatbush, and is the common ancestor of the Vanderbilts in this vicinity. On the 12th of Oct. 1640, a Jan Aertsen was apprenticed to Peter Wolphertsen Van Couwenhoven, for three years, who may have been John Aertsen Vanderbilt. He m. 1st, Dierber Cornelis; m. 2d, Feb. 6th, 1650, Anneken Hendricks, from Norway, and he m. 3d, Dec. 11th, 1681, Magdalentje Hansz. wid. of Harman Eudaardsz. and had children: *Aris Janse*, of Flatbush, who m. Oct. 6th, 1677, Hillegonde or Hilletie, dau. of Rem Janse Vanderbeeck, and d. after 1711; Jacob Janse, of Flatbush, m. Aug. 13th, 1687, Marretje, dau. of Dirck Janse Vander Vliet, and wid. of Andries Onderdonk; Marritje Janse, m. Rem Remsen; and Jan Janse who m. Helena.

Aris Janse had children: Jan Aertse, bap. Aug. 11th, 1678, m. Hillitie Remsen; Jaunetje or Annetje Aertse, bap. Jan. 9th, 1681, d. young; Jannetje Aertse, bap. Sep. 17th, 1682; Femmetje Aertse, bap. Sep. 14th, 1684; Rem Aertse, bap. Aug. 29th, 1686, m. Margrita ———; Aert, of Flatbush, bap. June 11th, 1693, d. after 1751, m. March 14th, 1717, Seytie Stryker; *Jeremias*, of Flatbush, bap. Oct. 19th, 1695, m. Nov. 11th, 1715, Pieternella, dau. of Cornelis Pieterse Wyckoff, of Flatbush; and Cornelius, b. Jan. 11th, 1697, d. Jan. 22d, 1782, m. Jannetie Wyckoff.

Jeremias, s. of Aris Janse and Hilletie, had children: George, bap. Dec. 15th, 1718; Hilletie, b. April 19th, 1721, d. Sept. 20th, 1779, m. May 5th, 1745, Leffert Martense; Pieternella, bap. March 5th, 1727; and *Jeremias*, of Flatbush, who m. Sarah Van Brunt, b. May 4th, 1728, d. March 12th, 1814.

Jeremias, s. of Jeremias and Peternella, had children: Elizabeth, b. April 1st, 1745, d. April 20th, 1813, m. Nicholas Williamson; *John*, of Flatbush, b. Feb. 16th, 1752, d. Nov. 23th, 1812, m. 1778, Maretie Ditmars, b. May 12th, 1758, d. Sept. 1st, 1830; Sarah; Catharine; Ida, and Elsie, bap. May 16th, 1766.

John, s. of Jeremias and Sarah, had children: Jeremiah, of Flatbush, b.

bush, b. Dec. 8th, 1785, d. May 16th, 1855. Resided in the old mansion house of his grand-father Johannes Bergen, and owned and occupied a portion of his father's farm at Gowanus.

Issue:

Ins. b. March 7th, 1805, d. Aug. 14th, 1806, of yellow fever contracted at Gowanus, while attending upon the family of her brother John V. Bergen, m. Dec. 20th, 1827, Samuel G. Lott, a farmer of Flatbush, and left issue. John b. Aug. 28th, 1830; d. Aug. 28th, 1831, John S., b. Feb. 7th, 1833, a minister in the Reformed Dutch Church. Theodore B., b. Sept. 14th, 1834; and Mary C., b. April 11th, 1837.

John V., b. Aug. 3d, 1806; d. July 30th, 1856, of yellow fever, m. Dec. 15th, 1831, Margaret, dau. of John S. Bergen, of Gowanus. Was for several years an Alderman of the 8th Ward of Brooklyn, and resided on and cultivated a portion of his father's farm at Gowanus. Had issue: Mary Gashe, b. Sept. 28th, 1832; Sarah Vanderveer, b. May 10th, 1834, d. Aug. 5th, 1856, of yellow fever; Margaret Maria, b. Aug. 15th, 1835, d. Aug. 13th, 1856, of yellow fever; Theodore, b. July 5th, 1837, d. Aug. 16th, 1856, of yellow fever; John De Hart, b. Aug. 15th, 1839, d. Aug. 18th, 1856, of yellow fever, Caroline H. b. Sept. 4th, 1841, d. March 11th, 1845; Miles H., b. Sept. 30th, 1843; Simon De Hart, b. Dec. 31st, 1845, d. July 5th, 1846; and Ida, b. Oct. 21st, 1847.

R.b...., b. Sept. 26th, 1808; m. April 28th, 1836, Maria Bergen, ds. of Jacob, and has issue: Jacob M., Phebe R. Theodore V. W., Susan, Isaac M., Sarah, Caroline, decd.; and Charles M.

Michael T., b. Aug. 7th, 1810; d. Oct. 2... 1844, single. Was engaged in mercantile business in the city of N. Y.

Jeromus V., Nov. 2d, 1812, m. March 5th, 1839, d... Ann, d.... de romus Lott,* of Flatlands, b. Aug. 29th, 1816. Divorced. Others born March 17th, 1778, d. Dec. 20th, 1853... John C. Vanderveer. Sarah, d. Dec. 8th, 1785, d. M... Theodorus Bergen, of Gowanus; Catalyn, b. ... son M... Henry. Mary, b. Dec. 12th, 1787, d. Nov. 4th, 1813. Han..., Sept. 14th, 1791, d. Dec. 24th, 1848, m. Sylvester Earle... June... 20th, 1794, d. Dec. 15th, 1842, m. Feb. 10th, 1817, Sarah Lott.

*Jeromus Lott, is a descendant of Hendrick Lott..... the sons of Peter Lott, the emigrant referred to... Wyckoff, wife of Grant Bergen. Hendrick... Jamaica, and m. Catrya or Katrina (son) De Witt... May 9th, 1654, and living as late as 1701. Had issue: Dorothy, b. Dec. 11th, 1688; Gertrude, b. May 4th, 1688; Pieter, b. March 4th, 1691, d... b. May 13th, 1692.

farm in the village of Flatlands, and has issue: Jerome L, b. Dec. 9th, 1841; Sarah Jane, b. March 19th, 1844; Theodore, b. Feb. 1st, 1846; Edgar, b. Jan. 22d. 1848: John Vanderbilt, b. Jan. 3d. 1851. d. young: Anna Maria, b. June 1st. 1853: and Irwin Eugene, b. Jan. 1858, d. young.

Mary. b. Oct. 26th. 1815, single.

Sarah, b. May 12th, 1818; d. Jan. 12th, 1848; m. Jan. 13th, 1836, Isaac E. Bergen, (s. of Jacob,) and left issue: Jacob I., Sarah Maria, and Theodore V.

Caroline, b. Sept. 12th, 1820; d. May 1st. 1861; m. Feb. 4th, 1845, the Rev. Samuel M. Woodbridge, pastor of the Protestant Reformed Dutch Church of South Brooklyn, and in 1865, a Professor in Rutger's College, New Brunswick. Issue: Caroline, b. Dec. 2d, 1845.

Ida, b. Nov. 26th, 1822: d. Aug. 17th, 1856, of yellow fever: m. Feb. 6th, 1850. Isaac E. Bergen, (s. of Jacob,) and left issue: George J.

Maria. b. Oct. 30th. 1693: and Antie, b. Aug. 23d, 1696, m. Folkert Folkersen.

Johannes, s of Hendrick and Katrina, b. May 11th, 1692, d. April 8th, 1775, resided in Flatlands, and had issue: Hendrick I., of New Jamaica, b. Nov. 7th. 1715, m. Rebecca, dau. of John Van Kerk: Joris, of New Utrecht. b. Oct. 3d, 1717, d. Aug. 26th, 1762, m. April 1737, Maria, dau. of Rutgert Van Brunt: Katrina, b Oct. 22d, 1719, d. Aug. 13th, 1769, m. Ap'l 21st, 1744, Derick Remsen: Johannes, of New Lots, b. Dec. 31st, 1721, d. Jan. 25th, 1782, m. April 6th, 1745, Jannetie Probasco: Maria, b. March 7th, 1723, d. Jan. 22d, 1804, m. Carl Boerum: Petrus, of Flatlands, b Nov. 20th, 1727, m. June 22d, 1745, Merretje Durland: Nicholas, b. May 6th, 1726, d. young: Nicholaes, b. Sept. 13th, 1728, d. Jan. 24th, 1766: Nieltien, b. Nov. 13th, 1730, m. Jacob Snediker: Folkert, b. Oct. 5th, 1732, d. April 1st, 1763: Antie, b. March 19th, 1736–7, m. 1759, Stephen Lott: Doretie, b. April 10th, 1740, m. 1759, John Van Leuwen: and *Jeromus,* of Flatlands.

Jeromus, of Flatlands, s. of Johannes, b. Jan. 26th, 1742–3, d. Feb. 19th 1794, m. 1763, Lammetie Rapalje, b. May 29th, 1743, d. Oct. 16th, 1825, and had issue: Antje, b. Dec. 3d, 1763, d. Aug. 22d, 1831, single: Maria, b. Nov. 30th, 1765, d. Jan. 10th, 1785, single: Catrina, b. May 29th, 1767, d. Sept. 28th, 1831, m. Garret Vanderveer, of Flatbush: Lammetje, b. Dec. 9th, 1768, d. July 15th, 1769: Lammetje, b. April 11th, 1770, m. Cornelis Nagel: Neeltie, b. Nov. 28th, 1771, d. Jan. 14th, 1832, m. Johannes Van Nuyse, of Flatlands: Aeltje, b. June 7th, 1773, d. May 28th, 1813, m. George Van Brunt, of New Utrecht: Johannes, of Flatlands, b. March 1775, d. July 24th, 1832, m. Elizabeth Van Sinderen: *Jeromus,* of Flatlands, b. Dec. 28th. 1776: Joris, of Flatlands, b. Sept. 29th, 1778, d. Jan. 15th, 1835, m. Wilhelmina, dau. of Peter Duryea: Daniel, of Bedford, b. March 5th, 1780, d. Oct. 25th, 1826, m. Maria, dau. of Lambert Suydam, of Bedford: Hendrick, b. June 23d, 1782: and Maria, b. Dec. 1st, 1785, d. Oct. 2d, 1811, m. Abraham Lott, father of the Hon. John A. Lott, of Flatbush.

Jeromus, of Flatlands, s. of Jeromus and Lammetie, b. Dec. 28th, 1776, d. Aug. 22d, 1831, m. Ann Suydam, and had issue. Maria, b. March 7th, 1811, d. Oct. 9th, 1824: Lambert, b. Dec. 5th, 1814: and *Jane Ann,* who m. Jeremiah Bergen.

Leffert T., b. Dec. 10th, 1824; m. April 24, 1850, his cousin, Mary C.
Earle, dau. of Sylvester Earle and Ida Vanderbilt, b. March 22d, 1827.
Engaged in business in the city of N. Y. Issue Sylvester Earle, b.
March 5th, 1852; De Witt, b. Oct. 4th, 1853; Irwin, b. July 13th 1855,
Ida Vanderbilt, b. Jan. 11th, 1857; Theodore Earle, b. March 16th, 1858,
and William A., b. July 26th, 1861, d. Jan. 30th, 1862.

Theodore, b. Oct. 16th, 1827; d. Oct. 24th, 1828.

LEFFERT BERGEN, (by 2d wife,) b. July 10th, 1789; d.
Aug. 22d, 1856, of yellow fever; m. April 10th, 1833,
his cousin *Phebe*, dau. of Jacob Bergen, of Brooklyn, b.
Feb. 20th, 1805, d. July 31st, 1856, of yellow fever. Resided on and owned the northerly portion of his father's
farm, at Gowanus.

Issue:

Michael, b. Feb. 16th, 1834; d. Aug. 14th, 1834.

Jacob, b. May 22d, 1835; d. Aug. 13th, 1836.

Michael, b. Oct. 4th, 1837; d. Aug. 19th, 1856, of yellow fever.

Catharine M., b. March 12th, 1839; m. 1861, John Wyckoff.

Jacob Eldert, b. Dec. 8th, 1840; d. Feb. 21st, 1853.

Leffert L., b. June 19th, 1842.

Jeremiah S., b. Dec. 4th, 1843; d. May 16th, 1844.

Rebecca L., b. April 9th, 1846.

CATHARINE BERGEN, b. Oct. 29th, 1791; d. Oct. 2d,
1828; m. March 11th, 1818, *Garret Couwenhoven*,[*] a farmer

[*] *Garret Couwenhoven*, is a descendant of Wolfert Garretsen Van Couwenhoven, the common ancestor of the Couwenhoven, Kouwenhoven or
Conover family in this country, who emigrated from Amersfoort, in the
province of Utrecht, in Holland, in 1630, with the colonists who settled
Rensselaerwick, near Albany, where he was employed by the Patroon as
superintendent of farms. He afterwards resided on Manhattan Island,
where he cultivated the Company's bouwery or farm No. 6 and in 1637, was
enrolled among the small burghers of New Amsterdam. On the 16th of
June, 1636, Wolfert Garretsen and Andries Hudde bought of the Indians
and obtained from Gov. Van Twiller, a part of for the westernmost of the
three flats on Long Island, (small prairies,) commonly known as the Flatlands, and called by them Castuteeuw or Kaskateuw which patent was rati-
fied on the 22d of August, 1658, to which premises it appears he never removed, on which they immediately commenced a settlement and where he
died in 1662. Aug. 2d, 1639, he purchased of Hudde his interest, a house,
barrack, barn and garden, on said patent, called Achtervelt, and Sept. 16
1641, he purchased of Hudde all his interest not previously disposed of in
the original patent. Wolfert's heirs, in 1666, conveyed the main portion of
these premises to Elbert Elbertse Stoothoff. This settlement was at first
named New Amersfoort, in honor of the place of Wolfert's nativity was

of New Utrecht. b. Aug. 27th, 1791. d. Sept. 6th, 1828.

Issue :—

Rebecca Lefferts Couwenhoven, b. June 29th, 1820; m. June 27th, 1838, Edward T. Backhouse, a merchant in N. Y., residing in Brooklyn, and has

afterwards commonly known as the Baai or Bay, and since as Flatlands. Wolfert's children, who all came over with their father, were Jacob Wolphertse, d. about 1670. m. 1st Hester Jansen. m. 2d. Sept. 26th, 1655, Magdalentje Jacobs, settled in New Amsterdam, where he carried on a brewery, was one of the nine men who from 1647 to '50, represented the principal classes of the community, and in 1649, one of the agents on the part of the community to Holland: *Gerret Wolphertse*, d. about 1645. m. Altie Cornelis, dau. of Cornelis Lambertse Cool, of Gowanus, who after the death of Gerret m. Elbert Elbertse Stoothoff, he settled on a farm in Flatlands, of which town he was a magistrate, in 1644; and Peter Wolphertse. m. 1st. Dec. 2d, 1640, Hester Symons Daws. m. 2d. Nov. 22d, 1665, Aeltje Sybrants. m. 3d. May 19th. 1699. Josyntie Thomas, was also a brewer on the corner of the present Whitehall and Pearl streets, New Amsterdam, where among other offices he held that of Schepen for many years.

Gerret Wolphertse, s. of Wolfert Garretse, had issue : Willem Garretse, b. 1636, living as late as 1727. m. 1st, 1660, Altie, dau. of Joris Brinckerhoff, m. 2d, 1665, Jannetie, dau. of Pieter Montfoort, resided at first in Brooklyn, and afterwards in Flatlands: *John Gerretse,* of Brooklyn, b. 1639, m. Gerdientje, dau. of Niscasius De Sille, Fiscal of New Netherlands: Neeltie Gerritse, bap. Sep. 20th, 1641, m. 1660, Roelof Martense Schenck of Flatlands; Marritje Garritse, bap. April 10th, 1643, m. Coert Stephense Van Voorhees, and d. prior to 1709.

John Gerretse and Gerdientje or Godarina, had issue : Garret Janse, d. about 1712, m. 1st, Lysbet, m. 2d, Aeltie Janse, bap. April 28th, 1678, m. Derick Brinckerhoff: *Nicasius Janse,* of Brooklyn, bap. July 8th, 1681, d. about 1749. m. Elsje: Cornelia Janse, m. Sept. 25th, 1694, Gerrit A. Middagh; Nelly Janse, m. July 27th, 1694, Jores Rapalie.

Nicasius Janse, of Brooklyn, and Elsje had issue: Geradina, b. Aug. 7th, 1705, m. Symon Van Wickelen; John, bap. Dec. 7th, 1707, d. young; John, of Brooklyn, d. about Aug. 1775, m. Catharine Remsen; *Gerret,* of New Utrecht, d. Nov. 17th, 1783, m. Sarah; and Peter, of Raritan, N. J.

Garret, of New Utrecht, and Sarah had issue: Nicholas of New Utrecht, b. Jan. 13th, 1742, d. Oct. 1st, 1778, m. May 1761, Nelly, dau. of Petrus Van Pelt, of New Utrecht, who d. Sept. 21st, 1817; Sarah, b. Oct. 28th, 1743, m. 1766, Martin Schenck, of N. J.; *Johannes,* b. Oct. 4th, 1746, d. Sept. 13th, 1823, m. 1st, Feb. 28th, 1768, Greta Ammerman, who d. Sept. 22d, 1780, m. 2d, Aug. 3d, 1781, Elizabeth dau. of Petrus Van Pelt, of N. U., who d. March 23d, 1786, m. 3d, June 24th, 1787, Catharine Steilenwerf, who d. June 30th, 1843.

Johannes, of New Utrecht, s. of Garret and Sara, had issue: by 1st wife, Antie, b. July 23d, 1769, m. Jacobus Van Nuyse; Jannetie, b. Sept. 17th, 1771, d. Sept. 6th 1774; Sara, b. April 22d, 1774, d. April 21st, 1854, m. John Hause; by 2d wife, Gitty or Gertrude, b. June 1st, 1782, m. Jan. 8th, 1801, Ruluf Van Brunt, of New Utrecht, and living in 1863; Margaret or Greetie, b. May 24th, 1784, m. Coert Gerritsen, of Somerville, N. J.; Elizabeth, b. March 23d, 1786, single; by 3d wife, Phebe, b. March 17th, 1789, single; *Garret I.,* of New Utrecht, b. Aug. 27th, 1791, d. Sept. 6th, 1828, m. March 11th, 1818, Catharine, dau. of Micheal Bergen; Jacob, b. Jan. 11th, 1793, d. July 22d, 1826, m. Aug. 28th, 1824, Ann, dau. of Roelof Van Nuyse, no issue; Nicholas, b. Oct. 30th, 1796, d. May 29th, 1841, m. Matilda Dingee, who d. Jan. 19th, 1861.

issue: Catharine Isabella, Mary Elizabeth, Rebecca, Edward, John Cowen Loven, George, Augusta, and William Garrett

John Jacob Couenhoven, b. Nov. 8th, 1821, d. May 2d, 1853, single. Engaged in mercantile business in N. Y.

Gertrude Ann Couenhoven, b. Nov. 15th, 1824, d. Feb. 27th, 1826.

Michael Bergen Couenhoven, b. July 4th, 1826, d. Oct. 27th, 1826.

Children of DERICK BERGEN and *Mary Burum*, of Brooklyn, N. Y., and of Newark, N. J.:

CATHARINE, d. about Oct. 6th, 1826; m. *Tunis Van Brunt*, of Jamaica, who owned and occupied a farm and grist mill in Queens Co.

Issue:

John Van Brunt, b. ——, 1797, d. Jan. 1832, in Illinois, and left several children.

Joost Van Brunt, b. May 5th, 1798; d. Sept. 22d, 1850, m. Oct. 27th, 1822, Jane Cornwell. Resided in Brooklyn, and in the tavern and omnibus business; left several children.

Richard Van Brunt, b. ——, 1800, m. Nov. 11th, 1819, Maria Tuthill, d. May, 1830.

Tunis Van Brunt, bap. Sept. 21st, 1802; m. Sarah Maria Toms; m. 2d, Mary Taylor. A merchant engaged in the pork-packing business in N. Y., Chicago and Philadelphia. Has issue, among whom, a s. Theodore, who m. Jane, dau. of John Berry, of New Utrecht.

Edgar Van Brunt, bap. May 13th, 1806, d. Jan. 13th, 1841, single.

Elizabeth Van Brunt, bap. April 29th, 1808, m. April 23d, 1833, Nicholas Wyckoff, of Jamaica, Queens Co.

Jeremiah Vanderbilt Van Brunt, bap. 1810; m. Sept. 23d, 1835, Catharine Duryea; engaged in the provision business in Philadelphia and has several children.

Polly Van Brunt, bap. June 30th, 1812.

Garret Van Brunt, m. about 1837.

Rebecca Van Brunt, bap. Dec. 14th, 1815, (a twin) m. —— Conway, of Philadelphia; died leaving surviving 3 children.

Catharine Van Brunt, bap. Dec. 14th, 1815, (a twin) m. —— Weiss(?), and d. about 1862.

Elsje Van Brunt, m. ——— Thorpe, and was lost with her three children some years ago, by the burning of the steamer Erie, on lake Erie.

MARIA BERGEN, living in 1835, and single.

REBECCA BERGEN, living in 1835, and single.

JOHN BERGEN, living in 1835.

MICHAEL BERGEN, d. prior to 1835, and single.

GARRET BERGEN, d. prior to 1835, and single.

Children of CORNELIUS BERGEN and *Gertrude Suydam*, of Flatbush, N. Y. :—

JOHN C. BERGEN, b. March 7th, 1786; m. Feb. 5th, 1826, *Belinda*, dau. of Cornelius Antonides,* of Flatbush. Owns and resides in Flatbush on the farm occupied by his father.

Issue :—

Cornelia Lozier, b. July 14th, 1827; m. May 10th, 1855, Rush J. Brown.

Gertrude, b. Oct. 1st, 1829; m. Sept. 26th, 1855, Abraham Lott, of Flatbush, s. of John A. Lott.

Maria, b. Aug. 4th, 1833, single.

Cornelius J., b. Oct. 17th, 1839; m. April 12th, 1860, Anna Maria, dau. of Stephen N. Stillwell, of Gravesend.

MARIA BERGEN, b. Dec. 31st., 1787; m. Dec. 16th, 1805, *Garret Kouwenhoven*, farmer of Flatlands, where she now resides.

Issue :—

Peter Kouwenhoven, of Flatlands, b. May 21st, 1807, single; d. in 1864.

Gitty Jane Kouwenhoven, b. Oct 4th, 1809; d. Nov. 18th, 1848; m. Dec. 27th, 1826, Michael Stryker of Flatbush; left issue.

Cornelius Bergen Kouwenhoven, b. Aug. 13th, 1813; d. Sep. 28th, 1813.

Cornelius Bergen Kouwenhoven, of Flatlands, b. March 6th, 1818; m. Sept. 6th, 1838, Mary Ann, dau. of Peter Williamson; has issue.

---

*Cornelius Antonides is a descendant of the Rev. Vincentius Antonides, who arrived in this country in 1705, from Bergen, in Friesland, and who with his colleague, the Rev. Bernardus Freeman, were pastors of the Reformed Dutch Churches on Long Island for many years. Antonides d. in 1744.

Sarah Mary Ko........, b. Sept. 20..., 1-20..., D... 20th, 1845, single.

Henrietta Benson Ko.... Ko......, b. Sept. 12th, 1826 m. Charles Clarkson.

Children of TUNIS BERGEN and *Anne Vandeveer,* of Brooklyn, N. Y.:

JOHN T. BERGEN, b. 1786; d. March 9th, 1855; m. 1st, *Margaret McLeod,* dau. of Donald McLeod and Ann Masterton, who d. Oct. 1811; m. 2d, *Maria F. McLeod,* her sister.

Owned and occupied at first the farm at Bay Ridge, purchased by his father of the Cropseys; afterwards resided in Brooklyn, and for some time engaged in the grocery business, and finally occupied a farm at Batavia, New York.

Was Captain of militia in the war of 1812; in 1821 appointed Sheriff by the Council of appointment, and served until Nov. 1822, when under the new constitution of the state he was elected to said office for three years; in 1828, he was again elected for three years, and was afterward elected a member of the 22d Congress for 1832 and 1833.

Issue by 1st marriage:

Tunis J., b. April 4th, 1810; m. April 2d, 1834, Catharine, dau. of Hendrick I. Lott,* of Flatlands, who d. May 8th, 1859, by who m children:

Hendrick I. Lott, was a descendant of Johannes Lott, of New Lots, a great grandson of Peter Lott, the common ancestor of the Lott family referred to in the foot notes under the head of Jane Wyckoff, wife of Garret Bergen, and of Jane Ann Lott, wife of Jeremiah Bergen.

Johannes, of New Lots, s. of Johannes of Flatlands and grandson of Hendrick, of Jamaica, was b. Dec. 30, 1721; d. Jan. 25, 1782, m. April 6th, 1745, Jannetie Barkulos or Probasco......, s.... Anne, b. April 14th, 1746, d. May 11th, 17...; Anne, b. Sept. 1th, 1747, d. Feb. 25th, 1829, m. 1782, Henry Staats, of Albany, Jarrret, b. March 10th, 1750, d. Nov. 27th, 1800, no issue; Johannes I., of Flatlands, b. Nov. 15th, 1752, d. March 27th, 1797, (sup.) m. Ire..... Margaret Van Nuys; Cataline, b. Feb. 13th, 1755, d. April 25th, 1842, m. Tipos Vos s rler m; Christopher, b. Jan. 28th, 1758, d. Feb. 34, 1803, m. E..... Br wr, dau; *Hendrick I.,* of Flatlands, b. Oct. 3d, 1760, d. Feb. 24th, 1849, m. July 15th, 1792, Mary Brownjohn; Jannetie, b. May 2d, 1764, d. Oct. 28th, 1832.

Hendrick I., of Flatlands, s. of Johannes and Jannetie, of New Lots,

18

m. 2d, his cousin, Margaret H. dau. of Cornelius Bergen, of Gowanus. Resides in the village of Flatbush, and in 1860, President of the Lafayette Insurance Company of Brooklyn.

Children by 1st wife: John L., b. March 19th, 1835; Mary, m. Oct. 21st, 1858, George S. Prince, of Flatbush; Henry L., b. March 27th, 1839; Margaret McLeod; William, b. May 20th, 1843; Adrian, b. Dec. 3d, 1847; Eliza V.; and Kate Vernon.

Cornelius J., b. Oct. 22d, 1814; m. Nov. 4th, 1838, *Helen N. Clarke*, no issue. Owned and occupied prior to 1860, a farm in the town of Islip, near the village of Babylon, Long Island. In 1863, a resident of Brooklyn.

Alexander J., b. Oct. 22d, 1814, (a twin with Cornelius J.); m. June 3d, 1836, Eliza W. Clarke. Owned and occupied, in 1865, a farm at Islip, Suffolk Co., L. I., and in 1861, one of the representatives of said county in the Legislature of the state.

Issue by 2d marriage :—

Margaret Ann, d. Feb. 1855, m. Harry Wilber, of Batavia, and had children: Helen Eliza, Harry, Florence Margaret, and Julia Allen.

Maria C. Prall, b. 1816; d. Feb. 21st, 1843; m. Robert W. Lober; no issue.

Eliza McLeod, m. Benjamin T. Hunt and has children: Maria Bergen, Eliza McLeod, Joseph Godney, and Josephine.

Catharine Delbert, b. 1821; d. March, 1829.

Henrietta.

Emily Augusta.

Donald McLeod.

Charles Edward.

Anna Matilda.

Henrietta Cornelia, m. Augustus N. Weller, and d. without issue.

Katharine Louisa, d. 1851.

Frances Adelaide, m. Willard N. Cross, and has children: Willard Bergen, and Henrietta Louisa.

John H., b. Oct. 27th, 1838; m. June 18th, 1863, Susan N., dau. of Gen. Philip S. Crooke, of Flatbush. Resides in Flatbush and practices law in Brooklyn.

Nearly all the children of John C. Bergen, by his 2d wife, reside in the vicinity of Batavia, N. Y.

had issue: Johannes H., of Flatlands, b. Aug. 20th, 1793, m. Dec. 28th, 1817, Gashe, dau. of Simon Bergen, of Gowanus; Elizabeth, b. Oct. 25th, 1796, m. March 25th, 1818, Dr. Adrian Vanderveer, of Flatbush; and *Catharine*, b. Aug. 11th, 1814, d. May 8th, 1859, m. April 2d, 1834, Tennis J. Bergen, of Flatbush.

CORNELIUS BERGEN, b. Feb. 22d, 1790; d. Aug. 26th, 1845; m. Oct. 8th, 1818, *Catharine Sice*,* b. Aug. 15th, 1798, d. Nov. 26th, 1847.

In early life engaged in mercantile business in the city of New York, afterwards owned and cultivated the homestead farm of his father in Gowanus, which he sold to Coope and Haynes.

Was a Lieut. of Militia in the war of 1812, and afterwards Capt.; in 1838 and 1839, represented the county of Kings in the Legislature of the state. Invented a self-sharpening plow, in use and popular for years.

Issue:—

Ann Van Brunt, b. 1821.

Margaret H., b. 1823; m. Tunis J. Bergen of Flatbush.

Rebecca, b. 1825.

Eleanor E. V. B., b. 1827.

Tunis C. b. Jan., 1830; m. Nov. 8th, 1853, Sarah Case.

Robert G. M. S., b. 1833.

Cornelius J., b. 1837.

Mary Ann, b. 1839.

Adrian Vanderveer, b. 1841.

Children of PETER BERGEN and *Mary* or *Polly Schoonmaker*, of Brooklyn, N. Y. :

PETER BERGEN, b. July 25th, 1801; m. June 19th, 1819, *Ann*, dau. of Simon Bergen, of Gowanus. Commenced life in mercantile business in the city of N. Y.; afterwards owned and cultivated the northerly one-half of his father's farm, in Gowanus. Sold his farm, since which engaged in mercantile business, in Brooklyn, and in green-house cultivation in the latter place, in gardening in New Utrecht, &c., and in 1863, resided in the city of N. Y. Held the office of Lieut. Col. of horse artillery. Alderman

* Catharine Sice was a dau. of Michael Sice, of N. Y., and Catharine Hubbard, the latter a dau. of Elias Hubbard and Margaret Lake, of Flatlands.

of th 8th ward of Brooklyn, in 1846 and 1847, and Comp-
troller in 1850.

Issue :—

Simon, b. May 4th, 1820: d. Sept. 27th, 1822.

Peter, b. Jan. 15th, 1823 ; m. Ann Phillips; emigrated to California,
where he d. April 19th, 1862. leaving no surviving children.

Mary Catharine, b. Oct. 3d, 1825. m. Henry Ansell.

Jane Ann, b. Sept. 8th, 1830. m. Tunis J. Johnson, s. of Parmenus Johnson, of Brooklyn.

Virginia, b. Dec. 13th, 1832. m. George Fletcher.

MARTENUS BERGEN, b. Feb. 21st, 1811 ; m. Dec. 15th,
1835, *Maria A. Lawrence,* dau. of Charles Kane Lawrence,* of Brooklyn. b. Dec. 25th, 1816.

Cultivated several years and owned the southerly one-
half of his father's farm, at Gowanus. Removed to Port
Washington, near Shrewsbury. N. J., where he owns and
cultivates a farm. Was a Capt. of horse artillery, and
Supervisor and Alderman of the 8th Ward of Brooklyn,
for a number of years.

Issue :—

Catharine, b. Dec. 6th, 1836.

Mary, b. Feb. 24th, 1838 ; d. July 16th, 1839.

Archibald T., b. Feb. 4th, 1840.

Susan L., b. Oct. 20th, 1842.

Martenus, b. Jan. 21st, 1845.

Charles Lansing, b. Feb. 18th, 1848.

Mary, b. Sept. 5th, 1850.

John L., b. Aug. 2d, 1852.

Cornelius, b. Oct. 25th, 1855.

* *Charles Kane Lawrence,* is a descendant of John Prescott Lawrence
and Abby O'Kane, of Fort Edward, N. Y., whose parents were William
Lawrence and Prudence Prescott, of Groton, Mass.

John Prescott Lawrence, of Fort Edward. had issue: *Charles Kane* ; Archibald Kane; William Prescott; Abbey, m. J. Hasbrouck: Maria. m. P.
Wetherill: and Sarah. m. J. Willoughby.

Charles Kane Lawrence, s. of John Prescott, m. Susan Duffield, whose
mother was a Debevoise, resided in Brooklyn. and had issue: John D. ;
Archibald D. ; *Maria,* m. Martenus Bergen; Margaretta, m. L. J. Lansing:
Adeline, m. S. Walmen; Cornelia W., single ; and Emily, m. Edgar Wash-
burne.

Children of JACOB BERGEN and *Catharine Elbert*, of Brooklyn, N. Y. :

MARIA BERGEN, b. May 23d, 1801; m. April 14th 1821, *Jeremiah V. Spader*, a farmer at the Wallabout, who d. some years ago.

Issue :

Jeremiah Vanderbilt Spader, b. Sept. 20th, 1825.
Catharine Bergen Spader, b. May 2d, 1827, m. Shafer Storms.

CATHARINE BERGEN, b. Feb. 16th, 1803 ; m. Jan. 13th, 1826, *Barent Johnson*, s. of Gen. Jeremiah Johnson, a farmer, at the Wallabout, where they reside.

Issue :--

Jeremiah Johnson, b. June 22d, 1827.
Catharine Johnson, b. July 30th, 1829.
Sarah Ann Johnson, b. Jan 26th, 1832.
Jacob Bergen Johnson, b. May 22d, 1835.
Tunis Johnson, b. June 3d, 1839.

PHEBE BERGEN, b. Feb. 20th, 1805; d. July 31st, 1856, of yellow fever; m. April 10th, 1833, her cousin, *Leffert Bergen*, of Gowanus.

Issue :

Michael.
Jacob.
Michael.
Catharine M.
Jacob Elbert.
Leffert L.
Jeremiah S.
Rebecca L.
For births, &c., of the above, see Children of Leffert Bergen.

AGNES BERGEN, b. Oct. 25th, 1806, d. Aug. 31st, 1856, of yellow fever; m. Jan. 7th, 1834, *John Bergen*, s. of J. S. Bergen, of Gowanus, who also d. of the same disease,

Issue :—

Catharine Eldert.
John S.
Jacob J.
Maria.
Phebe Ann.
Margaret.
Jeremiah Spader.
Simon.
Teunis Henry.
Teunis Henry.

For births, &c., of the above. see children of John Bergen.

MICHAEL BERGEN. b. July 28th. 1809 : m. April 28th, 1836. Rebecca. dau. of *Theodorus Bergen*. of Gowanus.

Resides on. cultivates and owns the farm late of John T. Bergen. at Bay Ridge. New Utrecht.

Issue :—

Jacob M., b. Sept. 1st. 1837.
Phebe R., b. Aug. 15th. 1840.
Theodore Van Wyck, b. Aug. 29th, 1842.
Samuel, b. Sept. 22d, 1845.
Isaac M., b. Oct. 7th, 1847 : d. July 29th. 1850.
Sarah Caroline, b. Aug. 29th, 1850 : d. Dec. 6th, 1851.
Charles M., b. May 19th, 1853.

ISAAC E. BERGEN. b. July 7th, 1811 : m. 1st. Jan. 13th, 1836. *Sarah,* dau. of Theodorus Bergen. of Gowanus. who d. Jan. 12th. 1848 : m. 2d. Feb. 6th. 1850, *Ida,* sister of Sarah. who d. Aug. 17th, 1856. of yellow fever : m. 3d. Dec. 4th, 1860. *Sarah Matilda.* dau. of Evert Suydam, of New Utrecht. who d. in 1863.

Resides on and owns the farm at Bay Ridge, New Utrecht. of 70 acres. (except a portion of which he has sold.) late of Nicholas R. Van Brunt.

Issue by 1st marriage :

Jacob I., b. March 15th. 1837 : m. Sept. 22d, 1858, Cornelia M. Betts, b. July 12th, 1837. Practices law in Brooklyn, and has children : Edward J., b. March 27th. 1860. and Amelia Marion. b. March 7th. 1863.

Sarah Maria, b. Dec. 18th, 1838; m. Nov. 10th, 1859, Benjamin Midgley.

Catharine Johnson, b. Nov. 17th, 1841; d. June 9th, 1842.

Theodore Vanderbilt, b. Sept. 8th, 1843.

Michael T., b. Nov. 22d, 1845; d. Aug. 27th, 1847.

Issue by 2d marriage:

George T., b. Aug. 25th, 1853.

JOHN TUNIS BERGEN, b. April 16th, 1815; single, and resides in the 8th Ward, Brooklyn.

ELDERT BERGEN, b. May 18th, 1818; m. July 26th, 1849, *Catalina,* dau. of John Johnson, of Jamaica, b. Oct. 23d, 1827.

Owns and cultivates a farm near Jamaica, Queens Co., N. Y.

Issue :—

John Johnson, b. Jan. 17th, 1851.

George Eldert, b. April 25th, 1853; d. Oct. 20th, 1853.

Carrie Maria, b. Oct. 5th, 1856.

Margaret, b. Jan. 18th, 1859; d. July 23d, 1859.

SARAH BERGEN, b. Aug. 22d, 1820; m. June 18th, 1851, *Daniel Backus Hasbrouck.* Resides in the city of Brooklyn.

Issue :—

Louisa Hasbrouck, b. March 18th, 1853.

Julia Hasbrouck, b. March 25th, 1856.

Mary Hasbrouck, b. May 5th, 1861.

MARGARET BERGEN, b. Aug. 25th, 1822; m. Oct. 25th, 1843, *De Hart Bergen,* of Gowanus.

Issue :—

Jacob De Hart.

Marietta.

Emma.

For births, &c., of the above, see children of De Hart Bergen.

Children of JOHANNES or JOHN BERGEN and *Rebecca Stryker,* of Flatlands, N. Y. :

TUNIS BERGEN, b. Feb. 19th, 1794; d. March 3d, 1831;

m. March 19th. 1818, *Harriet* or *Adrianna*, dau. of Jacob Voorhees.* of Flatlands, b. Sept. 25th, 1797.

Resided on his father's farm in Flatlands.

Issue :—

Rebecca, b. Jan 22d, 1819 ; d. Dec. 26th, 1840, single.

Martha, b. Aug. 12th, 1821, m. Dec. 15th, 1845, Rulef Woolsey, of Flatlands, and has children. Tunis Bergen, b. Nov. 11th, 1848; Catharine, b. March 30th, 1854, d. Aug. 6th, 1854; Harriet Ann, b. Nov. 18th, 1858. Rulef Woolsey, b. Oct. 17th, 1809, and d. Feb. 6th, 1860.

Jacob Voorhees, b. March 25th, 1824 ; m. March 27th, 1845, Mary Ann Stoothoff, is a farmer in Flatlands, and has issue : Gerret Stoothoff, b. June 8th, 1845 ; Rebecca, b. Sept. 11th, 1847 ; Martha Maria, b. Jan. 4th, 1851 ; and Margaret Jane, b. March 16th, 1858.

Maria, b. Oct 2d, 1829, single.

CORNELIUS BERGEN, b. Feb. 26th, 1798 ; m. March 10th, 1825, *Fanny*, dau. of Abijah Baldwin, of Flatlands,

---

* *Jacob Voorhees*, was a descendant of Jan Lucassen, a grand son of Steven Coerte Van Voorhees, referred to in the foot note on Antie Lucassen, wife of Hans Bergen, of Jamaica.

Jan Lucassen, s. of Lucas Stevense and grand son of Steven Coerte, was bap. Feb. 19th, 1675, m. Oct. 10th, 1699, Anna Van Dyckhuysen, who d. Jan. 5th, 1702, and resided in Flatlands; m. 2d. March 5th, 1704. Mayke Schenck, who d. Nov. 25th, 1736; m. 3d. Jan. 25th, 1737, Jannetie Remsen, who d. Aug. 24th, 1747, and had issue : Johannes Lucasse, b. July 19th, 1700, m. Jan. 28th, 1737, Jannetie Remsen, who d. Jan. 24th, 1747, emigrated about 1721, to Piscataway, Somerset Co., N. J.; Lucas b. Sept. 15th, 1707, m. 1st, Altie ——, m. 2d, Mary ——, d. about 1760; Roeloff, b. Aug. 19th, 1707, d. April, 1782; Stephen, b. March 24th, 1709, m. (prob.) Oct. 23d, 1753, Maria Leake; Antie ——; Petrus ——; Martenus; Isaac, of Flatlands, bap. March 23d, 1716, m. Sarah ——; Catlyntie, b. June 8th, 1718, m. (sup) Nov. 17th, 1773, Simon Van Arsdelen; Gerrit, b. Sept. 6th, 1720; Anna, b. July 15th, 1723, m. (sup.) Oct. 3d, 1743, John Ryers, of Brooklyn; *Abraham*, of Flatlands, b. June 8th, 1724, d. prior to 1808, m. May 9th, 1747, Adrianntje Lefferts; Sarah, b. Oct 1st., 1727, d. Nov. 29th, 1736; and Maria, b. April 5th, 1731.

Abraham, s. of Jan Lucassen and Anna, had issue: Marya, b. Sept. 25th, 1749, d. Aug. 12th, 1852, m. Hendrick Vanderveer; Pieter, b. Nov. 19th, 1751, d. March 10th, 1824; Yea, b. Jan. 19th, 1754, d. March 27th, 1852, m. March 28th, 1778, Tunis Snydam, of N. U.; Jan, of Flatlands, bap. Aug. 15th, 1756, d. Oct. 5th, 1828, m. Rensie Wyckoff; Abagail, bap. Feb. 8th, 1761, m. Hugh King; *Abraham*, b. July 3d, 1765, d. Aug. 18th, 1827, m. Maria Lott; and *Jacob*, of Flatlands, b. April 4th, 1766, d. May 9th, 1804, m. June 20th, 1795, Martha Hegeman, b. March 31st, 1776, d. Feb. 14th, 1848.

Jacob, s. of Abraham and Adriantje, had issue: *Adrianna* or *Harriet*, b. Sept. 25th, 1797, m. March 19th, 1818, Tunis Bergen; Rem Hegeman, b. Dec. 25th, 1799, d. a young man, single; and Jane, b. Sept. 1st, 1803, m. Nov. 14th, 1828, Peter Hughes.

Cornelius Bergen

d. March 31st, 1865, of malignant erysipelas. Owned and resided on the Island called by the Indians Wynpaggne, containing about 90 acres of upland, located in the salt marshes of Flatlands, and at present known as Bergen's Island.

Issue :—

John C., b. Jan. 19th, 1826; m. Jan. 19th, 1858, Mary T. Brower, of Dutchess Co. Resided with his father, and has children, Cornelius, b. Dec. 2d, 1858; John Tallmage, b. Sept. 21st., 1860, and Maria Elizabeth, b. Sept. 23d, 1862.

Mary C., b. March 31st, 1828; m. Oct. 11th, 1847, Daniel Van Brunt, son of Jaques, of New Utrecht, and has children : Anna Kate, Mary Frances, Elizabeth, Jaques, Rebecca, Rulif, and Jennie.

MARIA BERGEN, b. Dec. 30th, 1799, d. Jan. 27th, 1855; m. Dec. 26th, 1820, Henry Lott, a farmer, residing in Flatland Neck.

Issue :—

John Lott, b. Oct. 5th, 1821; d. Oct. 15th, 1842.

Samuel Stryker Lott, b. Jan. 14th, 1823; m. Nov. 3d, 1848, Johanna, dau. of Samuel S. Stryker, of Gravesend.

Catharine Lott, b. April 19th, 1824; m. May 2d, 1849, Nicholas Ryder, is dead.

Rebecca Lott, b. Sept. 5th, 1827, m. Jan. 24th, 1849, John Duryea.

Maria Lott, b. Jan. 4th, 1839, m. April 8th, 1857, John H. Schenck, of Flatbush.

William Henry Lott, b. March 21st, 1841, d. Sept. 29th, 1841.

John Bergen Lott, b. April 7th, 1844.

JOHN BERGEN, b. Dec. 19th, 1802 ; m. Dec. 22d, 1825, *Helen Stoothoff,* dau. of Johannes W.,[*] of Flatlands, b.

[*] *Johannes W. Stoothoff,* was a descendant of Wilhelmus Stoothoff, the youngest s. of Elbert, and a great grand s. of Elbert Elbertse Stoothoff referred to in the foot note under Tunis Bergen and Johanna Stoothoff, of Brooklyn.

Wilhelmus Stoothoff, s. of Elbert and Johanna, resided on Flatlands, m. Nov. 9th, 1728, Altie Corte Voorhees, and had issue : Garret, b. Oct. 1st, 1730, d. Sept 22d, 1780, m. May, 1762, Mary Voorhees; Albert, b. Nov. 6th, 1735, d. Dec. 29th, 1785, m. Sept. 31, 1784, Phebe Adriance; Johannis, b. Jan. 4th, 1738, d. June 20th, 1806, m. Mar., 1759, Catharine Bogart; *Wilhelmus,* b. May 3d, 1741, d. Sept. 21st, 1803, m. Dec. 1762, Heal-

Sept. 14th, 1806. A resident and late storekeeper in the village of Gravesend.

Issue :—

Rebecca Ann, b. Dec. 15th, 1826; m. June 23d, 1847, John Cole, of New Utrecht, and since of Staten Island.

Eliza Jane, b. Dec. 2d, 1828; m. Dec. 1st, 1850, John Van Pelt Wyckoff, of New Utrecht.

John, b. June 27th, 1830; a carpenter by trade.

H d n, b. Feb. 13t , 1836, d. 1863.

Johann m, b. Sep. 2d, 1839.

Tunis, b. June 7t , 1842; a carpenter by trade.

Cornelius, b. Oct. 15th, 1846; d. March 5th, 1851.

JOHANNA BERGEN, b. Oct. 14th, 1805; d. Aug. 17th, 1851; m. June 17th, 1829, *Stephen J. Voorhees*, of Gravesend.

Issue :—

Jacobus Voorhees, b. March 27th, 1830; m. Jan. 13th, 1852, Eliza Jane, dau. of Henry Van Dyke, of Gravesend.

Rebecca Voorhees, b. July 20th, 1832; d. May 31st, 1836.

ANN BERGEN, b. Nov. 17th, 1810; m. Jan. 11th, 1830, *George Kouwenhoven*,[*] a farmer of Flatlands.

tie Voorhees, b. Aug. 27th, 1746, d. Sep. 19th, 1819; Petrus, b. July 7th, 1745, d. Aug. 22d,1750; Abraham, b. April 19th, 1750, d. Aug. 13th, 1786, m. Catharine P quart; and Perus, b. Nov. 19th, 1752, d. July 30th, 1812, m. Nov. 1773, Leah Vanderbilt.

Willielmus, s. of Willielmus and Al ie, resided in Flatlands, and had issue: Abraham, b. Jan. 9th, 1760, m. Oct. 1783, Elizabeth Bogert; Sara, b. March 8th, 1767, m. 1st, John Van Pelt, m. 2d, Rutgert W. Van Brunt, of New Utrecht, d. Aug. 29th, 1849; Willielmus, bap. Dec. 4th, 1768; Cornelius, Sept. 1 h, 1770, d. Sept. 11th, 1813, m. Aletta Van Duyne; *Johannes W.*, bap. Oct. 23d, 1774, m. Rebecca, dau. of Roelof Lott,d.——; D ew, b. Apr 12th, 1776, d. April 9th, 1826, m. Cornelia Van Sinderen, Hieltie, bap. May 10th, 1778, m. George Lott; Gerret, bap. Oct. 29th, 1780; Arttie, bap. June 18th, 1783, d. July 29th, 1848, m. John R. Lott, of Flatlands; and Jannetie, bap. Aug. 15th, 1786, m. John I. Stoothoof.

Johannes W., s. of Willielmus and Heiltie, resided in Flatlands, and had issue: Elizabeth, m. Richard Amberman; *Heltie*, m. John Bergen, of Gravesend; Willem, d. young; Cornelia, d. young; Johanna, m. James C. Rhodes, of Brooklyn; and Sara , m. Henry Harteau.

[*]*George Kouwenhoven*, is a descendant of Willem Gerretse Van Couwenhoven, a grandson of Wolf rt Garretse Van Kouwenhoven, referred to in the foot note under Catharine Bergen and Gerrit Couwenhoven, her husband.

Willem Gerretse, s. of Gerret Wolphertse, and grand son of Wolfert

Issue:—

Gerretse, was born in 1636, living as late as 1725...

Rebecca Stryker Kouwenhoven, b. April 21st, 1833, m. 1864, John Williamsen.

Tunis Bergen Kouwenhoven, b. March 10th, 1835; d. April 12th, 1835.

Tunis Bergen Kouwenhoven, b. Oct. 28th, 1836; d. May 8th, 1837.

Joanna Kouwenhoven, b. Dec. 12th, 1838.

Anna Maria Kouwenhoven, b. April 29th, 1840; d. Aug. 28th, 1840.

Ida Kouwenhoven, b. April 8th, 1842; d. Nov. 16th, 1842.

John Bergen Kouwenhoven, b. Sept. 5th, 1843.

Phebe Maria Kouwenhoven, b. Aug. 22d, 1846; d. Aug. 1st, 1847.

Sarah Dubois Kouwenhoven, b. Oct. 10th, 1848.

Peter Kouwenhoven, b. Nov. 17th, 1849.

Theresa Kouwenhoven, b. Jan. 6th, 1854; d. July 30th, 1854.

GARRET BERGEN, b. Feb. 22d, 1813; m. July 19th, 1848, his cousin, *Catharine*, dau. of Tunis T. Bergen, of Flatbush. Owns and resides on a farm in Flatlands.

Issue:—

Rebecca Maria, b. Nov. 18th, 1849.

Jane Ann, b. May 10th, 1852.

Gerretta Abna, b. July 19th, 1854.

George Tunis, b. Jan. 25th, 1859.

Children of GARRET BERGEN and *Jane Wyckoff*, of Brooklyn, N. Y.:—

TEUNIS G. BERGEN, b. Oct. 6th, 1806; m. Dec. 19th, 1827, *Elizabeth*,* dau. of Rulef Van Brunt, of Bay Ridge, N. U., b. July 24th, 1804.

Gravesend, b. Oct. 27th, 1794, m. 1st May 29th, 1917, Susan, dau. of Peter Leake, m. 2d, Altie Bennem; Peter, of Flatlands, b. June 21st, 1799, single; William, of Flatlands, b. Sept. 7th, 1802, m. Oct. 14th, 1824, Phebe, dau. of Garret Stryker, of Gravesend; Maria, b. Oct. 2d, 1803, m. Aug. 25th, 1825, John Williamsen, of Flatlands; and *George*, of Flatlands, b. April 3d, 1808, m. Jan. 11th, 1830, Ann, dau of John Bergen.

* *Elizabeth Van Brunt* is a descendant of Nicholas Rutgersz, eldest s. of Rutger Joostin Van Brunt, referred to in a foot note under Lammetie Bergen, and Rutgert Van Brunt, her husband.

Nicholas Rutgersz m. Aug. 19th, 1683, Helena, dau. of Jaques Cortelyon, the surveyor, and d. in 1684, leaving issue, *Nicholas*, bap. August 31st, 1684, d. about 1714. Helena, after the death of her 1st husband, m. 2d., Deonys Teunis, the common ancester of the Denyse family, of this vicinity, and m. 3d, Hendrick Hendrickse, and resided on part of the Nyack tract, near Fort Hamilton.

Nicholas, s. of Nicholas Rutgersz, and Helena, m. Mary, dau. of Roelof, Jansz Verkerkken, of Buuren, in Holland, who, with his father, Jan Jansen Verkerkken, and some of his brothers, emigrated in the ship Rosetree,

Resides on and owns a farm at Bay Ridge, N. U., where he has resided since 1829, and mainly occupied as a surveyor. Held the offices of Ensign, Capt., Adjutant and Lieut. Col., in the militia, and finally that of Col. of the 241st Regt. Was Supervisor of the town of New Utrecht, from April, 1836, to April, 1859, 23 years in succession, a member of the Constitutional Convention of the state in 1846, repeatedly a member of Democratic State Conventions, and a delegate to the Democratic Convention at Charleston in 1860, to nominate a candidate for the Pro-

in 1663; had issue, Nicholas, a minor, in 1717; *Roelof*, a minor, in 1717 and Jaques, also a minor, in 1717.

Roeloofe, of New Utrecht, s. of Nicholas and Mary, m. Elsie, bap. June 27, 1731, dau. of Isaac Snedker, of New Lots, said Isaac being a s. of Garret of Flatbush, and a grandson of Jan Snedeker, one of the earliest settlers of Flatbush, and the common ancestor of the Snedeker family of this country, who d. in 1679. Roeloofe d. about 1768, and had issue, Mayke, bap. May 20th, 1733, d. young; Catryna, bap. July 6th, 1735, d. young; Helena, or Lena b. 1737, m. July 23d, 1757, Richard Prest, Schoolmaster of Gravesend, an Englishman, who removed to Freehold, N. J.; Nicholas bap. Jan. 17th, 1739, m. about Dec. 1768, Tryntie or Catharine Neefus, and removed to the Raritan River, N. J.; Isaac b. Sept. 18th, 1741, d. Jan. 10th, 1808, m. Annetie or Johanna Voorhees, of N. J.; *Jaques* b. Sept. 24th, 1746, d. Aug. 20th, 1811, m. June 1773, Mary or Maria, dau. of William Johnson and Mary Monfort, of Gravesend, b. Dec. 27th, 1754, d. Dec. 31st, 1845; Mayke, bap. May 5th, 1751, m. Jan. 1769, George Neefus, m. 2d. Myers Coe; Garret, b. April 25th, 1754, settled in N. J.; Abraham, b. April 25th, 1754, (twin with Garret), d. Nov. 30th, 1828, m. Eva Wilson; Roelof, m. a Neefus, and settled in Goshen, Orange Co., N. Y.; and Sarah, m. 1st Court Van Voorhees, of N. U., m. 2d, Aert Van Pelt, of N. J., afterwards of Flatlands.

Jaques, s. of Roeloof and Elsie, resided at Bay Ridge, N. U., had issue, Maria, b. Dec. 23d, 1775, d. 1863, m. Jan 2d, 1809, Jacobus Denyse, of N. U.; *Roelf*, b. Jan. 10-16, 1777, d. Aug 12th, 1833, m. Jan. 8th, 1801, Geertie, or Gertrude, dau. of John Cowenhoven, of N. J., b. June 1st, 1782, and living in 1863; Elsie, b. May 5 1778 m. Harmanus Barkeloo, and emigrated to Butler Co., Ohio, where she d. leaving several children, who have also all d. leaving no issue; Annor Anna, b. Jan. 1st, 1781, d. May 3d, 1859, m. April 3d, 1800, Cornelius W. Bennet, of Gowanus, afterwards of Gravesend; Jane, b. May 24, 1782, d. ———, m. John Bragaw, of Newtown; Mercy or Mayke (a twin with Jane,) b. May 2d, 1783, d. an infant; Catharine, b. Aug. 15th, 1784, d. June 20th, 1856, m. May 15th, 1808, Stephen I. Voorhees, of Gravesend; Mercy or Mayke (a twin with Catharine,) b. Aug. 15th, 1785, d. May 8th, 1851, m. April 9th, 1806, Peter Wyckoff, of Gowanus; Lena or Helen b. Jan. 30th, 1788, m. June 3d, 1811, Winant I. Bennet, of Bay Ridge, N. U., and afterwards of Staten Island; and Sarah, b. Aug. 7th, 1789 m. Jacobus Van Nuyse of N. U.

Rolif, of Bay Ridge, N. U., s. of Jaques and Mary, or Maria, had issue Jaques, b. May 20th, 1802, m. Dec. 19th, 1822, Ann, dau. of Daniel Barre, of N. U.; and *Elizabeth*, b. July 24th, 1804, m. Tunis G. Bergen.

sidency, where he favored the claims of Daniel S. Dickinson, and opposed the adoption of the resolutions which caused the breach between the Northern and Southern Democracy. In 1864, he was elected Representative in Congress, for the 2d Congressional District of the state, by a majority of about 4,800.

Issue :—

Jane, b. April 24th, 1830, m. April 24th, 1851, Peter L. Cortelyou, s. of Isaac and Sarah Cortelyou, of Flatbush; they reside on a farm at Mount Pleasant, near Middletown Point, N. J., which he owns, and have children, Isaac. b. Jan. 21st, 1852; Tennis B. b. Feb, 22d, 1855; John b. Dec. 12th, 1857, and Elizabeth b. Feb. 24th, 1861, d. July 12th, 1864.

Gertrude, b. Oct. 9th, 1831, d. July 16th, 1865, of typhoid fever, m. Oct. 6th, 1853, William G. Kouwenhoven, son of George Kouwenhoven, of Flatlands, at which place they resided on a farm, and have children; Tennis B., b. Sep. 13th, 1854; Anna, b. Dec. 28th, 1855, and Elizabeth Bergen, b. ———. 1865.

Garret T., b. July 4th, 1833, m. April 10th, 1856, Sarah, dau. of Isaac *

---

* *Isaac Cortelyou* was a descendant of Jaques, the eldest s. of Jaques Cortelyou, the surveyor, the common ancestor of the Cortelyou family in this country, referred to in the foot note under the head of Derick Bergen, and Deborah Cortelyou his wife.

Jaques, s. of Jaques, the surveyor of New Utrecht, m. 1st, Marretie Hendricks Smock, and m. 2d, Altie, d. about 1732; issue, Altie or Meeltje, b. 1691; Geertji, b. 1693, m. Hendrick Van Leauwen; Helena, b. 1695, d. prior to 1726; Jaques, b. Sept. 26th, 1697, d. April 4th, 1705; Hendrick, b. 1699, d. 1705; Neetji, b. 1703; Marya, b. 1706; *Jaques*, b. 1707, d. 1765, m. Mary; Hendrick, b. 1711, m. 1st, Antie Voorhees, m. 2d, Catryna, emigrated to Somerset Co., N. J., and is the common ancestor of what may be termed the New Jersey Cortelyous; Dyna, b. 1715; Frederick, b. Nov. 1716; and Altie b. 1722; the three last not being mentioned in the will of their father, all probably d. before its date in 1726.

Jaques of N. U., s. of Jaques and Marretie of N. U., b. 1707, d. 1765, had issue; Jaques, b. Oct. 8th, 1731, d. Sept. 20th, 1747; Antie, b. 1733, m. Col. Rutgert Van Brunt, of Gravesend; and *Isaac*, b. Aug. 11th, 1736, d. Oct. 3d, 1811, m. Altie Repalje.

Isaac of N. U., s. of Jaques and Mary of N. U., had issue, Martha, b. April 21st, 1767, d. Jan. 7th, 1850, single; Jaques, b. March 21st, 1768, d. April 26th, 1821, insane and single; Aletta, b. July 13th, 1769, m. Albert O'Blenis; Angletie, b. Oct. 7th, 1770, d. Dec. 15th, 1826, m. April 12th, 1792, Leffert Martense, father of the late Garret L. Martense of Flatbush; *John or Johannes*, of Flatbush, b. Feb. 2d, 1772, d. June 27th, 1855, insane, m. July 3d, 1794, Catharine, dau. of Peter Lefferts, of Flatbush; Isaac, b. Dec. 20th, 1774, d. May 29th, 1839, insane and single; Daniel, b. Sep. 13th, 1777, d. Feb. 2d, 1823, single; and Hendrick, b. March 11th, 1779, d. single.

John or Johannes, of Flatbush, s. of Isaac and Altie, of N. U., had issue.

and Sarah Cortelyou, of Flatbush, b. Jan. 1st, 1831, resided in 1860 on a
farm near Keyport, N. J.; in 1863, on the farm of his father, at Bay Ridge,
N. Y., and has children. Teunis G., b. Feb. 20th, 1857; John G., b. May
14th, 1858; Jaques Van Brunt, b. Sep. 12d, 1859; and Francis H., b.
May 7th, 1862.

Leonard A., b. April 27th, 1835; d. Nov. 6th, 1836.

Elizabeth C., b. April 13th, 1837.

Johanna, b. April 1st, 1839.

Van Brunt, b. April 29th, 1841; graduated as a civil engineer at the
Rensselaer Institute, of Troy, N. Y.

Leonard, b. April 23d, 1844; d. Jan. 8th, 1846.

PETER G. BERGEN, b. March 31st, 1808, d. Aug. 2d,
1865; m. 1st, May 1st, 1837, *Jane* dau. of Van Brunt
Magaw,* of Gravesend, b. Sept. 7th, 1814, d. Jan. 6th,

Peter Lefferts, b. Feb. 15th, 1796, d. Nov. 14th, 1801; *Isaac*, of Flatbush,
b. Oct. 8th, 1797, d. Nov. 10th, 1845, m. Nov. 22d, 1819, Sarah, dau. of
Timothy T. Cortelyou, of N. U.; Jacob, b. Oct. 16th, 1799, d. Dec. 26th,
1800; Aletta, b. Aug. 5th, 1801, d. Aug. 16th, 1822 single; and Jane, b.
Aug. 5th, 1801, (a twin with Aletta,) died Nov. 2d, 1806.

Isaac, of Flatbush, s. of John or Johannes and Catharine, had issue
Catharine Lefferts, b. April 12th, 1821, m. Oct. 13th, 1858, William K.
Williamson, of Flatlands; Timothy T., b. Aug. 1st, 1822, d. of issue; John,
b. March 12th 1824, d. March 30th, 1851, single, and a lawyer by profession; Isaac, b. Dec. 10th, 1825, d. Oct. 6th, 1826; Anna K. C., April 4th,
1828, m. Jan. 27th, 1859, Horatia G. Onderdonk, of Manhasset, Queens
County; Peter L. b. Nov. 6th, 1829, m. April 24th, 1851, Jane dau. of
Teunis G. Bergen, of Bay Ridge; Isaac, b. Jan. 16th 1832, d. April 16th,
1841; Sarah T., b. Jan. 1st, 1834, m. April 10th, 1856, Garret T. Bergen,
s. of Teunis G. Bergen, of Bay Ridge; and Jacob Lefferts, b. May 2d,
1836, m. Sep. 14th, 1856, Adeline Brower.

* Van Brunt Magaw, b. Sept. 7th, 1783, d. March 18th, 1831, m. March
14th, 1795, Adrianus, b. March 14th, 1795, d. April 1st, 1851, dau. of
Lawrens Voorhees, of Flatbush, b. Aug. 23d, 1769, and Jannetie dau.
of Samuel Gerretsen, said Lowrens kingst s. of Arcyon Voorhees, of
Flatbush and Adriantje Hobbert, a grandson of Albert Lowrens Voorhees
and Arrije antie Ditmarse, and a great grandson of Lowes Stevens Voorhees and Jannetie Mennes. Van Brunt Magaw was the only s. of Col.
Robert Magaw, of the Revolutionary war, who d. at Carlisle, Penn., in
1795, and who m. April, 1773, Marietje, b. Jan. 30th, 1762, d. Aug. 1st,
1803, dau. of Col. Rutgert Van Brunt and Alta Cortelyou, who two thirds
resided on the Pennoyer patent, now, 1864, of Samuel Smith, in Gravesend. Said Rutgert, (who was s. of Cornelis Rutgerts referred to in the
foot note under Rutgert Van Brunt and Lammetje Brunt, had issue
Elizabeth, b. Nov. 9th, 1758, d. Jan. 27th, 1761; Marietje b. Jan. 30th,
1762, d. Aug. 15th, 1803, m. Col. Robert Magaw; Rutgert, b. March 8th,
1764, d. Feb. 14th, 1768; Jaques, b. April 30th, 1766, d. June 5th, 1771;
Rutgert b. Aug. 8th, 1768, d. Nov. 14th, 1769; Ann, b. Nov. 9th, 1771,
d. April 2d, 1782; Elizabeth, b. Aug. 20th, 1774, m. June 22d, 1817, t
George Cowenhoven, of N. U.; Catharine, b. April 2d, 1775, d. Feb. 19th

1854; m. 2d, Jan. 12th, 1858, *Phebe Ann*, sister of Jane, b. March 21st 1822. d. Feb. 16th, 1861, by whom no issue.

Resided on the corner of 3d avenue and 18th street, Brooklyn, and engaged in mercantile business in the city of N. Y. From 1841 to 1846, was one of the associate Judges. of the County Courts, in Kings Co., N. Y.; 1841. Supervisor of the 8th and 9th Wards of the city of Brooklyn, and a member of the Board of Education of the city since its organization.

Issue by 1st marriage :

Van Brunt Magaw, b. March 4th, 1839; d. June 8th, 1865. Shortly after the rebellion broke out, he joined the 13th regiment of National Guards of Brooklyn, who at the time were stationed at Annapolis, Md., thence removed to Baltimore, and at the expiration of their three months' service, returned to Brooklyn. In the fall of the same year he accompanied his regiment to Suffolk, Va. Before the three months expired for which the regiment was engaged, he accepted a 1st Lieutenancy in the 131st Metropolitan regiment, of N. Y., which was mustered into service on the 9th of September, 1862, and shortly after sailed for Annapolis, Md., where they were detailed to guard some ten thousand paroled rebel soldiers. From thence with his regiment he accompanied Gen. Banks' expedition to La., and arrived at New Orleans on the 15th of December. They were engaged in the various expeditions of Gen. Banks' department at Baton Rouge, Donaldsonville, Brashear City, on the Teche, Franklin, Vermillion Bayou, Alexandria on the Red river, and Port Hudson. From the latter place, on its surrender, his regiment removed to Carrolton and Brashear City, and through nearly the whole of this campaign he was constantly exposed and always to be found where duty called him, acting as Adjutant. At Brashear City he was Post Adjutant for several months and afterwards filled the office of Assistant Quarter Master and Assistant Inspector General of the

1826. m. John Garretsen, of Gravesend; and Ann, b. Nov. 15th, 1777. d. Nov. 21st, 1795.

Van Brunt Magaw and Adrianna had issue: Mary, m. Rev. Isaac Labagh; Jane, m. Peter G. Bergen; Catharine Aletta, m. Van Brunt Wyckoff; Phebe Ann, m. Peter G. Bergen; Robert, m. Alice Devenport; Lawrence V., m. Lemma, dau. of Peter Wyckoff, and sister of Van Brunt Wyckoff; and Lott, who is single.

Col. *Robert Magaw* and Marietta had issue. Elizabeth, b. Jan. 8th, 1780. d. Aug. 14th, 1803, m. Peter McCarty; and *Van Brunt*.

V. B. M. Bergen Lieut

La Fourche military district. While employed on this duty he regiment was ordered north and sent to the Shenandoah valley, under the command of Gen. Sheridan. He was however detained by Gen. Cameron, who was in command of the La Fourche district as Assistant Inspector General until Gen. Canby superseded Gen. Banks, who decided that this position should be filled by a line officer, and not by one of inferior rank. Gen. Cameron then appointed him Ordinance Officer, with his head-quarters at Thibadeaux, where he remained until ordered north to join his regiment in the Shenandoah valley ; on which, after an absence of two years, he visited the home of his childhood, and on hearing of the battles of Sheridan, in which his regiment was engaged in the valley, he hurried off to join them, and participate in the laurels they were winning. While on his way he was detained at Harper's Ferry in assisting the movement to Sheridan of a provisional detachment of some twenty-two hundred men, of which on Col. Kitchen, (an old school-mate,) being appointed commander, he was appointed Ordinance Officer, a responsible position, in which, together with all the offices he held, he performed his duty faithfully and to the satisfaction of his superiors. In the Shenandoah valley he contracted a heavy cold, which fell on his lungs, producing consumption ; the change from the warm climate of the south being too great for his system ; on which on the 10th day of Dec., 1864, he obtained a furlough, and returned home to breathe his last among his sympathising friends.

Garret P., b. June 18th, 1842, m. Sept. 3d, 1863, C. Louisa, dau. of John Morrison, of Brooklyn. Engaged in mercantile business in the city of N. Y.

Adriana, b. May 30th, 1845.

LAMMETIE or LEMMA BERGEN, b. Oct. 6th, 1812 ; m. Jan. 15th, 1834, *Teunis S. Barkeloo,** of Brooklyn, b.

---

* *Teunis S. Barkeloo*, is a descendant of Jaques Barkeloo, referred to in a following foot note under the head of John G. Bergen and Elizabeth Barkeloo his wife, which was a son of Harmanus and Sara, a grandson of William Williamse and Maria, and a great grandson of William Janse Van Borkelo, the emigrant.

Jaques Barkeloo resided at Bay Ridge, N. Y., was b. Feb 21st 1747, d. April 8th, 1815, m. 1st, Catharine, dau. of Hendrick Suydam, July 5th 1753, d. May 24th, 1788, m. 2d, Feb. 1791 Maria Bogert, who after the death of Jaques m. Simon Cortelyou, of N. Y., and d. Sept. 9th, 1841 aged nearly 73. Jaques had issue by his 1st wife Sarah, b. June, d. 1771, m. Johannes Ross, and emigrated to Ohio ; Feet b. Nov. 22d, 1776 d. April 26th, 1826, m. 1st, a Van Dyck, of Gravesend, by whom no issue, m. 2d. Jan. 20th, 1802, Adriantie or Harriet, dau. of Teunis Styou m. of N. Y., who d. June 5th, 1828 ; Harmanus m. Eliza dau. of Jaques Van Brunt, of N. Y., emigrated to Ohio, where he and all his children d. Henry, m. Cornelia, dau. of Winant Bennet, of N. Y. emigrated to Ohio,

20

April 21st, 1803.   Resides on 3d avenue, near 35th street, Brooklyn.

Issue :—

Harriet Barkeloo, b. Nov. 22d, 1835; m. May 5th. 1856, Charles E. Buckingham. and resided in California.

Johanna Barkeloo, b. July 2d, 1837.

Lemma Barkeloo. b. March 26th. 1840.

JOHN G. BERGEN, b. Dec. 4th. 1814; m. Sept. 21st 1835, *Elizabeth*, dau. of Harmanus Barkeloo,* of Brooklyn, formerly of N. U., b. June 22d, 1813.

where he d., but his wid. and children returned to Long Island: Jaques L. bap. Nov. 5th. 1780. m. Mary, dau of Thomas Pearsall, of Brooklyn, emigrated to Ohio; John, bap. Feb. 19th. 1786, emigrated to Ohio; Catharine, m. Wiggins, and emigrated to Ohio: issue by 2d wife: Margaret, b. Jan. 16th, 1798, m. Jacob Wardell, d. Aug. 11th, 1834; and Maria, bap. July 6th. 1791, d. single.

Evert, s. of Jaques and Catharine, was at first a storekeeper at Bay Ridge. N. U., and afterwards engaged in mercantile business in Brooklyn. Had issue by 2d wife: *Teunis S.*, b. April 23d. 1803, m. 1st, Catharine, dau. of Simon Bergen of Gowanus, who d. May 10th. 1832, m. 2d, Lemma, dau. of Garret Bergen of Gowanus; Cornelia, b. Oct. 8th. 1805, d. Oct. 27th, 1806; Catharine, b. July 12th, 1807, d. Sept. 22d. 1807; Eida, b. Nov. 29th. 1803, d. Sept. 23d. 1818; and John, b. Nov. 21st, 1820, emigrated to California.

* Harmanus Barkeloo, was a descendant of William Janse Van Borkeloo, or from Bored o, Borkulo, Borkelo, and anciently written Borkeloe and Boreeloe, an extensive community near Zutphen, in the province of Gilderland in the Netherlands, who m. 1st, a lady whose name has not been ascertained. m. 2d. about 1666, Lysbeth or Elizabeth Jans, a widow, who previously m. 1st, Christoffel Jans, by whom a s. Johannes Christoffel, and m. 2d, Jan Cloesen. He emigrated to this country from Borkeloo in the earldom of Zutphen, Holland, residing at first in New Amsterdam, following the occupation of a butcher, afterwards removing to Flatlands, d. Nov. 1683, and had issue Jannetie Williamse, of Flatlands m. May 18th. 1679, Jan Barentse Van Driest, the ancestor of the Johnsons, of Gravesend, and of Gen. Jeremiah Johnson, of the Wallabout; Cornelia Williamse, Jan Williamse, of Gravesend, who took the oath of allegiance in 1687; *Willie Williamse*, of Flatlands, m. Maria dau. of Jaques Cortelyou, the surveyor, took the oath of allegiance in 1687, will dated April 2d, 1745; Dirk, b. in Flatlands, m. Sept. 17th, 1709, Jannetje Van Aersdalen; David bap. March 31st, 1678; and Coenrad, bap. Dec. 5th, 1680. In Feb. 1662, William Janse was on a visit at his native place in Holland, and returned in June of the same year, accompanied by his brother Harmen Janse, who may not previously have been in New Netherland, and who had a son Hans Harmense, who settled in New Utrecht, and with his sister Jannetje came over in 1658.

Willeam Willianse, s. of William Janse, resided in N. U. on the portion of the Nyack tract which his wife inherited from her father, and had issue: Jaques, who emigrated to N. J.; Wilmitien, living in 1709: *Har-*

Resides and owns a part of the house he occupies at G
wanus; was a member of Assembly of the .... and
Supervisor of the 8th and 9th Wards of Bro...
1846, 1849 and 1850, and of the 8th Ward in 18...
since its first establishment, one of the ....
the Metropolitan Police District, composed ... ...
New York and Brooklyn and surrounding ....

Issue:

Jno. Wyckoff, b. June 3d, 1838; d. June 26th, 18

Winnie Henry, b. Jan. 10th, 1840; m. Oct. 15th ... ...
of William Spader, of Middletown Point, N. J. ... ...
City of Brooklyn.

Jno. Wyckoff, b. Jan. 26th, 1841.

...... m. Sarah Terhune, and whose will is dated Sept ...
Helen, whom, Michael Blouw, and removed to N. J.
Hendricks, s. of Wm. Williamse and Maria, resided in S. ...
Maria, m. May 27th, 1719, Casper Crops ..., Gerb. ...
the passage, and the ancestor of the Crops ....
...... d. Nov. 10th, 1788, at Somerville, N. J., ...
1675, Elizabeth Duryea; Johannes, bap. Sept. 1 ...
ma., b. May 5th, 1739, d. May 29th, 1819 in J...
of N. Y.; Sarah, b. June 14th, 1741, m. Nov. 5th 1...
.... of New York; and Jaspers, b. Feb. 21st, 174...
..... 1st Catharine, dau. of Hendrick Suy an...
1788, m. 2d, Feb. 1790, Maria Bogert.
Henricks, s. of Hermanus and Sara, resided in N. J...
Sarah, bap. April 1st, 1766, m. Rev. Peter S.....
7th, 1768, d. an infant; Catharine, bap. Jan.....
Clerk of Red Hook; Harmanus, bap. Aug. 3...
...... H., b. Nov. 3d, 1773, d. Aug. 1776, 1812 ... M...
s Mayor, of N. Y., b. June 11th, 1780, d. May...
Nov. 17th, 1775, m. Hannah Seward, was ... ...
...... b. and father of the late Judge Barst.....
James, bap. July 26th, 1778, m. Catharine Ir...
18.., 1780, single and living in 1867; El...
...... ly d. young; and Nancy, b. May 1...
.... rneus Duryea.
Hermanus H., s. of Harmanus and I. ... ...
.... Iron works in Brooklyn, had issue: H....
Sept. 9th, 1805; Harmanus, b. June 15t ...
.. Potter, of N. J., resides in Louisiana; H ...
14, 1833, Elias H. Hubbard; Tunis Suy...
...th, 1851, single; Elizabeth, b. June 22d, 18...
...., b. Aug. 28th, 1815, single; Abraham ... S...
.... 1845, Aurelia M. Merrit, resides in N. J. ...
... June 24th, 1847, Isaac P. Gennings; ...
.... William, b. Sept. 16th, 1826, m. Jan. 18...
.. South Carolina, and who d. March 30th, 18...
.. wife.

Maria Adriana, b. Nov. 15th, 1842.
Frances Henrie, b. April 5, 1844.
Edward, b. Oct. 20th, 1846; d. Feb. 8th, 1847.
Herman Suydam, b. Sept. 25th, 1848.
Sarah Elizabeth, b. Sept 9th,1850.

GARRET G. BERGEN, b. April 6th, 1817; m. Oct. 14th,
1841, *Mary*, dau. of Elias Hubbard,* of Flatlands, b.
Jan. 23d, 1819, d. Dec. 5th, 1858; m. 2d, April 17th,
1861, *Sarah*, dau. of Garret P. Conover and Sarah Hubbard, (dau. of Elias and sister of Mary,) of Middletown
Point, N. J.

Resides on and owns a part of the homestead farm of
his father, at Gowanus.   Was Supervisor of the 8th Ward
of Brooklyn, in 1860.

Issue by 1st marriage :

Tennis G., born May 17th, 1847.
Huldah Holmes, b, Feb. 11th, 1851.
Mary Jane, b. Dec. 16th, 1854 ; d. Aug. 23d, 1855.
Ella, born Jan. 1st, 1856; d. July 19th, 1856.
Elias H., b. Nov. 17th, 1858; d. Dec. 30th, 1858.

By 2d marriage :

Francis Henry, b. May 14th, 1863.
John W. Holmes, b. Nov. 6th, 1864.

* *Elias Hubbard*, of Flatlands, a descendant of Henry Hubbard, referred
to in the foot note under John S. Bergen, and Mary or Polly Hubbard,
his wife, was born Dec. 1st, 1776, living in 1863; m. Jan. 14th, 1801,
Huldah Holmes, of Monmouth Co., N. J., b. Oct. 27th, 1779, d. April
4th, 1851; had issue : Ellen, b. Jan 28th, 1803, m. Dec. 7th, 1820, Nicholas
R. Van Brunt, of N. U., and since of Brooklyn ; Sarah, b. May 22d, 1805,
m. ——, Garret P. Conover, of N. J.: Elias H., b. Sept. 26th, 1807, m.
Mar. 4th, 1833, Ida Barkeloo, d. Sept. 5th, 1845 ; Asher Holmes, b. Nov.
17th, 1809, m. Oct. 27th, 1840, Catharine Amelia Pearsall ; John H., b. Mar.
28th, 1812, single; Margaret, b. Jan. 18th, 1815, m. May 10th, 1848,
Peter P. Conover, of Keyport, N. J.: James, b. Feb. 19th, 1817, single ;
Mary, b. Jan. 23d, 1819 ; d. Oct. 5th, 1858, m. Oct. 14th, 1841, Garret G.
Bergen ; and Catharine Holmes, b. April 8th, 1821, d. Dec. 5th, 1825.

Garret G.W Bergen

Children of TUNIS T. BERGEN, by his 1st wife, *Nelly Martens*, and by his second wife, *Jane B. Stillwell*, of Flatbush, Long Island:

By 1st wife:

JOHANNAH BERGEN, b. June 15th, 1804; m. Dec. 25th, 1821, *Nicholas William on*, of Flatlush, b. Nov. 12th, 1798, d. Aug. 23d, 1842. She resides on the farm purchased by her late husband, in Flatlands.

Issue:

Eleanor Williamson, b. Nov. 6th, 1822; m. Feb. 24, 1842, John S. Brown, of Flatlands, and has children, 3 sons and 1 dau.
Elizabeth Martens Williamson, b. Oct. 5th, 1827; d. Sept. 29th, 1851.
Jane Ann Williamson, b. July 28th, 1830; d. Oct. 19th, 1830.
William Williamson, b. Mar. 20th, 1835; m. — 1863. Ryter

ADRIAN BERGEN, b. Nov. 24th, 1806; m. May 28th, 1828, *Eliza*, dau. of John or Johannes Van Nuyse,[*] of Flatlands, b. May 11th, 1807.

Resides on and owns a farm in N. U., inherited from his grandfather, Adrian Martense. Held the office of Justice of the Peace and Captain in the militia.

* John or Johannes Van Nuyse was a descendant of Jan or Jacques Jansen Van Nuyse, commonly written on our old records, Auke Jansen, the common ancestor of the Van Nuyse family in this country. Auke Jansen, with his wife, Magdalena Pieterse, and some of his children, emigrated about 1651, from Amsterdam, in Holland, to New Amsterdam, now New York, and was by trade a carpenter, which occupation he followed in this country. His birth place was probably the village of Nuys, in the union containing 78 houses and 150 inhabitants. ... Van Nuyse. Jan 12th, 1653, he purchased a house and lot on the west side of the great highway in New Amsterdam ... on May of the same year. In 1654 he was engaged as constable ... of the first church in Midwout (Flatbush), which was formed about 1660. In 1661 he resided at ... from Holland ... and about 1665 finally settled in Flatbush of which place ... was ... in 1673, and one of the representatives of the town at a convention of delegates from the Dutch towns held at New Orange, New York, on the — day of March, 1674, to confer with Gov. Colve. On the death of his wife Magdalena, he m. 2d, in — 1666, Lysbeth Jans, who d. July Catrina and m. 3d, — Gurtie, wid. of Jan Jansen ... his last two wives. Had issue by 1st wife, Antone Auerse, b. Dec. 4th, 1661, Winant Pieterse Van E..., b. 21, ... Jan Workman, of Brooklyn; Gertruyd Aukersz, ...

Issue :—

John Van Nuyse, b. April 25th, 1829; m. Dec. 23d, 1852, Jane Ann, dau. of Charles Lott, of N. U.,* cultivates a part of his father's farm in N. U.

Eliza Eden, b. Jan. 16th, 1833; m. June 3d, 1852, Dr. James E. Dubois, who d. Sept. 13th, 1856, of yellow fever, having issue: Francis Adrian, and Sarah Louisa.

Jannetje Aukersz, m. 1666, Rienier Arendsz, whose will is dated in 1700; Jan Aukersz, b. in Amsterdam, resided in Flatbush, m. 1st, July ———, 1673, Barbara Provoost, m. 2d, April 4th, 1680, Eva Janse, dau. of Jan and Gurtje Jacobse; Peter Aukersz, bap. Oct. 13th, 1652; Abigail Aukersz, m. Leffard Pieterse, the ancestor of the Leffert family of this vicinity; *Jacobus Aukersz*, of N. U., m. April 26th, 1685, Maria or Mary Willems; and Femmetje Aukersz, bap. Mar. 4th, 1662, m. Oct. 8th, 1680, Jan Stevense Voorhees.

Jacobus Aukersz, of N. U., at one period resided in Flatbush, had issue: *William*, of N. U.; Auken, of N. U., m. Dec. 1, 1715, Aeltje Ammerman; Jan of N. U.; Isaac; Magdalena; Maregrieta; Elizabeth; Maria; and Jacobus.

William, of N. U., s. of Jacobus Aukersz, had issue: *William or Wilhelmus*, of N. U., who m. Magdalena Joost; Jan, of N. U., m. Mar. 17th, 1716, Adriaantje Wyckoff.

William, s. of William of N. U., had issue: William or Wilhelmus, d. Sept. 12th, 1779, m. Mar 30th, 1751, Annatje, dau. of Jan Verkerk; *Joost or George*, of Flatlands, bap. Sep. 16th, 1716; d. about 1792; m. April 26th, 1744, Elizabeth Emmans; and Jacobus, of N. U., m. Sarah, dau. of Tunis Raphalje.

Joost or George, s. of William and Magdalena, had issue; Sarah, bap. August 19th, 1750; m. ———, 1781, William Van Nuyse, her cousin; Wilhelmus, bap. March 8th, 1752, and b. in April, d. Sept. 25th, 1805, m. Nelly Hubbard, b. ———, 1757, d. Feb. 13th, 1832; Joost, m. Jane, dau. of Peter Vanderbilt, of N. U.; Elizabeth, b. Feb. 2d, 1762, d. July 25th, 1851, without issue, m. Jan. 18th, 1801, Winant Bennet, of Yellow Hook, N. U.; *Johannes*, of Flatlands, b. Nov. 25th, 1763, d. Oct. 16th, 1826, m. ———, Nelly Lott, b. Nov. 28th, 1771, d. Jan. 11th, 1832; Jacobus, d. single; Hellen, m. 1764, Jacob Stellenwerf.

Johannes, s. of Joost and Annatje, had issue: George, of Flatlands, b. Sept. 10th, 1802, d. Sept. 11th, 1831, m. April 12th, 1827, Margaret, dau. of John Ditmars, of Flatlands, and left surviving a dau., Cornelia D., who m. J. Holmes Van Brunt, of N. U.; Jeromus, of Flatlands, b. Jan. 2d, 1805, d. Sept. 29th, 1852, m. Jan. 10th, 1838, Ann Eliza Brinkerhoff, b May 8th, 1813, and left no issue; *Eliza*, b. May 11th, 1807, m. May 28th, 1828, Adrian Bergen, of N. U.; Lemma, b. July 24th, 1809, m. Dec. 29th, 1835, Cornelius Suydam, of Flatbush; Maria, b. March 24th, 1810, d. Sept. 1st, 1863, single; Eleanor, born Jan. 15th, 1813, d. Jan. 25th, 1853; m. March 4th, 1833, Tunis Bergen, of N. U.; and Magdalen, b. Sept. 23d, 1816, m. Dec. 28th, 1842, Garert Convenhoven, of N. U.

* *Charles Lott*, is a descendant of Abraham Lott, of Flatbush, s. of Englebert, and grandson of Peter, the common ancestor of the Lott family of this vicinity, referred to in the foot note under Jane Wyckoff, wife of Gerrit Bergen.

Abraham Lott, of Flatbush, b. Sept. 7th, 1684, d. July 29th, 1754, m. Nov. 15th, 1709, Catharine, dau. of Elbert Hegeman, b. Nov. 11th, 1691,

JANE BERGEN, b. Sept. 15th, 1808; m. Oct. 23d, 1827, *Joseph R. Crommelin*, of Brooklyn, b. Feb. 25th, 1798, d. Oct. 4th, 1858.

Issue:

Adrian Martens Crommelin, b. Sept. 25th, 1828; m. Nov. 26th, 1863, Maria, dau. of James Van Nuyse, of N. U.

Charles John Crommelin, b. Oct. 27th, 1829; d. Jan. 13th, 1855.

Theodore Crommelin, b. Aug. 23d, 1831; m. Sept. 16th, 1862, Ann Eliza Downs, and has children: Susan Downs and Amelia Louisa, twins, b. Aug. 11th, 1863.

Richard Crommelin, b. Sept. 4th, 1833; d. Aug. 14th, 1834.

Mary Jane Crommelin, b. Feb. 24th, 1835.

Amelia Ellen Crommelin, b. July 10th, 1837.

Joseph R. Crommelin, b. June 22d, 1840; d. June 17th, 1841.

Harriet Ann Crommelin, b. Jan. 23d, 1844.

Gertrude Elizabeth Crommelin, b. Jan. 18th, 1847.

Maurice Dwight Crommelin, b. Jan. 25th, 1851.

d. Nov. 19th, 1741, and had issue: *Jacobus*, d. 1757, m. Teuntie, dau. of Simon De Hart, of Gowanus; Englebert, b. May 7th, 1719, d. Nov. 17th, 1779, m. Dec. 4th, 1742, Maritie, dau. of Johannes Ditmers, b. Jan. 8th, 1723, d. April 17th, 1797, whose great grandson is the present Judge John A. Lott, of Flatbush; Abraham, who m. Gertrude, dau. of Andrew Coeyman; and Cornelia, who m. John Vanderveer, of Keuter's Hook.

Jacobus, s. of Abraham and Catharine, had issue: Simon, of N. U., b. Feb. 24th, 1742, d. Dec. 1st, 1807, m. March 1770, Annatie, dau. of Jacobus Van Nuyse, b. March 2d, 1753, d. Aug. 24th, 1832; Maryke, bap. Aug. 9th, 1747; Jacobus, bap. July 7th, 1752; Abraham, bap. Aug. 13th, 1753; Angenietje; Catharine, and Jan.

Simon, of N. U., s. of Jacobus and Teuntie, had issue: *Jacobus*, of the Wallabout, b. April 2d, 1771, d. Sept. 8th, 1831, m. Feb. 16th, 1804, Jane Titus, b. May 7th, 1785, d. April 20th, 1843; Sarah, b. July 10th, 1774, d. 1853, m. Oct. 24th, 1793, John Denyse, of N. U.; and Anna, bap. May 9th, 1782.

Jacobus, of the Wallabout, s. of Simon and Annatie, had issue: *Clarissa*, of N. U., b. Nov. 11th, 1806, m. Jan. 27th, 1829, Helen Ryder, Anna, b. Oct. 12th, 1808, m. Nov. 26th, 1828, Andrew Stockholm, Sarah, b. Feb. 1st, 1811, m. Dec. 5th, 1832, Sylvester W. Brower, Catharine, b. June 4th, 1814, m. May 27th, 1834, John Titus, Jane, a twin with Catharine, June 4th, 1814, d. April 6th, 1834, single; James, b. Dec. Aug. 8th, 1842, Augusta Rogers, m. 2d, July 3d, 1850, Catharine M. Gerrick, Simon, b. Dec. 25th, 1822, m. Nov. 5th, 1856, Jane Walters; Frances, b. Sept. 15th, 1844, Amelia Van Allen; and Aaron, of N. U., b. April 12th, 1828, m. Sept. 15th, 1841, Cynthia, dau. of Jeremiah E. Lott, of N. U.

Charles, of N. U., s. of Jacobus and Jane, had issue: James C., b. Oct. 14th, 1829, m. Sept. 30th, 1854, Phebe M. Snyder; Jacobus, b. Sept. 27th, 1834, m. Dec. 23d, 1852, John V. N. Bergen; Catharine A., b. May 9th, 1839, m. Nov. 17th, 1858, Bernard Lawrence, of N. U. and Sarah Elizabeth, b. April 7th, 1843.

TUNIS BERGEN, b. Dec. 25th, 1810; m. 1st, March 5th, 1833, *Ellen*, dau. of John or Johannes Van Nuyse, of Flatlands, b. Jan. 13th, 1813, d. Jan. 25th, 1853; m. 2d, Dec. 18th, 1855, Eliza, dau. of Alonzo G. Hammond, of Flatbush.

Resides on and owns a farm in N. U., inherited from his grandfather Adrian Martense. Held the office of Capt. in the militia.

Issue by 1st wife:—

Ellen Maria, b. Jan. 15th, 1842.

MARIA BERGEN, b. May, 1813; d. April 29th, 1849; m. May 15th, 1828, *Frederick D. P. Crommelin*, of Brooklyn.

Issue:—

Edward Augustus Crommelin, b. Aug. 25th, 1829.

William Frederick Crommelin, b. June 22d, 1831.

Maria Louisa Crommelin, b. March 30th, 1833; m. William, s. of Abraham and Sally Bergen, of Flushing, and has children: Sarah Maria, John William, and Hannah.

Oliver Henry Crommelin, b. March 27th, 1836.

Sarah Margaretta Crommelin, b. Dec. 3d, 1838.

Daniel Livingston Crommelin, b. May 13th, 1840.

Children by 2d wife:

DANIEL BERGEN, b. March 5th, 1817; m. Feb. 8th, 1843, *Phebe Ann Simonson*, b. Jan. 29th, 1824.

Owns and resides on a farm in Jamaica South, Queens County.

Issue:—

John Simonson, b. Nov. 11th, 1843.

Jane Matilda, b. Aug. 26th, 1845.

Tunis Adrian, b. March 21st, 1847.

William Frederick, b. March 7th, 1849; d. Sept. 17th, 1850.

Vanderveer, b. March 1st, 1851.

Garret, b. March 2d, 1853.

Annie Simonson, b. March 9th, 1856.

Henrietta Palmer, (a twin with Annie S.) b. March 9th, 1856.

JOHN T. BERGEN, b. Oct. 4th, 1819, single, and lost an arm by an accidental discharge of a cannon. Resides with his mother in Flatbush, and at one time engaged in the hardware business in Brooklyn.

CATHARINE J. BERGEN, b. July 31st, 1827; m. July 19th, 1848, her cousin *Garret Bergen*, of Flatlands.

Issue :—*Rebecca Maria, Jane Ann, Gretta Alva*, and *George Travis.*

LEMMA ANN BERGEN, b. July 3d, 1831; m. July 4th, 1849, *Stephen Halsted*, b. Feb. 1st, 1831.

Issue :—

Jane Augusta Halstead, b. August 4th, 1851.
Eva Malena Halstead, b. April 1st, 1854.
Charles Alva Halstead, b. March 16th, 1857.
Stephen Clarence Halstead, b. Oct. 18th, 1859.

SARAH MATILDA BERGEN, b. July 7th, 1836; m. Feb. 6th, 1856, *Gilbert Granger Raynor*, b. Sept. 12th, 1832.

Issue :—

William Harvey Raynor, b. July 25th, 1856.

ELMIRA ROSETTA BERGEN, b. May 15th, 1839; m. July 2d, 1856, *George A. Raynor*, b. Nov. 22d, 1833.

Issue :—

Francis Bergen Raynor, b. Feb. 23d, 1859.

JORES (GEORGE) HANSEN BERGEN.

Descendants in the line of JORES (GEORGE) HANSEN BERGEN and *Sara Stryker*, of Brooklyn, N. Y., the third son of *Hans Hansen Bergen*, the first settler:

Third Generation.

LAMMETJE BERGEN, bap. Dec. 26th, 1679; m. *Joris Remsen*, s. of Rem Remsen and Marritie Vanderbilt, a grandson of Rem Jansen Vanderbeeck and Jannetje dau. of Joris Jansen de Rapalie. She d. in early life, her husband marrying a second wife.

Issue :—

Joris Remsen, b. 1706; d. at Haverstraw, N. Y., in 1741, leaving surviving a s. Tennis.

SARAH BERGEN, bap. March 13th, 1681. No farther trace.

AALTJE BERGEN, bap. Oct. 15th, 1682 ; d. about 1724; m. Aug. 17th, 1707, *Rem Remsen*, s. of Joris Remsen,[*] and Femmetje, dau. of Derick J. Woortman, a grandson of Rem Jansen Vanderbeeck and Jannetje, dau. of Joris Jansen de Rapalie. Rem and Aaltje occupied the paternal Remsen farm, located on the East river in the vicinity of Atlantic street, Brooklyn.

[*] Joris Remsen purchased Oct. 10th, 1706, (see Lib. 3, p. 76, of original record in Kings Co. Reg. off.) of his father-in-law, Derick Janse Wortman, his Brooklyn lands, consisting of the patents of Jan Manje, Andries Hudde and Claes Janse Van Naerden, located on the East river, with a river front extending about from Atlantic to Clarke streets, and lying N. E. of the patent of Frederick Lubbertse.

Issue :—

George Rem.• n, d. between 1735 and 1743, m. Jane, dau. of Peage Nagel, of Flatbush, and inherited his father's farm. Had children ; Rem, Philip and Aletta, who m. Wyckoff Van Nostrand, John and others.

HANS JORISE BERGEN, bap. Aug. 31st, 1684; m. Aug. 16th, 1711, *Sytje*, dau. of Evert Van Wicklen,* of New Lots.

Jan. 28th, 1722 3, Hans Jorisse Bergen and Sytje, his wife, conveyed for £172, to Cornelius Evertse, "one half part of all that land, meadow, creek, grist mill, mill dam, and beach of the old dwelling house, bolting house and bolting mill, (the new dwelling house only excepted,) situate in Brookland at a place called "Marty's Hook," as in fence and as bought Feb. 9th, 1713, by said Hans Jorise Bergen of Aert Aerson (Middagh.") The above premises contained 20 2-5 acres.+

Hans Jorise's family is entered in 1738, on the census of Brooklyn, as consisting of two white males above 10, two white males under 10, and 3 white females over 10 years of age.

Issue :—

George.
Evert, b. 1717.

JANNETJE BERGEN, bap. May 27th, 1688; m. Jan. 21st, 1711, *Hendrick Vroom*, of Brooklyn, probably a s. of Hendrick Corsen Vroom and Josica Pietersz Van Kesh.

* Evert Van Wicklen, emigrated from Holland in 16-- at the --n 1687 he resided in Flatlands, in which year his name appears on the lists of those who took the oath of allegiance as "Evert Janssen Van W-----" Amongst other children had a s. Garrit --- So-- of L----- --l--ts---- in New Lots and Jamaica South.

+See Lib. 4, p. 309 and 336 of conveyances in Kings Co. Reg---
These premises were on the patent of John H--s, the p-- was ----t to 1710, by Middagh, and was located on the land now -----d by the U-- Navy Yard. Marty's or Martyne's Hook was the prop-- of Br--klyn form-- ed by the Wallabout bay, west of the Navy Yard, and opp---si-- to C-r-lear's Hook in the city of New York.

After her death, Hendrick Vroom, m. Jan. 18th, 1745,
Dortie Demont, a widow.

Issue :—

Petrus Vroom, bap. March 25th, 1722.

ANNETJE BERGEN, bap. March 9th, 1689–90 ; m. March
12th, 1720, Anouret or Arnout Abrahamsz.

Issue :—

Marrytie Abrahamsz, bap. May 17th, 1724.

JAN BERGEN, bap. May 17th. 1694. No further trace
and probably d. young.

JORIS or GEORGE BERGEN, d. prior to April 8th, 1749 ;
m. Framyntie ———.

June 10th, 1737, George Bergen, of Brooklyn, and
Framyntie, his wife, conveyed to Israel Horsefield, premises in Brooklyn, bounded N. 57 deg. W. 9 ch. and 60 l. in
breadth, by land of said George Bergen ; S. 39 deg. W.
90 l. ; S. 27 deg. 30 min., W. 23 ch. and 54 l. in length,
by land of Hanse Jacobse Bergen ; S. 56 deg. E. 4
ch. ; S. 19 deg. 30 min. W. 5 ch. and 9 l. ; S. 49 deg. 30
min. E. 3 ch. and 54 l. into the meadows at or near Gowanus creek ; and N. 30 deg. 30 min. E. 30 ch. in length, by
land of Carel De Bevoise, containing 25 7-10 acres.* These
premises were a portion of the tract his father bought of
Maritje Gerretse. On the census of Brooklyn, in 1738,
George Bergen's family is entered, one white male over
10, two white males under 10, two white females above
10, two white females under 10, and one black male under 10 years of age. Oct. 8th, 1742, his name appears on
a deed containing the names of residents of Brooklyn, relating to a parsonage located in Flatbush.

The name of a " George Barger," appears on the re-

---

* See Lib. 5, p. 150 of con. in K. C. Reg. off.

cords of the town of Hempstead, in 1726, who may have
been this George.

Issue :

Abraham, bap. Sep. 2d. 1726.
Probably other children, of whom no trace, except the census.

Fourth Generation.

Descendants of HANS JORISE BERGEN and *Sytje
Van Wycklen*, of Brooklyn, N. Y.: -

JORES or GEORGE BERGEN, m. by tradition, *Miss Hoogland*,* and afterwards a second wife, *Maria* — . Settled on a farm at New Windsor, near Cranberry, Middlesex county, N. J.   His will is dated Oct. 7th, 1784, and
recorded in Liber 26, pages 284, &c., in the office of the
Secretary of State in N. J., and proved at Princeton, Oct.
20th, 1784, his sons John and Jacob being executors.

Issue by 1st wife :

John B., b. March 27th, 1739.
Peter.
George, b. Feb. 14th, 1743.

Issue by 2d wife :—

Margaret.
Maria.
Synthe.
Dinah.

---

* Cornelis Dircksen Hooglant, emigrated to this country at an early period, kept the ferry from New Amsterdam to Brooklyn, and Dec. 12th,
1645, received a patent for a plant.[?] near the Brooklyn side of the ferry.
He appears to have gone to the Fatherland for a season, and returned ag
to this country, arriving in April, 1662, in the ship Hope, with his wife,
son aged 24, and dau. aged 2 years.

Direk Janse Hooglant, of Maerseveen, who m. Oct. 8th, 1632. Ann to
Hans Bergen, wid. of Jan Clercq, also came to this country at an early period, and from these two individuals the Hooglants in this country are
all probably descended.

Martha or *Metje*, bap. Dec. 9th, 1751.
Lamatie.
Sarah.
Jacob.
Christopher,

EVERT BERGEN, b. 1717: d. Nov. 17th, 1776; m. *Jane* dau. of Dennise Hegeman.* In his younger days resided in New Lots, which at the time was in the boundaries of the town of Flatbush, probably with his grandfather, Evert Van Wicklen. Purchased in 1737, and settled on a tract of 140 acres of land at Roysfield, Hillsborough township, Somerset Co., N. J., three miles from Somerville. Also purchased a farm at Whitehouse, nine miles from Somerville. Brought a pear tree with him from Flatbush, to N. J., which tree bore fruit until 1861, over 120 years, when it was blown down during a violent hail storm.

There is a tradition among his descendants, that at the time of his settlement at Roysfield, among other animals he brought with him a colt: that after a time the colt was missing from the pasture field in which he was confined, probably from the insecurity of the imperfect fencing of a newly settled locality; and that the colt was found at his old home in Flatbush, to reach which the animal must have swam across the kills to Staten Island, and across the Narrows to Long Island, the route then usually traveled. They say the ferryman who carried over passengers, vehicles and animals in scows, had no knowledge of having carried back the colt, which course would have been

---

* Dennise Hegeman was probably a descendant of *Adrian Hegeman*, who emigrated from Holland, was b. about 1638, m. Catharine, and settled in Flatbush, L. I., of which place he was Secretary as early as 1670. His children were, Joseph, Abraham, Hendricus, Jacobus, *Denys*, Isaac, Benjamin, Elizabeth and Adrian.

Denys, s. of Adrian, m. Lucretia, d. prior to 1704, and had children, *Dallius* and Adrian.

Dallius, s. of Denys, m. Gertrude, settled on the Raritan river and probably had a s. Dennise, the father of *Jane*, who m. Evert Bergen.

Issue:

John, b. Sept. 26th, 1746.
Jane or *Yaantie*, bap. Aug. 5th, 1750.
James, b. Sept. 11th, 1753.
Evert, b. 1756.

Descendants of JORES or GEORGE BERGEN and *Framyntie*, of Brooklyn, N. Y. :-

ABRAHAM BERGEN, bap. Sept. 2d, 1726; m. ----   .

April 8th, 1749, Abraham Bergen, son and heir of George Bergen, and Framyntie Bergen, widow of George Bergen, both of Brookland, conveyed for £270, to Israel Horsefield, land in Brookland, bounded N. by land of Leendert D'Grauw, and land of Carl D'Beavois; S. E. by land of Carl D'Beavois; and N. W. by the road, as now in fence, containing 7 acres.

Of the names of the descendants of Abraham Bergen, no positive proof has been found, but from the continuation of the family names and other circumstances, the probability and almost certainty is that he had issue:

John.
George.
Sara.

Fifth Generation.

Descendants of GEORGE BERGEN and ---- *Hoagland*, his 1st wife, and *Maria*, his 2d wife, of Cranberry, N. J.

JOHN B. BERGEN, b. March 27th, 1739; d. June 2d, 1808, of dropsy, in his 70th year; m. June 8th, 1763, Sarah Stryker, b. Aug. 25th, 1745, and d. Sept. 15th, 1821.

Was a farmer residing in the county of Middlesex, N. J., about five miles from Cranberry and six from Princeton, where he owned a large plantation and a family of negroes : he also owned two other farms in the same vicinity. In person he is said to have been nearly six feet in height, well proportioned, and generally in the enjoyment of good health ; in his habits he was pious, engaging daily in family worship. One of his grandsons says, he recollects his Dutch horse whip of many strands, very elastic, its handle wrapped ornamentally with brass wire, which he carried between his knees and seldom used, but when he did it was always with effect and not soon forgotten. He was among the patriots serving with the Jersey blues in the militia in the war of the Revolution, and his insignia of office was a long staff with a spear and slender battle axe attached, which after the war he preserved and kept in the garret of his house. As in many other cases, his old papers, books and deeds were preserved for many years, but at length, being in the way of the wife of his youngest son, who by paying legacies became the inheritor of the homestead, they were thrown into an old barrel in the garret, and became the resort of such as wanted waste paper. After many years a suit was brought against the homestead, or a part thereof, on some alleged old claim, in which the plaintiff recovered, for the very deed which guarded against that claim was found pasted on the inside of a window curtain of flowered paper, and in its tattered form was useless as evidence.

Issue :—

George I., b. June 16th, 1764.
Abram, b. Oct. 4th, 1767.
Margaret, b. Nov. 7th, 1769.
John I., b. June 18th, 1773.
Ida, b. Nov. 22d, 1775.
Peter I., b. July 10th, 1779.

Jacob I., b. Nov. 9th, 1782.
Christopher, b. April 27th, 1785.

PETER BERGEN, m. *Jane Van Nuyse* or *Ne* , of Somerset Co.

Was a farmer residing at South Brunswick, N. J., about three miles from Cranberry.   His will is dated in 1813, and proved Oct. 16th, 1824.

Issue :–

John P., b. Sept. 30th, 1765.
Peter P., b. July 28th, 1783.
Martha.
George.
Margaret.
Jane.

GEORGE BERGEN, b. Feb. 14th, 1743 ; d. Sept. 14th, 1785 ; m. *Helena* or *Lena Hoogland*, b. Oct. 30th, 1743.

Was a farmer and miller near Penn's Neck, N. J.

Issue :—

Margaret, b. April 13th, 1765.
John G., b. April 3d, 1767.
George, b. March 19th, 1769.
Christopher, b. July 2d, 1771.
Peter, b. Feb. 24th, 1774.
Dinah, b. Sept 30th, 1775.
Sarah, b. July 16th, 1778.
Mary, b. May 5th, 1780.
Ida, b. Nov. 22d, 1781.
Peter G., b. Aug. 30th, 1783.

MARGARET BERGEN, (by 2d wife) : m. –   *Post*

MARIA BERGEN, m. *Christopher Hoogland*, of Stoutack or Sourland, N. J.

Issue : –

George Hogeland.
Christopher Hogeland.
Jane Hogeland.

SYNTHE BERGEN, m. –   *Post*.

22

DINAH BERGEN, m. —— *Slayback.*

MARTHA or METJE BERGEN, bap. Dec. 9th, 1751: m. *Luke Cowenhoven,* of Dutch Neck, N. J., s. of Lucas, b. June 3d, 1716, who emigrated from Flatlands, L. I. to N. J., and grandson of William of Flatlands: said William being a son of William Gerritse, a grandson of Gerrit Wolphertse, and great grandson of Wolfert Gerritse, the common ancestor of the Cowenhoven family of this country.

Issue:—*Ann.* b. June 10th, 1770, d. Nov. 24th, 1860: m. Jan. 10th, 1788, John P. Bergen, of Cranberry Neck.

LAMATIE BERGEN, d. about 1784: m. 1st, *Garret Cowenhoven,* of Conn's Neck, N. J., s. of Lucas, and grandson of William of Flatlands: m. 2d, —— *Smith.*

Issue by 1st husband:
Ann. m. Peter I. Bergen, of Penn's Neck.

SARAH BERGEN, m. *John Hogeland,* of Shanack or Sourland, some 15 miles west of Princeton N. J., and living in 1812.

Issue:—
Martin Hogeland.
Bergen Hogeland.
George Hogeland.
Peter Hogeland.

JACOB BERGEN, d. 1781, m. 1st, *Elizabeth Cowenhoven,* dau. of Lucas, and grand dau. of William, of Flatlands: m. 2d, *Margaret Van Arsdale.* *

Was the keeper of a hotel at Princeton, N. J. His will is dated Jan. 1781, proved March 5th, 1781, and recorded in the office of the Secretary of State of N. J., in

---

* Syman Jansen Van Arsdalen, the common ancestor of the Van Arsdale family in this country, m. Pieterje Claasen Wyckoff, (a sister of Pieter Classen Wyckoff, the common ancestor of the Wyckoff family,) and settled at an early period in Flatlands, where he owned a farm. None of his male descendants at present reside in the country towns of Kings county.

which his residence is given as of the eastern precinct,
Somerset Co. Margaret's will is recorded in the same office and dated Feb. 21st, 1795, in which her residence
is given as of Rocky Hill, Somerset Co. On the records
of conveyances, books A and B, in the County Clerk's
office, in Somerville, there are records of several deeds in
in 1778-9 and 1780, signed by Jacob Bergen, Commissioner, supposed to be the Jacob who m. Margaret Van
Arsdale.

Issue :—

Christopher.

Mary.

Margaret, by 1st wife.

Jacob, b. 1763, by 2d wife.

According to a tradition, *Christopher,* s. of Jacob Bergen,
had a large family of children, and settled in one of the
western states ; there were Bergens, according to the Rev.
J. G. Bergen, residing in Kentucky, not traced, who may
have been his descendants.

Descendants of EVERT BERGEN and *Jane Hegeman,*
of Roysfield, Somerset Co., N. J. :

JOHN BERGEN, b. Sept. 26th, 1746 ; d. June 6th, 1828,
in his 82d year ; m. *Alche* or *Alle Rapalye,* b. Jan. 6th,
1744, and d. April 17th, 1815.

Inherited from his father and occupied the Whitehouse
farm of 318 acres, in Somerset Co., N. J.

Issue : —

Evert, b. June 23d, 1771.

Maria.

Cornelius, b. April 29th, 1775.

Jane.

Syche, b. April 17th, 1784.

JAMES BERGEN, b. Sept. 11th, 1755 ; d. Jan. 30th,
1830 ; m. May 20th, 1779. *Ann* or *Annache,* dau. of

Zacheus Von Voorhees,* b. Feb. 20th, 1761, and d. Jan. 11th, 1852. in her 91st year.

Inherited from his father and occupied the homestead farm in Roysfield, N. J., to which he added by purchase 220 acres. Dying intestate, his land was equally divided among his children.

Issue :—

Evert J., d. Oct. 30th, 1780.

Mary, b. May 5th, 1786.

John V., b. Feb. 19th, 1790.

Zacheus, b. Oct 1st, 1792.

June, b. March 15th. 1791 : d. Oct 10th. 1795.

Jane, b. Oct. 4th. 1797.

James, b. Aug. 30th. 1799.

* *Zacheus Van Voorhees*, is a descendant of Coert Stevense Van Voorhees. referred to in the foot note under Hans Bergen and Antie Lucassen, of Jamaica. L. I.

Coert Stevense Van Voorhees, emigrated with his father in 1660, from Holland, and m. Marretje Garretse Van Kouwenhoven, his will being dated Aug. 26th, 1677. He settled in Flatlands. L. I., and had children, Stephen Coerte. of Flatlands. who m. Eagge or Achai Jans. and d. Feb. 16th, 1723–4 : Meinard Coerte. of N. Utrecht. m. Jan. 9th, 1660. Maria Pia or Pieters. and d. about 1706. his will being proved on the 20th of Feb. of that year ; *Albert Coerte*, of Flatlands and N. U., d. about 1748, his will being proved April 14th of that year. m. 1st. Sarah Williamsen. m. 2d, Margrietje ———, m. 3d. May 12th. 1743. Willemptje Suydam, and also, supposed to have m. Ida Vanderbilt : Garret Coerte of Flatlands and N. U., d. 1703. will proved Sept. 23d. 1704. m. April 26th, 1685. Willemtje Pieters : Altie Coerte. m. April 16th, 1687, Joost Rutgerse Van Brunt, of N. U. : Cornelis Coerte. of Flatlands, bap. Jan. 23d. 1678. m. Altje ——— ; Annatie Coerte, bap. Dec. 5th, 1680 : and Johannes Coerte, bap. April 22d, 1863. m. Barbara ———, and settled in east N. J.

Albert Coerte, of Flatlands and N. U., and s. of Coert Stevense, had children, *Coert*. d. May 31st, 1757. m. Aunatie ———, who d. Jan. 30th, 1760 : Elizabeth, bap. Dec. 10th. 1695, m. Rutgert Van Brunt, of N. U. ; Mary, m. John Van Nostrand : Margaret. m. 1st, Petrus Stoothoff, m. 2d, David Nevius : Altie, m. Wilhelmus Stoothoff. and d. Feb. 25th. 1743 ; Ann, m. Hendrick Cortelyou, of N. J., and Neeltie, m. Christopher Hoagland.

Coert. s. of Albert Coerte. of Flatlands and N. U., had children, Coert of N. U. and afterwards of N. J.. d. about 1762. m. Sarah Van Brunt ; Albert Coerten, of Gravesend and N. U., m. 1st, May 10th, 1720, Adriaentje Ditmars. who d. April 14th. 1721. m. 2d. Dec. 1st, 1744. Ida, wid. of John Vanderbilt : *Zacheus*, who emigrated to Somerset Co., N. J., and d. in 1770 ; Bernardus, of Gravesend and N. U., m. Fammetie Latter, and d. in 1769 ; Jannetie. m. Wilhelmus Van Brunt, of N. U., and Annatie, who m. William B. Gifford.

Zacheus, of N. J., s. of Coert and Annatie, had children, *Ann*, who m. James Bergen of N. J., Coert, John and Mary.

EVERT BERGEN, b. 1756; d. Dec. 6th, 1777, of small pox. Single. Was a soldier in the American army, and engaged in the battle of Monmouth, in the war of the Revolution.

JANE BERGEN, d. March 20th, 1812; m. 1st, *George Rapalye*; m. 2d, *Abraham Voorhees*; m. 3d, *Jeromus Rapalye*. No issue.

Descendants of ABRAHAM BERGEN, of Brooklyn, N. Y. :—

JOHN BERGEN : a John Bergen, m. in the city of N. Y., Feb. 20th, 1760, *Margaret Van Deursen*, as per N. Y. R. Dutch Church records, who was probably John, s. of Abraham ; he also m. a 2d wife, resided in the city of N. Y., and was a soldier in the war of the Revolution.

Issue :

George, by 1st wife.

Abraham, by 2d wife.

Frances, by 2d wife.

GEORGE BERGEN : a George Bergen, of N. Y., m. March 25th, 1756, *Magdalena Britt*, as per N. Y. R. Dutch Church records. He probably d. shortly after his marriage, for May 9th, 1759, by same records, Magdalena Bergen, widow, m. Ebenezer Turrell. No farther trace.

SARA BERGEN : a Sara Bergen, as per above records, m. Sept. 20th, 1750, *John Wandell*. No farther trace.

--

Sixth Generation.

Descendants of JOHN B. BERGEN and *Sarah Stryker*, of near Cranberry, N. J. :

GEORGE I. BERGEN, b. June 16th, 1764; d. Feb. 1825; m. 1789, *Rebecca*, dau. of Judge Jonathan Combs, of Middlesex Co., N. J.   His widow two years after his decease m. the Rev. Mr. Keuner, a Baptist preacher from Virginia, and d. in 1846.   He was near six feet in height, energetic, persevering, religious, and with his wife members of the church from early youth, training their children to serve their Creator.   The ancestor of Jonathan Combs, it is said, came from Scotland, in the old ship Caledonia, which brought the first emigrants from the land of stern Presbyterianism; they seeking a home in the wild country from the intolerance of Papal and Episcopal power and persecution.

When George I. approached manhood, in consequence of his health not being considered good enough for a farmer, he taught school for several years.   After he was married he became a country merchant, and established the first store at Hightstown, Mercer Co., N. J., two miles south of Cranberry and ten east of Princeton.   Here he prospered for eight years, having no competitors.   Then he rented his property at Hightstown for three years, and with his brother Abram, joined in the purchase of a farm two miles distant, on which were grist and saw mills, cider works and distillery, tan yards and store.   To this place he expected to carry his customers with him, but he was disappointed, three new stores being started in Hightstown when he left.   On the termination of his lease he sold out his interest in the farm and distilleries, and returned to his old location, but he never recovered his old stand point in trade.   Consequently three years afterwards he sold out, and bought at Pluckermine, in Somerset Co., 18 miles west of New Brunswick, a farm of 70 acres, with good improvements and a capacious store. Here he carried on a large and prosperous business, several stores in the country around closed, and to prevent competition he set up another small store four miles dis-

tant. He dealt largely in pork and other produce, our
country at the time supplying Napoleon's, and the other
European, armies with food. Money was plenty and pri-
ces high. Down came the embargo in 1808, followed by
the non-intercourse act; then in 1812 the war, and in
1815 the sudden peace, on which the whole country was
flooded with British goods. The result was, that he, to-
together with his son David, who at the time was a merchant
in New Brunswick, with many others who were engaged
in business, failed. To retrieve their misfortunes, George L.,
his son David, and two married sisters, with their families
left New Jersey in June, 1818, for Kentucky, where his
sister Margaret and her husband John Voorhees, and two
sisters of his wife, Rebecca Combs, with their husbands,
Peter Conover and Peter Cox, then resided; they having
emigrated in 1790, to settle at Red Stone, near the present Wheeling, then the ultima thule. There they tarried
less than a year. Peter Conover* and Peter Cox were
among the first who made their boats and rafts to go down
the Ohio river.

At the time George L. emigrated, they resided in Wood-

* *Peter Conover*, was a s. of John Conover, said John being one of the
sons of William Gerretse and Altie Brinkerhoff, a grandson of Gerret
Wolphertse and Altie Cornelise Cool, and a great grandson of Wolfert
Garretse Van Couwenhoven, the common ancestor of the Conovers in this
country, referred to in the foot notes under Catharine Bergen and Gerrit
Couwenhoven, and Ann Bergen and George Kouwenhoven, descendants
of Michael Hansen Bergen.

John Conover, s. of William Gerretse, was b. Sept. 9th, 1681, m. to a
supposed Cuba or Jacoba Vanderveer and settled on a farm in Monmouth
Co., N. J., in 1705, on which a Peter Conover now resides. John had
children, William; who m. Sada Lane Cornel's, whom. Hendrick ———;
Peter, who m. Rebecca, dau. of Judge Jonathan Combs, of 1st Des ———;
who m. Mary Uplike, and Gerrit, who m. 1st Nellie Van Mater, and 2d,
Ann, dau. of Peter Schenck. All of these children settled at first at
Penn's Neck, except Gerrit, and removed thence to Kentucky; subse-
quently some of them to Indiana Gerrit and ———— settled to ———— in
New Jersey.

Peter, s. of John Conover and Jesse, had children, Jonathan Combs; who m. Sept. 1st, 1808 Martha ———; George
D. Bergen; Mary Ann, who m. Dec. 1st, 1819 Jonathan Combs Bergen,
and probably others.

ford County, Kentucky, within 12 miles of Lexington. Within a year these families intermarried. Old Major Conover was a large landholder and reputed to be rich, but in the troublesome times then in Kentucky, and by old Virginia land claims, the result was his castle fell, and he determined in 1824, to sell his homestead, and all his, and George I.'s family decided to make their home in Indiana. The old Major, his son Combs Conover, who had married Martha, a dau. of George I., and Jonathan Combs Bergen, (s. of George I.) who had married Mary Ann, a dau. of the Major, and George I., constituted the exploring party. They parched corn, ground it in their hand mills and mixed it with plenty of maple sugar, filled their saddle bags with it and other food, and set out on their expedition. They made a stand near where Indianapolis, the seat of government now is. One night, while they were around the fire, where they were making their claim, they were suddenly roused by the cry of "who's here,"—*hoosier*,—and from this has come the name of the Indianians—*Hoosiers*. The lone traveler on horseback spent the night with them. Said he. "what are you doing here?" "Making a claim for settlement." "Why will you do it in this towering forest, where the trees are so tall and thick on the ground that the sun can never penetrate to the earth ; where before you can open a farm you will all be gray among the stumps, when by going 150 miles west you will find the most beautiful prairie land all ready for the plough?" Said one in reply, "we have heard of the Sangamy country, by the rangers from the Indian war, but we have heard it is very wet and sickly." "Go and see for yourselves, I have just come from there." The result was, that next morning they mounted their horses, and by their pocket compass steered due west, and in one year from that time, they and their families were settled on a beautiful prairie, about 30 miles west of Spingfield, Illinois, which they named Jersey prairie. Such is a brief detail of the circumstances which led one branch of the Bergen family, as given by the Rev. John G. Bergen, son of George I., to the great west.

Issue: (All b. in New Jersey.)

John G., b. Nov. 27th, 1790.
Daniel Coats, b. Jan. 2d, 1795.
Margaret, b. 1796.
Jonathan Combs, b. May 20th, 1799.
Martha, b. June 14th, 1801.
Abram Stryker, b. Aug. 17th, 1804.
Sarah Bedell, b. 1807.
George Spafford Woodhull, b. July 6th, 1809.
Ida Van Ness, b. Oct. 11th, 1811.
Joseph Woodhull Scudder, b. 1815.

ABRAHAM BERGEN, b. Oct. 4th, 1767; d. April 13th, 1826; m. 1st, April 17th, 1778, *Catharine Voorhees*, who d. May 4th, 1792; m. 2d, April 7th, 1796, *Hannah*, dau. of Jacob Fisher, b. Feb. 28th, 1772, d. Sept. 11th, 1849.

Was a farmer near Cranberry, N. J., and for many years a Trustee and Elder in the Presbyterian church in said village.

Issue: -

Sarah, (by 1st wife,) b. 1790.
Mary, (by 2d wife,) b. Jan. 19th, 1797.
John A., b. Sept. 21st, 1799.
Jacob F., b. May 27th, 1802.
Margaret, b. Sept. 5th, 1805.
George, b. Sept. 10th, 1808.
Daniel, b. Dec. 12th, 1813; d. March 1st, 1841
Hannah Virginia.

MARGARET BERGEN, b. Nov. 7th, 1769; d. March 20th, 1805; m. *John Voorhees*, and emigrated to Kentucky; no issue.

JOHN I. BERGEN, b. June 18th, 1773; d. Aug. 8th,

23

1840; m. *Mary Mershon*. b. July 17th, 1775 : d. Oct. 18th, 1824.

Was a farmer at Scott's corner, Middlesex Co., N. J., about 4 miles from Cranberry.

Issue :—

Maria Schenck, b. Sept. 27th, 1797.
Enoch, b. Feb. 28th, 1801.
Christopher, b. June 2d, 1803.
Samuel Mershon, b. Nov. 16th, 1805.
Elias, b. Sept. 8th, 1808.
Sarah Stryker, b. Sept. 29th, 1810.
William Elwood, b. Nov. 13th, 1816.

IDAH BERGEN, b. Nov. 22d, 1775 : d. about 1854; m. *John Van Ness*, of Cranberry, N. J.

Issue :—

John Bergen Van Ness, m. Sarah Snediker.
Abraham Van Ness, m. Lammata Baker.
Diana Van Ness, m. Isaac Snediker.
Maria Van Ness, m. Isaac Snediker after the death of Diana.
Catharine Van Ness, m. Crukjee, a Frenchman.
George Van Ness, m. a Miss Dey.
Sarah Van Ness.
Peter Van Ness.

PETER I. BERGEN, b. July 10th, 1779 : d. about 1855; m. *Anna Conover*, dau. of Gerret and Lammatie Conover.

Was a farmer at Penn's Neck, N. J.; a short, fleshy, and active man, and an elder and the principal support of the church at that place.

Issue :—

Garret.
Lammattie.
John C.
Sarah.
George.

JACOB I. BERGEN, b. Nov. 9th, 1782 ; d. April 13th, 1836 ; m. Feb. 4th, 1806. *Syche*, dau. of John Bergen, of White-house, N. J., b. April 17th, 1784.

Was a portion of his life a farmer near Cranberry, N. J., inheriting and occupying the farm on which his father resided, afterwards removed to New Brunswick, and a number of years a member of the consistory of the Protestant Reformed Dutch church of said city.

Issue :—

Cornelia, b. Dec. 13th, 1806.
John W., b. June 28th, 1808.
Abram, b July 12th, 1810.
Matthew Egerton, b. Dec. 25th, 1813.
Simon Hillyer, b. June 13th, 1816.
Sara Maria, b. Oct. 6th, 1821.

CHRISTOPHER BERGEN, b. April 27th, 1785; d. Dec. 24th, 1844; m. Aug. 25th, 1808, *Mary Disbrow,* b. Oct. 11th, 1789, d. April 8th, 1846.

Was a farmer at Cranberry Neck, N. J.

Issue :—

Samuel Disbrow, b. Aug. 25th, 1809.
Sarah A., b. Feb. 1st, 1811.
Ida Van Nest, b. Jan. 25th, 1813.
Alfred, b. Sept. 2d. 1815.
John Stryker, b. Oct. 21st. 1819.
James Williamsen, b. Jan. 16th, 1823.
Symmes Henry, b. July 15th, 1826.
Mary, b. Jan. 20th, 1828.
Elizabeth Voorhees, b. Jan. 2d. 1830.

Descendants of PETER BERGEN and *Jane Van Nuyse,* of near Cranberry, Somerset Co., N. J. :—

JOHN P. BERGEN, b. Sept. 30th, 1765; d. Jan. 11th, 1850; m. Jan. 10th, 1788, *Anna Conover,* dau. of William, of Cranberry Neck, a s. of Lucas, and grandson of William of Flatlands, b. June 10th, 1770, d. Nov. 24th, 1860. Was a farmer at Cranberry Neck, Middlesex Co., N. J.

Issue :—

Elizabeth, b. Jan. 31st, 1789.
Peter C., b. Aug. 21st, 1792.

who d. Aug. 1848.

Issue by 1st wife :—

Catharine, b. April 2d, 1805.

Jane, b. June 19th, 1807.

Elizabeth, b. Nov. 17th, 1810.

John, b. April 23d, 1812.

William, b. Dec. 28th, 1814.

Henry D., b. July 23d, 1817.

Ann, b. Feb. 18th, 1820; d. June 20th. 1820.

Children by 2d wife :

Vincent D., b. Dec. 29th, 1821.

Peter T., b. Sept. 29th, 1824.

Caroline, b. May 9th, 1829.

MARTHA BERGEN : m. *John Baily*, and had issue.

GEORGE BERGEN ; m. *Margaret*, dau. of George Bergen and Lena Hoagland, of Penn's Neck. Emigrated west, and d. prior to 1813, the date of his father's will, leaving surviving issue.

MARGARET BERGEN : m. *John Duncan*.

JANE BERGEN : m. *Henry Davis*, and d. prior to 1813, the date of her father's will, leaving surviving issue.

Descendants of GEORGE BERGEN and *Lena Hoagland*, of near Penn's Neck. N. J. : -

MARGARET BERGEN, b. April 13th, 1765 ; d. July 10th, 1812 ; m. *George*, s. of George Bergen, and emigrated west.

JOHN G. BERGEN, b. April 3d, 1767 ; d. April 24th,

---

* Theunis Dey, of New Amsterdam, m. Feb. 4th, 1685, Anneken Schouten, and had children : Derick, bap. March 27th, 1687, and Sara, bap. June 10th, 1688. He was probably the common ancestor of the Dey family of this country.

1812; m. Dec. 23d, 1789, *Elizabeth Conover*, b. Feb. 21st, 1773. Was a miller near Cranberry Neck.

Issue:

Lawrence, b. Sept. 3d, 1792
Helena, b. May 3d, 1794.
Rulef, b. Sept. 17th, 1796.

GEORGE BERGEN, b. March 19th, 1769; m. 1st, *Mashia Scudder*; m. 2d, *Elizabeth Scudder*; m. 3d, *Polly Conover*, by whom no issue.

Issue by 1st wife:—

Joseph.
Elijah.
Ellen.
Lydia.

By 2d wife:

Sarah.
Harriet.
William.
Isaac.
Ezra.

CHRISTOPHER BERGEN, b. July 2d, 1771. Married and emigrated to Indiana.

PETER BERGEN, b. Feb. 24th, 1774; d. young.

DINAH BERGEN, b. Sept. 30th, 1775. Suppose she emigrated west.

SARAH BERGEN, b. July 16th, 1778; m. *Elijah Voorhis*.

Issue:—

Eli Voorhis.
Catharine Voorhis, m. Vincent Perrine.
Margaret Voorhis, m. Joseph Mount.

MARY BERGEN, b. May 5th, 1780; m. *Nathan Davis*.

Issue:—

Isaac Davis.
Lewis Davis.
John Davis, m. Ann Perrine.
Eli Davis.

Margaret Davis, m. Edward Holcum.
Ida Davis, m. Humphrey Mount.
Dina Davis, m. John Evered.

IDA BERGEN, b. Nov. 22d, 1781; m. *Lewis Riggs.*

Issue :—

Lena Riggs.
John Riggs.
Maria Riggs, m. John Chamberlin, and emigrated to Ohio.
Elias Riggs, m. Rachel Baird.
C.tharine Riggs.
George Riggs, m. 1st, Lydia Hampton; m. 2d, Sarah Ann Perrine.
William Riggs, m. Catharine Ann Mount.

PETER G. BERGEN. b. Aug. 30th, 1783; d. Dec. 1st, 1856; m. *Susan Mershon*, who d. April 23d, 1846.

Was a blacksmith at Perrinesville.

Issue :—

Alice, b. June 26th, 1806.
George.
Margaret, d. July 10th, 1812.
Catharine, d. Feb. 24th, 1827.
James, b. March 3d, 1814.
Ellen, b. March 10th, 1816.
John, d. May 13th, 1838.
Emily, b. Oct. 3d, 1822.
William Mount, b. Oct. 7th, 1824.
Gertrude Ann, b. Feb. 23d, 1827.
Jane Eliza, b. May 10th, 1829.

Descendants of JACOB BERGEN and *Margaret Vanarsdale*, of Princeton, N. J. :—

MARY BERGEN. m. —— Hews, and resided in Sussex Co., N. J.

MARGARET BERGEN, m. Samuel Mershon, and resided in Sussex Co., N. J.

JACOB BERGEN, b. ——, 1763; d. May 17th, 1851, in his 88th year; m. Mary McClow, wid. of Simon Brokaw, who d. Sept. 12th, 1838, in her 84th year.   Simon's father, Burgan Brokaw, his descendants say, came from Holland, and purchased 1100 hundred acres of land in Somerset Co., N. J.   About 1804, Jacob Bergen purchased a farm at Branchville, near the head of the Raritan River, on which his s., Cornelius, now (1865) resides.   On the baptism of his son Jacob, in the Reformed Dutch Church at Somerville, his wife's name is entered on the record as Mary Brokaw, and on that of his son Cornelius, in the same church, as Mary Mallom.

Issue :—

Jacob, b. Oct. 3d, 1794.

Simon, b. April 22d, 1797.

Mary, b. March 9th, 1800.

Cornelius, b. Sept. 12th, 1802.

Descendants of JOHN BERGEN and *Allie Rapalye*, of Whitehouse, N. J. :—

JANE BERGEN, b. ———, 1770; d. April 23d, 1851, in her 81st year; m. ———, *Simon Hillyer*.

Issue :—

John B. Hillyer, ———; m. Hannah Heyer.

Maria Hillyer, ———; m. Stephen Emmans of Gravesend.

William Hillyer, ———; m. Ann Davis, and resides at Boundbrook, N. J.

EVERT BERGEN, b. June 23d, 1771; d. March 3d, 1856; m. Jan. 5th, 1793, *Nancy* or *Ann Van Duerson*, b. March 21st, 1769; d. July 16th, 1861.

Was a farmer at Whitehouse, N. J., near Somerville.

Issue :—

John, b. Dec. 5th, 1793.

William, b. Sept. 11th, 1795.

Ann, b. Sept. 15th, 1797.

James, b. Nov. 27th, 1799.

Maria, b. Nov. 20th, 1801.

Aletta, b. May 9th, 1804.

Stats, b. July 15th, 1806.

Jane, b. May 6th, 1808.

George, b. May 13th, 1810.

MARIA BERGEN, b. ———, 1772; d. July 30th, 1865, in her 84th year; m. ———, *Matthew Egerton.*

Issue :—

John Egerton.

Evert Egerton.

William Egerton.

CORNELIUS BERGEN, b. April 29th, 1775; d. Jan. 31st, 1831; m. Nov. 5th, 1811, *Nancy Hart.*

Was a farmer near Somerville, N. J.

Issue :—

Alche or *Aletta*, b. Feb. 23d, 1813.

Susonna, b. Aug. 13th, 1816.

John C., Dec. 15th, 1820.

Cornelius, b. Nov. 1st, 1822.

James, b. Nov. 10th, 1823.

Maria, b. Oct. 27th, 1825.

Abagail, b. Oct. 13th, 1828.

SYCHE BERGEN, b. April 17th, 1784; m. Feb. 26th, 1806, *Jacob I. Bergen*, s. of John of Cranberry, N. J. Residing, 1860, with her dau., Sarah Maria, wife of Charles Webber, in Brooklyn, N. Y. Has six children, whose names are given under that of her husband.

Descendants of JAMES BERGEN and *Ann Van Voorhees*, of Roysfield, N. J. :

EVERT J. BERGEN, b. Oct. 30th, 1780, m. Sept. 14th, 1804, *Jane Stryker*, dau. of John, and grand dau. of Peter Stryker,* of Flatbush. Jane d. Feb. 28th, 1845.

---

* *Peter Stryker*, is a descendant of Pieter, s. of Jan, the first settler of the Stryker family of Kings Co., N. Y., referred to in the foot note under John Bergen and Rebecca Stryker, of Flatlands, N. Y.

Pieter, s. of Jan, resided at Flatbush, was b. Nov. 1st, 1653, d. June 11th, 1741, m. May 30th, 1681, Annetje Barends or Jooste, who d. June 17th, 1717, and had issue : Lammetie, b. March 20th, and died April 9th, 1682 ; Lammetie, b. Feb. 16th, 1683, d. July 26th, 1690, of small pox : Jan, of Flatbush, b. Aug. 6th, 1684, d. Aug. 18th, 1770, m. 1st, Margrieta Schenck, who d. Aug. 1721, m. 2d, Feb. 17th, 1722, Sara, dau. of Michael Hansen Bergen; Barent, b. Sept. 3d, 1686, d. July 3d, 1690, of small pox : Jacob, b. Aug. 24th, 1688, m. (sup.) Dec. 17th, 1710, Annetie Vander Beek ; Barent, b. Sept. 14th, 1690, d. Oct. 27th, 1746, m. Feb.

Issue : --

James E., b. Sept. 14th, 1805.

John E., b. March 12th, 1808.

Jane, b. June 7th, 1811.

Ann or *Joanna*, b. June 7th, 1813.

Mariah, b. April 18th, 1815.

Peter S., b. March 25th, 1818.

Phebe, b. March 25th, 1819.

MARY BERGEN, b. March 5th, 1786 ; d. March 12th, 1861 ; m. Nov. 16th, 1802, *Abraham I. Staats*, who d. in 1840.

Resided on a farm near Roystield, N. J.

Issue :—

John A. Staats.

James B. Staats.

Evart B. Staats.

16th, 1717, Libertje Hegoman, who d. June, 1758 ; Hendrick, b. Dec. 3d. 1692, d. May 17th, 1694 ; Sytie, b. Dec 17th, 1694, m. (sup.) March 14th, 1717, Aert Vanderbilt ; *Pieter*, of Flatbush, b. Feb. 12th, 1697, d. Dec. 24th, 1776, m. May 18th, 1720, Jannetie Martens, dau. of Marten Adrianse, b. July 31st, 1702, d. Jan. 1st, 1794 ; Hendrick, b. Feb. 18th, 1699, d. Aug. 19th, 1739, m. (sup.) Marritje or Mary ; and Lammetie, b. Dec. 21st, 1700, d. Sept. 14th, 1763, m. 1st, Nov. 4th, 1721, Johannes Lott, who d. in 1732, m. 2d, Christianus Lupardius, s. of Dominie Lupardius.

Pieter, of Flatbush, s. of Pieter and Annetje, had issue : Annetie, b. March 20th, and d. April 13th, 1721 ; Sara, b. July 3d, 1722, m. (sup.) Dec. 10th, 1743, Cornelius Cornell ; Antje, b. Oct. 5th, 1724, d. April 17th, 1725 ; Jannetie, b. Oct. 5th, 1724, m. Oct. 5th, 1745, Jacob Messerole ; *Pieter*, of Flatbush, b. Dec. 22d, 1730, m. May 23d, 1752, Jannetie, dau. of John Van Kerk, who d. Feb. 21st, 1761, m. 2d, June 23d, 1764, Femmetie Schenck, b. July 29th, 1760, d. Dec. 11th, 1844 ; Gerrit, b. Oct. 13th, 1733, d. March 26th, 1783 ; and Jan, b. Feb. 15th, 1739, d. March 15th, 1742.

Pieter, of Flatbush, s. of Pieter and Jannetie, had issue : *John*, of N. J., b. Sept. 1st, 1753 d. July 13th, 1794, m. ——— . Phebe ——— ; Jannetie, b. Dec. 31st, 1756, d. July 8th, 1740, m. ——— John Fish ; Peter, of Flatbush, b. April 20th, 1766, d. Aug. 3d, 1832, m. Polly or Maria Cornell, and had no issue ; and Garret, of Flatbush, b. July 12th, 1776, d. July 8th, 1819, m Feb. 2d, 1804, Anne, dau. of Jacob Polhemus.

John, of N. J., s. of Pieter and Jannetie, had issue Jane, b. ———, d. ———, m. Sept. 14th, 1804, Evart J. Bergen ; Sarah, b. ———. d. ———. 1830, m. ———, Joseph Bennet ; and Peter, b. ———. d. April 17th, 1827.

24

JOHN BERGEN. b. Feb. 19th. 1790: m. May 29th, 1830. *Phebe*, d. of Joseph Totten. of Newtown, L. I., who d. Aug. 29th. 1850.

Is a merchant at New Brunswick. N. J., and resides at No. 148 George St.

Issue:—

Ann Eliza, b. March 3d. 1831.
Mary Louisa, b. Oct. 4th, 1832.
James Augustus, b. Oct. 22d, 1836.
Catharine T., b. April 28th, 1838.

ZACHEUS BERGEN. b. Oct. 1st. 1792; m. Jan. 18th, 1816. *Mary Simonson*, b. April 29th. 1790.

Is a farmer at Roysfield. Somerset Co.. N. J., occupying and owning about 140 acres. the original homestead tract of his grand father. Evert Bergen.

Issue :

Johanna V., b. Sept. 4th. 1817.
Elizabeth S., b. Aug. 14th, 1819.
Mary Stouts, b. May 5th, 1822.
Gertrude V., b. June 19th. 1825.
James, b. Dec. 19th, 1827.

JANE BERGEN. b. April 12th, 1797: m. Oct. 4th, 1817. *William Wilson*. Owns and resides on a portion of her father's farm at Roysfield, N. J.

Issue :—

Minard W. Wilson, b. Nov. 18th, 1818, m. July 31st, 1841. Elizabeth White. Is a professor of Music, in Brooklyn, N. Y.

Martha V. Wilson, b. Feb. 7th. 1820 ; single.

Henry W. Wilson, b. March 2d, 1822; m. Nov. 23d, 1847, Rebecca Hood. Is an architect at Newark.

James B. Wilson, b. Feb. 14th, 1824; m. April 17th, 1857, Mary E. Porter. Is a clergyman at Long Branch.

John B. Wilson, b. May 26th. 1826 ; m. Sept. 6th, 1835. Caroline Van Duyn. Is a mechanic in Newark, N. J.

Mary Jane Wilson, b. Dec. 21st, 1828 : m. Jan. 25th, 1860, David D. Munson,

Peter Q. Wilson, b. Sept. 18th, 1830, a clergyman at East Greenbush, near Albany, N. Y.; single.

Frederick F. Wilson, b. Sept. 18th, 1830, a clergyman at Schenectady N. Y.; single.

Eliza E. Wilson, b. March 27th, 1833; m. Aug. 8th, 1860, Harvey H. Barrett, an Engineer in the U. S. Navy.

Anna V. Wilson, b. July 11th, 1835; d. March 16th, 1853.

Louisa Wilson, b. Jan. 3d, 1838; single.

JAMES BERGEN, b. Aug. 30th, 1799; d. Aug. 16th, 1855; m. Feb. 17th, 1820, *Phebe Peterson*, b. Sept. 8th, 1801.

Was a farmer at Roysfield, owning about 140 acres of the homestead farm.

Issue :—

Garret P., b. Nov. 20th, 1820.

John J., b. June 27th, 1823.

James, b. Sept. 19th, 1825.

Vanderveer, b. Sept. 26th, 1827.

Zacheus, b. Sept. 1st, 1829.

Elizabeth, b. Oct. 12th, 1831.

Evart, b. June 24th, 1834.

Cornelius, b. Jan. 31st, 1838.

William, b. Aug. 10th, 1840.

Jan, b. Aug. 6th, 1846.

Descendants of JOHN BERGEN and *Margaret Van Deuser*, of the City of New York :

GEORGE BERGEN : d. about 1855; m. *Elizabeth Shocker*, who d. about 1837. Was a shoemaker, and resided in Dutch St., in the City of N. Y.

Issue :—

John, b. about 1797.

Frances, b. about 1800.

Abraham, b. about 1802.

Jane, b. about 1804.

George, b. June 20th, 1806.

Catharine.

William.

James, b. Jan. 20th, 1814.

Elizabeth.

Maria Louisa, b. Dec. 18th, 1819.

ABRAHAM BERGEN : d. many years ago.

Was a farmer at Bloomfield. N. J.. where he owned a small farm.

Issue :—

Sarah.

Hetty.

Margaret.

FRANCES BERGEN ; d. single.

Seventh Generation.

Descendants of George I. BERGEN and *Rebecca Combs*, of Jersey Prairie, Illinois. :

JOHN G. BERGEN, b. Nov. 27th. 1790. in N. J., m. Nov. 10th, 1812. *Margaretta Matilda*, dau. of Dr. Thomas Henderson, of Freehold. Monmouth Co.. N. J., an elder and trustee of the old Tennent Church, in said county, and a Judge and member of Congress. She d. Oct. 18th, 1853.

In consequence of the pious instruction and example of both his parents. his early impressions were of a religious character. and in his 13th year. he became a member of the church. In the Academy at Baskingridge, under the care of the Rev. Dr. Finley. he was prepared for college, entered the junior class at Princeton. and graduated when but 17 years old. He immediately commenced studying for the ministry with the Rev. Dr. John Woodhull, of Monmouth Co.. who, prior to the establishment of a Theological Seminary. had been appointed by the Synod of N. Y. and N. J.. Professor of Theology, and had trained a large number of young Ministers ; and at the

Rev. J. G. Bergen. D. D.

age of 20, he was licensed to preach the Gospel. It was his purpose, as soon as licensed, to mount a horse, and go to the West, which he had chosen as his field of labor; religion and the West having been early impressed on his mind, from letters which his parents had received from their sisters in Kentucky, giving an account of the wonderful revival of religion in all that region, about the year 1800. In the Spring of 1810, he was appointed one of the Tutors of Princeton College, which position, although at first declining, he was finally, on the solicitation of Dr. Stanhope Smith, and other friends, induced to accept, and which he held for two and one-half years, the two last as senior Tutor.

In September, 1812, he resigned the Tutorship, and in October accepted a call as Pastor of the Church of Madison, Morris Co., N. J., about 20 miles from the City of N. Y. and took charge on the 1st of Dec., having married Miss Henderson in Nov. This church, during his ministry, was blessed with several revivals, on one occasion as many as 69 members being added to the communion in one day. In 1817, a revival, with a lesser ingathering, took place. In 1821-2 a great revival took place in East Jersey, commencing with the church at Madison, continuing for more than 15 months, in which more than 100 communicants were added to his church. In 1826, twenty six were added. In 1828, his parents being on a visit to him from the West, he concluded that his work in the East was about completed, and that a door was opened for him in the West, to which place his early aspirations had been directed. On the 10th of September, 1828, he resigned his charge, and on the 22d, with his parents and family, started on wheels for his new destination. They traveled some 1,500 miles, averaging 33 miles a day, deviating from the nearest route to visit Lexington and Frankfort, in Kentucky, and arrived in Illinois in Nov; Springfield, in Sangamon Co., being the end of their journey. Springfield, at the time, was composed of about 35 log cabins and two or three small frame houses, without a place of Divine worship other than a log school house, just built. At the time there were no churches in those regions, except those built of logs, like the cabins everybody lived in, only larger and generally rougher, some with the bark on, and others hewed. All were covered with what are now called clap-boards; these boards were kept on the roof, not with nails, for these were very scarce and expensive, but with weight poles, and these were separated from each other by knees, as they were called. The floors were laid of puncheons, being logs split, and of the same the seats were made: these were supported by wooden legs in augur holes. On the second Sabbath after his arrival, he gave notice to the people that he came to Springfield, not to make an experiment, or to tarry a few months, as had been often done by others, but to live, labor and die on the field with his armor on: he said, "come, let us rise up and build a house for God." A meeting was held, a building committee organized, funds raised, and ere long was built and dedicated the first frame or brick meeting house in the State, known as the Sangamon Church: the Methodists of Springfield, who had been aroused by his exertions, completing one a few weeks later. When he came to the town there were but 6 members of the Presbyterian Church in it: during his ministry about 500 were added to his church, about one-half on confession of faith, and the balance on certificate from other churches. At the time it was the only Presbyterian Church in the County, some of the members living 40 miles apart. Out of it he has since organized six other Presbyterian Churches, two of them in the City, colonies from the first, the others in the surrounding country.   At the time he commenced laboring in the State, there were but seven Presbyterian ministers in it, he making the eighth, and now, 1865, the only survivor.   He helped form the first Presbytery, and afterwards the first Synod in the State, and was the first Moderator of the same.   At that time there were only 25 Presbyterian Churches in the State, and no Congregational or New School ones, although numerous Methodist, Baptist, Cambelite, Cumberland, &c.   Now there are in connection with the Old School Presbyterian General Assembly, two Synods and twelve Presbyteries, embracing nearly 200 ministers, and about 250 churches, the New School Presbyterians having about the same number, and the same may be said of the Congregationalists.   What an amazing progress in 33 years! from 8 ministers to 400; from 25 to 700 churches, other denominations advancing in proportion.   At the time, Illinois had but 150,000 inhabitants; now it has 1,750,000.   Springfield, from being a log house town, has become a stately city of 12,000 people, having many fine churches and buildings, and one private mansion which cost about $200,000.   It is the seat of government, having a magnificent State House, built of hard stone of various colors, quarried about six miles south of the place.   In 1848 he resigned his pastoral charge, and retired from the city to his farm in the vicinity, from which time he has devoted himself gratuitously to writing, mostly for religious periodicals, endeavoring to preach the gospel to the tens of thousands by the press; also to organize new churches, occasionally preaching in them.   Many of his articles are over the sobriquet of "The Old Man of the Prairies."   In 1854, without solicitation or knowledge on his part, the honorary degree of Doctor of Divinity was conferred on him by

the College of Danville, Kentucky. His wife having died
in Oct., 1853, in Nov., 1857, he married, as a second wife,
Susan Ann Lewis, widow of Henry Vanhof, who had
been an elder in his church, and for whom he had performed the marriage ceremony 20 years before, she being
a native of Baskingridge, N. J. In 1853, he was brought
to death's door by dysentery, the same disease which removed his first wife, but since his recovery his system has
been renovated; he weighs 50 pounds more than when
he resigned his charge, and his ability to endure fatigue,
study, and preaching, is now, 1862, greater than it then
was.*

Issue by 1st marriage; all b. in N. J. :

Jane Eliza, b. ——, 1813; d. March ——, 1857; m. April ——, 1833.
Robert Allen, of Kentucky, a merchant in Springfield, and during the
Mexican war a Major in the Quartermaster's Department, who d. Dec.
——, 1854. Had children, two sons: one d. in infancy, and the other
was a Capt. in an Illinois regiment, and took part in the battle of Belle-
mont, was for a time Provost Marshal of Columbus, and was in the
thickest of the fight at Fort Donelson, in the present great rebellion.

Catharine Henderson, b. Sept. ——, 1816; m. Nov. ——, 1836, Edward
Jones, a lawyer of the District of Columbia, s. of Walter Jones, an
attache of the Treasury Department of the United States since the days
of Alexander Hamilton. He was with Gen. Scott in the Mexican war, in
Gen. Shield's Brigade at the taking of Vera Cruz, and at the scaling of
Cerra Gorda. He d. in 1857, of disease contracted in Mexico. She had
issue: five children; the first three dying when about twelve months old:
John G. Bergen Jones, b. ——, 1855; and a daughter, Matilda Jones.

Amelia Matilda, b. July ——, 1818; m. ——, 1840, Joshua G.
Lamb, of Pennsylvania, a commission merchant at Alton, Illinois; no
issue.

Thomas Henderson, b. Dec. ——, 1820; m. April ——, 1849, Mary
Green, dau. of Rev. C. F. Cooly, D. D., and Catharine Henderson, of
N. J. Resides on a farm one mile east of Springfield; has no issue.

George, b. April ——, 1824; single, and resides on a farm adjoining his
brothers.

* The materials for this sketch of the Rev. J. G. Bergen, were furnished
by himself, also much that relates to his branch of the Bergen family.

DAVID COMBS BERGEN, b. Jan. 2d, 1795, d. July , 1834, in Kentucky; m. , 1813, *Nancy*, dau. of Judge Boyce, of New Brunswick, N. J. He was educated to be a physician, which profession he never followed, commencing actual life in the commercial establishment of John Pool, in New Brunswick. When his father's family removed from Kentucky, he remained in that State, and engaged in teaching until his death. Nancy Boyce was born Nov. 4th, 1788, and d. Dec. 4th, 1854.

Issue :—

Mary E., b. July 3d, 1814; m. March 27th, 1837, Jacob Dubois, a farmer of Warren Co., Ohio, and has children: Ann Elizabeth, b. May 16th, 1838; Nelson Rue, b. Jan. 15th, 1840, m. June 14th, 1860, Joanna Chase; Louisa B., b. March 1st, 1844, m. May 1st, 1862, Joseph Hendrickson, a carpenter; Jacob, b. Aug. 29th, 1849; and Mary Margaret, b. Jan. 1st, 1855.

John B., b. Jan. 27th, 1815; m. July 25th, 1842, Jane Maria Stelle. Cultivates a farm at Dayton, O., and has children: Edward Stelle, b. Jan. 22d, 1843; Mary Frances, b. Oct. 2d, 1846; Moses Parkmow, b. Oct. 31st, 1848; George Boice, b. Sept. 3d, 1850; d. aged 11 months; Anna Jane, b. Jan. 3d, 1852; and Cornelia Barkolow, b. Aug. 19th, 1854.

Louisa, b. Feb. 3d, 1818; m. April 9th, 1839, George L. Denise, of Franklin, Ohio, a smith and farmer, and has children: Ira Condit, b. Feb. 29th, 1840; Obediah Howes, b. Jan. 4th, 1842; Correna Ann, b. Feb. 25th, 1844, d. Oct. 24th, 1844; Charles Edgar, b. Nov. 4th, 1845; Julia Hines, b. May 28th, 1848; Sallie Belle, b. Oct. 14th, 1851; Henrietta Boice, b. Oct. 21st, 1857; and Carrie Stryker, b. June 11th, 1860.

George P., b. Jan. 1st, 1820, m. August 25th, 1857, Mary E. Bentley, of Albany. Is a graduate of Danville College, and studied Divinity at Princeton. At first settled for a number of years in Locktown, near Cincinnati; then accepted an appointment in the field of Domestic Missions at Omaha, Nebraska. After remaining two years, his health failing, he returned to Ohio, and accepted a call as Pastor of the Presbyterian Church at Bellefontaine, in that State. Has children: Paul David, b. July 19th, 1860, and George Bentley, b. Jan 11th, 1862.

Syche, b. March 12th, 1822; m. May 10th, 1842, Nehemiah Francis, a farmer in Warren Co., O., and has children: Richard, b. May 2d, 1844

25

Mary A., b. June 28th, 1847; Cornelia, b. May 10th, 1849; Otho Evans, b. Aug. 30th, 1851; Deborah, b. June 12th, 1853, d. Sept. 10th, 1853; George Bergen, b. July 20th, 1856; and Sally K., b. July 8th, 1860.

Cornelia Ann, b. Oct. 22d, 1826; m. Dec. 31st, 1844, Moses V. Barkaloo, oil merchant, Franklin, Ohio, and has children: William V., b. Jan. 25th, 1846; Elizabeth E., b. Sept. 15th, 1857; Emma R., b. May 12th, 1850; Anna E., b. Sept. 14th, 1852; Jennie B., b. Aug. 4th, 1854, d. Oct. 29th, 1859; and Louisa Denyse, b. June 16th, 1861.

Elizabeth Light, b. June 29th, 1830; m. July 2d, 1850, Dr. R. P. Evans, of Franklin, O., and has children: Forman Richard, b. Aug 29th, 1851; John Newton, b. May 19th, 1855, d. July 6th, 1856; Cornelia B., b. April 16th, 1857; and Jennie, b. March 31st, 1861, d. May 24th, 1861.

Susan B., b. Dec. 13th, 1823; d. Aug. 27th, 1854; m. ——, 1843, Joseph Denise, a farmer in Warren County, Ohio. Has children: George Bergen, b. June 19th, 1848, d. Aug. 12th, 1849; Clara, b. Nov. 10th, 1849; Elizabeth Evans, b. Oct. 30th, 1852; Susan B., b. Aug. 27th, 1854, d. young.

MARGARET BERGEN, b. ——, 1796; d. about 1837; m. ——, 1815. *Nathan Compton*, at first a merchant in New Brunswick, and afterwards a farmer in Illinois.

Issue :—

James Compton, a merchant in Augusta, Ohio.

John B. Compton, a merchant in Augusta, Ohio.

Thomas Henderson Compton, a resident of Indiana.

Rebecca Compton, m. William Lewis of Pennsylvania, a lawyer and a merchant.

JONATHAN COMBS BERGEN, b. May 20th, 1799; d. Dec. 15th, 1848; m. Dec. 1st, 1819, his cousin, *Mary Ann*, dau. of Peter Conover. Was a farmer and carpenter at Princeton, Cass Co., Illinois, and with his wife, a member of the Baptist Church, and for many years an officer in the same.

Issue :— -

David Combs, b. May 17th, 1824; d. Feb. 26th, 1847.

Hannah Rebecca, b. May 2d, 1827; d. Aug. 6th, 1850.

Catharine, b. Jan. 24th, 1831; d. March 10th, 1832.

P⁰⁰ L. S. Je'y 4th, 1857 m ——— , 1852 Dolle Conover, and a s a
dau., Aadie. By occupation a farmer.

Mary E b O, b. Oct 27th 1840; d Nov. 7th, 1840.

MARTHA D. BERGEN, b. June 14th, 1801 ; d. Sept. 9th,
1838 ; m. Sept. 16th, 1818, her cousin, *Jonathan Combs*,
s. of Peter Conover, a farmer in Illinois. They were
both members of the Baptist Church, and had several
children.

ABRAM STRYKER BERGEN, b. Aug. 17th, 1801 ; d.
Feb. 26th, 1848 ; m. 1st, Nov. 1st, 1824, *Elizabeth*, dau.
of James White, of Kentucky, b. Dec. 1, 1805, d. July
21, 1832 ; m. 2d, May 17th, 1833, *Fil Via A. Eldridge*,
wid. of ——— Sturtevant, of Vermont, b. May 17th,
1809.

Intending to enter the gospel ministry, he commenced
his preparatory studies for that purpose, but in consequence of the family removing west, the design was frus-
trated. Was at first a farmer in Illinois, then a merchant,
afterwards a successful land speculator, so that in 1837,
he was reputed to be wealthy, but the sudden crash of
that period swept away all his property like dew before
the morning sun. From that time until his death, he devoted himself to the work which his conscience had so often upbraided him for forsaking, and was intent upon redeeming the lost time, if it were possible. As an agent of the
Bible and Tract Societies, he visited from house to house
throughout the state of Illinois, carrying with him the
word of God, and many, very many, can testify to the
good work wrought within them through his instrumen-
tality. His last sickness of sixteen weeks was character-
ised by a christian fortitude and patience seldom exhibited
by mortal man. The influence exerted upon his neighbors and friends during that period, will never, while they
survive, be forgotten.

Issue by 1st wife:—

Mary Jane, b. Nov. 1st, 1825; d. Aug. 22d, 1834.

George I., b. Dec. 31st, 1827; m. Oct. 9th, 1849, Sylvia Maria Field, of Vermont, b. Sept. 15th, 1826, and has children: George A., b. Nov. 4th, 1852, d. Aug. 22d, 1854; Frank Delong, b. March 13th, 1856, d. Oct. 13th, 1856; Mary Lincoln, b. May 13th, 1859; and Loyal Harry, b. July 12th, 1861.

George I. Bergen carries on a carriage and wagon manufactory at Galesberg, Illinois, is the inventor of a valuable corn and seed planter is at present (1864,) a member of the Common Council of Galesberg, has held many important public trusts, and in 1862, was the defeated Union candidate for state Senator, for the district in which he resides, and ran 400 ahead of the regular ticket.

James W., b. Dec. 13th, 1829, m. March 28th, 1853, Lucretia Curry, of Illinois, b. May 6th, 1834, and has children: Abraham G., b. Sept. 13th, 1854, and George I., b. July 12th, 1859.

By 2d wife:

Margaret M., b. Feb. 24th, 1834; d. June 30th, 1835.

Wells G., b. May 25th, 1835; d. Feb. 21st, 1837.

Edward H., b. Jan. 3d, 1837; d. Aug. 14th, 1837.

Francis Louisa, b. Sept. 5th, 1841; d. Dec. 3d, 1844.

Susan A., b. Feb. 1st, 1844; m. June 27th, 1861, Rev. Rufus B. Guild, and has issue: George A., b. April 28th, 1863.

J. P. Williston, b. Feb. 1st, 1847.

SARAH BALDWIN BERGEN b. at Pluckamine, N. J., Jan. 26th, 1807; m. 1st, Dec. 24th, 1822, *Hezekiah Smith*, who kept a public house at Beardstown, on the Illinois river, and who d. Aug. 6th, 1834; m. 2d, March 25th, 1835, Moses Perkins, of New Hampshire, a hotel keeper at Burlington Iowa.

Issue by 1st husband: 8 children, 5 of whom d. under the age of 8 years, the survivors being:

Desdemonia E. Smith, who m. May 7th, 1848, John S. McClure, an attorney, who d. April 1854; she d. in June 1861.

Hezekiah Smith, who d. Aug. 6th, 1834.

Issue by 2d husband: 8 children, 6 of whom d. under the age of 6 years, the survivors being:

John L. Perkins, b. May 9th, 1837, m. June 19th, 1864, Laura J. Renshaw. Entered the army as Capt. of Co. D 25th Reg't Iowa Infantry, in Sept. 1862, and was promoted to Major of said Reg't on the 9th day of May, 1863. Served with his Reg't until Dec., 1864, when he was detached by Maj. Gen. C. R. Woods, commanding 1st Div. 17th army corps, as Chief of Staff. Was with Gen. Sherman in all his campaigns until the end of the war, when his Reg't was mustered out of the service at Washington, D. C.

Albert A. Perkins, b. Jan. 22d, 1840. Entered the army as 2d Lieut. of Co. D, 25th Reg't. Iowa Infantry, in Sept. 1862, was promoted to 1st Lieut. in Feb., 1863, to Capt. on the 9th of May, 1863, served with his Co. and Reg't until January, 1864. when he was detached as Acting Ass't Inspector Gen'l of 1st Divis. 15th army corps, and in November, 1864, was detached by Maj. Gen. P. Jos. Osterhause, commanding 15th army corps, as Act. Ass't Ins. Gen., of 15th army corps. Was with Gen. Sherman in all his campaigns up to Jan., 1865, when he was detached as Aid-de-Camp to Maj. Gen. Osterhause, and was with the Gen'l at the capture of Mobile, and carried despatches under a flag of truce from Gen. Canby to Gen. Taylor, (rebel.) concerning terms of Taylor's surrender, and then accompanied Gen. Osterhause to Jackson, Miss., where he left the Gen'l and reported to his regiment to be mustered out, on the expiration of the term of service.

GEORGE SPOFFORD WOODHULL BERGEN, b. July 6th, 1809; m. Feb. 16th, 1829, *Emily Wyatt*, whose father with a large family emigrated from Kentucky to Illinois. Is a farmer near Petersburg, Minard Co., Illinois, 20 miles west of Springfield, and himself and wife members of the Presbyterian church. Was named after the Rev. George Spafford Woodhull, pastor of the Presbyterian church of Cranberry, N. J.

Issue :—

Walter, b. Feb. 18th, 1830; m. Mr. H., and he completed his college course.

Lucy Ann, b. Dec. 3d, 1832; d. Feb. 2, 1868.

John Milton, b. July 10th, 1834, m. Feb. 2d, 1855, Mary Jane Moore. Is a farmer near Petersburg, Illinois, has four children, as above, and has children: Cordelia, b. May 20th, 1857; d. July 15, 1857; Edward Franklin, b. Sep. 19th, 1858; Henry Moore, b. Nov. 2, 1860; and Thomas Henderson, b. June 10th, 1863.

Susan Olive, b. March 22d, 1836; d. March 6th, 1857; m. June 6th, 1856, Milton Tate Moore, and had a son, George Allen, b. Feb. 27th, 1859, and d. Aug. 1859.

Benjamin Franklin, b. June 28th, 1838; m. 1st. Jan. 26th, 1859. Dulcene Moore, by whom issue: George Franklin, b. Aug. 26th, 1860; d. Dec. 3d, 1862; m. 2d. Oct. 24th, 1861, Elizabeth Clark, by whom issue: Annie, b. March 3d, 1863. Is a dry goods merchant at Petersburg, Illinois.

James Monroe, b. May 1st, 1840. Studying law near Petersburg.

Abram Samuel, b. April 13th, 1842.

Jacob Fisher, b. April 23d, 1844.

Jonathan Combs, b. April 2d, 1846.

Sarah Emily, b. Dec. 11th, 1848; d. March 25th, 1857.

Charles Henry, b. Dec. 19th, 1851.

The following article in relation to Susan Olive Bergen, written by the Rev. John G. Bergen, was published in the St. Louis Presbyterian, together with the accompanying stanzas, composed by her a short time before her last sickness :

"Hope in Death."

" Having just returned from visiting some of our feeble churches and desolate places ; having had the privilege of preaching to the destitute, holding prayer meetings, communion seasons, and Sunday school enjoyments ; having especially visited many of the grand children and other relics of my departed venerable friend, John Moore, on whom the sweet savor of his spirit and prayers rests with an unction blessed and blessing to the praise of our covenant-keeping God ; and having found the following *touching incident* and stanzas in a young family composed of his household and mine, I send them to you, hoping that these tender mementos of God's grace—this conjugal effusion of a young wife and mother's calm, peaceful and Heavenly desires, counsels, suggestions and anticipations, may alleviate some drooping spirit—point some wanderer to a better world—soothe some aching heart—encourage some child of affliction to look up, once earth bound soul to come away from fashion and forth to a throne of grace to receive the spirit of adoption, and to breathe the life of Christ in the soul amidst bodily agonies present or to come. These children of God had been wedded two years—to them short years and full of promise. Blooming in youth and health, in the midst of a large circle of relatives and friends, their home beautified by the family altar, enlightened by the lamp of Heaven, resounding with the songs of redeeming love gave them their sweetest seasons of communion at the throne of grace with the light of His countenance and the joy of His salvation.

"The last four months of her life—apparently without a cause other than her delicate condition—were months in which she felt and allowed the presentiment that she would not survive to be a living mother. Her spirits meantime were cheerful, but her conversation savored of the presentiment she indulged. I cannot but think wrongfully—though with a "lively hope by the resurrection of Jesus Christ from the dead." She survived the event, by which she was greatly sustained but a few days, and sweetly fell asleep in Jesus, leaving a living pledge of love to tender hearts and willing hands. A few days after her burial the following stanzas, full of tenderness and delicacy, as if touched by an angel's wing, were found in her escritoir. So far as I know they are original. Be it so or not, unless I am greatly mistaken, they will move the feelings of every reader to kindlier, holier sentiments, by their vein of generous nature, grief and wisdom, and well deserve a place in every heart, therefore I send them.

"Come near *me*, let me lay my hand
Once more upon thy brow—
And let me whisper in thy ear
Loves last and fondest vow.

"Perchance the hour may come,
When thou wilt win another form
To soothe thy heart and home,
When thou wilt welcome to thy board,
A younger, fairer face—
And bid thy child smile on her
Who takes its mother's place.

"But, think not, could I speak to thee,
That I would frown or blame
That it should love the stranger one,
And call her by my name,
For it may speak to thee of me—
My memory is its trust,
A word, a smile, a look like mine
Will call me from the dust.

"Yet make my grave no place of tears,
But let the dear one bring,
To cheer its mother's lonely home
The blossoms of the spring;
And ever there, thou mayest kneel,
And softly press the earth,
That covers her whose face once gave
A brightness to thy hearth.

"Then will the form of early years
Steal softly to thy side,
And for the hour thou canst forget
Thou hast another bride.
She may be all thy heart canst ask,
So dear, so true to thee!
But oh! the spring time of love!
Its freshness was for me."

May she be blessed who comforts thee,
And with a gentle hand
Of such there be, the trembling one
That would make a household band;
She cannot know the tenderness
That would fill its mother's breast,
But she can love it for thy sake,
And make it more than blessed.

Yet keep one place, one little place,
From all the rest apart—
One spot—which I will call a home
Within thy faithful heart—
And in the holy hour of dreams,
When spirits fill the air—
With tender eye and folded wing
I'll gently rest me there.

May God forgive this erring love
That is to mortals given;
It almost moves my soul back
From happiness and Heaven,
And yet I feel it will not die
When this frail life is o'er,
But watch till my loved ones come
To meet to part no more."

IDA VAN NESS BERGEN, b. Oct. 14th, 1811; m. 1st,
Sept. 2d, 1828, *James G. Kenner*, of Virginia, a son of
her step-father, who d. a violent death in 1837; m. 2d,
John W. Skidmore, who d. Jan. 5th, 1863, at St. Louis,
Missouri, where they had resided for many years. Resides
at present at Chillicothe, Peoria Co., Ill., and is a member
of the Baptist church. No children by 2d marriage.

Issue by 1st marriage:

John Lewis Kenner, b. Nov. 14th, 1829, at Preston, Ill.; m. Dec. 1st,
1850, Caroline Cornelia Smith, of N. Y. Resides on the Illinois river 20
miles west of Peoria, and has living 2 sons, John Lewis and Henry Burton.

26

ANN HENDERSON BERGEN, b. 1815; d. prior to 1862; m. 1832. *William Mallory*, of Ohio, who settled on Jersey prairie, Illinois, and at first kept a small store; then a farmer, and afterwards removed to Cincinnati.

Issue :—

William Mallory, m. a Virginian, and kept a bookstore in Cincinnati, sold out in the winter of 1860, and removed to the city of N. Y.

Eliza Mallory, m. 1857, W. McMullen, a stationer in the city of N. Y.

Descendants of ABRAM BERGEN and *Catharine Voorhees* and *Hannah Fisher*, of Cranberry, N. J. :—

SARAH BERGEN, (by 1st wife,) b. 1790; m. *Samuel E. Jones*.

MARY BERGEN, (by 2d wife,) b. Jan. 19th, 1797; m. *Joseph I. Rue*.

Issue :—

John Rue, m. a dau. of William Mount.

Hannah Rue, deceased.

Rebecca Rue, m. Wm. Scudder.

Abram Rue, m. Mary Voorhees.

Jacob Rue, m. ———— Conover, of Freehold.

Peter Rue, single, resides at Hightstown.

JOHN A. BERGEN, b. Sept. 21st, 1799; d. Aug. 25th, 1865; m. 1822. *Eliza* or *Elizabeth Duncan*. Owned and cultivated a farm between Cranberry and Hightstown, N. J.:

Issue :—

Mary Ann, b. Sept. 30th, 1823; m. March 6th, 1850, Elijah Voorhees Perrine, and has children: Elizabeth, Jane and Jacob Bergen.

Abram, b. April 23d, 1826; d. Jan. 23d, 1828.

Isabella, b. Oct. 24th, 1828; m. March 3d, 1853, Derick Perrine, and has children: John Bergen and Samuel.

Jacob, b. Sept. 23d, 1830; m. Nov. 14th, 1854, Sarah Emma Griggs, and has children: William McMullen and Charles Morgen.

Charles Morgen, b. March 1st, 1833; d. Aug. 15th, 1849.

Peter, b. Aug. 16th, 1835; m. Dec. 2d, 1857, Rebecca Roberts, and has children: Sarah Ann and Eliza Jane.

Samuel Jones, b. Oct. 31st, 1837.

John Scudder, b. Jan. 5th, 1848; d. Aug. 3d, 1848.

JACOB F. BERGEN, b. May 27th, 1802; m. Dec. 16th, 1833, *Eliza Jane Montgomery*, b. Jan. 3d, 1817. Emigrated west and settled on a farm at Princeton, Jersey prairie, Cass Co., 30 miles west of Springfield, Illinois.

Issue:—

Abram, b. March 11th, 1836; m. Sept. 1863, L. C. Thompson, and has a son George, b. Dec. 26th, 1864. Is an attorney and resides at Pekin, Ill.

John L., b. Sept. 5th, 1842; m. Dec. 2d, 1862 S. C. Stevenson, and has a dau. Louisa Mildred, b. Nov. 2d, 1864. Is a farmer and cattle dealer, and resides two miles south of Virginia, Cass Co., Illinois.

George Spafford, b. Nov. 1st, 1844. Is a minister of the gospel, unmarried. Sailed as a foreign missionary from Boston for India July 20th, 1865, and is connected with the old school Presbyterian church.

MARGARET BERGEN, b. Sept. 5th, 1805; m. *John C. Morris*, who resides at Plainsboro, near Princeton, N. J.

Issue:—

Virginia Morris, m. Dr. Scudder.

Caroline Morris.

Jane Morris.

Ann Morris.

George Morris.

CAROLINE BERGEN, b. Sept. 10th, 1808; m. Feb. 24th, 1829, *Cornelius Wyckoff*, a farmer at Cranberry, N. J.

Issue:—

Jacob F. Wyckoff, b. March 14th, 1830; m. Hinton, and is a merchant.

Abraham Bergen Wyckoff, b. Dec. 1835. Is a farmer.

Hannah Virginia Wyckoff, b. Oct. 11th, 1837, m. T. H. Harris, a merchant.

Kenneth A. Wyckoff, b. Jan. 1st, 1845.

HANNAH VIRGINIA BERGEN, b. Jan. 29th, 1813; m. Dr. *John V. D. Scudder*, of Cranberry Neck.

Issue :—

Johannah V. Scudder.
Sarah Scudder.
Edwin Scudder.

Descendants of JOHN I. BERGEN and *Mary Mershon,* of Scott's Corners, near Cranberry, N. J. :—

MARIA SCHENCK BERGEN, b. Sept. 27th, 1797 : d. Oct. 26th, 1824 : m. Sept. 1816, *David W. Griggs,* b. May 10th, 1792 ; d. 1819, a farmer near the cross-roads, Middlesex Co., N. J.

Issue :—

Mary Ann Griggs, b. July 1817 ; m. Martin Ryerson, of Long Island, and is dead.

John W. Griggs, b. Oct. 20th, 1818 ; m. Phebe Walter, and is a farmer near Jamesberg, on the Camden and Amboy railroad.

ENOCH BERGEN, b. Feb. 28th, 1801 ; d. Oct. 27th, 1824, single.

CHRISTOPHER I. BERGEN, b. June 2d, 1803 : m. Nov. 19th, 1828, *Mary Rue,* who d. July 17th, 1864. Is a farmer, and resides in the village of Cranberry, N. J.

Issue :—

Enoch, b. July 25th, 1830 ; m. Nov. 21st, 1855, Catharine Ann Davidson, b. Feb. 7th, 1836.

Peter R., b. Oct. 11th, 1832 ; m. Feb. 21st. 1856, Cornelia Forman.

Sarah Stryker, b. April 8th, 1835 ; m. Nov. 1st, 1855, Howard C. Scudder.

Anna Wilson, b. Sept. 9th, 1837.

William E., b. Feb. 4th, 1842.

SAMUEL MERSHON BERGEN, b. Nov. 16th, 1805 : d. about March, 1856, single. A hatter by trade.

ELIAS BERGEN, b. Sept. 8th, 1808 ; m. *Phebe Rue.* Is a farmer at Dutch Neck, N. J.

Issue:

Henry, b. May 16th, 1835; m. Anna Arabella Laird

Rebecca, b. July 5th, 1838

Gilbert, b. Dec. 19th, 1844.

Edgar, b. May 21st, 1847

SARAH STRYKER BERGEN, b. Sept. 29th, 1810; m. Oct. 9th, 1829, *Thomas S. Snediker*, of Jamesburg, N. J.

Issue:

Mary Ann Snediker, b. April 1st, 1832; m. Oct. 5th, 1864, Austin L. Richardson, of Brattleboro, Vermont, and resides near Jamesburg, N. J.

Sarah Elizabeth Snediker, b. June 7th, 1841.

Emmeline Snediker, b. July 12th, 1844.

Isaac Snediker, b. June 21st, 1847.

Willard Snediker, b. Dec. 22d, 1850; d. Sept. 11th, 1859

WILLIAM ELLWOOD BERGEN, b. Nov. 13th, 1816; m. *Emmeline Chamberlin*. Is a farmer at Cranberry, N. J.

Issue:

Hannah Virginia, b. Aug. 25th, 1844

Mary, b. May 18th, 1846.

Sarah Stryker, b. Aug. 11th, 1848; d. Sept. 1st, 1856.

Elizabeth, b. Sept. 13th, 1850; d. Sept. 1st, 1856.

Sarah Stryker, b. July 17th, 1852.

Ella, b. June 4th, 1857.

John, b. March 7th, 1860.

Descendants of PETER I. BERGEN and *Anna Crozer*, of Penn's Neck, N. J.

GARRET BERGEN, d. young; m. *Mary Hope*. Was a farmer near Dutch Neck.

Issue:-

Harriet, m. Charles R. Stoucker.

LAMMATTA BERGEN; m. *Elias Updike*.

JOHN C. BERGEN, m. *Gertrude Dennen*. Is a farmer at Dutch Neck.

Issue:

Ann, m. John P. Brown.

Caroline, m. Peter S. Stout

Sarah, m. John R. Stutts.

Peter, m. Adeline Applegate.

Elizabeth, m. Simon Everett.

Susan, m. Abraham M. Skilman, of Brooklyn.

Lammatta, m. Daniel D. Davidson.

George D.

Joseph II.

Asa F., deceased.

SARAH BERGEN, d. 1855; m. *Abraham Terhune,* of Princeton.

Issue :—

2 children.

GEORGE BERGEN; m. *Matilda Dey.* Is a farmer at Dutch Neck, near Penn's Neck, N. J.

Descendants of JACOB I. BERGEN and *Syche Bergen,* of Cranberry, N. J. :—

CORNELIA BERGEN, b. Dec. 13th, 1806; d. Feb. 4th, 1851; m. Feb. 22d, 1826, *Denyse Thompson,* of Freehold, N. J.

Issue :—

Jacob Bergen Thompson, b. Dec. 7th, 1826; d. Dec. 23d, 1827.

William I. Thompson, b. June 7th, 1828.

John Bergen Thompson. b. May 4th, 1830.

Joseph Conover Thompson, b. Dec. 27th, 1832.

Cornelia D. Thompson, b. Feb. 15th, 1834.

Stephen Emmans Thompson, b. Oct. 27th, 1836.

Tunis D. Thompson, b. Oct. 13th, 1839.

Charles II. Thompson, b. Aug. 23d, 1843.

JOHN W. BERGEN, b. June 28th, 1808; m. Oct. 22d, 1831, *Catharine V. Vanderbilt,* b. March 22d, 1807; d. Dec. 15th, 1844; m. 2d, March 3d, 1846, Mary Hunt, who d. July 20th, 1858; m. 3d, May 16th, 1860, Susan P. Large. Was a merchant at Lambertsville, N. J., on the Delaware river.

Issue :

Helena C., b. Aug. 4th, 1832; m. April 4th, 1860, Henry D., son of Peter P. Bergen.

Jacob, b. Jan. 5th, 1834 ; d. April 28th, 1863.

Dennis C., b. May 24th, 1837; m. Oct. 15th, 1863, Julia Bergen.

John Henry, b. Aug. 13th, 1839; d. June 10th, 1858.

Syche Mariah, b. Oct. 31st, 1841 ; m. July 23d, 1865, James Oliver.

Catherine Jane, b. April 3d, 1844 ; d. Aug 20th, 1845.

By 3d wife :

Charles Emae, b. Jan. 21st, 1862.

William Earnest, b. Sept. 14th, 1864.

ABRAHAM BERGEN, b. July 12th, 1810; m. *Elizabeth Vanderveer.*

Resides at Saddle River, N J., and has no issue.

MATTHEW EGERTON BERGEN, b. Dec. 25th, 1813; m. Dec. 25th, 1830, *Sarah Dehart,* who d. March 17th, 1841 : m. 2d, Nov. 9th, 1844, *Gitty A. H. Manly.* Late a farmer ; in 1862, resided in George street, New Brunswick, N. J.

Issue by 1st wife :—

Henrietta, b. Jan. 23d, 1831 ; d. Oct. 1st, 1855 ; m., 1852, Conover Cortelyou, and had children : Sarah Jane Cortelyou, b. 1853, and Henrietta Cortelyou, b. 1855.

Jacob I., b. Sept. 26th, 1833 ; d. Oct. 1st, 1855.

Hannah Maria, b. Nov. 21st, 1836 ; d. Aug. 25th, 1838.

By 2d wife :—

Aaron M., b. March 3d, 1845.

Sarah S., b. Aug. 23d, 1848.

Charles D., b. Aug. 20th, 1850; d. Aug. 8th, 1851.

SIMON HILLYER BERGEN, b. June 13th, 1816; m. June 13th, 1836, *Mary Voorhies,* b. Dec. 13th, 1820. Late a manufacturer; in 1862, resided in George street, New Brunswick, N. J.

Issue :—

William Voorhies, b. July 28th, 1837 ; m. Oct. 12th, 1839.

Jacob, b. April 17th, 1839.

Mary Ellen, b. June 21st. 1846.

Cornelia, b. Feb. 22d, 1849.

John Hillyer, b. May 21st. 1852.

Peter Voorhies. b. June 18th, 1856.

SARAH MARIA BERGEN. b. Oct. 6th. 1821: m. Sept. 7th, 1857. *Charles Webber*. of Brooklyn. N. Y. No issue.

Descendants of CHRISTOPHER BERGEN and *Mary Disbrow*. of Cranberry Neck. N. J.:—

SAMUEL DISBROW BERGEN, b. Aug. 25th. 1809; m. Nov. 25th. 1835. *Charity Voorhees*. b. Sept. 22d. 1804. Is a storekeeper at Princeton. N. J.

Issue :—

Mary D., b. Nov. 2d. 1836.

Martin Voorhees. b. Feb. 12th, 1839.

Christopher A.. b. Aug. 2d, 1841.

Peter Voorhees. b. Feb. 1st. 1844.

Jennie S., b. Nov. 28th. 1847; d. June 16th, 1848.

Samuel D., b. Oct. 3d, 1850: d. Feb. 26th. 1851.

Samuel D.. b. April 9th. 1852.

SARAH A. BERGEN. b. Feb. 1st. 1811: d. Oct. 17th. 1844: m. Feb. 5th. 1834. *David Perrine*.

Issue :—

James Henry Perrine, b. 1835: d. young.

Christopher Perrine. b. Nov. 1841: d. Dec. 3d. 1860.

Mary Bergen Perrine, b. July 1833: m. Perrine.

IDA VAN NEST BERGEN. b. Jan. 25th. 1813: d. Sept. 2d. 1851: m. Feb. 5th. 1834. *George A. Hutchinson*. b. Jan. 21st. 1810. who after the death of Ida. m. April 20th. 1854. Julia Smith.

Issue :—

Marianna Hutchinson. b. Dec. 27th, 1834.

Thirza Anderson Hutchinson. b. Aug. 17th. 1836; d. June 17th. 1864: m. May 22d. 1861, H. Harrison Woolsey. who d. June 19th. 1864.

Emma Hutchinson, b. July 13th, 1838.

Alfred Bergen Hutchinson, b. April 1st. 1840.

Sarah M. Hutchinson, b. Jan. 31st. 1842.

Elizabeth Bergen Hutchinson, b. March 13th, 1841; d. July 6th, 1846.

Lewis E. Hutchinson, b. March 12th, 1846; d. Dec. 21st, 1852

George Augustus Hutchinson, b. March 26th, 1848

Symmes Bergen Hutchinson, b. Sept. 2d, 1851.

ALFRED BERGEN, b. Sept. 2d, 1815; d. Sept. 6th, 1849; m. Feb. 2d, 1842, *Mary T. Ward*, b. March 1st, 1821.

Was a physician and emigrated west, from whence he removed to Freehold, N. J., where he died.

Issue:

Alfred Ward, b. Oct. 29th, 1842; m. March 28th, 1864, M Virginia Lowell; is an accountant and resides at Paterson N. J.

Henry Williamson, b. March 13th, 1846 is a clerk, and resides at Newark, N. J.

JOHN STRYKER BERGEN, b. Oct. 21st, 1819; m. Dec. 6th, 1843, *Lydia Wyckoff*, d. Aug. 11th, 1845; m. 2d, Sept. 1848, *C. Amanda Hunt*, b. Sept. 6th, 1829. Is a farmer at Cranberry Neck, and no children by 1st wife.

Issue :

Symmes, b. Aug. 9th, 1849.

Elston Hunt, b. Oct. 15th, 1852.

JAMES WILLIAMSON BERGEN, b. Jan. 16th, 1823; m. Nov. 3d, 1847, *Abagail W. Scudder*, b. April 26th, 1830. Is a farmer at Scott's Corners, near Cranberry, N. J.

Issue :—

Isaac Scudder, b. Jan. 26th, 1849.

Elizabeth Ward, b. Oct. 4th, 1851.

John Stryker, b. July 4th, 1854.

Howard Scudder, b. March 28th, 1857.

Disbrow, b. May 5th, 1859.

Julia Scudder, b. Dec. 1st, 1861.

Mary Disbrow, b. Sept. 2d, 1864.

SYMMES HENRY BERGEN, b. July 15th, 1826; m. Nov. 28th, 1860, *Mary S. Lalor*, b. May 24th, 1834.

Is a physician, emigrated west, resides at Toledo, Ohio, and has no issue.

27

MARY BERGEN. b. Jan. 20th. 1828 : d. Feb. 11th. 1849 : m. Nov. 4th. 1847. *William Hooper.*

Issue :—

Mary Hooper. b. Jan. 23d. 1849.

ELIZABETH VOORHEES BERGEN. b. Jan. 2d. 1830 ; m. April 2d. 1850. *Caleb Condit Ward*. b. Dec. 7th. 1798. d. April 30th. 1860.

Issue :—

Caleb Condit Ward, b. Oct. 2d. 1851 : d. young.
John Condit Ward. b. April 24th. 1855.

Descendants of JOHN P. BERGEN and *Anna Conover*. of Cranberry Neck. N. J. :—

ELIZABETH BERGEN. b. Jan. 31st. 1789 : m. Jan. 8th. 1806. *Isaac Story*. of Kingston. N. J.

Issue :

John B. Story. m. Cornelia Conover. A farmer. and resides near Middletown. Monmouth Co.. N. J.

PETER C. BERGEN. b. Aug. 21st. 1792 : d. Dec. 24th. 1857 : m. 1st. Dec. 16th. 1813. *Lydia*, dau. of Dr. James Anderson. who d. Oct. 14th. 1828 : m. 2d. *Hannah*, dau. of James Mount.

Was the proprietor of the mill known as Bergen's mill in Middletown township. Monmouth Co.. N. J.

Issue by 1st wife :

Ann C. b. Oct. 15th. 1814 : m. Sept. 13th. 1832, John J. Lake, of Kingston. Middlesex Co.

James A. b. March 29th. 1816 : m. May 4th, 1842. Adelia or Cordelia, dau. of Thomas Ely. of Middletown. Is a farmer and has children : Ann Amelia. b. March 29th. 1844 : Lydia A.. b. Feb. 13th. 1856 and Peter C.. b. Aug.. 1848, resides in Monmouth Co.

Helen. b. Aug. 31st, 1817 : m. Feb. 10th. 1841. Smith Conover, of Red Bank.

Elizabeth B.. b. May 31st, 1819 ; m. Dec. 27th, 1837. Thomas Smith, of Manalapen.

John P., b. June 23d, 1823; m. Feb. 16th, 1859, Lydia, dau. of Richard Mount, of Manalapen, Monmouth Co., where he resides, is a farmer, and has children: Laura K. b. Feb. 23d, 1860, and Johnson Lake, b. June 30th, 1862.

Lydia A., b. Jan. 5th, 1825; m. Oct. 25th, 1848, Anthony Wilson, of Manalapen.

Matilda, b. Oct. 10th, 1828; d. Nov. 27th, 1863; m. March 12th, 1851, Peter F. Perrine, of Monaoea.

Issue by 2d wife:

Emma, b. April 3d, 1833; m. Jan. 1st, 1855, William Smith, of Smithville.

Cornelia, b. Nov. 12th, 1835; m. Dec. 31st, 1857, Matthew Perrine, of Perrinesville.

Virginia, b. Oct. 21st, 1838; single, resides at Perrinesville.

Edward, b. June 19th, 1841; single, and resides in the city of N. Y.

Descendants of PETER P. BERGEN and *Nancy Day*, of N. J. :—

CATHARINE BERGEN, b. April 2d, 1805; single.

JANE BERGEN, b. June 19th, 1807; m. *George Van Ness*. Reside in Pennsylvania.

Issue :—

Nancy Van Ness, d. aged 21.
Sidney Van Ness, d. aged 24.
John Van Ness.
Peter Bergen Van Ness.
George Van Ness.
Ida Van Ness.
William Van Ness.
Henry Van Ness.
Ellen Van Ness.

ELIZABETH BERGEN, b. Nov. 17th, 1810; m. *David Stonaker*. Reside at Plainsboro, N. J.

Issue :—

Alfred Stonaker.
Vincent Stonaker.
Elizabeth Stonaker.

John Stonaker.
Rebecca Stonaker.
William Stonaker.
Howell Stonaker.
Peter Stonaker, d. when a child.

JOHN BERGEN. b. April 23d, 1812; m. *Rose Ellen Applegate.** His children that are living are all married.

Issue :—

Sidney.
Sarah Ann, d. aged about 18.
Elizabeth, m. Charles Parient.
Ruth, m. Alfred Burris.
Emily.
Catharine.
Margaret.
Helen.
Vincent, d. when a child.

WILLIAM BERGEN. b. Dec. 25th, 1814; d. Jan. 22d. 1863 ; m. *Margaret Helen Vanderhoff*, who resides in New Brunswick.

Issue :—

Julia Ann, b. March 7th, 1838.
Martha June, b. May 17th, 1840; d. Nov. 29th, 1842.
Sarah, b. March 29th, 1842.
Alfred, b. March 19th, 1844.
Peter, b. Oct. 15th, 1848 ; d. Aug. 15th, 1851.
Theodore, b. April 7th, 1851.
William, b. Sept. 9th, 1854.

HENRY D. BERGEN, b. July 23d, 1817 ; m. 1st, *Maria Effingham ;* m. 2d, April 4th, 1860, *Helen*, dau. of John W. Bergen. Is a farmer near Cranberry, and had two children by his 2d wife, who d. young.

VINCENT D. BERGEN. b. Dec. 29th, 1821 ; m. Nov.

----

* Rose Ellen Applegate is probably a descendant of Thomas Applegate, an Englishman, who was among the early settlers of Gravesend, and Nov. 12th, 1646, purchased of John Ruckman, a plantation in said town. Many of the early settlers of this town removed to New Jersey.

24th, 1840, *Helen Hutchinson*, b. Aug. 28th, 1829. Is a farmer and resides in the village of Cranberry.

Issue:

Willia n Hutchinson, b. Nov. 28th, 1846.
Martha Ann b. July 27th, 1848

PETER T. BERGEN, b. Sept. 29th, 1824; killed Sept. 26th, 1843, by a fall from a horse, when about 20 years old.

CAROLINE BERGEN, b. May 9th, 1829; m. *John V. Snedeker*. Reside in Trenton.

Issue:—

Catharine Virginia Snedeker.
William Snedeke
Isaac Snedeker.

Descendants of JOHN G. BERGEN and *Elizabeth Conover*, of Cranberry Neck, N. J.:

LAMMETIE BERGEN, b. Sept. 3d, 1792; d. May 27th, 1817; m. Feb. 28th, 1811. *William Nutt.*

Issue:

Elizabeth Nutt, b. March 20th, 1812
Sarah Nutt, b. Aug. 2d, 1814.

HELEN BERGEN, b. May 3d, 1794, single.

RUTES BERGEN, b. Sept. 17th, 1796; d. Sept. 1st, 1859; m. April 9th, 1818. *Harriet Newbold*, b. Nov. 20th, 1799. In early life a shoemaker and tanner currier, at Milford, 1 1-2 miles south of Hightstown, N. J., afterwards a miller.

Issue:

John R., b. March 4th, 1819 d. Mar 12 1816, Js a boot and shoe dealer at Red Bank, married Ellen J. in B. J. Nov 1846, and Elizabeth, b. Oct. 8th, 1848.

William Ely, b. Aug. 20th, 1820, m. Sept 23d, 1849, Deborah Lockstreet Snyder, b. June 28th, 1825, a widow Is a clerk in Federal and store of his brother John R., and has children: Hannah Virginia, b. Aug. 9th. 1850, and Jane Ann, b. May 20th. 1854.

Lewis R., b. May 9th, 1823; m. Dec. 23d. 1850, Elenor Emily Horner. Is a boot and shoe dealer at Long Branch. No issue.

Lydia Ann, b. Nov. 7th, 1825; m. March 11th, 1849, William Mount Bergen, s. of Peter G., and has children: Sarah Elizabeth, b. Dec. 4th, 1852, and Lewis, b. Jan. 21st, 1857.

Andrew Jackson, b. March 27th, 1834; single. Is a miller at Colt's Neck, N. J.

Elizabeth, b. Nov. 4th, 1838; m. Dec. 31st, 1855, Charles H. Matthews, of Colt's Neck. No issue.

Descendants of GEORGE BERGEN and *Marshia* and *Elizabeth Scudder*, of N. J. :—

Issue by 1st wife :—

JOSEPH BERGEN. Enlisted in the navy and not heard of since.

ELIJAH BERGEN, d. about 20 years old.

ELLEN BERGEN, d. when about 10 years old.

LYDIA BERGEN, m. —— *Conover*, and died about one year after her marriage.

Children by 2d wife:

SARAH BERGEN, m. *Benjamin Hunt*.

Issue :—

George Hunt, m. Mary Hazard.
Marshia Hunt, b. Sept. 10th, 1820; m., 1843, Harmanus Carreboom. from whom she is divorced. Resides near Cranberry.
Daniel Hunt, d. young.
Ellen Hunt, d. young.
Hatty Hunt.
Emily Elizabeth Hunt, d. young.
Scudder Hunt, d. young.

HANNAH BERGEN, m. 1st, *Randell Dey;* m. 2d, *Eze-kiel Willson*.

Issue by 1st husband:

Elizabeth Dey.
Theodosia Dey.
Phebe Dey.

By 2d husband:

Lydia Wilson.
Hart Wilson, and others.

WILLIAM BERGEN, m. *Susan Reed.*

Issue:—

Alice, b. June 26th, 1806.
George, b. Nov. 9th, 1807.
Margaret, b. Oct. 8th, 1809.
Catharine, b. Nov. 6th, 1811.
James M., b. March 3d, 1814.
Elenor, b. March 10th, 1816.
John M, b. May 25th, 1818.
Emily R., b. Oct. 3d, 1822.
William M., b. Oct. 7th, 1824.
Gertrude Ann, b. Feb. 23d, 1827.
Jane Elizabeth, b. Sept. 19th, 1830.

ISAAC BERGEN, m. *Margaret Hoffman.*

Issue:—

Mary, d. young.
Virginia, m. William Winner.
George.
Rosalia.

ELIZA BERGEN, m. 1st. *Stephen Bowns*; m. 2d. *William Lutes*

Issue:—

Martha Bowns.
Stephen Bowns.

Descendants of PETER G. BERGEN and *Susan Mershon* of Perrinesville, N. J.:

ALICE BERGEN, b. June 26th, 1806; m. Jan. 29th, 1840, *Shafford Mount* b. Oct. 29th, 1813, of Cranberry, N. J.

Issue :—

William Henry Mount, b. Dec. 18th, 1843.

GEORGE BERGEN, m. *Mary Jane Mount.* Emigrated west in 1846, and resides at Monroe, Butler Co., Ohio.

Issue :—

Mary Jane, m. William Chamberlin.
William.

JAMES BERGEN, b. March 3d, 1814 ; m. Sept. 17th, 1839, *Amy Potts.* Was a farmer in Ocean Township near Marlborough, Monmouth Co., N. J., at present, (1865,) at Long Branch.

Issue :—

Thomas, b. Oct. 3d, 1840 ; m. Mary Ellen Woolley, b. April 4th 1848, d. May 29th, 1865.
Susan, b. Oct. 1st, 1842 ; d. Oct. 8th, 1845.
Charles W., b. July 13th, 1847.
Mary Ellen, b. July 1st, 1849.
John W., b. March 3d, 1854 ; d. Nov. 29th, 1860.
Willie M., b. Feb. 20th, 1862.
Martha J., b. Dec. 11th, 1864 ; d. May 4th, 1865.

ELLENOR or ELLEN BERGEN, b. March 10th, 1816 ; d. March 4th, 1853 ; m. June 10th, 1845, *Lewis Lucas.*

Issue :—

Susan Elizabeth Lucas, b. Oct. 24th, 1846.
Henry Lucas, b. Feb. 26th, 1848.
Julia Ann Lucas, b. Jan. 11th, 1851.

EMILY BERGEN, b. Oct. 3d, 1822 ; m. Feb. 8th, 1843, *Noah Applegate,* a farmer near the village of Cranberry, N. J.

Issue :—

Margaret Ann Applegate, b. Dec. 20th, 1843.
Peter B. Applegate, b. May 28th, 1846 ; d. Aug. 7th, 1847.
John Stults Applegate, b. May 6th, 1851.

WILLIAM MOUNT BERGEN, b. Oct. 7th, 1824 ; m. March

1st, 1849, *Lydia Ann*, dau. of Rutes Bergen, b. Nov. 7th, 1825. Is a blacksmith at Colt's Neck, N. J.

Issue:

Sarah Elizabeth, b. Dec. 4th, 1852

Lewis R., b. Jan. 21st, 1857.

GERTRUDE ANN BERGEN, b. Feb. 23d, 1827; single.

JANE ELIZA BERGEN, b. May 10th, 1829; single, and resides with her sister Gertrude Ann, at Hightstown, N. J.

Descendants of JACOB BERGEN and *Mary Borgan*, of Princeton, N. J.:

JACOB BERGEN, b. Oct. 3d, 1794; m. Oct. 3d, 1816, *Ellen Boorum*; d. Sept. 19th, 1864. Was a farmer at Farmer, Seneca Co., N. Y., to which place he removed, from N. J., in 1820.

Issue:--

Cornelius, b. Aug. 10th, 1817; d. May 3d, 1821

Sylia Maria, b. May 2d, 1819; m. March 11th, 1837, Ira Patridge, a farmer in Michigan, and has children: Ellen Ann Patridge, b. May 29th, 1838, who m. July 4th, 1853, Joseph Haven, of Michigan; Larned D. Patridge, b. Dec. 27th, 1839; Ebenezer B. Patridge, b. Aug. 11th, 1842; John W. Patridge, b. Oct. 19th, 1844; Louisa Maria Patridge, b. Feb. 20th, 1847 d. Oct. 26th, 1849; Alida Jane Patridge, b. March 3d, 1850; Martha L. Patridge, b. Oct. 3d, 1856; and Sarah M. Patridge, b. Nov. 30th, 1858.

Deborah Ann, b. Nov. 15th, 1820; m. Sept. 1844, Alfred Symonds, an Englishman, a resident of Griggstown, N. J., who d. Jan. 1853, and had one child, John Alfred Symonds, b. Sept. 13th, 1855, d. Jan. 1854

Cornelius, b. Feb. 5th, 1823; m. Emmeline, dau. of David Laberette. Is a flax manufacturer at Fentonville, Michigan, and has one child, Ellen Adalaide, b. July 30th, 1844.

Lucy, b. Nov. 5th, 1824; m. Nov. 22d, 1848, Delaus W. Glover, a harness maker, at Geneva, Ontario Co., N. Y., and has children Dewitt L. Glover, b. May 6th, 1850; Eugene H. Glover b. Oct. 7th, 1854, and Mary Glover, b. Aug. 27th, 1857.

Belden S., b. May 11th, 1827; m. May 14th, 1860, Juliette Rider, who d. Feb. 24th, 1861; m. 2d, June 9th, 1863, Emily Everts, wid. of — Larison Is a farmer at Mecklenburg, N. Y.

28

Peter P., b. Aug. 11th. 1829. Single. and a manufacturer of barrel, staves. &c.. at Farmer, N. Y.

John H.. b. Jan. 29th, 1832; d. Oct. 21st. 1850. Single.

Jacob. b. March 24th, 1834. Single, and is a cabinet maker and furniture dealer at Farmer, N. Y.

Christopher Q., b. Aug. 6th, 1836; m. March 4th. 1862. Mary Ann Morehouse. Is a manufacturer of barrel staves and heading at Farmer. N. Y. and has a son, Albert E.. b. Nov. 21st. 1863.

Jane D., b. Sept. 9th, 1838; d. Aug. 25th. 1840.

SIMON BERGEN. b. Aug. 22d. 1797; d. April 7th. 1842; m. Sept. 1821. *Margaret Daly.* b. May 9th, 1802. who d. Oct. 3d. 1845. Was a farmer at Flagtown. Somerset Co., N. J.

Issue :—

Cornelius, b. 1822; m. Mary Ewing of Lexington, Ky., is a carpenter, and resides in Louisville, Ky., and has children: Cornelia, Kate. Mary, Zillah, Stonewall Jackson and Frank.

Catharine Ann. b. March 5th. 1824; single, and resides in the city of N. Y.

Jacob. b. 1826; m. Lydia Saunders. who d. about 1861, having had 3 children. all deceased. Is a car builder at Jeffersonville. Indiana.

Mary Jane. b. 1834; m. Henry P. Cone. of California. and has issue: Bile Zurita, b. Nov. 16th. 1855.

John B. D.. b. 1839; emigrated to Louisville. Kentucky. Is a carpenter by trade. and when last heard of was in Tennessee.

MARY BERGEN. b. March 9th. 1800; m. Nov. 4th, 1819. Isaac Covert. who d. April 20th. 1860.

Issue :—

Mary Covert. b. Sept. 26th. 1820; m. Oct. 31st. 1839, Thomas Davis. and has children: Isaac Covert, b. Sept. 14th. 1840; John T. Covert. b. Sept. 9th. 1844; William T. Covert. b. Oct. 19th. 1846; Mary M. Covert. b. Oct. 5th. 1850. and Abraham S. Covert. b. Aug. 23d. 1857.

Jane Covert. b. Feb. 25th. 1824; m. Feb. 6th, 1845, Albert B. Hoogland. and has children: William N. Hoogland. b. Nov. 15th. 1845; Isaac C. Hoogland, b. Nov. 21st. 1847; Anna M. Hoogland. b. Feb. 16th. 1850; Mary L. Hoogland. b. June 11th. 1852. and Uriah V. Hoogland, b. Aug. 9th. 1858.

J. Berger

Martha ..... b. Feb. 22d, 18.. ...... m. Nov... ... ... Major Van Camp, an .... Irene Van Camp, b. June 16, 18.. d. Apr. 4th, 1857, Joan Van Camp, b. Dec. 6, 18.. ... M... ... ... J. Van Camp, b. Mass. ... 1s... d. J... ... ... B... Crop, b. Feb. 2d, 1s.d. d. Apr. 27.. 18.. and Martha N. b. V... ..... b. Nov. 14th, 1862.

CORNELIUS BERGEN, b. Sept. 12th, 1s.2, m. Nov. 14th, 1832, *Helen Van Derpe*, of Trenton. Is a ..... at Branchville, N. J.

Issue:

Jacob, b. Jan. 20th, 1831, d. S... 20th, 1s.... m. P... 1s... Louisa Sirken, an Ibsel Trent, June 8... d... ... 18.. C... ... to Nov. 6th, 1862.

Christian, b. Oct. 3d, 1837, m. Nov. 1.. 1s.5, Peter O. Brokaw, and has children: Anna L. Brokaw b. Oct. 12... 1s.8, Helen Brokaw b. Aug. 22d, 1860; and Garretta Brokaw, b. Oct. 23d, 1862.

Mary Ella, b. Jan. 19th, 1847.

John Q., b. Oct. 25th, 1851.

Descendants of EVART BERGEN and Ellen Van Dursen, of Whitehouse, Huntingdon Co. N. J.:—

JOHN BERGEN, b. Dec. 5d, 1793; d. Aug. 7th, 1811. Death caused by being thrown from a wagon, driven by a runaway team of oxen. Single.

WILLIAM BERGEN, b. Sept. 11th, 1795; d. Sept. 27th, 1831. Single.

ANN BERGEN, b. Sept. 15th, 1797; m. ..... 1s15. *John Messler*, son of Dr. Messler, of Somerville, and resides at Blairstown, Warren Co. N. J.

Issue:—

Evart B. Messler, b. Feb. 6th, 1817; ....

Cornelius Messler, b. Dec. 18, 1818; ....

William Messler, b. Aug. 31st, 1820; .... Mes...

John Messler, b. May 21st, 1823; m. I... ... ...

Abraham Messler, b. Oct. ..., 1825; ..... Wood...

Mary Messler, b. Dec. 23d, 1829; d. A... S... 18..

Isaac Messler, b. Sept. 3d, 1831; farmer at Blairstown.
John Livingston Messler, b. Oct. 19th, 1835; farmer at Blairstown.
Simon Hillyer Messler, b. Aug. 13th, 1839; farmer at Blairstown.

JAMES BERGEN, b. Nov. 27th, 1799; single; farmer at Whitehouse.

MARIA BERGEN, b. Nov. 20th, 1801; m. March 7th, 1818, *James Park*, a farmer at Whitehouse, N. J., who d. Aug. 1st, 1854.

Issue :—

Evert Bergen Park.
David Park.
Staats Park.
William Park.
Mary Ann Park.
Adeline Park.
John Park.
Elias Park.
Hannah Park.
Eugene Park.

ALETTA BERGEN, b. May 9th, 1804; m. Feb. 3d, 1836, *James E.*, s. of Evert J. Bergen, of Roysfield.

STATS BERGEN, b. July 15th, 1806; m. *Christina Merlett;* farmer at New Germantown, N. J., and has children :

John Newton, of Pinckney, Livingston Co., Michigan.
Evert B., of Pinckney, Livingston Co., Michigan.
George, of New Germantown.
William.
Anna.
Jane.

GEORGE BERGEN, b. May 13th, 1810; single.

JANE BERGEN, b. May 6th, 1808; d. May 11th, 1826.

Descendants of CORNELIUS BERGEN and *Nancy Hart*, of Somerville, N. J. :—

ALETTA or ALCHE BERGEN, b. Feb. 23d, 1813; m.

Nov. 12th, 1831, Nicholas Hartford of New Brunswick, and has issue:

Jane Hartford, b. Nov. 2d, 1832.
Mary Ella Hartford, b. Aug. 2d, 1834.
John Hartford, b. March 1st, 1836.
David Webster Hartford, b. Jan. 20th, 18—.
Henry Clay Hartford, b. July 30th, 1838, d. Aug. 2d, 1844.
Charles B. Hartford, b. Sept. 1st, 1840.
William V. Hartford, b. March 20th, 1842, d. Dec. 1st, 1855.
Susannah B. Hartford, b. March 2d, 1844.
James B. Hartford, b. June 15th, 1847, d. Dec. 11, 1851.
Sarah B. Hartford, b. June 20th, 1849.
William Hartford, b. May 9th, 1852, d. Jan. 20th, 1857.

SUSANNAH BERGEN, b. Aug. 15th, 1816; d. Feb. 8th, 1840; m. March 13th, 1833, Record Ten Eyck, of North Branch, Somerset Co., and had issue:

John V. Ten Eyck.
Cornelius B. Ten Eyck.
Susannah Ten Eyck.

JOHN C. BERGEN, b. Dec. 15th, 1820, d. March, 1864, m. June 13th, 1841, Aletta Van Doorn, and had issue:

* Aletta Van Doorn is —

Phebe Emma.
Cornelius J.
Sarah Ten Eyck.
Jane.
Dennis Van Dyne.
John Smith.
Peter Van Dyne.

CORNELIUS BERGEN, b. Nov. 1st, 1822; m. July 5th, 1845, *Gertrude Van Dyne*, resides in New Brunswick, and has children :

Elizabeth Mary, b. Oct. 19th, 1845.
Anna Gertrude, b. Jan. 2d, 1848.
Abby Louisa, b. Dec. 13th, 1851; d. Sept. 16th, 1858.
Cornelius, b. May 13th, 1860.
John J., b. June 6th, 1864.

JAMES BERGEN, b. Nov. 10th, 1823; m. Dec. 31st, 1845, *Phebe Hutchinson*, resides in New Brunswick, and has children :

Anna Mariah, b. Feb. 5th, 1847; d. Aug. 1st, 1852.
John H., b. Feb. 7th, 1851, d. Feb. 23d, 1852.
James H., b. Nov. 21st, 1852.
William D., b. June 10th, 1855.
Samuel R., b. Sept. 8th, 1859.
Ella C., b. Dec. 2d, 1862.

MARIA E. BERGEN, b. Oct. 27th, 1825; m. Sept. 14th, 1849, *John Smith*, of North Branch, and has children : Benjamin Smith, Cornelius Smith, Abagail Bergen Smith, who d. Feb. 24th, 1854, George Smith, and James Smith, who d. Sept. 15th, 1856.

ABAGAIL BERGEN, b. Oct. 13th, 1828; single.

Descendants of EVERT J. BERGEN and *Jane Stryker*, of Hillsborough, N. J. :—

JAMES E. BERGEN, b. Sept. 14th, 1805; d. March 25th, 1859; m. Feb. 3d, 1836, *Aletta*, dau. of Evert Bergen, of Whitehouse. Was a farmer at Roysfield, N. J. No issue.

JOHN E. BERGEN, b. March 12th, 1808; m. Feb. 23d, 1837, *Catharine Wilson*. Is a farmer residing near Somerville.

Issue:—

George, b. Nov. 15th, 1840.
Anna Maria, b. April 18th, 1847.
Sarah Aletta, b. Oct. 4th, 1850.
Catharine Jane, b. July 19th, 1853.
Cornelius, b. May 12th, 1857.

JANE BERGEN, b. June 7th, 1811; d. Feb. 8th, 1847; m. May 19th, 1834, *Michael Neefus*, of Flatbush, Long Island.

Issue :—

Eliza Jane Neefus, dec'd.
Sarah Neefus.
Peter Neefus.

ANN or JOANNA BERGEN, b. June 7th, 1834; m. Sept. 14th, 1836, *William Van Arsdale*, and settled on a farm at Rariton, Henderson, Co., Illinois.

Issue :—

Abraham B. Van Arsdal, b. March 1st, 1838.
Evert Bergen Van Arsdel, b. Oct. 24th, 1839, d. Sept. 2d, 1841.
Peter Van Arsdal, b. May 20th, 1840, was a member of the 14th regiment Illinois cavalry, during the last two years of the Rebellion of the southern states.
James B. Van Arsdal, b. Nov. 29th, 1842.

MARIAH BERGEN, b. April 18th, 1815; m. July 9th, 1844, *Elijah Rouuser*, of Bound Hook, N. J.

Issue:—

Nelson Rouuser, b. 1847.

PETER S. BERGEN, b. March 25th, 1819; m. Aug. 7th, 1845, *Rebecca M. Dilts*. Is a farmer at Roysfield.

Issue :—

Evert, b. July 11th, 1846.
Daniel, b. Nov. 8th, 1847.

Julia, b. March 22d, 1850.

Francis, b. Dec. 1st, 1851.

Henry, b. July 28th, 1853; d. Nov. 17th. 1858, of scarlet fever.

Ellen, b. April 9th. 1857; d. Nov. 17th. 1858, of scarlet fever.

PHEBE BERGEN, b. March 25th, 1819; (a twin with Peter.) Single.

Descendants of JOHN BERGEN and *Phebe Totten*, of New Brunswick, N. J. :—

ANN ELIZA BERGEN, b. March 3d, 1831; single.

MARY LOUISA BERGEN, b. Oct. 4th, 1832; single.

JAMES AUGUSTUS BERGEN, b. Oct. 22d, 1836; single.

CATHARINE T. BERGEN, b. April 23d, 1838; single.

Descendants of ZACHEUS BERGEN and *Mary Simonson*, of Roysfield, N. J. :—

JOHANNA V. BERGEN, b. Sept. 4th, 1817; single.

ELIZABETH S. BERGEN, b. Aug. 14th, 1819; m. Sept. 25th, 1844, *Simon Van Liew*, a merchant in Somerville.

Issue :—

Frederick Van Liew, b. March 14th, 1849.

Joanna Van Liew, b. Dec. 5th, 1850.

MARY STAATS BERGEN, b. May 5th, 1825; single.

GERTRUDE V. BERGEN, b. June 19th, 1825.; m. Aug. 12th, 1846, *John A. Voorhees*, a farmer in Roysfield.

Issue :—

Catharine T. Voorhees, b. May 16th, 1847.

Mary B. Voorhees, b. Feb. 18th, 1850.

Abraham Voorhees, b. March 9th, 1854; d. May 26th, 1858.

Abraham Augustus Voorhees, b. Oct. 7th, 1862.

JAMES BERGEN, b. Dec. 19th 1827; m. Oct. 18th, 1852, *Mary V. Staats*. Is a farmer at Roysfield.

Issue :—

Lizzy, b. June 26th, 1856.

Garret P. Bergen

Margetta, b. April 4th, 1859
Zachees, b. June 25th, 1861

Descendants of JAMES BERGEN and *Phebe Patterson*, of Somerville, N. J.:

GARRET P. BERGEN, b. Nov. 20th, 1820, m. April 10th, 1849, *Mary K. Thompson*; m. 2d, Oct. 14th, 1861, *Henrietta Thompson*, sister of Mary. Resides in Brooklyn, N. Y. Engaged in the railroad business, and a few years ago was a defeated candidate for the state Assembly.

Issue by 1st wife:—

Mary L., b. Dec. 29th, 1849.
Emma S., b. Aug. 30th, 1854

Issue by 2d wife:

Samuel W., b. Aug. 26th, 1862.
Charles C., b. Sept. 24th, 1864.

JOHN J. BERGEN, b. June 27th, 1823; m. Feb. 17th, 1847, *Mary Ann Park*. Engaged in the lumber trade in Somerville.

Issue:—

James, b. Oct. 1st, 1847.
M. Fannie, b. July 15th, 1849.
William, b. Sept. 12th, 1852.
Maria Emma, b. Oct 19th, 1855.
Emma L., b. Dec. 15th, 1857; d. Aug. 30th, 1858

JAMES BERGEN, b. Sept. 19th, 1825; m. April 18th, 1855, *Jane Tunison*. Late a merchant at Somerville, in 1862, a Justice of the Peace.

Issue:—

Edward Growth, b. March 11th, 1856, d. June 15th, 1856
Sarah C., b. Aug. 30th, 1858.
Ellen F., b. April 10th, 1861.
Jane Estelle, b. April 26th, 1863
29

VANDERVEER BERGEN. b. Sept. 24th. 1827; d. April 19th. 1858; single.

ZACHEUS BERGEN. b. Sept. 1st, 1829; m. Oct. 23d, 1856. *Sophia C. Thompson.* Is a merchant in New York, and resides in Brooklyn.

Issue:—

George Clifford, b. Aug. 8th, 1859.
Frederick T., b. Feb. 16th, 1862.

ELIZABETH BERGEN, b. Oct. 12th, 1831. Resides at Somerville. Single.

EVERT BERGEN, b. June 24th, 1834; *Mary Elizabeth Husted.* Is a cooper and resides in Brooklyn.

Issue:—

Edward, b. Nov. 6th., 1862.

CORNELIUS BERGEN, b. Jan. 31st, 1838; m. Oct. 1860. *Sarah Jane Bullard.* Resides in Brooklyn, and late in flour and feed business. Holds the commission of Lieut. in the Union army, engaged in suppressing the rebellion of 1861, and wounded in one of the engagements.

Issue:—

Mary, b. June 1st, 1861.

WILLIAM BERGEN. b. Aug. 10th. 1840; single. Engaged on railroad at Somerville.

ANN BERGEN. b. Aug. 16th. 1846. Single, and resides at Somerville.

Descendants of GEORGE BERGEN. of the city of New York :—

JOHN BERGEN. b. about 1797; d. about 1832; single. and resided in the city of N. Y.

FRANCES BERGEN. b. about 1800; d. about 1849; m. George Thompson and no issue.

ABRAHAM BERGEN, b. about 1802; single, and is a farmer near Binghampton, N. Y.

JANE BERGEN, b. about 1804; m. *John Maynard*, and is now a widow residing in the city of N. Y.

Issue:—

William Maynard.

James Maynard.

GEORGE BERGEN, b. June 20th, 1806; m. *Jane* who d. Sept. 20th, 1861, ag. 50. Is a shoemaker in the city of N. Y.

Issue:—

George, b. 1832; d. Jan. 30th, 1862.

Mary, b. 1843; d. Jan. 15th, 1862.

CATHARINE BERGEN; m. ——— *Hill*, and is now a widow residing in the city of N. Y.

Issue:—

William Hill.

Clara Hill.

WILLIAM BERGEN, d. young.

JAMES BERGEN, b. Jan. 20th, 1811; m. 1842, *Mary Laffaty*. Resides in the Eastern District of Williamsburgh of the city of Brooklyn, and is a boot and shoemaker.

Issue:—

Mary, b. Sept. 13th, 1847.

Jane, b. Nov. 10th, 1849, d. Feb. 1854.

Sarah Frances, b. June 20th, 1852; d. Feb. 7th, 1853.

Charles, b. July 15th, 1854.

Jane Margaret, b. Jan. 25th, 1857.

ELIZABETH BERGEN, d. when about 18 years of age.

MARY LOUISA BERGEN, b. Dec. 1st, 1819; m. *William Crosley*, and resides in the city of N. Y.

Issue:—

Sarah Crosley, b. 1840.

Charles Crosley, b. 1846.

Frances Crosley.
Thomas Crosley.
Benjamin Crosley.
Adele Crosley.

Descendants of ABRAHAM BERGEN, of Bloomfield, N. J. :—

SARAH BERGEN: m. *James Smith,* of Bloomfield, and is now a widow residing in Newark.

Issue :—
Garvine Smith.
Jannette Smith.
Louis Smith.

HETTY BERGEN ; m. 1st, —— *Galispie ;* m. 2d, —— *Bartlett,* by whom one child. Resided in Bloomfield and Boston, at which latter place she d.

Issue by 1st husband :—
Margaret Galispie, now deceased.

MARGARET BERGEN,: m. —— *Kidney,* and is dead. Resided in Bloomfield.

Issue :—
Abraham Kidney.
Sarah Kidney.

JACOB HANSEN BERGEN.

Descendants in the line of *JACOB HANSEN BERGEN* and *Elsje Fredricks Lubbertse Vander Krest*, of Brooklyn, N. Y., the fourth son of *Hans Hansen Bergen*, the first settler.

Third Generation.

HANS JACOBSE BERGEN, bapt. May 12th, 1678; d. prior to March 1719; m. Dec. 11th, 1707, *Sarah*, dau. of Jeronimous Rapalie and Annate Denuyse, and grand-dau. of Joris Jause de Rapalie, b. Nov. 4th, 1687.

Owned and resided on a portion of his grandfather Lubbertse's patent, in South Brooklyn. It also extending to the head of Freeke's mill pond, and amounting to about 200 acres. He also purchased, Feb. 9th, 1713, of Aert Aersen Middagh, an undivided half of the mill and premises thereto attached, since known as Remsen's mill, at the Wallabout, on lands at present occupied by the U. S. Navy Yard. This mill was built by Middagh in 1710, on lands probably originally patented to Jan Haes, a natural pond in the marsh, requiring a short dam, affording the necessary facilities. Jan. 28th, 1722-3, Hans Jacobse conveyed his interest in these premises to Cornelius Evertse.

On the census of Brooklyn, in 1738, his family is entered as consisting of two white males above 10, two white males under 10, and three white females above 10 years of age.   In 1730, he was one of the Commissioners of common lands of Brooklyn, his associates being Hans Machielse Bergen and John Rapalje.

His will is dated Sept. 11th, 1743, and proved March 12th, 1749, in which he devises to his eldest son Jacob £25 : to his wife Sarah the use of his personal and real estate during life ; after the decease of his wife, one fifth of his estate to his son Jacob, one-fifth to his dau. Antie, wife of Garret Cowenhoven, one-fifth to his dau. Elsje, wife of Rem Remsen, one-fifth to his dau. Catelynte, wife of Michael Bergen, and one-fifth to his dau. Sarah Bergen.

The following copy of an original paper* in the archives of the N. Y. Historical Society presented by Peter A. Jay, gives some curious information in relation to the localities occupied by Jacob Hanse and Jores Hanse, (two sons of Hans Hansen Bergen,) and by their descendants. The paper is endorsed :

"ISRAEL HORSEFIELD, | Copy of what witnesses
                ads. | can say."
ON D. OF HANS BERGEN. |

Also endorsed in hand writing of Gov. John Jay, "see Remsen's Evid. respecting Nutten's Island." Underneath is the following endorsement by Peter A. Jay : "The first two pages of these notes, are I believe in the hand writing of John Chambers, an eminent counsel, afterwards Judge of the Supreme Court of the Colony—the note on the margin is in the writing of John Jay, his nephew and executor of his widow.

                                   P. A. JAY."

---

* A copy of this paper is published in Valentine's Manual of the city of N. Y., of 1849, in which on a careful comparison with the original, a few errors were found.

The trial appears to have taken place in 1741, but no records have been seen throwing light upon its results.

"Gerrit Dortland says he is 86 years of age. Was born at the ferry, and lived after at Brookland, knew Frederick Lubbert's land since a boy, says that he knew where Frederick Lubbertse lived, which is S. Westward of Sebring's mill,* and it was commonly esteemed that Frederick Lubbertse's line was near to his house. Remember Joost Francey in possession of land that George Bergen and Israel now have; fences went to the creek, about sixty years since he knew them; has now seen the fences and think they stand as then. Remembers Jan Evertse Bout in possession of Bevois land, was a man of 75, and married a girl of 16. Says he help't him to make his fences; work't there two years and fences stood as now, was then about 23 years old; never then heard that Frederick Lubbertse made any pretension to these lands nor any for his right till now.

"Maritie Bevois says is aged 84 years, near 85, was born in New York; it's last May 63 years since she came to live at Brookland; knew Frederick Lubbertse lived where Hans Bergen now lives. Remembers was going to the place where Brewer's mill+ is now from Brookland by the house of Lubbertse and saw many little hills in the way from the house to the mill along the creek and enquired what the hills were, and was answered by them with her that it was the Indian corn land; knows where Mancuoell lived a little below Tomractie; knew the land of George Bergen to have belonged to Merite Gerritse or Ex. She let it to Israel Francey (Marate Ex.) lived at

---

* This is evidently an error. I ... s ... ... wi th ... w ... re
from Sebring's mill, an l n rth nortcw ... I r ... ... l ... t r ... ...
Brower's, at th head f a sno ... ... a ... ... l th pr ...
ent Hoyt and Warren streets.

+ Brower's Mill.

New York. She remembers Francey on it about 60
years ago. that Francey lived on it till Maratie sold it
it to George Hanse. father of George Bergen. Remembers it to be always in fence, and that the fences
stood as they now stand and the same of the other lotts ;
has lived at Brookland ever since she removed from York
as before.

"Heard Jeromus Remsen's mother say. that there was
only a small creek between Nutton Island and the shoar.
and that a squah carried her sister over it in a tub : that
that sister was the first born in this country.*

"Says that George Bergen's half-sister† lived at Bevois
place on rent. and had a mind to buy Maratie's Ex. place
but was disappointed. and complaining of it with tears
said it was her brother Jacob Hanse Bergen and brother
Michael that were the cause of Jorey's buying it and dis-
appointing her.

"Joost Van Brunt. aged 77 years and upwards. born and
lived at New Utrecht. says when he was about nine years
old. when the Dutch came to take New York. he came
with his father. mother and brothers in a wagon down the
hollow near Tommeties, and they said that the other side
of the hollow was Fred Lubbertse's land. Says that a
great deal of the land is wash't away against Nutten Isl-
and. and it went farther out than now. but can't say how
mutch. Remember to have seen meadow before Sebring's
house. but how far out he knows not : has seen the fences
at Bergen's and does not remember to have seen them

---

* Jeromus Remson's mother was Jannetie, dau. of Joris Jansen de Rapalie : her sister Sarah, who m. successively. Hans Hansen Bergen and
Tunis Gysbert Bogaart, was the eldest child of Joris Jansen de Rapalie.
and reputed to be the first born of Europeans in the conutry, in which
respect the testimony of the witness agrees with what is generally ad-
mitted. According to this witness. Sarah was the one carried over in a
tub.

† This half sister, was one of Sarah de Rapalie's children. by Bogaart,
her second husband.

otherwise than as now. That he was an arbitrator about dividing the land between Sebring and Bergen about 14 or 15 years ago, and that there was no pretence that lands in question were part or that they claimed any right there.

"Jeromus Remsen, aged 77 years, was born about Brookland, and lived all his days there. Knew Frederick Lubbertse lived where Hans Bergen now but had little acquaintance with him remembers about 55 years ago, that Jacob Hans Bergen, father of Lessor, lived at Lubbertse's place, that he came to this depon't to get a pr. of shoes made, that then he told the depon't he had been at York with Maratie Gerretse to ask if she would sell her place, and that she had said she would, and said that he was going to his brother George Hansen, at Flatbush, to get him to buy it; that George Hansen bought it soon after and lived there; that he was there a long time before the date of the deed; that deed was only given at last paym't:* that the year depon't was married, which was 1688, the said Joris Hanse, being a carpenter, agreed to do a job of work for depon't, if depon't would plow for him, and that depon't did plow for him the very land now in question, close up to the meadows, that it was then in fence and fences stand now in the very place they were then. Never heard of any pretence, and says that if he had any he would not have gone to advise his brother; says that he turned his plow ag't the fence of the land of Bevois, and that fences stood then as now so far as he thinks. Says that he has heard his mother say she was carried off Staten Island by a Squah, and that it was all sedge and meadow, only a creek between Staten Island and Long Island; his mother's sister was first born in this country.

* The deed is dated Sept. 13th. 1698

30

its now 116 or 117 years since she was born ;* his mother
was four years younger : he heard often from other people
that there was but a small creek between Nutten and
Long Island.†

" Abraham Lott, aged 57, remembers between 30 and 40
years that fences stand at George Bergen's as now ; says
was an arbitrator; was shown then the will of Fred. Lubbertse, who devised to his own two daughters each one
plantation as then in fence, and to his wife's two sons‡
other lotts : seems pretty sure the words were as then in
fence; heard no discourse of any claim of neighbour's
land out of fence.

" Peter Stryker, aged 44, says that being on a jury of
view about 6 or 7 years ago, Jacob Hanse, father of Hanse
Bergen, said at his house on talking of Worpus, there's
Worpus,§ pointing with his finger thro' his window to the
head of the creek by his garden; remembers about 30
years the land in fence as now and no claim till within
this year or two.

---

* From this testimony it appears that Jannatie, dau. of Joris Jansen de
Rapalie, who m. Rem Vanderbeek, the common ancestor of the Remsens
and the mother of Jeromus, was also carried from Nutten (now Governor's)
Island to Long Island, by a squaw; that her sister (Sarah) was born about
1625, which agrees with the recorded date of her birth. Quære: from the
witnesses reference to his mother's sister Sarah, might it not be inferred
that he intended to be understood that Sarah, and not his mother Jannetie,
was the one carried over, as previously testified to by Maratie Bevoise, and
that the tradition referred to the same person.

† On the margin against this paragraph, is the following in the hand
writing of John Jay: "his mother carr'd from Nutten to Long Island by
a squaw. Sworn 1741, at ye Tryal."

‡ These were Cornelius Corssen and Peter Corssen, children of Tryntje
Hendricks, the wife of Frederick Lubbertse, by Cornelius Peterson Vroom,
her first husband.

§ "Warpoes" was a term bestowed on an eminence in the vicinity of
the present Chatham square, situated near the small lake or pond called
the Kolek, in the city of New York, and was probably the site of an Indian
village. This term is stated by Schoolcraft to be apparently a derivation
from Wawbose, a hare. The "Worpus" pointed out by Jacob Hanse,
may also have been the site of an Indian village, a large Indian burying
ground being located in the vicinity, where remains were exhumed a few
years ago in leveling the ground for city purposes; and besides Indian
maize lands are referred to in that region in the early patents.

"Peter Winans, aged 79, born at Bedford and about 8 or ten years old when he came to live at Brookland; knows the land in dispute upwards of sixty years ago, and believes the fences stand now much as they did then; ab't 40 or 45 years ago he went to live at Staten Island; he remembers Nicholas Baker* who was husband of Maritie Gerretsen, first lived upon the land of George Bergen, and the witness's father and Joost France hired it of Maritie Gerretsen, or her husband, and his father left it to Joost France. He remembers Jan Evertse Bout, who lived upon the land sold by Carel De Bevoise to Israel, above 60 years agoe; he knew Fred Lubbertse, and never heard he made any pretense on any of their lotts. Knew old George Hanse Bergen, father of the present George, in possession of the premises above 40 or 45 years agoe, when France's time was out, and he was often in the house.

"Benjamin Van Deventer, aged 71 years, said he knew Jan Evertse Bout the son of the patentee that he had heard and understood that the father was owner of both the place of Bergen+ and Debevois, that he made a will and died before his son was born; that 63 years ago he remembers Annetje Pieterson, widow of Jan Evertse Bout the elder,‡ in possession of the land of Carel Debevoise, they lived on it about 12 years at least or more."

---

* Maritie's husband was Nicholas Jans[...]

+ The deed from Maritie Gerretse to Joost France [...] plantation patented by K[...] Wolpert[...] above described the one half of the neck of land with garden thereunto [...] to Jan Evertse Bout.

‡ Annatie Pieterson or Pieters[...] widow of Jan Evertse [...] the elder, her first husband [...] Andrew Jan[...] Jans[...] among others she had a son Jacob[...] Staats, who owned land [...] at Gowanus. Jan Everts Bout [...] Gov. Kieft, a patent for land at M[...] Gowanus, bounded [...] westerly by land of Gerret Wolpherse[...] including the meadows, together with [...] 18

The tradition as given by these witnesses that Nutten
or Governor's Island and Long Island were so closely connected at the time of the early settlement of the country,
is doubted by many intelligent persons, and there is nothing in the early maps of the vicinity favoring its accura-
cy.* Old traditions on being compared with the documentary evidence of the time, are found to be very unre-
liable. No docks until about the period of this trial were
built east of Wall street, that could have the least effect
in diverting the currents of the East river towards Buttermilk channel.+ It is well known to residents in the bay

morgens and 270 rods, for which a confirmatory patent was granted, Feb.
14th, 1667, by Gov. Nicolls. This patent, in addition to the land on the
north side of Gowanus Creek, apparently covered a tract south of said
creek on which was located Brower's mills, since of Freecke and Denton,
that of Freecke being known as the old Gowanus mill, having been erected
prior to 1661. This will, according to the affidavits of Jan Cornelisse
Buys and Dirk Jansen, of Sept. 12th, 1698, (see Lib. 2 of con. p. 179, K.
C. Reg. off.,) in 1667 Bout gave " the corn and meadows and place whereon the mill is grounded," to the children of Adam Brower. By a recital
in a deed dated April 30th, 1707, of Sybrant Brower to Abram and Nicholas Brower, (see Lib. 3 of con. p. 201, K. C. Reg. off.,) it appears that a
conveyance had been executed by the heirs of Jan Evertse Bout and "Tunis Nuyse," (Denyse,) to Adam Brower, their ancestor, for the neck of
land on which the mill was located. March 1st, 1695, Annitie Para, widow of Jan Evertse Bout, Sen., and of Andries Janse Juriance, and now wife
of Jan Janse Staats, who appears to have been in possession of the land
north of the creek, for £150, conveys the same to Jurian Andriesse, her
son, bounding said land as lying on the south side of the Kings highway,
on the west side of Machiell Hansen (Bergen,) and on the east side of
Jores Hansen (Bergen,) and Lambert Andriesse, the latter probably also
her son. Feb. 19th, 1707-8, Jurian Andriesse for £400, conveyed the
above premises, giving the quantity as 27 morgen, more or less, to Carell
Debevois. Debevois afterwards conveyed to Israel Horsefield, who appears to have been in possession at the time of the lawsuit. It may be
that the Evertse's who a few years ago owned land and resided west of
Fulton ferry, were descendants of Jan Evertse Bout, Jun., having dropped the sirname of Bout and retained that of Evertse, Evarts or Everet.

* See map in Van der Donck's " Description of New Netherland," printed in 1655, a copy of which may found in the Hon. Henry C. Murphy's
translation of the " Vertoogh of New Netherland and Breeden Raedt," printed N. Y., in 1854, in which Governor's Island appears to be as distant
from Long Island as on modern maps.

+ One writer quaintly supposes this name to have been derived from this
channel having been the passage through which the wives and daughters
of the residents of Gowanus wended their way in their canoes or row
boats loaded with buttermilk to the market of New Amsterdam. In these
early days most of the citizens or burghers of New Amsterdam, as in

of New York, that the loss by abrasion on its shores is caused mainly by the waves during storms and high tides, and very little, if any, by the ordinary currents. The theory advanced by some, that the docks of the city changed the current so as to sweep away the intervening meadows and form a fordable creek from a deep, wide and navigable strait, does not appear to be very tenable.

Issue :

Jacob, bap. Dec. 12th, 1708.

Antie.

Elsje.

Catalyn'te.

Sarah.

FREDERICK JACOBSE BERGEN, bap. Nov. 27th, 1681 ; d. prior to 1762 ; m. *Gerretye*, dau. of Gerrit Vechte.*

Resided on Staten Island on a farm, in the north precinct or division, which he purchased of Catharine, wid. of George Hooglant, 20 acres of which he sold, June 10th, 1727, for £110, to John Van Pelt. May 2d, 1726, he also sold for £225, to Garret Kroezen, 80 acres lying on the great plain in the rear of the land patented to Cornelius

---

other new and sparsely populated cities, probably kept cattle of their own, leaving little demand for outside milk. The name was most probably derived (and of this there can be little doubt,) from the abundant white froth or foam on the water in a part of the channel, produced by the ripple caused by the meeting of the tide of that portion of the East river which passes through said channel, with the tide of the North river. Hence also from the spray and white color of the water, the name of Buttermilk falls on the Hudson, near West Point.

* *Claes Arentse Van Velten*, with his wife Laurence, 3 children and a boy, emigrated from Norch or Nora a community in the province of Drenthe, Holland, in the ship Bonte (spotted cow) arrived in New Netherlands in April, 1660, settled, as near as can be ascertained, in the Eighth ward of Brooklyn, on the farm late of Aert and Jaques Cortelyou, extending from 1st to 5th streets, and erected in 1699, the old stone house known as the Vechte or Cortelyou mansion. His children were Hendrick Claesz, of Brooklyn, who m. Oct. 10th, 1686, Gerretye Remsen Wiegelpenning, and *Gerrit Claes*, of Staten Island, who m. Sept. 25th, 1682, Jannetje Crocheron, of Staten Island, and m. 2 , March, 1614, Magdalentje Jans. Of the other children who came over with him have no account.

Gerrit Claesz, s. of Claes Arents, had issue *Gerretye*, who m. Frederick Jacobse Bergen, and probably other children.

Corson and Company, which plot he had recently purchased of Hendrick Kroesen and others.* On the Richmond county records his name is written "Frederick
Berge." About this period farmers were in the habit of
turning out their cattle on the commons for pasturage,
each owner having a distinctive mark, which was recorded on the public records. March 5th, 1740, on the county records of Richmond Co., it is recorded of "Frederick
Berge," that "the ear mark of his horse kind, cattle,
sheep, &c., is a swallow tail at the end of the right ear,
and a half moon or half circle in the upper part of the left
ear."

In 1715, he was a private in Capt. David Aersen's company of Brooklyn: in 1738, a Lieutenant of militia in
Richmond Co., and in 1727 and 1728, a deacon in the
Reformed Dutch church on the north side of Staten Isl-
and. From Richmond Co. he removed to Somerset Co.,
N. J., where he owned and cultivated a farm and died,
his will being dated May 28th, 1757, proved Nov. 22d,
1762, and recorded in the office of the Secretary of State
of N. J., in which he devises his farm to his son Jacob.

Issue :—

Jacob, bap. July 19th, 1719.
Gerritie, bap. April 29th, 1722.
Henry or *Hendrick*, bap. Sept. 26th, 1725.
Elsje, bap. March 12th, 1732.

JACOB JACOBSE BERGEN. bap. Jan. 20th, 1684: d.
1750: m. *Margaret, Maritje* or *Maria Croesen.*

Resided on Staten Island, and in 1738,† he held the office
of Lieut. in the militia in Richmond Co., and in the same
year was a deacon in the Reformed Dutch church, at Port
Richmond on the north side of the Island. July 3d,

---

* See Lib. C, p. 258, and Lib. D, p. 4, of con., in off. of Clerk of Richmond Co.

† Written "Jacob Berge," see vol. IV. Doc. His. of N. Y.

1745, the Rev. Cornelius Van Santvord for £360, conveyed to "Jacob Burgher," Jun., of Staten Island, cordwainer, a parcel of land located on the north side of the Island on the Kill Von Kull, in breadth 485 feet, also, the one third part of 80 acres of woodland, and 5 acres of salt meadows.* Aug. 11th, 1746, "Jacob Barregan," shoemaker, and Margaret his wife, of Richmond Co., quit claim, release, &c., to Jacob Bennet and Cattrenah his wife, of Gowanus, against all manner of actions, &c. Oct. 11th, 1746, "Jacob Bergen" and Margaret his wife, convey to Peter Van Pelt and "Christopher Schass," a farm at Gowanus, and woodlot No. 43, in the first Division, containing 5 acres, the farm being bounded N. W'ly by Cornelius Van Duyne; E'ly by the Flatbush wood lots; S. W'ly by woodlot of Jan Bennet, known as No. 44.† These premises are the same which Johannes Bergen bought March 7th, 1751, of Peter Van Pelt and "Christophel Scharse," and which he conveyed to his brother Derick Bergen. They are located in the vicinity of 15th and 16th streets, and mainly designated on Butt's map as land of John Dimon and heirs of Rachel Berry.

His will is dated Sept. 22d, and proved Dec. 13th, 1750. In the body of his will his name is written "Jacob Berge," but signed "Jacob Bergen." He devises to his son "Jacob Berge," a negro woman, &c.; to Elsje, wife of Johannes Van Wagene, and his dau. Cornelia, each a negro girl, directs his lands in Richmond Co. to be sold, and appoints his son-in-law, Johannes Van Wagene, his brother-in-law Cornelius Kroesse, and Daniel Corson, executors.‡

Issue :—

Elsje, bap. July 29th, 1722

* See Lib. D, p. 509 of con. in off. of Clerk of Richmond Co.
† See Lib. G, p. 2, of con. in Kings Co. Reg. off.
‡ See Lib. 17, p. 279, of wills, Sur. off. City of N. Y.

Cornelia, bap. Jan. 1st, 1728-9.
Jacob, bap. Sept. 31st, 1731.
Cornelis, bap. Sept. 4th, 1737.

SARAH JACOBSE BERGEN, bap. Aug. 5th, 1688. Dec. 21st, 1723, "Sarah Jacobse Bergen" and Jores Bergen were sponsors at bap. of Neeltje, dau. of Thomas Middleswart and Geertje, and Sept. 26th, 1725, "Sarah Bergen" and Jacob Corsen were sponsors at Staten Island at bap. of Hendrick, s. of Frederick Bergen and Gerritje Veghte. No farther trace.

CATRYNA JACOBSE BERGEN, m. *Johannes Slecht,* of Staten Island.

Issue:—

Cornelia Slecht, bap. April 17th, 1720.
Catharine Slecht, (twin with Cornelia,) bap. April 17th, 1720.

MARRETJE JACOBSE BERGEN, m. Nov. 17th, 1719, *Gysbert Boogart, Jun.*

Issue :—

Jacob Boogart, bap. April 7th, 1723.
Jan Boogart, bap. July 29th, 1732-3.

BRECKJE JACOBSE BERGEN, m. *Jan Croesen,* of Staten Island. Nov. 17th, 1720, Breckje Bergen, Elsje Bergen, and Jacob Carsen, were sponsors on Staten Island, at bap. of Cornelia and Catharine, twin children of Johannes Sleght and Catharine Bergen.

ELSJE JACOBSE BERGEN, m. *Hendrick Croesen,* of Staten Island. Nov. 17th, 1720, Elsje Bergen and others, sponsors at bap. of the twin children of Johannes Sleight and Catharine Bergen.

Issue :—

Cornelius Croesen, bap. Oct. 19th, 1709.
Neeltje Croesen, bap. 1715.
Cornelia Croesen, bap. Oct. 30th, 1716.

CORNELIA JACOBSE BERGEN, m. _Dick Crocen_, of Staten Island, Jan. 1st, 1729. Cornelia Crocen (Bergen) and Hendrick Crocen were sponsors at bap. on Staten Island, of Cornelia, dau. of Jacob Bergen and Maria Crocen, and Sept. 4th, 1737, at bap. of Cornelus, s. of the same parties.

Fourth Generation.

Descendents of HANSE JACOBSE BERGEN and _Sara Rapalie_, of Brooklyn, N. Y.:

JACOB BERGEN, bap. Dec. 12th, 1708; d. about 1767; m. _Antie_ ———. Resided on and owned a portion, if not the whole, of his father's farm, in Brooklyn, probably occupying the old dwelling house of his ancestor, Frederick Lubbertse, located near the junction of Hoyt and Warren streets.

On the census list of the residents of Brooklyn, in 1838, his family is entered as consisting of two white males above 10, two white females above 10, one white female under 10, one black male above 10, and one black female above 10 years of age.

Oct. 8th, 1742,* among other residents of Brooklyn, he signed a deed relating to the parsonage of the Reformed Dutch church, located in Flatbush. April 7th, 1750,† Jacob Bergen and Rem Remsen Jun., conveyed to John Rapalie a right of way over their lands in Brooklyn.

April 18th, 1750,‡ Jacob Bergen and Antie, his wife, conveyed to John Rapalie, for £700, 159 acres in Brook-

* See Lib. 5, p. 117, of deeds in Kings Co. Reg.'s off.
† See Lib. 5, p. 169, of deeds in Kings Co. Reg.'s off.
‡ See Lib. 5, p. 161, of deeds in Kings Co. Reg.'s off.

31

lyn, being the premises afterwards conveyed by Rapalje
to Robert Stoddart, and by the latter, Dec. 21st, 1799,
(except a portion previously conveyed to Coles,) to Jacob,
s. of Hans Bergen and Catryntie, located in the vicinity of
Court street and Gowanus Creek, and designated on Butts'
map as land of Jacob Bergen and Jorden Coles.

April 30th, 1750, Sarah, (wid. of Hans Jacobse Bergen,) Jacob Bergen, Gerret and Antie Couwenhoven, Rem
Remsen, Rem Remsen, Jr., and Sara Remsen, signed a bill
of sale for a negro boy named Tyte, aged about 19, to
Michael Bergen, which boy formerly belonged to Hans
Jacobse Bergen. March 7th, 1755, (deed not recorded,)
Jacob Bergen and Antie, his wife, of the Wallabout, con-
veyed to Martin Ryerse, 150 acres of land situate at the
Wallabout, bound W. by land of John Ryerse, S. by land
of Cornelius Vanderhoven and the King's highway or
road leading from the ferry to Jamaica, and E. by land of
Jeronomus Rapelje, Harman Andriesen and Jacobus Lef-
ferts. These premises have since been known as the John
Ryerson farm, and probably were inherited either by Sara
Rapalje, Jacob Bergen's mother, or by Antie his wife.

His will is dated Sept. 10th, 1766, and proved April 25th,
1767.* In it he bequethes his estate, real and personal,
in "Brookland" and in the town of Brookhaven, Suffolk
Co., to his wife Antie, during widowhood; on her decease
or re-marriage, his Brookland lands to his grand son Rutgert Van Brunt, subject to a legacy of £12 per annum to
his dau. Sarah, the mother of said Rutgert, now the wife
of Thomas Roberson; his Brookhaven lands to his grandson Jacob Van Brunt, subject to a similar legacy of £12
per annum to his dau. Sarah; to his grandson Thomas
Roberson, a minor, £400; his grand dau. Sarah Roberson,
a minor, £400; and appoints his wife Antie, brother-in-

---

* See Lib. 25, p. 172, Sur. off. city of N. Y.

law Michiel Bergen, cousin John Van Horn, and friend
Johannes Bergen, executors.

It is probable that Jacob Bergen during his lifetime, (although the deeds have not been seen,) sold other portion
of his patrimonial estate, and that he purchased a portion of
Gerret Wolphertse Van Couwenhoven's patent, (since of
George Bergen, and afterwards of Horsefield,) and a portion
of Jan Evertse Bout's patent, (since of Debevoise, and afterwards of Horsefield,) said purchased lands lying between
the northerly portion of his patrimonial estate and those of
Van Rossum's patent, (once of Michael Hanse Bergen and
late of Powers.)   This probability is founded on the fact
that the Van Brunts, the descendants of his dau. Sarah,
owned said portions of Van Couwenhoven's and Bout's
patents, and that they resided in the ancient dwelling
house located on the Bout patent, which the spirit of im-
provement, caused by the spread of the city, some 20 years
ago swept out of existence.

Issue :—

Sarah.

ANTIE BERGEN, m. *Garret Couwenhoven,* supposed to be
the ancestor of the Cowenhovers, at present residing in
New Utrecht.

ELSJE BERGEN, m. *Ren Remsen,* of Brooklyn.

Issue :

Geory B   n
Hans or Jo's B   n, bap. Nov 25th   174
Rem Remsen.
Sarah Rem   .

CATELYNTIE BERGEN, m. *Michael Bergen,* of Hans
Machielse, who resided on and owned what was lately
known as the Power's property in Brooklyn.   She survived her husband and d. in Gowanus at the house of Tunis
Bergen her husband's brother.

Issue :—

Sarah, m. Aug. 30th, 1759. Capt. John Grant.

Teshe, m. July 3d. 1759, Stephen Terhune.

SARAH BERGEN. Not married at the date of her fath er's will. No farther trace.

Descendants of FREDERICK JACOBSE BERGEN and *Gerretye Vechte*. of Staten Island. and afterwards of Somerset Co., N. J. :—

JACOB BERGEN, bap. July 19th, 1719: m. *Margaret Lane*. By his will dated Jan. 5th, 1781, and proved March 5th. 1781. he appears to have resided in the Eastern Precinct. Somerset Co., N. J. Jacob Bergen. (supposed to be this Jacob.) as a Commissioner, conveys land in 1778–79, and '80. as per book A. pages 1 and 241. and per book B. pages 51 and 53. in the County Clerk's office, Somerville, N. J. His wife's. (Margaret.) will is dated Feb. 21st, 1795.

Issue :—

Jacob. b. July 7th, 1756.

Hendrick.

Charity.

Elsy.

And another dau.

GERRITIE BERGEN, bap. April 29th. 1722: m. *John Van Dyck*, as per her father's will.

HENDRICK BERGEN. bap. Sep. 26th. 1725. Named in his father's will. Supposed to have remained on Staten Island. when his father emigrated to N. J., and probably d. shortly after his marriage.

Issue :—

Henry. b. Oct. 23d, 1757.

ELSIE BERGEN. bap. March 12th. 1732: m. *Koenraet Ten Eyck*. as per her father's will.

Descendants of JACOB JACOBSE BERGEN and *Maritje Crowson* of Staten Island. :

ELSIE BERGEN, (written in some places Elsje Berger,) bap. July 29th, 1722; m. Nov. 9th, 1747, *Johannes Van Wagene*, of Staten Island.

Issue:—

Johannes Van Wagene, bap. July 19th, 1748.

CORNELIA BERGEN, bap. Jan. 1st, 1728-29; m. *John Swim*, of Staten Island.

Issue :—

Maria Swim, Oct. 5th, 1760.

JACOB BERGEN, bap. Sept. 31st, 1731; m. *Grietje* or *Margaret Panel*. Resided on Staten Island; his wife was a cousin of Christoffel Scharse, of Brooklyn, and a legatee in his will, dated June 25th, 1794. April 23d, 1751, "Jacob Bergen and Margaret," his wife, of Staten Island, for £417, sold to Cornelus Krousen, the premises his father bought in 1745, of the Rev. Cornelius Santvord,* of the Reformed Dutch church. May 17th, 1773, he gave a receipt for money to the estate of Peter Van Pelt, of Gowanus.

Issue :—

Maria or *Mary*.
Jacob, bap. May 9th, 1745.
Gerritje, bap. June 10th, 1747.
Adriaen, bap. May 31, 1749.

CORNELIS BERGEN, bap. Sept. 4th, 1737; probably d. young, not being named in his father's will.

*See Lib. D. p. 283 and 285 of Con. Richmond Co. Conveyances.

Fifth Generation.

Descendants of JACOB BERGEN and *Antie* of Brooklyn, N. Y.:—

SARAH BERGEN: d. March 13th, 1792; m. 1st, Jan. 19th, 1745, *John Van Brunt*, of New Utrecht, (s. of Rutgert, commonly known as the rich brother.) John Van Brunt in 1751, was accidentally drowned in Flatland bay. Sarah m. 2d, April 16th, 1754, *Thomas Robinson*.

Issue by 1st husband :—

Rutgert Van Brunt, who inherited and resided on the Brooklyn lands of his grandfather, Jacob Bergen; m. Dec. 3d, 1767, Lena Van Horn, and d. Sept. 19th, 1781, leaving children: John Van Brunt, b. Jan. 30th, 1769, d. Jan. 27th, 1793. single; Lana Van Brunt, b. Nov. 5th, 1772, m. 1st, Jan. 22d, 1793, Jeremiah Vanderbilt, and m. 2d, John Bocka or Bockee, by whom children: Jane Sophia, Helen and John I.; Jane Van Brunt, b. Feb. 14th, 1775, d. Sept. 9th, 1798. single; Jacob Van Brunt, b. Feb. 12th, 1780, m. March 16th, 1799, Esther Vanderbilt, d. Oct. 1st, 1810, leaving children: Helen b. Oct. 22d, 1800, who m. Jan. 13th, 1818, George Martense, of Flatbush, and Jane b. May 14th, 1803, who m. Oct. 2d, 1821, Samuel Gerritsen, of Gravesend.

Rutgert Van Brunt by his will dated Jan. 20th, 1781, and proved Dec. 18th, 1781,* devised to his sons John and Jacob, the homestead farm in Brooklyn; John devised by will dated June 26th, 1793, and proved July 30th, 1793,† his undivided half of the homestead to his brother Jacob and his sisters Laura and Jane. Jane devised by will dated May 10th, 1797, and proved Dec. 20th, 1798.‡ her interest in the homestead farm to her brother Jacob. Feb. 12th, 1801, John Bockee and Laura, his wife, released their interest in the homestead farm to Jacob Van Brunt, thus making him the sole owner thereof. Jacob devised by will dated July 26th, 1808, and proved Nov. 14th. 1810,§ the westerly one-half of said homestead farm to his dau. Jane, and the easterly one-half to his dau. Helen.

Jacob Van Brunt, b. July 10th, 1747; d. July 27th, 1813; m. Phebe Woodhull, b. Dec. 24th, 1752, d. April 9th, 1799.

---

* See Lib. 34, p. 390, in off. of Sur., in city of N. Y.
† See Lib. 1, p. 131, in off. of Sur. of Co. of Kings.
‡ See Lib. 1, p. 256, in off. of Sur. of Co. of Kings.
§ See Lib. 2, p. 130, in off. of Sur. of Co. of Kings.

Inherited from his grandfather Jacob Bergen, his lands in Brookhaven, (East Setauket,) Suffolk Co.

Issue :—

John Van Brunt, b. Nov. 17th, 1772, d. Sept. 16th, 1811, m. Jerusha Hedges. Inherited his father's farm and had children—James R., b. Jan. 8th, 1798, m. May 26th, 1840, Ruth Bayles, inherited and resides on his father's farm; Sarah A., b. Aug. 29th, 1800, m. Daniel H. Skidmore; Ann Maria, b. April 15th, 1803, d. March 21st, 1844, m. William M. Smith; John, b. June 19th, 1806, d. April 9th, 1842, m. March 6th, 1828, Caroline Dickinson; Jacob, b. Oct. 9th, 1808, m. Harriet Norton, and Antoinette, b. Dec. 16th, 1812, m. Adam D. Bayles—James Van Brunt, b. Dec. 9th, 1774, d. June 8th, 1793, single; Sarah Van Brunt, b. April 17th, 1777, d. March 29th, 1863, m. Justus Coe, Nathan Van Brunt, b. Aug. 2d, 1779, d. June 1st, 1780; Joanna Van Brunt, b. April 2d, 1781 d. June 4th, 1783; Benjamin Van Brunt, b. Aug. 4th, 1785, d. Nov. 7th, 1790; Rutgert Van Brunt, b. April 3d, 1789, d. Nov. 7th, 1795.

Issue by 2d husband :-

Thomas Robinson.
Sarah Robinson.

Descendants of JACOB BERGEN, (s. of Frederick Jacobse,) of Somerset Co., N. J. : –

JACOB BERGEN, b. July 7th, 1756; d. Sept. 2d, 1782; m. *Tunche Van Dyke*, b. March 1st, 1758; d. Jan. 25th, 1826. Was a farmer at Rocky Hill, N. J.

Issue :—

Aaron, b. Oct. 12th, 1777.
Matthew, b. Oct. 2d, 1779.
Margaret, b. July 31st, 1781.

HENDRICK BERGEN: d. 1816; m. *Mary or Polly Cowenhoven* dan. of Peter, sister of Joost or Joseph and Nicholas, of New Jersey, and cousin of Johannes Cowenhoven, of New Utrecht. Owned and resided on, at first, a farm within about one mile of New Brunswick. Afterwards owned and resided on a farm at Hillsborough, near Somerville, N. J., where he died. Will dated Dec. 17th, 1815, and that of his wife in 1826.

He owned a number of slaves on whom, probably in consequence of having no children of his own, his and the affections of his wife, were entwined. Negroes are known to be proverbially fond of poultry, and from this infirmity his were not exempt. They were in the habit of pilfering hen roosts, and when the stock of their master failed would depredate on that of the neighbors. For this they were frequently arrested, and being tried before a Justice of the Peace, sentenced to the whipping post, the punishment at that time usually inflicted for petit larceny. In these cases uncle Hendrick, as he was styled, would make feeling appeals in their behalf, and submit to paying fines to screen his negroes from punishment, and when this failed would be moved to shed tears to serve them.

No issue.

CHARITY BERGEN; d. 1822; m. *Abraham Quick*, a widower, a Colonel in the Revolutionary war, who d. in 1805, and who owned and cultivated about 500 acres of land at Ten Mile Run, N. J., on which some of his descendants now reside. *Charity* was born to command and did command up to the time of her death, she managing and giving all directions for the farm, of which she was left in possession, after the death of her husband. They had 14 slaves, and amongst her peculiarities, as related by one of her descendants, was her taking her stand morning, noon and night, in the door leading from the family room to the kitchen, with a well filled flask of apple whiskey or apple jack in her hand, when the slaves coming in for their meals would be called by name, beginning with the oldest, and each be allowed to take a good stiff dram of the raw stuff, and then retire from the door, hat in hand, with a "dank gij vrow," or, thank you Missus.

The custom of giving drams to their negroes was quite

common among the descendants of the early settlers a half
century ago. The author well recollects an amusing incident which occurred in the old homestead in his younger
days, at the time when his grandmother was an invalid.
Among the negroes employed on the farm was a freedman
named Tite, who, whenever he wanted a dram, would pro-
ject his head through the doorway into the dwelling room,
catch the eye of the old lady, and without uttering a word
commence rubbing his lips with his finger. She, under-
standing the pantomime, would take from the closet the
bottle and give the darkey his dose. On one occasion, by
mistake, she filled the glass with spirits of turpentine,
which Tite in his haste took down in one swallow, when
instead of "thank you Missus," the burning sensation he
experienced, caused him to exclaim with rolling and extended eyes, "O, Missus, what have I taken? what have I
taken? I will die, I will die!" Death, however, did not
ensue, the ostrich-like stomach of the negro disposing of
the burning fluid without injuring the patient.

Issue: —

Abraham Quick, b. about 1770, is now 92 years old and is a farmer,
owning some 330 acres at North Bran... Somerset Co. N. J. Here
Abraham resides on a farm la... ... is great uncle Hendrick Bergen.

Jacob Quick, b. May 17th, 1772, d. Jan. 21st 1857 and was a farmer at
Ten Mile Run.

John Quick, d. about 1817, a farmer at Ten Mile Run.

Margaret Quick, d. about 1835; m. Henry Lockwood, a farmer of Lexington, N. J.

Ann Quick, d. 1851; m. when quite advanced in years, Christopher
Hoagland, a farmer of Griggstown.

Peter Quick, d. 1831; settled on a farm near... ...

Elsie Quick, d. 1838 or '39; m. John F. Post of Ten Mile Run.

All the children of Abraham and Charity Quick, except Ann, left...

and they reside within a circle of 20 miles from the old homestead, and are amongst the most respectable in the community.

ELSEY BERGEN. Named in her brother Hendrick's will, as follows: "the residue (of my estate) to be equally divided between my brother Jacob's children and Elsey the widow of ——— Schenck, dec'd, that is to say, the one-half to be divided equally between the heirs of Jacob, Charity the widow of Ab'm Quick, dec'd, heirs of Margaret and Elsey Bergen, the other half to my sister Elsey, the widow of Lucas or Lewis Schenck, dec'd." Schenck died probably shortly after her marriage. Elsey resided with her sister Charity until about 1837, when she removed to Ab'm Quick's, at North Branch, where she d. in 1840 or '41. Ab'm Quick says he has no knowledge of her ever having been married.

Descendants of HENDRICK BERGEN, (s. of Frederick Jacobse,) of Staten Island:—

HENRY BERGEN, b. Oct. 23d, 1757; m. May 14th, 1783, *Polly* or *Mary Tyson*, b. about Aug. 20th, 1765, d. March 20th, 1809. Henry resided on Staten Island, was a blacksmith and farmer, wrote his name Barger, which method of spelling his descendants have continued to this day. He d. Dec. 23d, 1804, and was buried in the cemetery of the Moravian church at New Dorp, of which church he was a member. A regular record of births, &c., has been kept in this church from 1764, when it was first established. Most of his descendants appear to have been buried in the above named cemetery, they holding to the doctrines of said church. Dec. 13th, 1784, John C. Dungan for £150, conveyed to "Hendrick Barger" a lot of about 40 acres in the manor of Castleton on Staten Island, and also another lot of about 56 acres in the same manor.*

---

* See Lib. E, p. 165, of con. in off. of Clerk of Richmond Co.

April 21st, 1785, "Hendrick Barger, of Staten Island, and Mary his wife, conveyed for £180 to Randolph Drake 54 acres, lying on the road to Ryer's ferry."

Aug. 1st, 1796, "Henry Barger, blacksmith, and Mary his wife, conveyed for £450, to James Johnson about 13 acres on the road to Van Deusen's ferry, on Staten Island.†

Sept. 6th, 1797, "Henry Barger" conveyed for £675, to John Braisted about 26 acres on the road leading from Van Deusen's ferry to Richmond.‡

Issue:--

Jacob, b. Oct. 27th, 1784.

David, b. Nov. 16th, 1788.

Mary or *Polly*, b. Nov. 16th, 1788

John, b. Aug. 10th, 1793.

Henry, b. Sept. 3d, 1797.

Descendants of JACOB BERGEN and *Grietie Bennet*, of Staten Island:--

MARY or MARIA BERGEN, m. 1st, *James Newberry*; m. 2d. ------ *Stillwell*.

May 12th, 1792, John Newberry, late of Kings Co. bought a plot of land on Staten Island, of William Drake, which plot Drake conveyed June 11th, 1793, to "Henry Barger," and on the 25th of the same month, the latter conveyed the same to Mary Newberry, the wife of John, so as to place the title in his wife.§

Issue:

Ruth Newberry, b. Oct. 21, 1781, married ---- Deny, Deacon of Brooklyn; d. Oct. 15th, 1862

Catharine Newberry, b. July 9th, 1785, d. Dec. 1st, 1841. March 13th, 1828, John Stillwell, of Brooklyn.

* See Lib. E, p. 172, of conveyances of Clerk's office of Richmond Co.

† See Lib. F, p. 162, of conveyances of Clerk's office of Richmond Co.

‡ See Lib. F, p. 389, of conveyances of Clerk's office of Richmond Co.

§ See Lib. E, p. 426, of conveyances of Clerk's office of Richmond Co.

Sarah Bennet Newberry, b. June 1st, 1796; d. June 23d, 1843; m. Dr. Reynolds.

Mary Ann Newberry, b. Oct. 22d, 1798; d. April 16th, 1800.

Mary Ann Newberry, b. March 25th, 1801; m. Uel Reynolds, brother of the Doctor.

JACOB BERGEN, bap. May 6th, 1745; m 1783, *Catharine McLean.* No farther trace.

GERRITJE BERGEN, bap. June 10th, 1747. No farther trace.

ADRIAEN BERGEN, bap. May 3d, 1749. No farther trace.

Sixth Generation.

Descendants of JACOB BERGEN and *Tunche Van Dyck* of Rocky Hill, N. J. :—

AARON BERGEN, b. Oct. 12th, 1777; d. Jan. 27th, 1849, m. Nov. 11th, 1801, *Eliza,* dau. of Thomas and Betsey King, of Lenington, N. J., b. Oct. 21st, 1781, d. March 11th, 1815. Resided at one period at White Plains, Westchester Co., N. Y., and the latter part of his life at Princeton, N. J., where he kept a regular country store. In 1796, his name appears as a subscriber for six copies of " Watson against Paine," printed by Ab'm Blanvelt, New Brunswick. April 21st, 1819, he conveyed land to Matthew Bergen, as per book J. p. 532, of con. in County Clerk's off., Somerville.

Issue :—

Eliza Bergen, b. Nov. 16th, 1802; d. April 12th, 1803.

Maria Bergen, b. April 6th, 1804; m, 1st, —— Peters: m. 2d, —— Evans, of Peacher's Hill, Kentucky. At present a wid. and has no children.

Eliza B—, b. March 16, 1865 —— Jeremiah, 1827. Ralph Gulick, of Princeton, N. J. b. Oct. 7th, 1805 d. about 18— Had children Peter Gulick b. May 12th, 1828, d. March 26th, 1831. John Ann Gulick, b. Nov. 30th, 1830, d. Feb. 26th 1857. Elizabeth Gulick b. Feb. 19th, 1832 d. May 3d, 1853, m. Sept 17th, 1851, Thomas Davis. Mary Gray G. b. Aug. 23d, 1835, d. May 15th, 1854. Jason Van Dyke Gulick, b. Nov 7th, 1838, m. Nov. 27th, 1860, Julia Downing and resides at Princeton, N. J. William Henry Gulick, b. Jan. 1st, 1840, d. Dec 28th, 1859; and Addison Alexander Gulick, b. Sept 24th, 1843, resides at Princeton.

Jacob Van Dyke Bergen, b. Sept. 14th, 1805 d. Oct. 2nd 1853, m. 1st, Betsy Downey, by whom no issue; m. 2d, Mary Ann, dau. of John Blackwell, who d. shortly after her husband. Was a store keeper at Princeton, N. J.

Issue:

Matthew Bergen, b. Nov 15th, 1850; Mary Bergen, b. Jan. 25th, 1853.

Jane Bergen, b. Dec 6th, 1809, m. April 11th, 1838, Vincent Gulick, of New Brunswick, b. Jan. 17th, 1811, d. July 20th, 1857.

Issue:

Ann Eliza Gulick, b. April 8th, 1839, d. April 30th, 1838; Augustus Gulick, b. Nov. 1st, 1840, d. Dec. 23d, 1863. Ann Amanda Gulick, resides at New Brunswick. Mary Gulick, b. Aug 31st, 1843; d. June 22d, 1846. Emma Gulick, b. June 7th, 1847; and Mary Gulick, b. June 30th, 1850.

Henry Bergen, b. April 18th, 1812, of White Plains, Westchester Co., N. Y., m. Aug. 31st, 1841, Martha H. Berger who d. April 27th, 1846, without issue; m. 2d, May 15th, 1847, Hannah N. —. After the death of his mother resided for a number of years on the Wyck Bergen, near Somerville, after which he went to —. The most important epoch in his life was when he connected himself, about 20 years, while residing at Princeton, with a congregation of the Presbyterian church of that place. On this he loved to comment with great spirit and will which he has been careful never since that time. It connects with a period when connected with the Congregational church. To the last he gave the experience that when closely attached to the Mary —— to the best life or hopes for in the future whether it ——— population and enjoyment, and he will carry — to the future. At the age of 21, he commenced studying with a view to the gospel ministry, at Kingsborough, N. Y., and entered the Academy at Lee, prepared to enter college, Mass., graduated in 1849, after which studied Theology at Princeton, N.

J., and in the spring of 1841, was licensed to preach. In Oct., 1841, after his marriage with Miss Mary H. Badger, of Boston, Mass., he came to northern Illinois as a missionary of the A. H. M. Society, and in January, 1842, was advanced to the gospel ministry at Elgin, in said state, by the Fox River Union, since which he has labored in various places in northern Illinois, residing at present in Galesberg. On the death of his first wife, by whom no children, he married Miss Harriet O. Norton, of Ridgefield, Ill. His two oldest children are at present connected as students with Knox College, at Galesberg.

Issue :—

Henry Baldwin Bergen, b. Oct. 18th, 1848; Mary Jane Bergen, b. Sept. 19th, 1851; George Matthew Bergen, b. Nov. 21st, 1854; John Albert Bergen, b. Dec. 11th, 1858, d. Aug. 23d, 1860; Edward Martyn Bergen, b. Oct. 26th, 1861.

Matthew Bergen, b. March 24th, 1814; d. July 4th, 1849; m. Martha Stevens, of Hannibal, Missouri. He and his wife died of cholera, within a few hours of each other, near St. Louis, Missouri, where he had settled; which disease also carried off during the same summer three of his children. His children were: Charles, Mary and Edmund, who all d. of cholera; Anna Maria, (oldest child,) m. a Mr. Watson, and resides at St. Louis, and Alice.

MATTHEW BERGEN, b. Oct. 2d. 1779; d. Oct. 16th, 1843; m. *Rebecca Monfort,* late in life and left no children. Resided after arriving to years of maturity in the city of N. Y., where he kept a grocery store, but the last years of his life were spent at Kingston, N. J., where he died.

MARGARET BERGEN, b. July 31st, 1781; d. Nov. 28th, 1860; m. 1806, *Andrew Gaddis,* b. Dec. 18th, 1779; d. Dec. 16th, 1836. A farmer at North Branch, on the Raritan, N. J.

Issue :—

Ann Gaddis, b. Aug. 7th, 1807; d. Nov. 16th, 1822, single.

Jacob Bergen Gaddis, b. Nov. 9th, 1810; m. March 8th, 1831, Eliza C., dau. of Judge Oalcatt, of New Brunswick, is president and superintendent of the New Jersey Lighterage Co., at Jersey City.

David A. Gaddis, b. April 7th, 1817; m. Oct. 22d, 1836, Sarah E, dau. of Elisha E. Bird, of Flemington, and is freight agent of the N. J. R. R. and Trans. Co., residing at Newark.

John Van Dike Gaddis, b. Aug 26th, 1816, d. Dec 1st, 1863, m. John dau. of Rev. Ab'm D. Wilson, of Fairview, Ill. where he practiced medicine until his health failed, when he removed to Jacksonville in the same state, where he d.

Catharine Ann Gaddis, b. Oct 31st, 1818, m. Samuel, son of Henry Sloan, of Bedminster, N. J.

Matthew Bergen Gaddis, b July 11th, 1821, d. March 6th, 1822

Descendants of HENRY BARGER, (Bergen,) and *Polly Tyson*, of Staten Island:

JACOB BARGER, b. Oct. 27th, 1784; d. Aug. 12th, 1833; m. *Hannah Cole* or *Hannah Winants*. Resided in the city of N. Y., where he d.

May 22d, 1809, his brother David Barger, and Nov. 18th, 1809, his brother-in-law William Beatty and Mary his wife, conveyed to him their interest in the farm of their father, Henry Barger, dec'd, located in Southfield, Staten Island, containing 99 acres of upland, and a plot salt meadows.

Issue :—

Susan W. Barger.
Mary Barger, m. Ogden M. Rogers, of N. Y. Bowlder.
Eliza Ann Barger.
Catharine Barger, deceased.
Henry Barger.
Abraham Barger, deceased.
Catharine Mese eau Barger, b. 1812, d Nov 23d, 1814
Jacob Barger.
Abraham Barger.
Hannah Barger.
Pricilla Barger, m Feb. 1848, Charles Smith of Brook'yn.

Found it difficult to obtain information of the children of Jacob Barger, and there may be others of them now leased

DAVID BARGER, b. Nov. 16th, 1788; m. Jan. 29th, 1812, *Sarah*, dau. of Jacob and Elizabeth Cortelyou, of Staten Island, b. March 21st, 1796. Is a blacksmith by trade, residing at first at Westfiel l, on Staten Island, from whence with his family he removed to Rochester, Michigan.

Issue :—

Mary Barger, b. Jan. 5th, 1813; m. June 11th, 1837, Amos Brown. No issue.

Henry Barger, b. Oct. 11th, 1819; d. July 13th, 1820.

Eliza Ann Barger, b. Nov. 6th, 1821. Single.

John Williams Barger, b. Nov. 9th, 1823; m. Nov. 22d, 1853, Mary Cain, who d. Feb. 6th, 1855; m. 2d, Dec. 16th, 1857, Susan Keler. No issue.

James Guion Barger, b. Sept. 23d, 1833.

MARY or POLLY BARGER, b. Nov. 16th, 1788; d. March 18th, 1850; m. June 22d, 1806, *William Beatty*, of Staten Island.

Issue :—

Henry Beatty, b. Feb. 28th, 1807.

William Beatty, b. Nov. 24th, 1809.

Emmeline Beatty, b. May 31st, 1811; m. John D. Kinsey

Elenore Mary Beatty, b. May 2d, 1812.

John Edmond Beatty, b. Sept. 23d, 1818. Is dead.

Edwin Beatty, b. March 29th, 1821. Is dead.

Hiram Beatty, b. April 19th, 1824. Is dead.

Mary E. Beatty, b. Nov. 23d, 1826; m. Jacob Best.

JOHN BERGER, b. Aug. 10th, 1793; d. 1860, at the residence of his brother Henry; m. *Ann Lake*.

HENRY BARGER, b. Sept. 3d, 1797; m. *Matilda Ann Frost*, who d. March 14th, 1837. For many years a merchant in N. Y., and at present a resident of Paterson, N. J. At one time Col. of the regiment of horse artillery in the counties of Kings and Richmond.

Issue :—

Henry Barger, b. Aug. 8th, 1829. Single.

Samuel F. Barger, b. Oct. 19th, 1832. Single. Practices law in the city of N. Y.

Hester M. Barger, b. Nov. 9th, 1834. Single.

35

36

ERRATA.

For "m. June 3d, 1836, Eliza W. Clarke." read "m. July 3d, 1835, Eliza, dau. of Daniel Clarke, Esq., of the City of N. Y.," in the 12th and 13th lines of page 138; and at the end of the 15th line of the same page, add "Had issue 6 children, among whom were daughters Hellen and Margaret, all of whom d. in infancy, except Victor B. b. July 5th, 1836, m. Nov. 1858, Cornelia J. dau. of Genl. Richard A. Udall, of Islip, and Cornelius J. who d. June 1862, a young man, in China. Victor B. has children, Eliza, Cornelia and May."

For "Itsue," read "Issue," in the 16th line of page 146.

For "William Kouwenhoven," read "William G. Kouwenhoven," in the 2d line of page 147; and for "2745," read "1745," in the 27th line of the note on the same page.

For "Kovwenhoven," read "Kouwhenhoven," in the 3d and 4th lines of page 148,

For "Antie," read "Antie," in the 16th line of page 150.

For "Arrayen," read "Arryaen," in the 20th line of the note on page 151; for "Marietie," read "Marritie," in the 25th line, and for "Marrietie," read "Marritie," in the 30th line of the same note.

For "which," read "who," in the 3d line of the note on page 153.

Strike out "its first establishment," and insert in place thereof "1860," in the 5th line of page 155.

For "Eagge," read "Eagle," in the 7th line of the note on page 172.

Strike out "Michael," and insert "Jores or George," in the heading on page 173.

For "Abraham," read "Abram," in the 17th line of page 177.

For "Christopher," read "Christopher I.," in the 8th line of page 178.

For "Denser," read "Denrsen," in the 24th line of page 187.

For "Burgan," read "McClow," in the 9th line of page 217.

Strike out "Covert," and insert "Davis," in the 30th, 31st and 32d lines of page 218.

For "Evart," read "Evert," in the 19th line of page 219.

For "Elen," read "Ellen," in the 4th line of page 221.

For "Patterson," read "Peterson," in the 3d line of page 225.

For "Dennyse," read "Denyse," in the 9th line of page 229.

Strike out the word "form," and insert "from," near the commencement of the 6th line of page 237, so that the sentence will read "from a fordable creek."

For "Laura," read "Lana," in the 25th and 27th lines of page 246.

For "Jene," read "Jane," in the 12th line of page 247.

For "Charity," read "Charity," in the 20th line of page 248.

ADDITIONAL ERRATA.

Erase the 24th line of page 119.

Erase "Sept. 12th, 1894," and insert "August 20th, 1801," in the 1st line of page 120.

Erase "May" and insert "December," in the 5th line of the note on page 121.

Erase "8" and insert "9 in the second line of page 123.

Erase "1821" and insert "1831" in the 4th line; also, "1832" and insert "1831" in the 16th line, and "1835" and insert "1832" in same line; also "24" and insert "21" in the 18th line; also "Feb. 9th," and insert "Feb. 27th" in the 26th line; and also "wood" and insert "ward" in the 28th line of page 127.

Erase "1854" and insert "1855" in the 9th line of page 130.

Erase "1811" and insert "1814" in the 8th line of page 137.

Erase "1823" and insert "March 1, 1822," in the 14th line; also "1825" and insert "March 12th, 1824" in the 15th line; also "Jan. 1830," and insert "Jan. 10, 1829" in the 17th line; and also insert after b. "Feb. 16th" in the 19th line of page 139.

Erase "1863" and insert "1864" in the 3th line of page 142.

Erase "John G." and insert "John C." in the 3d line of page 151; also, "March 14. 1705," and insert "November 2d, 1811, in the 17th and 18th lines of the note on same page.

Erase "fall" and insert "spring" in the 16th line of page 152.

Erase "Jan. 20th" and insert "June 24th" in the 13th line; also "June" and insert "January" in the 14th line of the note on page 153.

Erase "23d" and insert "21st" in the 9th line; also "1897" and insert "1827" in the 12th line of the note on page 154.

Erase "Louisiana" and insert "Alabama" in the 28th line of the note on page 155.

Erase "23d" and insert "22d," and "15th" and insert "11th" in the 8th line; also "11th" and insert "6th" in the 10th line; and also insert after 1863 in said 10th line "Susan D., d. Aug. 19th, 1864; Amelia L., d. Aug. 23d, 1864," of page 159.

Erase "1831" and insert "1828" in the 9th line; also insert after the 14th line. "Lafayette, b. July 25th, 1862; Jessie Tennis, b. Jan. 21, 1864; and Lemma Amelia, b. April 30th, 1866;" also erase "1833" and insert "1830" in the 20th line; also insert after b. "Dec. 29th, 1857, d." in the 22d line; and also insert after said 22d line "Jennie Louisa, b. Jan. 18th, 1864," of page 161.

Erase the 27th, 28th, 29th and 30th lines of page 170; also the 1st to 9th lines inclusive of page 171.

Erase "MICHAEL" and insert "GEORGE" in the heading of page 173; also insert "blacksmith" after N. Y. in the 19th line of same page.

Insert "Catharine Coombs, b. July 8th, 1792." after the 7th line of page 177; also, for "Abraham" read "Abram I." in the 18th line.

Insert "John Schenck, b. about 1814, d. 1816," after the 11th line of page 178.

Erase the 15th to 23d lines inclusive of the same page, and insert:

"Issue:—Elias Van Ness, of Dutch Neck, m. Sarah Schenck.

John Bergen Van Ness, of Dutch Neck, m. 1st, Lammata Baker; 2d, Mary Snediker.

Abraham Van Ness, of near Hightstown, m. Harriet Dey.

George Van Ness, of West Windsor, m. Jane, dau. of Peter Bergen.

Diana Van Ness, m. Isaac Snediker, of Dutch Neck.

Christopher Van Ness, d. aged about 15.

Maria Van Ness, m. Isaac Snediker after the death of Diana.

Sarah Van Ness, m. Marco Crechee, a Frenchman, and moved west.

Peter Van Ness, removed to Illinois, where he married.

Catherine Van Ness, m, William Perrine, of Dutch Neck."

Also on 24th line of same page erase "about" and insert "Aug. 10th;" and at the end of 25th line add "b. Nov. 17th, 1782; d. Jan. 18, 1855."

in the 9th line, insert "b. Dec. 16th, 1814 ; d. Jan. 12th ;" after "Bergen," in the 13th line, insert "b. April 2d, 1818."

Erase "1839" and insert "1859," and add "Clorissa Felter, b. Aug. 14th, 1839, and has issue, Izora E., b. April 16th, 1864." in the 35th line; and after "Jacob" insert "I.," and after "1839" insert "m. Sept. 27th, 1863, Maria Stevens, b. July 2d, 1846, and has issue, Edward Stevens, b. Oct. 18th, 1864." in the 36th line of page 207.

Erase "James" and insert "John B." in the 21st line ; also "Middletown" and insert "Millstone" in the 23d line of page 210.

Erase in 3d line of page 214, so as to read "Lewis R., b. March 9th, 1823 ; m. Dec. 22d, 1850, Helen Imlay." Add to the end of the 4th line, "surviving." Insert in the 12th line, after George, "G.," so as to read "George G. Bergen." After the 15th line so as to read "Joseph S. Bergen, b. Aug. 12th, 1793." After 16th line add "Lydia Bergen, b. Sept. 30th, 1794 ; d. Sept. 15th, 1813." After 17th line so as to read : "Elijah V. Brew, b. Oct. 1, 1796 ; d. Nov. 20, 1798." After 17th line add: "Sarah Bergen, b. Nov. 22d, 1798 ; d. June 15, 1828. Elijah Bergen, b. April 30th, 1800 ; d. August 4th, 1821. Jesse Bergen, b. Jan. 25th, 1804 ; d. May 16th, 1805." After 18th line, so as to read, "Eliza Bergen, b. July 22d, 1806 ; d. Sept. 25th, 1813." After 19th line add, "Mary Bergen, b. Feb. 23d, 1808 ; d. Sept. 16th, 1811." Erase the 21st line. After "Sarah Bergen" in 22 line, insert "by 1st wife." After "Hannah Bergen," 32d line, insert "by 2d wife, b. Dec. 29th, 1810," on said 214th page.

Insert "G" after "William," and "b. Sept. 2d, 1835," after "Bergen," in 8th line of page 215. Erase so forth to last characters, five, and insert "Johanness, b. Feb. 27th, 1838, Stephen W., b. Aug. 19, 1839, Stephen B., b. Dec. 14, 1841, Sarah, b. Feb. 10, 1842, John (?) R. b. May 14, 1843, Elizabeth N. vend ? r 22d, 1844, Charles D., b. Jan. 7th, 1847 ; d. Aug. 20th, 1852, Mary, b. Dec. 25th, 1849 ; d. Aug. 21st, 1872, Wesley ? , Dec. 22d, 1850 ; d. Sept. 15th, 1851, Isaac H., b. Aug. 30, 1853, Isabel, b. Aug. 5th, 1855, George, b. Aug. 17th, 1858, Emma, b. Nov. 20, 1860." In the 21st line after "Isaac" insert "H." and after "Bergen," "b. F b. 23d, 1813." On the 27th line of said page 215, erase "Eliza," and insert "Elizabeth Bergen, b. March 13th, 1813."

Insert in the 3d line of page 216, after "George Bergen," "b. Nov. 9th, 1807 ;" after the issue of George Bergen, in the 7th line, add "Margaret Bergen, b. Oct. 8th, 1809," and "Charles Bergen, b. Nov. 6th, 1811." After "James," in the 8th line, insert "M.," so as to read "James M. Bergen ;" after the 25th line, add "Joan M. Bergen, b. May 27th, 1818."

Erase "May 10th, 1828" in the 7th line of page 217, and insert "Sept. 10th, 1834."

Erase "Bergen" and insert "McCloon" in the 9th line ; erase "farmer" and insert "miller, carpenter and joiner," in the 12th line ; erase "d. Jan. 1854," in the 20th line ; erase "Genevah" and insert "Genoa" in the 31st line ; and erase "Mary" and insert "May" in the 32d line of page 217.

After "N. Y." insert "see following portrait" in the 5th line of page 218.

Erase "son" and insert "brother" in the 27th line of page 219.

At the end of the 19th line insert "d. April, 1850 ;" at the end of the 21st line insert "m. Mary Ann Huston, dau. of Geo. Huston ;" erase "20th, 1840," and insert "9th, 1842." in the 23d line ; at the end of the 25th line insert "m. Amanda Jane Huston, dau. of Geo. Huston ;" and erase "Nov. 29th, 1842," and insert "Oct. 30th, 1844," in the 26th line of page 223.

Erase "1825" and insert "1822" in the 21st line of page 224.

Erase "June" and insert "January" in the 2d line of page 225.

Add to 15th line of page 241, "In 1737 was Captain of Militia."

Erase "No further trace" and insert "m. Sept 20th, 1750, Johannes Wendell, of Albany, b. 1720, and had issue :—Johannes, bap. June 3d, 1751 ; and Francyntia, bap. Nov. 12th, 1752," in the 5th line of page 244.

Erase "Coe" and insert "Roe" in the 13th line of page 247.